CW00517507

# TO BE A KING

## (Volume I)

Harbinger Media Group, LLC

**TO BE A KING, Volume 1 and 2** is dedicated to the memory of my mother, Grace (Tocco) Lindbloom, and my grandparents, Peter Paul and Grace Tocco.

# Acknowledgements

First and foremost, I must make it clear that this book would not be what it is without the love, support, and professional knowhow of my amazing wife Maria. She is blessed with such incredible talent that it defies description. There is so much about her that the world will never know or see—her wit and charm, her intelligence, and her incredible sense of humor. I struggle even trying to put into words what she means to me. She waited 6 years for me while I was in prison, faithfully supporting me, always there without fail. She devoted her life to not only preparing a home for me when I walked out of prison, but she also paved the way for me to publish this book, working endless nights and weekends on the editing, proofing, formatting, marketing, and the dozens of other tasks that come with publishing a novel. She is my biggest fan and believes in me more than any person on this planet. I truly believe she was made by God just for me, and sent from Him to be my Earth angel and protector. I have experienced no greater joy in life than having the honor and privilege to call her my wife. She is beautiful and extraordinary in every sense of the word. It defies all logic and the nature of the universe that a woman like her would even show interest in a man like me, let alone love me as fiercely as she does. Yet here we are… proof that God is real and He has a great sense of humor. I MARALAN you, Birdy!

Second, I must say a special thank you to all those who never gave up on me while I was in prison. They are few and far between, but they were my anchor and inspiration. I now have many "friends," but only a select few showed their true love by supporting me during the 13 years I was locked up. Billy Usher, my best friend and business partner, never even had to read this book to know I had written a masterpiece. He simply said, "If you say it's a masterpiece, Al, then it's a masterpiece. I'll do anything in my power to help you get it published." And he has. Billy, you have never wavered in your genuine love and support for me. You're a true friend and brother. I love you and am eternally grateful for your friendship.

Joe Rubino, you are one of only two Earth angels that God has sent me in my life. There is not enough room on this page for me to express my love and gratitude for you. I'm awed by who you are and what you do as a father, husband, and true Christian. You were the first one to read this book outside of prison, over 7 years ago, and ever since you have been telling people it will be a best-seller. It's an honor to call you my *"goombadi."* Thank you for your love and support.

John Campis, you are my longest living friend, and more of a brother to me than mere friend. I am honored to be the godfather of your boys, and there are no words to express the special friendship we have. When we are together, we don't even need to talk. We just know each other's thoughts. I always have so much fun with you, and I know it's mutual. Together, we revert to giant caveman kids! Thank you for always being my champion. It's an honor to call you family.

And, of course, my father, George Lindbloom. He has never given up on me and has always been there for me, through thick and thin. As bad of a son I have been at times, he has been a great father to me. And for that I am eternally grateful. Love you, Dadeo!

I have a few special acknowledgments for several friends who, no matter what has been said about me, have been a supporting, encouraging presence in my life since my release from prison: Mark Hammerschmidt, Joey Mazzola, Pashko Gojcaj, Gino Bianchette, Dana Harvey, Jose Llombart, Mark Monday, Jeff Miller, Pat O'Brien, Brian Pfeifer, Ronny Boggs and Dan Schetter.

Also, there are a couple of Facebook cyber friends I'd like to also thank for always supporting and encouraging me: Craig Timmins (of *National Crime Syndicate*) Jedidiah Wilson, Dante Giovanetti, Andrew Green, and Michael White. Thanks, fellas, for believing in me and having my back from day one!

—Gunner A. Lindbloom

*"Significantly reduced in numbers—recent FBI accounts place Motor City Mafia membership at roughly 25 made members with about 75-100 associates, compared to nearly triple that in the 1970s—as well as headline grabbing exploits, there have only been five Mob-related homicides in the last two decades, the Detroit crime family is the most functional, healthy, and financially profitable Mafia syndicate in the entire country. While other regional Mob families have been destroyed from within by internal squabbling and government defection, the Motor City Mafia has only had one made member ever turn federal witness, an astronomical feat considering the current underworld landscape. The Detroit faction of La Cosa Nostra remains a silent but ultimately very real and deadly presence in the American gangland culture while exhibiting no signs of slowing down. And, although membership is aging, a new generation will eventually ascend to take the reins of the local Mafia and lead the storied crime family into the future, and most likely, beyond."*

-Scott M. Burnstein, *Motor City Mafia*

www.gangsterreport.com

# PROLOGUE

## KEY LARGO, FLORIDA

As Stanley led the don out onto the patio terrace behind his beachfront home, he chuckled inwardly, remembering the first time he added the prefix "don" to his friend's name. The don had mildly rebuked him, saying, "Stan, you don't have to call me Don. That's just a bunch of Hollywood bullshit Puzo made up. They only say it to old men back in the Old Country. We're friends. Call me Pete, *capisce*?"

But Stanley had associates in Miami—upper echelons of the Trafficante Family, Florida's resident Mafia faction—who had explained to him that Peter Paul Falcone was one of the ten most recognized Mafiosi in the country. Santos Trafficante had come right out and said, "Falcone is a Boss, Stan... From the Old Country. He should always be addressed as 'Don Falcone' in private. To not do so is considered a blatant act of disrespect." So whenever they were alone, Stanley always made sure to address his lifelong friend with the prefix "don."

As Stanley stepped over to the patio bar, he stole a quick glance back at his old friend. They locked eyes, and the memories came flooding back. They had many memories throughout their half-century friendship. Some good, some bad. But the one that always stood out was one he wished he could forget. It happened nearly fifty years ago, yet it was so clear in his mind that it could have happened yesterday. He shivered at the mere thought of it. The savage brutality of it. The manic look in those eyes. Even after all these years, a single look into those menacing dark eyes could make him shudder with fear. And for

1

good reason. Peter Falcone was the most dangerous man he'd ever known.

"Please, Don Falcone, take a seat," Stanley said politely, handing him a cigar, gesturing toward a canopied patio set. "Make yourself comfortable. I'll get you a drink."

Don Falcone sat at the table and slowly took in his surroundings. He loved the Floridian weather. Even now, in the middle of winter, the weather was warm and pleasant. Far off to the west, the sun was setting below the horizon, casting a ghostly orange iridescence into the evening sky. A distant thunderstorm was quickly making its way across Florida Bay, heading directly toward them, its preceding breeze carrying an ambrosia of impending rain and briny ocean air. On the beach, several hundred feet behind Stanley's home, a flock of pelicans were waiting patiently for their nightly tidal feast. It was a beautiful tableau that seemed to tug at the don's soul.

As Don Falcone watched Stanley pour them drinks, he breathed deeply, filling his aged lungs with the warm air. He savored the heady, humid fullness in his expanded lungs, tasting it, relishing it, as if the air itself was some kind of intoxicating drug. It reminded him of another time, another place, another life. Visions of his childhood in Sicily danced through his head. So beautiful and tranquil were the lush Nebrodi Mountains of his beloved Sicily. Since arriving in America so long ago, not a day went by that he didn't yearn to return home to the temperate climate of his youth. Unfortunately, obligations to *La Famiglia*, his family, and *La Borgata*, his community, had always kept him firmly rooted in Detroit, where the winters were long, dreary, and brutally cold. He had always envied Stanley's life in the tropical Floridian sun, a life of leisure and relaxation the don had never been afforded in his line of work. He sometimes wondered if the man had ever seen snow. But then he remembered their time together in the Marines, when they had fought side-by-side in the biting snow and blistering cold of South Korea.

Stanley Dunn, retired businessman and six-term Floridian Senator, was a serial hedonist who had spent the better part of a century living in Florida. He planned to live out his remaining days there, relaxing by the beach, indulging in the finest spirits, eating the finest foods, smoking the finest cigars, and sampling the finest young beauties money could buy. He had lived a long life of excess and was quite proud of his many accomplishments. But he was even more proud of his family. His daughter was a successful plastic surgeon in Miami. His youngest son owned a lucrative financial consulting firm in Houston. However, his eldest son was his true pride and joy— and naturally so. Jonathan Randall Dunn was the current United States President. Who, just as of last week, had been elected to a second term in office.

A self-made millionaire, Stanley had amassed his fortune through a number of lucrative business ventures, some more scrupulous than others. A few of those ventures had involved the menacing old Sicilian now seated on his patio. In fact, Don Falcone had helped him get started in business.

Upon completing his obligation to the Marines, Peter Falcone returned to Detroit and quickly made a name for himself in the local underworld, aligning himself with a collective of powerful Italian associates known as the "Combination," which later became known as the "Partnership" and eventually the "Syndicate." It was these shadowy underworld associates, many of whom had powerful political allies, who had put Stanley on the road to success. Though it had been many years since he had any actual business dealings with the don, they always tried to stay in touch, albeit discreetly because of the nature of the don's business. Yet it was a relationship that had lasted over a half-century. From time to time the don and his wife would come down to vacation during the winter months, occasionally bringing with them their entire family. But these winter visits had grown less frequent over the years. Usually, several years would lapse between visits. But the don never lost touch and always made sure to send a gift basket for the holidays.

It had been several years since the old mob boss paid Stanley a personal visit, and the fact that he showed up this evening unannounced, accompanied by two young men who appeared to be bodyguards, had Stanley feeling a bit uneasy. He could tell from the look in the don's eyes that this was not merely a social call. So why was he there? And why the imposing bodyguards? It was almost as if they were expecting trouble. Whatever the case, Stanley hoped a couple of fingers of Glenfiddich single malt scotch would ease the bad feeling he had in is gut.

Doing his best to seem unruffled, Stanley handed the don a tumbler of scotch. "So, Don Falcone, you didn't bring Gracie down this time," he stated matter-of-factly, referring to the don's wife, hoping a bit of subtle probing would get him some answers.

The don shrugged and took a sip. "No," he replied tersely, a single syllable delivered in an impassive monotone. "And I've told you a thousand times, Stan, you don't have to call me 'don.' That's just Hollywood malarkey."

"Sorry, Don Falcone," Stanley goaded, grinning. "I'm getting old. Sometimes I forget these things."

Don Falcone gave him a look. "Smartass," he mumbled, and then turned his attention to the ocean.

Stanley didn't want to come across as intrusive, so rather than come right out and ask him what was on his mind, he continued to exercise discretion.

"Well, I hope Gracie and the rest of your family are well," he said, offering him a look of genuine concern.

"This is a damn fine cigar, Stan," the don said, carefully examining the smoldering stogy as if he hadn't even heard Stanley's last remark. He then fell silent again as he pulled deeply from the cigar and continued staring out at the darkening ocean.

4

"It's a Cohiba," Stanley declared proudly, deciding he had no choice but to play along. "Special edition. Best batch to come out of Havana this year…"

For the next hour, the two old Marine comrades sipped scotch and engaged in nostalgic banter, reminiscing on old times as dusk turned to night. Eventually, as the alcohol ran its course, Don Falcone began to relax and loosen up. As always, the two old friends reveled in each other's company. Life was behind them now. Their wars had been fought. Some lost, but most won. Nowadays, fewer things in life were more precious than a quiet evening with an old friend, sipping good drink with a fine cigar. As the evening wore on, they laughed and caught up on time lost, as well as recounted tales of old. But Stanley was no fool. Studying the old don's face, he noticed there was something just below the surface. A deep pain. Or was it worry? Could it be fear? It was definitely something. Whatever it was, it was exacerbated by those foreboding obsidian eyes.

"Let me get you a refill," Stanley offered, taking the don's empty glass over to the bar.

Don Falcone motioned a finger across his throat. "No more of that Scottish poison," he said, his peasant Sicilian accent still detectable even after all these years. "Too strong. Gives me heartburn and makes me sluggish. Do you have any decent *vino rosso*?"

"Vino what?" Stanley asked, hovering over the bar with the expensive bottle of premium scotch.

"Red wine," Don Falcone chuckled softly. "Sometimes I forget I'm speaking Italian. Part of getting old, I suppose."

"We're all getting old, my friend," Stanley countered, setting the bottle of scotch on the bar. "Let me go inside and check my cellar. I think I have just the thing."

"Any red will do," Don Falcone offered, waving a hand indifferently. "I'm not picky."

5

"Nonsense," said Stanley, flashing him a cryptic grin. "I've been saving a certain bottle for just such an occasion..."

Ten minutes later, Stanley returned from his wine cellar with an aged bottle of red wine. "The very best I've got," he declared, holding the bottle out to him. "Almost twenty years ago I was vacationing in Tuscany with my second wife, Katrina. We met the Marchese Incisa della Rocchetta's son. He gave me five bottles of this. It was a gift in memory of his father, who I'd met in Rome while on a diplomatic mission. It's called Sassicaia, made in the Emilian Apennines of your homeland. Even back then a bottle was worth a couple grand. This is my last one. I've been saving it for a special occasion. I figured tonight is as good as any."

Don Falcone looked surprised but not all that impressed. "Yes, I know of Sassicaia. Very good vino, paisan. But not from my homeland. My homeland is Sicily. How many times have I told you this? There is a big difference between Sicilians and mainland Italians. Starting with Sicilians make better wine. They just don't share it with the rest of the world. They keep it for themselves. But I'll give it to you, Sassicaia is a decent red. What year you got there?"

"Eighty-five," Stanley grinned, twisting in a corkscrew, pleased that he was able to impress the don.

"Ehhh..." Don Falcone shrugged, unimpressed, having no idea that it was the finest vintage the vineyard had ever produced. "It's all wine to me. It's made for drinking, not hoarding in some dusty cellar."

Stanley grinned and yanked the cork out with an audible pop. "My sentiments exactly," he agreed, filling a crystal wineglass and handing it to the don. "Here you are, old man. Personally, I like the stronger stuff. Brandy, cognac, scotch." He patted his bulging belly. "Keeps the ol' fire burning. Helps ward off the aches and pains. Deborah, God rest her soul, always said I liked it a little too much. Said it would kill me someday. But I say to hell with that! I've lived this goddamn long. I've earned the right to indulge. I'm an old man. I need a little kick in the ass once in a while."

The don chuckled, a low rumble reminiscent of the approaching thunder. "Salute," he said, touching his glass to Stanley's tumbler. As he took a long sip of the aromatic wine, he found himself studying his gracious host. He hated how they had been forced to be distant over the years. He genuinely liked Stanley and they had quite an interesting history, one that spanned almost five decades. At the ripe old age of eighteen, they had met in Korea as platoon-mates with the 26th Marines, Advanced Recon Squadron Delta. Both had been full of piss and vinegar, high on patriotism and short on common sense. But their friendship had been an unlikely one, especially considering how they had come from two very different worlds. Back then the don was nothing but a bellicose young private with a chip on his shoulder. After witnessing his father's murder on the streets of Trapani—his hometown in Sicily—his mother had sent him to live with a great aunt in Detroit. He had been a terribly unruly teenager, with a deep-seated propensity for violence. He spent his days running the streets, hanging around a local gang of hustlers and petty criminals, all of them Italian. Though his aunt did her best to be good surrogate mother, she was unable to control him. Most of his teenage years were spent ducking the law and running errands for a crew of local Mafiosi. Stanley, on the other hand, had been raised by two adoring parents in the middle-class suburb of Sarasota, Florida. While the don had been a raucous, crude, ill-tempered ruffian, Stanley had been an introverted, reserved, genuine intellectual. Yet for reasons neither of them could explain, they forged a unique brotherly bond that had endured a lifetime.

Silently sipping his scotch, Stanley was also studying the don. Memories flooded his head, and he suddenly recalled the story of how the don had ended up in America. He'd never been made privy to the particulars, but one night after drinking heavily the don had slipped up and shared the whole story. Apparently,

7

there had been some kind of ongoing war between local Mafia factions in the don's hometown back in Sicily. A "vendetta" he had called it. Several members of his family had been killed in this vendetta, including his two older brothers and his father, as well as a number of uncles and cousins. When he was the last living male Falcone, his mother put him on a boat and literally shipped him off to live with distant relatives in Detroit, where there was a large Italian community. After six years of legal troubles and living as an illegal alien, he was offered a chance to cleanse his criminal record and gain legal citizenship by volunteering for one of the armed services. Since his mother had died back in Sicily, leaving him nothing to return home to, he enlisted in the Marines, if only because he'd heard that it was the toughest branch of the military. After completing his four-year commitment to the Marines, he returned to Detroit and slowly muscled his way through the ranks of the city's local mob syndicate. An exceptionally ruthless and cunning young Mafioso, he eventually established himself as a leader in his "*borgata,*" the Italian word for community. In time, he eventually rose to become Detroit's *Capo de Tutti Cappi*, the city's supreme Boss of Bosses. But that was many, many years ago. He had long since settled into semi-retirement after relinquishing his position as the Syndicate's leader to his son-in-law, Leoni.

Taking another long pull from his cigar, Stanley now decided it was time they stopped dancing around the subject and got to the real reason the don was there. "It's great to see you Don Falcone, but..." he began, and then paused, snapping the don from his nostalgic reverie. "It's been what, four, five years?"

"Probably more like seven," Don Falcone admitted with a touch of shame, also pulling deeply from his cigar.

"Why?" Stanley asked. "Why so long? You know you and your family are always welcome in my home." He took a sip and gave him an earnest look. "But tell me, Don Falcone... old friend... is there something on your mind? I mean, you've never

8

just showed up at my home like this unannounced. And, well... you seem a bit distracted."

Don Falcone said something in Italian to his bodyguards, dismissing them with a wave of his hand. They immediately stepped out onto the back lawns, out of earshot but close enough to maintain a vigilant eye on him.

"You're very perceptive, old friend," said the don, turning softened eyes on him. "There is indeed something serious we need to discuss."

"And that is?" Stanley asked.

Don Falcone was silent for a long moment before finally answering, "I have a favor to ask, paisan. A big one."

As the don's ebony eyes bored into him, Stanley felt a wave of trepidation wash over him. His old friend's amiable mask had vanished. No longer did he look like a harmless old man. His back suddenly seemed straighter, accentuating his full height and bulk, instantly drawing Stanley's eyes to shoulders that looked like bowling balls and hands that resembled baseball mitts. Clad in a white linen shirt, suspenders, black slacks and a massive diamond pinky ring, he still very much looked like what he was—a mob boss. Yet imposing as he was physically, it was his eyes that were most unnerving. They were the piercing dark eyes of a hungry lion. Giant pupils without irises. Black as obsidian. Fearless. Threatening. Violent. Stanley remembered those eyes well from their time together in Korea. Even their hardline gunnery sergeants seemed to shrink when he turned those eyes on them. Though he was just above average height at 5'11", he had always been powerfully built. A solid mass of muscle. And during their tour together in Korea, he'd been a renowned brawler, always ready for a good fight.

Looking at his old friend, Stanley inadvertently shivered as the memory came flooding back. It was the same one that still gave him nightmares. It happened nearly fifty years ago, yet in his mind he could see it with such clarity that it might have happened yesterday. They were on a weekend pass to Seoul, and Stanley witnessed his friend fly into a murderous rampage. In fact, it was the single most terrifying night of his life. It was also the first time he witnessed just how ruthless and bloodthirsty his young Italian platoonmate could be. After a long night of heavy drinking and womanizing, they had found themselves in a bar packed with tough local Koreans and a few American GIs. They were minding their own business, enjoying the company of some local girls, when several Army privates began fighting with a group of local Korean thugs. Apparently the Koreans had grown tired of the American GIs hogging all the hookers. It was an ugly exchange, with the Americans getting the worst of it. That is, until Private Falcone and Corporal Dunn jumped into the fray. For nearly twenty minutes the brawl continued, with bottles flying, tables crashing. Eventually, several American MPs burst in and broke it up before things escalated into something worse than a battle of fisticuffs.

After the fight, with both of them nursing their share of lumps and bruises, Private Falcone and Corporal Dunn followed a pair of nubile and, in hindsight, overly zealous young prostitutes to a seedy back-alley opium brothel, completely unaware that they were being setup. Stanley had just pulled down his pants when five Korean thugs—all of them drunk and hell-bent on revenge—burst in and began beating him savagely. Just down the hall, the same thing was happening to Private Falcone. But being that he was the smaller of the two, the Koreans had only dedicated three of their ranks to Private Falcone. A big mistake. A fatal mistake. Private Falcone had grown up in Sicily, where violence was the norm. Then later, as a teenager, he had made his bones as a young hustler on the mean streets of Detroit, where he had become more than proficient with a knife. Even during his tenure as a Marine, he never left the barracks without his grandfather's Latama switchblade, which he kept neatly concealed in a custom sheath strapped to his forearm. So when three Korean thugs burst in on him while receiving fellatio, he didn't hesitate. Drunk and naked from the waist down, he fought off his attackers with vehement aggression. Within seconds, two of his attackers were thrashing on the floor in bloody heaps, writhing in death throes. The third, stabbed and bleeding out, ran for his life before he met the same fate.

Meanwhile, Stanley was down the hall, on the floor of his own room, naked and fighting for his life as five drunken thugs beat him savagely. But just as he was about to lose consciousness, the door burst open and Private Falcone came charging in. Time seemed to freeze as he watched his platoonmate fly into a murderous rampage. When the bloodbath was over, three more Koreans were dead and Stanley lay quivering on the floor, naked, bloody, clutching his broken ribs. Private Falcone, who was covered head-to-toe in blood, quickly helped him dress and half carried him to a nearby alley, where he stole an Army jeep and drove him to an American Army hospital. It was this night Stanley branded the don with a moniker that would last a lifetime. From that night on, Private Falcone became known as Pete "The Butcher" Falcone.

"A favor?" Stanley asked, blinking away the gruesome images of that distant memory.

"Yes, paisan," Don Falcone answered, sounding uncharacteristically apprehensive. "A very important favor. One I hate to ask but... I must."

Stanley looked into those intimidating dark eyes and noticed something he had never seen before. Vulnerability. Even desperation. That's when he knew this favor would involve Stanley's eldest son.

"Well, old friend, let me have it," he prompted, casually taking a sip of his scotch, doing his best to sound indifferent. "We go way back. Favors make the world go 'round. Lord knows you've done plenty for me. If it's within my power, I'll do anything to help you."

The old don set his glass of wine on the table and again locked eyes with him. "It's my grandson," he said, sounding dejected. "He needs your help…" He then leaned forward and dove into a lengthy explanation of the entire situation.

For nearly twenty minutes Stanley listened attentively, absorbing the don's every word, captivated by what he was hearing. It was almost like something out of a movie. Some thirty years ago, the don's only son, Antonio, had been murdered. Stanley remembered meeting "Tony" on several occasions. A tall, handsome, powerfully built man who looked like a younger version of the don. They even had the same unnerving dark eyes. The younger Falcone had been an upcoming star in their underworld organization, and was the don's pride and joy. But Antonio's murder had left him with a terrible void in his life. Even worse, the loss of his only son had left him with only a single heir who could carry on his family name—Antonio's infant son Omnio, the last Falcone. At the time, baby Omnio was a mere three months old, but he quickly became the don's new pride and joy. Now, as Stanley listened to the urgency and emotion in the don's voice, it was clear that this grandson meant the world to him, for he explained that Omnio was the rightful heir to the Falcone Family throne.

When the don finally made his request clear, Stanley leaned back in his chair and pondered it for a long moment, silently considering the potential fallout. "Don Falcone," he began in his most saccharine voice, "I'm going to be honest with you because I know you appreciate candor and you have always been straight forward with me." He paused and looked him in the eye for a moment. "You're one of my oldest and dearest friends. You know I'd do anything to help you. But I'm sure you understand that what you're asking is…" He shrugged and took a sip of scotch to calm his nerves. "Well, it's complicated. There are many variables to consider, and the timing is bad. Very bad. I mean, if someone on Capitol Hill or in the mainstream media caught wind of it, they'd have a goddamn field day. Congressional oversight committees live for shit like this. Imagine the rumors that would fly. Obviously, I mean no

12

disrespect to you or your family, but as you know there have been rumors over the years. Rumors that I have ties to... Well, to you and your associates. And it's been hard to deflate these rumors."

Don Falcone nodded pensively. "Yes, I know, Stan. It's why I've kept my distance over the last few years. Believe me, the last thing I want is those fuckin' hyenas in Washington hurling shit at your boy..."

The don stood and topped off his glass of wine. The fact that his hand was slightly trembling did not go unnoticed by Stanley. After gulping down the entire glass, he took a deep breath and continued, his eyes filled with emotion, his words forced and at times even rambling.

"...But this is very important to me, Stanley. *Very important!* Not just to me, but to my entire community. My Famiglia! Omnio is very dear to me. We're cut from the same stone. Sicilian stone. He honors the old decrees. Loyalty. Honor. Respect. He puts Our Thing first over himself. That's a rare thing in our Community these days. I have other grandsons, but he is the only one who can carry on my family name. I know I can't expect you to understand what that means to someone like me, but you must try. I'm Sicilian, and to a Sicilian the continuance of our Family name is everything. It's how we honor our ancestors. Omnio must carry on my name or I will dishonor mine. He must be given a second chance..."

Again he paused to revere the memory of his lost son. "Omnio is his father's legacy," he continued, his eyes glazing over with emotion. "He's an extraordinary young man. Just brilliant. He has potential to be something special. He's not like my other grandsons. They're a bunch of entitled, selfish brats who only think about themselves. They fight and bicker with each other like women. Every last one of them thinks he deserves their button. I can barely keep them from each other's throats. They weren't like that when Omnio was still around.

13

They feared him. He kept them all in line. Even the other skippers. But now..."

He stopped and again refilled his glass, the trembling of his hand even more pronounced. "My Family has never had a secure foothold in the Syndicate. Some of the others have been there for three, four generations. They're bigger and have more men on the street. They have people, even their own family, in the unions and government. I had to fight tooth and nail for my place in the Community. It took me a lifetime to earn the respect of the other *capiregime*, the Commission. Now I'm afraid my disgraceful son-in-law and his brats are going to destroy it all. As long as I'm alive, they stay in line. At least to some degree. But when I'm gone..."

His words trailed off and again stared up at the foreboding dark clouds that were nearly upon them. For several minutes he just stood there, leaning over the terrace balustrade, watching the approaching storm, his mind flashing back in time, reliving the many mistakes he had made in life. There was so much regret, so many things he wished he could go back and do differently. But it was too late now. He had to deal with the cards he'd been dealt, the choices he had made.

Stanley had never seen the don like this, so downtrodden and emotional. Nor had he expected him to divulge such intimate knowledge of his organization's inner workings. Most of it was far beyond his comprehension, and frankly, it scared him. These were matters not meant for his ears. But the don was a friend. A good friend. Stanley had no idea what to say in response, so he said nothing. He simply sat there silently sipping his scotch and puffing on his cigar, waiting for the don to continue.

"Omnio is not like them," Don Falcone finally spoke, his words barely a whisper. "And you know what gets me, Stan? Even after how they treated him so unfairly, he still loves them. They're his blood. To him, there is nothing stronger than blood. That is the true Sicilian way. I wish with all my heart that the

14

Commission would've given him a chance to take over. He was my choice, you know. He was always my choice. I knew he was the one even when he was just a little bambino. He was a born leader. His younger cousins used to follow him around like he was some kind celebrity. They called themselves *La Quattro Duchi*. The Four Dukes. And he was their Omnio, their King. But when they grew up, they became jealous of him. He was always bigger, stronger, smarter. More cunning. He..."

Again he let his words trail off, unable to continue, overcome with emotion. For several minutes his hands trembled, his face flushed with anger as he thought about how unjustly his beloved grandson had been treated by their own family. Their *Famiglia*.

The don's prolonged lapses of silence prompted Stanley to finally speak. "You said they treated him unfairly. What do you mean by that, Peter?"

Don Falcone looked at him with much softer eyes. It had been many years since his friend had addressed him without the prefix "don." But he didn't mind. After all, they were old friends. Very old. And he'd never been fond of the title anyway. He knew it was intended to be a show of respect, but it always made him feel like he was a character in some kind of Hollywood production.

"My grandson has lived a tough life," he answered, deciding that he might as well tell him everything. "He's what is known in Sicily as a *dragoni difetto*, or *tam messosangue*, a disparaging term used to describe a member of our community who is not pure Sicilian. It literally means born with a birth-defect. Here in America they just say *difetto*. Defective. You see, his mother was Jewish, and because of it, our rules forbid him from ever rising above the rank of a street soldier. So the others have ostracized him. His uncles and cousins turned their backs on him. But he didn't care. He struck out on his own, just as I did when I was a young man. And he was well on his way until..."

He took a long sip of wine and once again attempted to settle his

15

trembling hands. "There was an incident between him and his cousin Anthony. I can't get into that with you, but it led to this. The Commission ruled. I was in prison at the time, so there was nothing I could do to stop it. They allowed this thing to happen. They said he was a lone wolf. A maverick. Said he was becoming a danger to the Community, that I was giving him special treatment, that I was treating him like he was a full..."

He glanced at Stanley and decided he had already said too much. "Anyway, that's none of your concern," he said, a message passing between them. "But it's true, I did treat him differently. Because he deserved it! He earned it. I didn't care that he wasn't pure Siciliano. He was a brilliant young man, a mastermind who could squeeze blood from a rock. Even without the Syndicate's backing he was making a name for himself on the street. His men loved him. They were completely loyal and dedicated to him. He reminded me of myself at that age. I, too, started out a lone wolf. And look what I accomplished. Omnio may be a *difetto dragoncello* but his heart is that of a thoroughbred Sicilian. The others, they just never gave him a chance. And now, because of his mixed blood, he's suffering. As soon as I was sent away, they all conspired to get rid of him. First they tried to kill him." He jammed a meaty finger at Stanley. "Which of course they deny. He was too crafty for them. Outsmarted them from every angle. When they couldn't kill him, they took away his police protection. And when that didn't work, they set him up! The bastards should be ashamed. Where's their fuckin' honor? This isn't how Our Thing works. It goes against everything we're supposed to stand for. It's that little shit Anthony's fault. He's an emotional, jealous little worm. When he saw Omnio once again upstaging him..."

He took another sip of wine, the alcohol only adding fuel to his anger. "They were scared of him," he continued, waving a hand in disgust. "Every goddamn last one of them. Not just his uncles and cousins, but the entire Syndicate. Even some of the Commission *capi*. They feared he would someday become more than even they could handle, which he probably would've had they left him alone. I know they only let him live out of respect for me. Believe me, I know this. If The Round Table wants you dead, that's it, you're dead. End of story. But I also know that if they would have given him half a chance he could've been a great leader for our *borgata*. Maybe even the Boss. I know he could have fulfilled this dream if it wasn't for Anthony, that goddamn cockroach grandson of mine. The only reason I didn't get rid of his sniveling little ass was because of the love I have for his mother. He'll never be half the man Omnio is. Men like Omnio founded Our Thing in Sicily over two thousand years ago. Bold and fearless men of honor. Now his life is wasting away in that place because of what? Because his cousin was jealous of him? It disgusts me to even think about. That's why I'm here tonight, Stanley. You're the only one who can help him. I would never come to you like this if it wasn't of the utmost importance. If you do me this one last favor, I'll be forever in your debt. Without it, my name, my Family dies with me."

Stanley was bewildered. What the don was asking was next to impossible and considered ethical taboo for someone in his position. Unfortunately, the only person on earth who could grant such a favor was his eldest son, the President of the United States. But he did owe the don. The man had saved his life. More than once, actually. While stationed in Korea, Private Falcone had actually saved his life on several occasions. Later in life, it had been a young Don Falcone who introduced him to the world of big business. In fact, the don had been integral to Stanley's success in business. Then, throughout his political career, it had been the don's powerful business associates and political contacts in Miami who helped him maintain his tenure as a Floridian Senator. Though the don had never been one of the Mafia's top chieftains on a national level, he was feared, respected, and well-connected throughout his underworld organization. And he had come through for Stanley on many occasions, never denying him a favor. Stanley knew he owed the man more than he could ever repay. If it weren't for him, his own children wouldn't exist, for he would have surely been killed and forgotten in some filthy opium brothel back Seoul, Korea, over fifty years ago.

Stanley now stood and sauntered over to the terrace balustrade to stand next to him. For a moment, he just stood there, sipping his drink while staring out at the approaching thunderstorm. It had been threatening to rain most of the evening, yet the sky had produced nothing more than a few faint flashes of lightning and distant rumbles of thunder. But the storm was nearly upon them now. Mother Nature was about to unleash her full fury on Southern Florida. The temperature had dropped fifteen degrees in the last ten minutes. The sky was an inky, swirly mass of grayish-black clouds, illuminated by occasional bolts of lightning that crackled like Tesla coils from cloud to cloud. The once low rumbles of distant thunder now boomed ferociously from the heavens. Taking it all in, Stanley felt almost as if the gods were talking to him, warning him not to do this. But as he took a long pull from his smoldering cigar, he glanced over at those dangerous obsidian eyes and realized that he feared Don Falcone more than he feared the gods. He *had* to do this. It was a matter of honor. He owed it to him. It wasn't going to be easy, that's for sure. It would have to be kept completely sub rosa. If there were any leaks prior to it, a congressional oversight investigation could result. The FBI would be in an uproar. The Attorney General would be outraged. The media pundits would have a field day.

"Don Falcone..." Stanley began, fumbling for words. "I... I just..."

Don Falcone, sensing his apprehension, set a hand on his shoulder. "Stan, consider this an old friend's dying wish."

Those words hit Stanley like a brick and instantly made his trepidation over a potential scandal vanish. He took a step back and looked at the don incredulously. The man was old, yes, but not that old. For a man in his early seventies, he still looked healthy and fit. He was bulky around the waist, but his swarthy olive skin lacked the excessive wrinkles and liver spots that were so common with men his age. Although his hair was a whitish-silver, he still had a thick mane of it, every strand slicked back just so with pomade. He still moved with the grace of a predatory cat, and those onyx eyes looked sharp enough to cut diamonds. He did not look like a dying man.

"What do you mean 'dying wish?'" Stanley asked, confused.

Don Falcone looked up at the undulating clouds and, almost as if right on cue, the heavens above came to life with a brilliant flash of lightning and subsequent thunderclap. "I'm not well, paisan," he said earnestly. "I have a problem with my prostate. Cancer. And to make matters worse, the goddamn Feds are trying again to pin a RICO case on me. Say they got new evidence. Say I didn't do enough time the first time around."

Suddenly feeling in need of another drink, Stanley stepped over to the bar and poured himself two more fingers of scotch. "Not enough time?" he asked, unsure what that even meant. "I don't understand, I thought you did your time? Eight years, if I remember correctly."

"To hell with 'em," the don answered, waving a hand dismissively. "I'm tired of fighting those *puttanas*. They'll never give up until they see me die behind bars. But time isn't on their side. I'm dying, Stan. I got cancer. It's spreading. The docs say maybe six, seven months at the most. Go figure. I survived a blood vendetta in Sicily when I was a kid. I survived a war in Korea with you. I survived God knows how many indictments. I even make it through eight years in the clink. And it ends up being my goddamn prostate that takes me out. Pretty ironic, don't you think?"

Stanley, at a loss for words, leaned against the balustrade with a look of utter disbelief. He had always revered his old friend as an almost mythical figure. The eminent Don Falcone. The Butcher. Invincible. Indestructible. An immortal who would live on forever in infamy. But Stanley was now struck with the

19

realization that the man was indeed mortal, subject to the hands of time like everyone else. He was dying. And to add insult to injury, the government was still trying to lock him up. The heartless bastards couldn't just let the old man die in peace. They would chase him to the grave and slap an indictment on his casket. It was sad to see such a once vibrant and powerful man look so tired and weary.

Stanley drained the last droplets of his glass and set it down, deciding he'd had enough for now. "Another indictment?" he asked, still confused. "But I thought you retired years ago?"

"I did," the don shrugged. "But RICO has no statute of limitations. This new indictment dates back ten years, when they charged half the Syndicate with Operation Game Tax. Some shylock banker got pinched for laundering Mexican dope money and the Feds offered him immunity if he ratted us out. Bastard squealed like a stuck pig. Brought up all kinds of shit from way back. Some as far back as thirty years. Said I was in charge of the skim at the Stardust and Frontier hotels in Vegas. Now they have that rat bastard locked away tight in some Arizona Army base. The lawyers say he's willing to testify at my trial. The feds got him surrounded by a small army of military police. Can't even get to him. He's gonna say I helped the Syndicate extort Hoffa out of Teamster money to build the casinos and skim from them. If he makes it to the stand, I'll get twenty-to-life. Not that it matters. I only got a few more months."

Stanley studied him for a long moment. The once so menacing Mafioso suddenly looked like a defeated shell of the man he once was—a man who had saved his life and always been there for him when he needed him. Stanley knew he could never deny him this dying wish. He would never be able to live with himself.

"Well, Don Falcone, old friend..." he began, offering him a genuine smile. "I have not forgotten how you and your associates helped John get elected. Your campaign contributions. Your influence over the automotive unions. The help your political friends gave us in the primaries. Shit, now that I think about it, he may have never even gotten elected if it weren't for you. So, in a sense, I suppose he owes you this favor just as much as I do. I'll speak to him this week and see what he says."

The don's eyes suddenly turned cold and almost threatening. "Stan, you must insist! I'm counting on you. Your boy is my only hope."

Stanley looked into those eyes and swallowed the lump in his throat. "I will, Peter," he assured him, glancing at the two bodyguards, both of them suddenly staring at him with threatening looks of their own. "I'll tell John this is something he must do. But you have to understand that it won't happen until the end of this new term. That's almost four years from now. Not until his last days in office. That's when they all do it. Less time for the media to turn it into a fiasco. The vultures in the Hoover Building will bitch and moan for a few weeks when they catch wind of it. The A.G. will probably raise a stink. But hopefully we can sweep it under the rug without too many people noticing. If we're lucky, no one will really notice. Or care. But if they do want to make a fuss about it, fuck 'em. Jonathan will be done in Washington for the most part. And to tell you the truth, I don't foresee the media, or anyone else for that matter, looking too deeply into this. I mean, Pete, I say this with the utmost respect for you and your grandson, but in the eyes of the government he's a relative nobody. From what it sounds like he was never even a serious player in your organization. I'm sure the mainstream media won't even know who he is. And we'll do our best to keep it that way."

The don was still glaring at him, but the slightest grin played at the corners of his mouth. "Give me your word," he insisted, stretching out one of his massive hands. He said it as a request, but Stanley knew that it was an order.

"You have my word," Stanley said, grasping the meaty hand firmly. "Don't worry, old friend. As God is my witness, I promise you, Don Falcone, that whatever happens with your health between now and then, I will see that this is done when the time comes. I swear it on the lives of my grandchildren."

The don's slight grin morphed into a full smile as he pulled Stanley into a powerful embrace. "Thank you, paisan. You're a good man and a good friend. I knew I could count on you to handle this for me. You have done my Family a great service, one I can never repay. I hope that you get a chance to meet Omnio yourself. He's a bright star in these darkest of times for Cosa Nostra. In his blood runs the last vestiges of the old ways. We need boys like him to keep Our Thing from dying... to teach and lead the next generation. If there is anything that I can do for you, anything at all, please let me know. My life now belongs to you."

Stanley stepped back from his embrace and offered him a look of genuine love. "Don Falcone, you've already done more than enough for me. It's my honor to help you. My own family, my children and grandchildren, they wouldn't exist if it wasn't for you. The success I've had and everything I've accomplished in life, I owe it much in part to you. What kind of man would I be if I didn't do this for you?" He grinned and gestured toward the bar. "All I ask is that you stay a bit longer and have another drink with me. Let us reminisce more on the old times, back to when women loved us for more than just our money and power. Tonight we get drunk and recount our war stories. Speaking of, do you remember that night in Seoul, when we took on a bar full of Korean thugs?"

Just as the sky began unleashing a deluge of pelting rain, a manic grin appeared on the don's face. Paying no attention to the sudden downpour, he rolled up his sleeve and revealed an old leather sheath strapped to his forearm. In it was his grandfather's Latama switchblade, the very same knife from that night in Seoul so long ago. "How could I forget?" he said with a wink, and then they both burst into a fit of laughter and dashed inside to escape the rain.

# CHAPTER 1

## JESUP MEDIUM SECURITY FEDERAL CORRECTIONAL INSTITUTION JESUP, GEORGIA

It was mid-afternoon, and for once the inmates were behaving. From the south gun-tower, corrections officers Cox and Younger swept their eyes from inmate to inmate, looking for any signs of trouble. A number of heavily-muscled men were lifting weights under a tin-roofed "weight pit," the clanks of iron-on-iron creating a dissonant backdrop for the rap music that was blaring from several boom-box radios. A few prisoners were running laps on the dirt track that skirted the barbed-wire perimeter fences. Here and there inmates preformed calisthenics on the pull-up and push-up bars. A crowd had gathered to watch a heated basketball game on the main macadam court. A softball game was underway on the diamond, where a group of spectators had gathered in the bleachers to place wagers on their favorite team. As always, the prisoners were segregated into groups based on ethnicity, gang, or crime. In one set of bleachers, a group of high-level drug dealers were smoking cigars and playing dominos. The yard's north corner was dominated by several Latino gangs. Black Muslims dominated the south corner. A group of computer hackers, identity thieves, and other white-collar criminals occupied the picnic tables in the center of the yard, the most exposed and unsafe place to be. It was a classic scenario of strength in numbers. Some groups were larger and more dangerous than others, and often they were at odds with each other, but all seemed peaceful on the yard today, most likely a result of spring's early arrival.

Today the two correctional officers found themselves watching one specific group of inmates, a tight-knit group that always ran together, a group other inmates respected and feared, a group of Italians who were allegedly high-level mobsters. This was a federal penitentiary, not a state prison where criminals were housed with every facet of low-life street thug—rapists, murderers, armed robbers, drug dealers, larcenists, petty thieves, etc. The inmates here tended to be more of society's upper-crust criminals; high-level drug dealers, upper-echelon gang leaders, corrupt bankers, insider stock traders, book-cooking accountants, gun smugglers, corrupt lawyers, unscrupulous businessmen, various computer hackers, and a multitude of other criminal masterminds. And of course, there were the mobsters—the Italian Mafiosi who sat firmly atop the criminal totem pole.

Corrections Officer Michael Cox was a fairly new employee of the Federal Bureau of Prisons, only having worked at Jesup FCI for several months. But he had quickly learned the who's who of the inmates. "So that's him?" he asked his partner, peering through a set of Nikon binoculars, referring to one of the Italians.

His partner, Officer Jim Younger, had been working at Jesup FCI for nearly twenty years and planned to retire in less than two. Having grown up in the foothills of southern Georgia, Officer Younger was a backwoods bumpkin with no education beyond eighth grade. He looked, sounded, and acted like what he was—an Appalachian hillbilly. Yet he wasn't entirely stupid. He was an old veteran who always kept abreast of what was happening on the Jesup FCI compound, which he considered to be "his" compound as much as the warden's.

"Yeah, that's him," Officer Younger confirmed, looking at the same man through the scope of his Mini-14 assault rifle.

"So that's it, eh?" Officer Cox asked, still studying the heavily-muscled inmate seated in the softball bleachers. "Just like that they're gonna let him go?"

Officer Younger lowered his rifle, shrugged apathetically and spit a mouthful of chewing tobacco through the tower's open window. "It seems so," he answered tersely, preparing himself another wad of chew.

"How?" Officer Cox mused, mystified, finding it hard to believe such a thing was possible.

The Italian in question was one Omnio Falcone. Since transferring to Jesup almost a year ago, he had been a model inmate, always quiet and keeping to himself. For the most part, he only associated with what the Jesup faculty had dubbed "The Mob Squad," a group of roughly twenty Italian/Sicilians, most of whom were from New York. The Mob Squad was one of the most secretive and tight-knit groups in the prison, always sticking together on the yard, in the chow hall, and in the housing units. Upon Falcone's arrival at Jesup, the Mob Squad's leader, an old New York mobster named Vittorio Salestro, had taken a special interest in him. They were rarely seen apart. While on the yard, they would sit in the bleachers and talk for hours, or sometimes walk side-by-side on the track, always followed closely by several of Salestro's henchmen.

Warden Edward Gonzales had issued a staff-wide memorandum requesting that his faculty try to learn why the old mob boss was so infatuated with the new arrival, but the memo had done little good in terms of helping him learn anything. The vast majority of his staff were on Vittorio Salestro's payroll. And the ones who weren't had no way of penetrating the Mob Squad's inner circle, for the mobsters almost exclusively conversed amongst each other in a unique Sicilian dialect of Italian that was indiscernible to even the most seasoned interpreter. Though the Italians made up the smallest gang on the yard, they were by far the most powerful, controlling the sale of drugs, which the corrections officers brought in for them, and

25

the protection racket, which they enforced using contracted black and Latino gangs. They also controlled all facets of gambling on the compound, collecting a 10% vigorish from every book, every sports ticket, every craps game, and every poker table. For the right price, they could even arrange for a woman to be snuck in during the nightshift for a few hours of indulgence in one of the conjugal visiting trailers, a perk the Italians took full advantage of. They ran nearly every aspect of illicit activity in the prison, and they did it all right under the warden's nose. Each evening, after the warden went home for the night, Jesup FCI became alive with illicit activity, all of it run by the Mob Squad and overseen by corrupted corrections officers. Assisting the mobsters was very lucrative for corrections officers who traditionally made less than $50,000 a year. Working with the Italians at Jesup could, and often would, result in tripling that.

Officer Younger had learned the monetary perks of assisting the Italians many years ago when he first began his tenure as a corrections officer. Since then, many of the incarcerated Mafiosi at the facility had helped him compile a substantial retirement fund, as well as help him purchase a beautiful home in Savannah and a luxurious hunting cabin in the hills of Kentucky. However, his partner on this peaceful spring afternoon was not yet privy to the financial benefits of assisting the Italians of Jesup FCI.

Nevertheless, today Officer Younger was just as perplexed as Officer Cox about the handsome young Italian they were watching. Not even the warden himself knew how the newest member of the Mob Squad, a young man they had never even heard of before his arrival there a year ago, obtained an actual presidential pardon. On very rare occasions certain federal inmates received such pardons on a President's last day in office, but these presidential pardons almost always went to white-collar criminals who had powerful friends with vast sums of donative money. This guy appeared to be a relative nobody, from nowhere, just some random thug from Detroit. It made no sense.

"So nobody has a clue as to how he pulled it off?" Officer Cox asked incredulously, watching Omnio Falcone, Inmate #427265, through his binoculars.

"Far as I know, nobody knows how he did it," Officer Younger answered.

"Not even the warden?" asked Officer Cox, well aware of the fact that his partner was the warden's personal lapdog and ears of the compound.

"Nope," Officer Younger answered curtly, working a gob of tobacco into his lower lip. "I spoke to him myself. Said he got the papers from Washington about a month ago. Real hush-hush. Nobody's saying nothin'. Some hotshot Washington suit warned him to keep his mouth shut about it. I figure CIA. You don't wanna fuck with them CIA. Brought papers signed by the President himself. Tomorrow morning, the guy walks outta here a free man."

Officer Cox glanced at his rot-toothed partner and the first thought that popped into his head was that the man must have read too many spy novels. Then a second thought occurred to him: Officer Younger was probably too stupid to read. "So, who is this guy?" he asked, pushing such thoughts from his mind. "I mean, he had to know someone way up the ladder."

"No idea," Officer Younger answered, spitting a glob of sticky brown tobacco toward the window, some of it landing on his chest, most of it splattering against the wall under the window. "And I really don't care. Far as I know, he's just some punk greaseball from Detroit. Nobody special. Had a grandfather who did a stint here a while back. Some kind of shot-caller. Heard he ended up dying in a fire. I remember the old bastard. Real quiet. Had an accent. Always carried a shank. Stabbed a couple niggers for trying to extort him, if I remember right..."

He stopped, frowned, and let loose a fart that seemed to reverberate off the inside of the gun tower. "...Ahhh, I needed that," he said, shaking his leg, allowing a foul, rotten-egg stench to escape his pants and waft throughout the cramped gun tower. "Anyway, the kid came down with a million-and-one years. A lifer. Mile-long rap sheet. All kind of crazy charges—guns, extortion, conspiracy, armed robbery, you name it. They got him on the RICO this time. They all come down on the RICO. But no headline Godfather shit. Just your basic loser. He's only been here a year, but them old guineas really seem to like him."

Officer Cox tried not to gag from the smell. He found Officer Younger to be a crude, foul, disgusting bigot with the intelligence of an adolescent. He hated getting stuck in the gun towers with him. But such was his bad luck of the draw today. So, trying to ignore his wretched partner, he focused his attentions on the group of Italians gathered in the bleachers. There was at least a dozen of them, mostly younger men standing protectively around Vittorio Salestro and Omnio Falcone, both of whom were whispering in hushed tones.

"Yeah, well, Salestro seems to have taken a real liking to him," he said, stating the obvious. "He must know someone."

Officer Younger shrugged. "Just another dago thug, far as I'm concerned. They come, they go. Like I said, I remember his grandpappy. Looked just like him. Just older and shorter. They all end up here sooner or later. He'll probably be back if someone don't kill him first. Fuckin' guineas are always killin' each other. They worse than goddamn niggers. When the feds lock 'em up they all find a way to get transferred here. I always wonder how they do it. Call in a few favors, I figure. They like the weather down here. It's halfway between New York and Miami. That's where most of them come from. Less travelin' for their families come visit time…"

He stopped talking and appeared to be in deep thought for nearly a minute. "Funny thing is…" he finally continued, rubbing the gray stubble on his chin, looking as if he was trying to solve a profound riddle. "That Falcone character—they call him King— he's never even got himself a visit. Not one since he's been

28

here. Over a year. Most of them get visits, but he don't even have no one listed on his visiting list. Don't make no calls neither. Warden had me look at his file. Fuckin' guy never even gets mail. He lists no family, no emergency contacts, nothin'. Never even put in a phone list. He only got one letter since he's been here. There's a copy of it in his file. I read it. Came from Italy, or Sicily, or wherever the fuck they come from. Had no return address. Real short and cryptic."

"Yeah?" Officer Cox asked, suppressing a smile, surprised his partner even had the word 'cryptic' in his lexicon. "What do you mean cryptic?"

Officer Younger thought for a moment, his tiny brain working overtime. "Not really sure," he answered. "All it said was something about being a leader. Then something about a Duchess. I figure it was some kind of hidden guinea message. It was signed 'The Butcher.' The warden asked me to try an' figure out what it meant. My guess was the guy must've worked at a butcher shop or somethin'…"


Don Vittorio Salestro was not an old man, but he appeared much older than his 58 years. Short, balding, and an easy fifty pounds overweight, he did not fit the mold of the typical Hollywood Mafioso. Nevertheless, he was an exceptionally dangerous and powerful Mafioso. In fact, he held one of only ten coveted seats on the Mafia's Commission, AKA "The Round Table," a reclusive ruling counsel of Mafia chieftains from all over the country, moderated by the five New York Bosses but overseen by a single supreme Boss in Sicily. Salestro was a cutthroat old-school gangster from Brooklyn. He had dropped out of high school at age fourteen to work full-time for his mentor, Joe "Scarface" Scarponi, a one-time legendary New York *capo* who, before being killed by a rival *capo* in his own Colombo Family, had been the Boss of his Brooklyn-based *borgata* for almost twenty years. Naturally, after the death of his

29

mentor, Salestro had avenged his mentor and then used extreme violence to take control of his Boss' Family and subsequent rackets. Since his incarceration, however, his son Gino had been acting as the Family's interim boss.

Now, with less than four years left on his ten-year sentence, Don Vittorio Salestro sat in the bleachers and studied the handsome young Detroit soldier seated next to him. "Your grandfather was right about you, Omnio," he said, almost philosophically, taking a pull from his cigar. "After getting to know you, I also see your potential. You're a listener and you believe in the Old Ways. There's not enough young *soldato* like you left."

"I get it from my grandfather," King said, offering him a smile. "He taught me well."

Salestro took another pull from his cigar and studied him. "So tomorrow you begin the next leg of your journey," he said matter-of-factly, giving him a fatherly pat on the knee. "I gave you all I can from here. You have my blessing. My Family will support you. Gino and the rest of our people will assist you when the time comes. But first you have to prove to your own people in Detroit that you deserve to be straightened out. And like we talked about, you'll need to bring food to the table for this. That's the key, kiddo. You have to make yourself invaluable. Gino talked to the other members of the Round Table. They say Detroit is a fuckin' mess. Says all the skippers are at each others' throats again. Since your grandfather died, there's been a constant power struggle over who should be Chairman up there. Your Uncle Leoni is still in charge, but word is that he's sick and wants his boy to take over. Sounds like some goddamn bullshit if you ask me. I don't believe in the whole nepotism thing. Not when it comes to Our Thing. Which, yeah, must sound crazy since my boy is running the Family in my absence. But he earned it. I'm a firm believer that you have to earn your stripes. And Gino earned his. He deserves to be where he is. I dare anyone to tell him he doesn't."

30

He took a quick drink from a water bottle that was filled with cheap Kentucky bourbon. "Anyway…" he continued, savoring the strong whiskey. "That's what I think. Just wanted to give you a heads up. Your people up there have lost control of the casinos." He gave him a cold look in the eye. "That's really got The Round Table pissed off. It's costing everyone money. So if there ever was one, now is the time for you to make your move. The Commission would like to see someone take control of the Detroit Partnership. Even by force. Although, they would never sanction such a thing at the Round Table. Most of the old-timers are still tight with the Detroit skippers. A few of them are family by marriage. Chicago's Tony LaPina has a daughter married into your Family. Big Al Provazanno, from Jersey's DeCalvalcante crew, his son married Sal Tocco's daughter since you've been gone. Joe Polizzi's son is married to the daughter of a Bonanno *capo*. They're not looking to start trouble. But clearly something ain't working up there. Most of the old skippers are dead or locked up. The ones still left, your uncles and cousins, they can't seem to get along. Who knows, maybe you're the one who can bring Detroit back under control and reunite the Partnership. I had Gino mention this to The Round Table, but they still have a problem with you being a *difetto*. Personally, I don't know why. After all, Lansky was a Jew. Seigel was a *difetto*. You come from good stock. Don Falcone was from the Old Country. Your father was a *caporegime* before he was killed…"

He paused to catch his breath and wipe sweat from his brow with a handkerchief. "…Either way, I'm happy to see you go, kiddo. That old Senator in Florida really pulled it off. Nobody gets a fuckin' Presidential Pardon. At least not one of us. Don Falcone must've had somethin' good on the old fucker. Either that or they were closer than we ever knew. Whatever the case, he pulled it off. This shit is over for you, paisan." He paused and took in the bustling prison yard. "This is no way to live. Now you can go home and get back to business. But you'll have to do it without the help of the other Detroit skippers. At least for now.

31

After all, you ain't took the oath." He gave him a look and pointed his cigar at him. "And we ain't gonna get into what happened with your cousin. All the Detroit *capi* bitched and moaned about that whole incident. Needless to say, Anthony and your uncle aren't going to be happy to see you back on the streets. But The Round Table has ordered them to leave you alone. We made a promise to your grandfather before he died, and that promise still stands. But you'll receive none of the Syndicate's protection. You'll be completely on your own up there. You'll have to start from scratch. But if you can gain control of at least some of their major operations and bring the Commission its share, I think you'll get your button. For now, this is between me, you, and my associates on The Round Table. Not even your allies in the Syndicate need to know about it. Not yet. But the skippers up there have been ordered to let you operate independently. And they will. If they don't, they'll have to answer to us."

King suppressed a grin. "Thank you, Don Salestro," he said warmly. "I appreciate you speaking to the Commission on my behalf. My grandfather tried once, but they refused to listen."

"That was before Detroit stopped bringing bread to the table. They've lost control of the streets up there. Their coffers are leaking like a sieve. They even got some *melanzana* mayor that won't work with them. Can you imagine? How the fuck did they let *that* happen?"

"I will do my best to help get things back in order."

Don Salestro eyed him affectionately. "I think you'll do fine, kiddo. Just remember what I taught you: Money and fear make the world go 'round. You know how it works. You did it once, you can do it again. Make them fear you and they'll always fall in line. Bring food to the table and they'll have to respect you. I knew your grandfather. I met him many times. He was an honorable man. Old-school, like myself. He didn't contribute much to The Table on a national level, but he never failed to pay his dues. When your *borgata* was making money, he broke bread with everyone, including The Table. My mentor, Joey Scarface, God rest his soul, was always talking about your nonno. Said he was a true don, a Man of Honor. He followed the rules. He did his part in Vegas. He handled that fuckin' Jimmy Hoffa. He honored *Omerta* when the feds put the clamps on him. He helped us get gambling legalized in Motown. He worked to make us stronger as a whole. That's how a *caporegime* is supposed to act. And people feared him because he didn't take no shit from no one. Not even us."

King grinned as memories of his beloved grandfather flashed through his head. Indeed his grandfather was not the kind of man who was easily bullied or pushed around. King now recalled one particularly humorous incident. A pair of undercover FBI agents had been parked across the street from his grandparents' home in Grosse Pointe, an affluent suburb just outside the Detroit city limits. He was very young then, no more than four or five, but he had been very perceptive. While playing out front with his Tonka toys, his grandfather was pruning tomatoes in the backyard garden. At some point, he looked up and noticed two strange men parked in an unmarked car across the street. When he noticed the men pointing a camera at him, he immediately ran back to report this to his grandfather, who flew into a fit of rage. After picking up a brick, his grandfather charged out into the street and hurled the brick at the FBI car, smashing out its window as he screamed Italian expletives at the two bewildered agents inside. Nonno Falcone was like that. He definitely did not take any shit.

"You must recruit good *cugine*," Don Salestro continued, interrupting King's nostalgic reverie, sounding as if he were plotting a corporate takeover. "Reliable soldiers. Italians are fine but Sicilians are better. Only from your community. They must know how to take orders and follow them without question. They must love you, respect you, and be prepared to lay down their life for you. Most of all, they must know the consequences of betraying you..."

He paused for a moment as a memory interrupted his train of thought. "...Fear, Omnio, is the key," he continued, sneering. "I remember, many years ago, Gino came to me with a seemingly trivial problem. Some punk *cafoon* ran off with ten pounds of his grass. Not much in the grand scheme of things—we were moving thousands of pounds at the time—but it was the principle of it. The kid showed no respect for Gino or the Family. I told Gino to find him and make an example out of him, but the kid went into hiding. After a few weeks we tracked down the kid's partner and threatened to kill his mother unless he gave up where his partner was hiding. The kid was from Reggio di Calabria. A fuckin' rat Calabrazzi. Punk had no heart. Gave his partner up quick." He expelled a rumbling guffaw and took a pull from his cigar. "But my boy is one cold sonofabitch. Rather than off the kid who actually stole the grass, he had the kid who stole the grass whack his rat Calabrazzi partner for giving him up. Put 'em both in the back seat of a stolen Eldorado and Gino gave the thief a clean piece. Made him pop his rat fink goomba right in the face so his momma couldn't have an open casket." He made a pistol with his finger and smiled. "POW! Blew the fucker's head all over the back seat. Gino ended up letting the thieving little punk keep the ten pounds. It wasn't the money, you see, it was the principle. An opportunity. The kid who stole the grass learned two valuable lessons. First, the consequences of crossing the Family. Second, the value of loyalty. Instead of losing his life for his infraction against us, it was his disloyal friend who paid the price. And for that, the kid swore his life to Gino. He's been one of our most loyal soldiers ever since. You see? It's all about fear. This, Omnio, is something that you must always remember."

King nodded his understanding. "I won't forget, Don Salestro. I'll never forget what you've taught me. I'm honored that you've vouched for me with the Commission."

Don Salestro grinned a toothy grin. "I'm sure you'll someday make it up to me. When I get out in a few years, you'll come to

New York and meet my Family. New York is a lot like Detroit. Sicilians have a long history there. Whole neighborhoods are Italians and Sicilians. We're like celebrities back in the old neighborhoods. You'll see. We'll eat and drink at Gino's club. He's the Boss of Brooklyn. They love him there."

"I'm sure they do, Vittorio."

"For now," said Don Salestro, setting a hand on King's shoulder affectionately, "may Madonna dell'Annunziata be with you. God knows you have more than a few enemies back home. I'm sure a lot of people up there won't be happy to see you back in the neighborhood. But fuck 'em. It's time someone in the Syndicate gets their shit together and sets your *borgata* back on track."

King glanced at the softball diamond, where several players had begun arguing. "I have a plan," he said, offering the old mob boss a conspiratorial grin. "I just need to get out of here."

"Yes," said Don Salestro, also turning toward the commotion on the softball diamond. "You've told me this plan. It's bold as hell and won't be easy, but if your men love you the way you say they do, you already have a head start. Just remember, your men have to fear you before they can love you. They must know the consequences of betrayal. They have to prove their loyalty by eliminating one of your enemies. And they must, **must** adhere to *Omerta*. When *Omerta* is broken..." He motioned a hand around the prison yard. "This is what happens. A fish never gets caught if it don't open its mouth. Capisce? Learn from what happened in New York. That rat Graziano, Vinny Massino, Tony Casso, Gotti. They fucked everything up. It all comes down to patience. *Col tempo la foglia di gelso diventa seta*. Vinny The Chin used to always tell me that. It means time and patience can turn a mulberry leaf into satin. The world belongs to the patient men. Look at us in here. If there is one thing you learn in here, it's patience. But it has only made us stronger, smarter, more ambitious. Remember that, my friend, and maybe someday you'll be Detroit's *Capo di Tutti Capi*."

35

Suddenly, without warning, one of the arguing softball players snatched up a baseball bat and began beating one of his antagonists savagely. Pandemonium ensued as the yard erupted into an all-out brawl between two sects of Latino gangs. Shanks and other various weapons were produced. Don Salestro's bodyguards instantly formed a protective shield around him and King. Nobody dared approached them.

Within a minute the emergency alarm was blaring, and nearly two-dozen officers came charging out onto the yard, all of them covered head-to-toe in full riot gear. Warning shots were fired from the perimeter gun towers. Cans of tear gas were dispatched. Inmates were tossed to the ground and ordered silent.

Ten minutes later the entire inmate population was back in their respective housing units, locked in their cells, the compound on emergency lockdown for the remainder of the day. Not that it mattered to King Falcone. He had less than fifteen hours before he would be a free man for the first time in eight years.


Several hours later, back in his cell, King Falcone packed an army-style duffle bag with the few meager belongings he had accumulated over the last eight years. There wasn't much: A cheap MP3 player; several books on Alexander the Great and other famous military strategists; a 13" color TV; several old photographs; and a letter he received nearly two years ago.

As he packed, he found himself staring at the letter. It was signed "The Butcher," which had been his grandfather's moniker. But his grandfather had died in a house fire two years before he received the letter, so he knew it wasn't actually from his grandfather. The letter had been postmarked from Palermo, Sicily, with no return address. He still had no idea who sent it, but he was forming an idea as to why it was sent. At the bottom of the single page, under the sender's signature, was a single line that read: "7 & Duchess. A true soldato is loyal till death."

His thoughts were interrupted when his cellmate, Lucky, a skinny black kid from St. Louis, saw him staring at the letter and decided to speak up. "Hey, King, what the fuck you staring at? You just blanked out."

King offered him a grin. He genuinely liked the guy. Lucky was young, only 22, and much smarter than he looked. Especially when it came to computers and all things technology. He was in prison serving eight years for hacking into a federal bank, where he had surreptitiously siphoned one dollar from over a million separate accounts, essentially making himself an instant millionaire. Had his girlfriend not snitched on him for refusing to buy her a new Mercedes-Benz, he would have actually gotten away with it. Women, King had thought to himself when Lucky told him the story of his downfall. They were so often the cause of a man's ruin.

"This letter," he answered, holding it up to his young cellmate, "I still don't know who actually sent it, and I'm trying to figure out what it means."

"Yeah?" Lucky asked, lighting a joint and holding it out to him. "Well here, Craig. Smoke some weed, Craig. Expand your mind, Craig. It's Friday… You ain't got no job… Let's get *hiiiiiiiiii!*"

King laughed and gave him a look. "Luck, how long have I been in this cell with you?"

"About a year. Why?"

"How many times have you offered to smoke weed with me?"

"Pretty much every day."

"And how many times have I actually smoked?"

"None. What's your point?"

"My point is this: What makes you think, after all this time, I'll suddenly want to smoke?"

"I don't know," Lucky shrugged. "Guess I figured since this is your last night you might want to indulge. You know, celebrate your release with a little puff-puff-give."

King chuckled and glanced at the smoldering joint, its sweet, pungent aroma already filling the cell. It had been many years since he smoked pot or even drank alcohol. He preferred to keep a clear head. But Lucky did have a point: This was a night for celebration, and smoking a little pot might help settle his nerves.

"What the hell," he said, taking the joint, inhaling deeply. Within seconds he felt a mellow buzz coming on.

"Yeah, mon," Lucky said, taking on a faux Jamaican accent. "That's that good ganja, mon. The rasta ganja, mon."

King shook his head and glanced down at the letter. Within seconds he once again found his eyes transfixed on the words scrolled across it.

"So what's it mean, brah?" Lucky asked, reverting back to his natural computer geek self.

"I still don't know who sent it," King answered, focusing his burning eyes on the piece of paper. "But I'm pretty sure it was sent to make sure I go see an old gumbadi."

"A gum-what?"

"Gumbadi," King laughed. "It means best man. You know, like at your wedding."

"You never told me you were married."

"I'm not. It can also mean good friend. Like best friend."

"You fuckin' Italians," Lucky said, puffing on the joint. "Ya'll think you're the Godfather. There ain't no Mafia. That shit is all Hollywood."

King just grinned and returned his attention to the single sheet of paper in his hand. Some people were just naive. People like Lucky would go through life never knowing how Cosa Nostra influenced nearly every aspect of modern society, from the federal government down to local municipalities, all overseen by a small group of powerful men that most of the world would never know existed. And that was exactly how they wanted it.

# CHAPTER 2

Omnio "King" Falcone spent his last night in prison tossing and turning, trying to find a comfortable position on his lumpy mattress. But he was far too anxious to sleep. He'd spent the last eight years formulating a master strategy that he promised to implement if a day ever came when he was released from prison. And that day had finally come. In a few hours, he would step back into the world a free man. And as he now lay on his bunk, tossing and turning, he found himself meditating on the minutiae of his strategic blueprint. Over and over he reviewed every step he'd have to take, every ally he'd have to make, every obstacle he'd have to overcome. It was all perfectly clear, real in his mind as the bars of his cell. Finally, he would face those who put him there.

All night he lay there, mostly staring at the concrete ceiling, wide awake, listening to Lucky's rhythmic breathing, the occasional toilet flushing in a nearby cell. The night seemed to stretch on forever. Then, finally, just after 7:00 in the morning, he heard the jingle of keys and approaching footfalls echoing off the cinderblock walls down the cellblock. He knew they were coming for him. His heart began to race, and suddenly Warden Gonzalez and Officer Younger were standing in front of his cell.

"It's time, Falcone," Warden Gonzalez said coldly, emotionless, motioning for Younger to key open the door.

As King gathered up his bedroll and duffle bag, Lucky jumped off his bunk and embraced him affectionately. "It was good knowin' ya, man," he said, and then offered him a wink.

40

"When you're tappin' that first ass, make sure you give her one for ya boy."

"I will, Luck," King chuckled, stepping out of the cell, making no attempt to look back at the 8'x10' broom closet that had been his home for the last year.

Warden Gonzalez and Officer Younger escorted him from his housing unit to the prison's control center, where he turned in his bedroll and prison-issue garb. Vittorio Salestro had arranged for a new Baroni suit to be deposited into his property, and though the designer suit was a bit tight around the neck and shoulders, it was much better than walking out wearing one of the khaki jumpsuits the prison usually provided indigent inmates upon their release. Don Salestro had also arranged for $3,000 to be wired into King's prison account, so at least he wouldn't be walking out completely destitute.

"So what's your plan, Falcone?" Warden Gonzalez asked, watching him put on the expensive black suit in a small Quarter Master annex.

King stepped in front of the wall mirror and began carefully tying his tie. "My plan?" he parroted, not even turning to acknowledge the warden. "Why, to take over the world, of course."

"Pinky and the Brain," Officer Younger mumbled under his breath.

Warden Gonzalez shot his dim-witted employee a look. "Pinky and the what?"

King was suddenly grinning, but he said nothing as he continued perfecting his Windsor knot in the mirror.

Officer Younger looked like a starved mutt cowering under its abusive master. "Pinky and the Brain," he said nervously. "It was a cartoon. Brain was a little mouse with a giant head... because he had a giant brain... that's why they called him Brain. He was always saying how he was gonna to take over the world."

41

King chuckled inwardly, having predicted Officer Younger would recognize the Brain's mantra.

Warden Gonzalez studied King for a moment, wondering if his officer had just made him the butt of some kind of inside joke. "Seriously, Mr. Falcone, what's your plans now that you're a free man?" he asked for the second time, ignoring his officer. "You going back to Detroit?"

With one final adjustment to his tie, King turned to face the warden, who stood a good half-foot shorter than him. "What I plan to do, and where I plan to do it, is none of your business." He gestured a hand around the room. "Here in this pathetic little world you think you control, you like to think you're someone special. But in my world, where I come from, you're nothing. I'm no longer one of your inmates, so my plans are none of your concern. You can take this prison and go fuck yourself with it. Now, if you don't mind, I have a bus to catch."

Face flushed with anger, the warden led him over to a discharge counter without saying another word. He figured he would surely see the arrogant young Mafioso again sooner or later. If they didn't get themselves killed first, they almost always ended up back in prison. And they almost always found their way back to Jesup. When this one did, Warden Gonzalez would make sure he paid for his insolence.

King was issued several items: papers to verify his official release from federal custody; a personal identification card; a bus ticket; and a state-issued debit card loaded with the amount of $3,090—the extra $90 from saving three months of his measly $30 monthly prison pay, which he earned working in the prison's surprisingly extensive library. During his eight years in prison, he always found a way to work in the library. He loved reading and learning, and he had spent much of his time holed up alone in his cell, self-educating on everything from history, politics, and sociology, to corporate business, venture capitalism, and the stock market. He studied history's greatest military minds, from Alexander the Great and Sun Tzu, to

George Patton and Douglas MacArthur. He read books penned by some of Wall Street's foremost investment strategists. He taught himself about banking, corporate structure and tax codes. He read books on cultural etiquette, fine foods and fine wines. From his studies he learned how to act worldly and cultured if needed, such as in the presence of powerful businessmen or men of influence, whom he knew would be integral to the success of his master plan. No longer could he walk around like he was just another street thug. For his plan to succeed, he would need to carry himself differently, with a touch of panache and sophistication. Even old-school bosses respected an educated, cultured and well-spoken man.

From the control center, Officer Younger escorted him outside to the prison's front gate. "Well, this is it, Falcone," said Younger, motioning an officer in an overlooking gun tower to open the gate. "You're a free man, now." There was an audible clank and a loud buzzing alarm sounded as an electric motor powered open the gate. "But you'll fuck up and be back."

King turned and narrowed his eyes on him menacingly. "That's right, I am a free man now," he said with projected contempt. "But you, you brainless idiot, will never be free. You'll forever be a redneck buffoon trapped in his own pathetic little world of nothingness."

With that, King Falcone stepped through the open gate a free man. Some fifty yards away he saw the bench where he was supposed to wait for a shuttle bus to pick him up and deliver him to a Greyhound station in town. Next to the bench was a dumpster that he headed straight for. Not wanting to keep anything that would remind him of his time behind bars, he deposited nearly the entire contents of his duffle bag in the dumpster. The only item he kept was a leather wallet he'd bought from an inmate who made it in a craft class several years before. Inside it were a few old photos, his new ID, the $3,090 state debit card, a bus ticket, and the ambiguous letter he received from Sicily three years ago. Everything else went in the dumpster. Fifteen minutes later, he loaded onto a crowded city shuttle bus that took him to a Greyhound station in Jesup, where he planned to catch a 10:00 AM bus north to Detroit.

In the lobby of the Greyhound station, several people were quietly waiting for buses to arrive. With nothing else to do, he sat on a bench and almost immediately smelled the distinct aroma of bacon, his favorite. Wondering where it was coming from, he peered out the front window and noticed a small cafe across the street. His stomach began growling with excitement. The old analog clock on the wall read 9:05. Plenty of time for him to eat a quick breakfast.

He smiled at woman quietly feeding a baby in a stroller a few feet away. "Excuse me, ma'am, do you know if there's a bank anywhere nearby?"

He was relieved to learn there was indeed a federal bank just around the corner. So, with almost an hour to burn and his stomach demanding food, he walked to the bank, cashed out his entire debit card, and headed straight for the little cafe. As he ate, though, he began noticing the café's other patrons discreetly watching him, which really wasn't all that surprising. Not only did he look like a starved animal, grunting and groaning as he scarfed down his food, but a man with his exotic looks, wearing a $3,000 suit, was not a common sight in a small town like Jesup. But regardless of their oblique stares, he devoured his food with impunity, as if he was the only person in the room. He simply did not care about exercising table etiquette. Not today. Not after being deprived of real food for eight years. He devoured his entire meal within five minutes and declared it the best meal of his life, if only because he'd forgotten how good "street" food tasted.

After he finished, he sat in his booth, feeling bloated and satisfied, quietly reading a local newspaper and sipping black coffee. At 10:05 he saw a Greyhound bus pull into the station across the street. Tucking the paper under his arm, he left a $10 tip on the table, thanked his waitress politely, and strolled from the cafe with a determined pep in his step, ready to meet his destiny.


After a layover in Atlanta and stops in Chattanooga, Knoxville, Lexington, Cincinnati, and Toledo, his bus arrived in Detroit twenty-one hours after leaving Jesup, just as the sun was coming up. At exactly 7:08 in the morning he debarked from the bus and stepped into a surprisingly busy Greyhound terminal. Making his way outside, he stopped on the sidewalk and breathed deeply for several minutes, taking in his surroundings. Home. His beloved city. All the familiar sights, sounds, and smells flooded his senses. The air was damp and cold, the sky gray and overcast. Morning dew slicked the cragged macadam of Lafayette Avenue, where the first of the city's morning commuters raced toward their downtown office buildings. The smells of garbage and automobile exhaust battled for odor supremacy. Steam wafted from manhole covers in the middle of the street. Police sirens sounded in the distance, echoing off abandoned buildings and modern skyscrapers alike. A pair of rough-looking black prostitutes eyed him salaciously while ignoring a snoozing bum sprawled on the sidewalk behind them. A malnourished mongrel rifled through a pile of garbage someone had deposited on the sidewalk.

"Home sweet home," he mused, taking in the scene with a smile. He couldn't wait to get to work. But first, he needed to get himself a hotel room and do some shopping. Yes, he needed a nice room with a hot tub to soak away the memory of prison. Then he would use the hotel's gym to get a little workout in. A good workout would settle his nerves and clear his head.

After hailing a passing taxi, he instructed its driver to take him to the Renaissance Center, the city's largest skyscraper, where he paid $450 dollars for an executive suite at the Detroit Marriott. When he stepped into the luxurious room, the first thing he did was he strip naked and order breakfast from room

45

service. The second thing he did was pour himself a glass of cognac from the mini bar and then submerge himself in a steaming hot tub. Within minutes the cognac began taking effect, relaxing him as the hot water loosened muscles that were stiff from the long bus ride. He was so comfortable, in fact, that he didn't even bother getting out of the hot tub to answer the door when room service arrived with his breakfast. He simply called out to the attendant and had it delivered straight to him as he soaked in the bubbling water.

"Can you do me a favor and have my suit cleaned and pressed?" he asked the attendant, handing her a $20.

"Yes, sir," the attendant answered with an appreciative nod. "I'll bring it down now and have the concierge return it to your room as soon as it's finished."

"Perfect," King said, and then settled back into the water to relax and enjoy his breakfast.

Rejuvenated after his breakfast-in-bath, he was ready for a good workout but had nothing to wear. So, with nothing else to do, he sprawled out on the room's sumptuous bed to take a brief nap while his suit was being cleaned and pressed. But he hadn't anticipated how incredibly comfortable the bed was. Having barely slept over the last several days, and after sleeping on a rock-hard prison mattress for the last eight years, the bed had a drug-like effect on him. Mere seconds after hitting the pillow he was comatose, and he didn't wake up for nearly six hours. When he finally did roll out of bed, he felt like a new man, his body completely recharged.

Since he'd slept the entire day away, he decided to postpone his shopping excursion and have a little fun. Tonight he needed to release a bit of pent-up energy. Particularly sexual energy. After all, he had been locked up eight years and had only occasionally taken advantage of the conjugal visiting trailers at Jesup. Hookers had never done much to arouse his libido. Early on in life, he had found that he only became aroused by women when they were genuinely aroused by him. The fact that hookers were paid professionals had always been a turnoff, to the point that he usually lost any desire for them. But tonight he wasn't interested in a hooker. Tonight he was interested in the company of a good girl. A nice girl. Perhaps a little romantic ambiance with a ride down Lakeshore Drive.

Deciding he knew just the place to find such girl, he quickly showered and used the room's complimentary assortment of toiletries to shave and ready himself for his first night on the town in over eight years. While he'd slept, the hotel's concierge had returned his suit, clean and pressed as requested, so after slipping into it he called the front desk and had them order him a cab. Ten minutes later he ducked into the backseat of a taxi that reeked of curry and was driven by an Indian driver with a turban.

"Eight Mile and Gratiot," he said, handing the driver a $20. "Players."

Like most taxicab drivers, this one had a lead-foot. Within a minute they were racing down the Lodge Freeway at nearly 90 mph. Fifteen minutes later the driver turned off East 8 Mile Road into the parking lot of Players Gentlemen's Club. Located on Detroit's northeast border, Players was one of the city's premier strip clubs. Known citywide for its beautiful girls, it was one of only three 4-star gentlemen's clubs in the entire city. Before going to prison, King and his crew had frequented the club often, usually as a place to conduct informal business meetings. He knew its owner, a little man named Salvatore "Little Sal" Finazzo, who was in fact just a front-man for the Syndicate, as were nearly all the strip-club owners in Detroit. Finazzo was a sleazy Italian pimp who worked for the Vito Adamo, boss of the Syndicate's powerful Toccio crew. A low-level flesh peddler, Finazzo liked to act as if he had Syndicate status because he was the brother-in-law to one of the Syndicate's top chieftains. In actuality, he was nothing but a lackey they used to throw the feds off their trail. But he had always treated King with respect whenever he dropped by, comping his drinks and meals, seeing that he was entertained by the finest girls the club had to offer.

47

King had always been cordial with the man out of respect for the Toccio crew, which was headed by Giacomo Toccio, one of the most seasoned and powerful *caporegime* in the Syndicate, second in power only to King's uncle, Leoni Gianolla, the Syndicate's current Boss of Bosses. But King never really liked Finazzo. Pimping women had never been part of his crew's operations, though he fully understood it was one of the Syndicate's most lucrative street rackets. Using strip clubs to prostitute women was extremely profitable and easy to do. But not all of the strippers were "working girls." Many were just regular girls. Some were college students by day, exotic dancers by night. A few were even nice girls who had found a very lucrative way to make fast money using their bodies without actually selling it for sex. And tonight he was hoping he might become acquainted with one such girl.

After tipping the taxi driver, he stepped into the club's entry foyer and was instantly met by a hulking bouncer. "I.D. and ten dollar cover," growled the huge bouncer.

King was a bit caught off guard because in his previous life no one had ever asked him for identification. Nor had he ever paid a cover charge. At least not there in Detroit. Before going to prison, he had been well known throughout the city. Club owners, managers, bouncers, they all knew him and his notorious crew. No one would have dared asked him for identification. By the time he was eighteen, he was a regular on the local club scene, and at nineteen he opened his own a nightclub. No matter where he went, owners, managers, and bouncers always gave him VIP treatment. But that was a different time. Things had changed. People—bouncers, management, owners—they were all new. He'd also changed. His old acquaintances probably wouldn't even recognize him if they walked right by him. After all, eight years was a long time. He went in at 24 and came out at 32. He had matured into a grown man, and the years of heavy weight lifting had added a lot of muscle to a frame that had already been muscular to start with.

King pictured the club's owner in is mind. Little Sal Finazzo. Short, maybe 5'5", with long greasy hair slicked into a pompadour. Always clad in a cheap suit. Lots of gold chains. Fake Rolex. Gaudy nugget bracelet. Too much cologne. Perpetual bad breath. A repugnant little man for sure, King remembered, but he considered asking for him. Then he figured name-dropping probably wouldn't get him anywhere with this robotic bouncer now demanding to see his identification.

"Actually, paisan, I don't have any I.D. on me," he explained to the bouncer, a mammoth Italian wearing a black tuxedo and bow tie. "I left in my hotel. But I'm pretty sure you can see I'm old enough to get in. I'm thirty-two."

The bouncer sized him up. "Sorry, pal. No I.D., no get in. You know how it works."

King glanced inside and spied several nubile young beauties gyrating around a set of poles on center stage. "So how much is it gonna cost me to get in?" he asked, removing a wad of cash from his inside pocket, knowing a shakedown when he saw one.

The bouncer glanced at the money and studied him for a moment. *Nice suit, which meant he had money. Handsome, like a movie star. Built like an NFL linebacker. Eerie black eyes that for some reason made him nervous.* "You ever been here before?" he asked, avoiding direct contact with those eyes.

"Sure," King shrugged. "But it's been a while. About eight years. Why?"

"You look familiar but I've only worked here for three years so it must be from somewhere else."

King nodded, mildly annoyed. "So what's the ticket, paisan?" he prompted, finding this whole charade ridiculous. After all, he knew the bouncer was just looking to make an extra buck.

"Fifty," said the bouncer, looking at the wad of cash.

49

King handed him a $50, brushed past him and headed straight for the bar, paying little attention to several girls who instantly locked lascivious eyes on him.

"Do you still serve Player's Punch?" he asked the bartender, a bubbly blond wearing a tuxedo top unbuttoned to display her ample cleavage.

"Of course," she answered. "It's our house special. Would you like one?"

"I would," he answered. "But not too strong. I'm a bit of a lightweight."

As she went to making his drink, he turned on his barstool and took in the scenery. The room was dark and filled with smoke, but there was just enough light for him to see across the club. Seated at tables and booths were well-dressed men, their eyes transfixed on half-naked beauties who were teasing them with the seductive movements of their bare hips and breasts. Rhythmic music poured from ceiling-mounted speakers. Scantily clad waitresses scurried about, delivering watered-down drinks to patrons who were already drunk with testosterone and lust. A heavy mixture of cheap perfumes lingered in the air. Several guys were in the middle of receiving lap dances, their eyes locked on nearly naked bodies as they whispered to their "dancer" in hushed tones, surely doing their best to wow them with inflated tales of generosity and large bank accounts. Seated in one of the preferred corner booths was a group of four Chaldean Arabs smoking cigars, talking loudly and laughing boisterously while several topless girls flitted around them like a flock of lusty-eyed nymphs. They were tossing money at the girls like it had no more value than the paper it was printed on, and they were clearly having the time of their lives.

"Here you are, sir," said the busty bartender, handing him his drink, a sweet concoction of coconut rum and fruit punch. "That'll be eight-fifty."

He handed her a $10 and motioned for her to keep the change. "You guys still make a good steak Siciliano?"

"Of course," she said, flashing him a flirty smile. "The best in town. Would you like one? Comes with a side of spaghetti and garlic bread."

"That would be wonderful," he said, slowly taking a sip of the strong, fruity drink, eyeing a curvaceous raven-haired beauty over the rim of his glass. "I'll also have an appetizer of bacon-wrapped shrimp. Steak medium. And tell the cook to add a spoon of sugar to my sauce. In fact, you can bring me a side of sauce and some fresh bread with the shrimp."

She punched his order into a computer. "Anything else?"

"Nope. Just make sure the cook adds sugar to the *sugo*. But only one spoon."

"One spoon of sugar to your sauce. Got it. I'll have your bread and sauce brought right out with your shrimp. Your steak shouldn't be too long. I'd say about fifteen minutes at most."

"Perfect," he said, and then returned his attention to the main floor. The sexy raven-haired girl was now staring straight at him as she gave an older man in a cheap suit a lap dance. He made sure she knew he was watching her, and the instant she finished teasing the old man, she collected her gratuity, slipped on a bikini top, and made a beeline straight for him.

"Want a dance?" she propositioned coquettishly.

He slowly took a sip of his drink and studied her for a moment. He could smell her perfume. It reminded him of the flowers his grandmother used to plant around their house every spring. Not strong. Faint and pleasant. She was short. The top of her head barely came to his chest. Maybe 5'2", about 130 pounds, and very curvy. Her jet-black hair was styled in a pageboy that gently curled under her chin. Her eyes were big and round, light blue with long natural lashes. Her fair skin had faint tan lines on breasts. She was compact and stout but not overly muscled. She was curvaceous, just the way he liked his women, and he wondered if her almost disproportionately large breasts were natural. She was more cute than beautiful, yet he found her extremely arousing. He'd always had a thing for short girls, especially brunettes built like this one.

"Sorry, shorty, but I don't get dances," he declined politely, casually sipping on his drink.

"You don't get dances?" she echoed, looking slightly disappointed. "Then why are you in a strip club?"

"Well," he shrugged, "they make a good steak here. Or at least they used to."

She gave him an incredulous look. "And I suppose the scenery is just a bonus?"

He tipped his glass to her. "Exactly!"

She stared up at him for a moment, taking him in. He was tall and powerfully built under his suit. Very good-looking. Boy, was he good-looking! It wasn't often a guy with his looks came into the club. Especially one dressed in a 3-piece suit. She wondered who he was, where he had come from, and why he was dressed so formally. There was definitely something very different about him. One thing that she found unusual was that he was yet to even glance at her breasts, which she considered her most endearing physical feature. Usually, every man she came in contact with stared at her chest as if they were under some kind of spell. And after a year of working there, she had grown to find it repulsive. It made her feel like a piece of meat. But not this mysterious Adonis. He looked her dead in the eye when he spoke, and because of it, she suddenly felt uncharacteristically insecure and exposed.

"So why don't you get dances?" she asked, trying to hide her breasts by folding her arms over them.

Just then the bartender set two small plates on the bar. One had his bacon-wrapped shrimp, the other slices of fresh Italian bread and a small ramekin of spaghetti sauce. "Your steak should be ready in a few minutes," she said, and then returned to pouring drinks.

King dipped a piece of bread in the sauce and popped it in his mouth. It was delicious. The bread was fresh and the cook had added just the right amount of garlic, oregano and sugar to the sauce. It wasn't his grandmother's *sugo*, but it wasn't bad for generic restaurant sauce. He dipped and ate another piece of bread and then finally returned his attention to the little brunette, who was still awaiting an answer as to why he didn't get lap dances.

"Not my style," he shrugged, washing down the bread with a sip of Player's Punch. "Never been. I'm not paying you to tease me. Why would I give you money just to get me worked up and then watch you run off and work the next mark?"

She reeled back and glared at him. "So you're judging me?"

"Of course not," he said, chuckling at her angry inflection. "Settle down, shorty. That's not what I meant. I respect your hustle. But, like I said, it's not my style."

This seemed to placate her slightly. "So what's your style?" she asked, intrigued by his uncanny ability to speak to her without ever glancing down at her chest.

He popped a shrimp in his mouth, savoring it for a moment before answering. "Well..." he began, then paused to take another sip of punch. "Giving you money to tease me just seems like a waste."

Now she looked even more offended. "A waste!" she spat, loud enough to turn the heads of several people within earshot.

"Yes, a waste. I mean, if I were to spend my money on you, it would be to take you out to a nice dinner. Maybe a movie afterwards. And if I like you, and you like me, we could go somewhere private and dance for each other. Just the two of us. Alone. No teasing."

She expelled a melodic giggle of incredulity. "Oh, shit, that's a great line, pal," she said, sounding genuinely impressed. "And original. I've never heard that one before. You're a slick one, I'll give you that. You're obviously a player."

He raised an eyebrow. "Not quite. That wasn't a line. You asked why I don't get dances, so I told you. That's all. It doesn't make ma a player."

53

"But you are. I can tell."

Feigning indifference, he took another bite of bread and glanced around the club, which seemed to be getting busier by the minute. "Not that I'm trying to get rid of you, shorty, but shouldn't you be working? I mean, you're not making any money standing here talking to me."

She hopped up on the stool next to him. "I could use a break," she said, brushing a lock of raven hair from her face. "How 'bout you let me buy you a drink?"

"How 'bout you let me buy you one?"

"You won't buy a dance, but you'll buy a girl a drink?"

He shrugged and glanced down at her body, making sure she saw it. "I suppose it's the least I can do. I mean, it's been a while since I've been in the company of a beautiful woman."

Suddenly she was blushing. "You think I'm beautiful?" she asked, coyly, feeling even more insecure and exposed than before.

"Very," he said, half-honestly.

She knew he was lying, but she could tell from the look in his eyes that he was attracted to her. He had been watching her since he stepped through the door. She would be lying if she said she didn't like it.

"You haven't been in the company of a beautiful woman?" she asked, staring up at him with intrigue. "What does that mean? How long has it been?"

He looked her deadpan in the eye. "Longer than you would believe."

"Try me."

He was about to answer when the door to the kitchen swung open and out stepped a man wearing a white chef's apron and matching hat. In his hand was a plate of steak and spaghetti. The instant he saw King seated at the bar his eyes went wide with recognition and disbelief.

"Holy shit!" the chef exclaimed. "I don't believe it. King Falcone in the flesh! Sugar in the sauce. I knew it had to be you!" He set the plate on the bar and extended a hand to him. "Goddamn, man, it's been forever!"

Joe Boulin had been a cook at Players for over twelve years, but he was no an ordinary cook. He practically ran the place. Having grown up in the rough, lower-middle-class suburb of Roseville, a small city just a few miles outside Detroit, he was a slick and effervescent street hustler, which was how he landed a job at Players in the first place. Over the years, he had taken full advantage of his position at the club, bedding innumerous strippers, acquiring countless connections and contacts, and selling cocaine, pot, and ecstasy to the revolving door of strippers who worked there. His main charge was not as the club's head cook or resident drug supplier, but rather it was to act as a liaison between the club's many regular patrons seeking the services of working girls, an operation overseen by Vito Vitale, the club's real owner. Everybody knew Joe. And since he worked at Players, people assumed he was well connected to the Syndicate's top brass. Which was partly true, since he did in fact, report to Vito Vitale, a Toccio captain. But King knew Joe was really just a small-time pimp and dope pusher, a puppet for the Toccio crew.

King gave him a firm handshake. "Hey, Joe, how ya doin?"

Joe stepped back and looked him over. "Jesus Christ, man!" he exclaimed. "You got big as a fuckin' house. But..." He shot a furtive glance around the club and lowered his voice to a whisper. "I thought the feds had you for good? Somebody said you were never coming home."

"Apparently, somebody lied to you, Joe," King said, grinning cryptically, noticing from the corner of his eye how the little brunette was studying him intently. "I'm back for good. Just got out yesterday."

Joe eyed him suspiciously, his mind flashing back in time. Back in the day, King Falcone had been a bit of a local legend around town. But he wasn't supposed to be there. He was supposed to be serving a life sentence in federal prison. Joe wanted to ask how he got out but knew better than to press the issue, for some things just weren't meant for his ears.

"Well, it's good to see you, man," Joe said, jerking a thumb over his shoulder toward the kitchen. "When your order came back, it was like a blast from the past. You're the only guy who ever asked for a spoon of sugar in the sauce. That's how I knew it was you. I remember you used to go ape shit when I forgot the sugar."

King chuckled. "Yes, well, you know us Sicilians. We prefer a touch of sugar in our *sugo*. It's a secret the rest of the world has yet to discover. So don't tell anyone."

Joe laughed and held his right hand up like he was swearing an oath. "Hey, your secret is safe with me, King. Mum's the word..." Again he cast a nervous glance around the club before lowering his voice to a whisper. "But hey, does Tony G. know you're home?"

King shrugged, feigning indifference. "Maybe, maybe not. But I'd appreciate it if you didn't tell anyone you saw me. I don't need any drama before I even get settled in."

Joe nodded his understanding, the message perfectly clear. Though King made him nervous, Joe had always liked him. The guy had a style and presence about him. He was a real Mafioso through and through, and he wasn't ashamed of it. Shoot, he was proud of it. He had never flaunted his status, but at one point he had been well-respected and feared by even the top bosses. He and his crew used to come into the club looking like real bigshots, always accompanied by a couple of intimidating bodyguards, just like in the movies. And even though none of them were Made Men, they were respected because of King's grandfather. Even Joe, a nobody cook at a strip club, knew of the legendary Pete "The Butcher" Falcone. The old boss had been a living legend before he died. King, the don's favorite grandson, had once run around the city like he owned it— because he could. Back then, nobody dared cross the favorite grandson of Don Falcone. That is, nobody outside his own family. At one point, King and his cousin, Anthony Gianolla, son of the Syndicate's current Boss, had some kind of falling out. It had been very hush-hush. Nobody knew exactly what happened, but it was right before King was indicted and supposedly sent away for life. That was the last Joe had ever heard of King Falcone. Nobody ever talked about him again. Yet here he was in the flesh, back in Players, wearing a 3-piece suit and ordering his signature breaded Sicilian steak and spaghetti with sugared meat sauce. And he was looking more menacing than ever. But he was alone, with no sign of his crew. Joe figured he would at least have Johnny New York with him. Back in the day, King never went anywhere without Johnny New York.

Joe now gave him a curious look. "So, King, did you stay in touch with any of your guys while you were away?"

"Not really," King answered, draining his drink and motioning the bartender for another. "Haven't heard from them in years. I guess most of them work for Anthony and my uncle now."

Joe gave him a surprised look. "What about Johnny New York? Wasn't he your right-hand-man?"

King displayed no outward reaction, but the mention of his best friend and *protettore* sent a wave of emotion surging through him. "Haven't heard from him either," he said stoically. "I told him to forget about me and focus on taking care of his family. He wrote a few times. Even came to see me once or twice. But we had nothing..." He shrugged. "I told him to move on."

The bartender set his drink on the bar. King took a quick sip and looked Joe in the eye. "You seen him lately?"

Joe nodded thoughtfully, knowing he was definitely missing something here. "Actually, yeah, I have. He runs Duchess. Over on Seven Mile. Place is a bit of a dive but he's got a few decent girls working in there."

The little brunette cleared her throat, as to let them know she was still there. King glanced down at her, wondering why she was still lingering. "On Seven Mile, you say? Seven and what?"

"Seven and Duchess," Joe replied. "Right on the corner. Why, you gonna go see him?"

"Maybe," King said, glancing at his plate of food, his mouth salivating in anticipation. "But right now, Joe, I'm starving and my dinner's getting cold."

Joe looked at the plate on the bar. "Oh, sorry, King," he apologized, and then waved over a handsome, middle-aged man wearing a sharp suit. "King, this is Jerry Bobcheck, our manager. Jerry, this is King Falcone. He's an old friend of Sal's."

Jerry extended a hand to him. "Pleasure to meet you, Mr. Falcone," he said, shaking his hand as if he was meeting a celebrity. "If you're a friend of Sal's you're a friend of mine." He waved over a behemoth bouncer who had been lurking in a nearby hallway that led to the club's dressing room. "Carmine, show this gentleman over to our best VIP booth. See that his meal and drinks are comped. And make sure the girls treat him right. He's a friend of Mr. Finazzo's so he gets the platinum treatment."

"I appreciate that," King said, and then offered Joe a parting handshake. "Thanks, Joe. It was good seeing you. Give Vito and Sal my regards. And remember what I said: You didn't see me." He turned to the little brunette, who was trying to act as if she hadn't been listening. "Excuse me, shorty."

A waitress carried his food while Carmine the bouncer led him over to a reserved VIP booth at the back of the club. "So you're King Falcone," said the bouncer, slowly looking him over.

King slid into the booth shot him a look. "You say that like you've heard of me."

The bouncer waited for the waitress to set his food down and leave before answering. "I've heard guys talk about you."

"Yeah?" King asked, looking up at him with a touch of surprise. "And what did they say?"

The bouncer suddenly looked uncomfortable. "Nothing really," he said nervously.

King raised an eyebrow. "Nothing?"

"Well..." the bouncer shrugged. "I mean, I've heard guys say you used to have a lot of pull around town. And..."

"And what?"

The bouncer suddenly looked like he wanted to run. "And you were serving life in prison."

"Well, they were misinformed," King said curtly, dismissing him with a wave of his hand.

As the bouncer lumbered off to resume his post by the dressing room, King turned his attention to his meal. It had been over eight years since he had tasted steak Siciliano, and it was just as delicious as he remembered. But he exercised perfect table etiquette, taking his time to savor every bite of the tender breaded steak. As he ate, a steady stream of silicone-enhanced beauties began stopping by his table to offer him lap dances, which he politely declined, although this didn't dissuade them from staring at him as he ate his dinner.

Ever since he was a young man, girls had always found the physical appearance of Omnio Falcone appealing. And now, as a grown man, his 6'2", heavily muscled frame gave him an even greater appeal. But there was something more. He emanated a certain energy, an aura of danger and mystery that women were drawn to like insects to light. His unique obsidian eyes seemed to bore into the soul of whoever he turned them on. No matter where he went, women of all ages stared at him with intrigue. Though he didn't usually mind how women appreciated his looks, tonight he was feeling a bit self-conscious about all the overt stares he was receiving. He just wanted to enjoy his dinner and maybe find himself a nice girl to take home.

Strangely, the one girl he had his eye on was the only girl who didn't approach him for a dance while he ate–the short brunette from the bar. He found her to be very attractive, and hoped that she might come over and join him for dinner. But she, for whatever reasons, was the only girl in the club acting like he didn't exist. And he wondered why.

After his meal, he ordered his third glass of Player's Punch. Just as he settled in to drink it, he watched the buxom little brunette take the stage for her requisite hourly striptease act. He made sure she knew he was watching her as she strutted around the poles seductively, and he noticed her glance at him several times. She even offered him a few discreet smiles. He became mesmerized by the movements of her hips and breasts. Maybe it was the alcohol muddling his perception, but she seemed to be dancing for him. By the end of her performance she was looking directly at him, their eyes locked as if they were the only two people in the room. Watching her, his heart began to race and he suddenly found himself sweating under his suit. He felt a stirring in his loins that he hadn't felt in over eight years. Something about her reminded him of a woman from his past, a woman who had once been very dear to him. Though this girl didn't possess the striking beauty of the woman from his past, they were built similar—short and petite with full breasts, muscular legs, and perfectly shaped round buttocks. He wanted her. Badly. He only hoped that she wasn't a hooker or junkie. She didn't look it, but looks could be deceiving. If she were, it would most certainly ruin her appeal. After all, he was looking for a good girl.

Indeed she was watching him watch her. As she stepped off stage, she felt a pang of trepidation when he began waving her over to his table. She hesitated, sensing he was trouble. She had begun working at the club over a year ago, and since then she had encountered every type of unscrupulous characters. Most were just run-of-the-mill perverts and sexual deviants, or men who had never seen an actual naked beautiful woman in real life. But there were also a lot of criminals and shady guys who frequented the club. Most commonly were drug dealers. Usually of the black persuasion, they were low-level street dealers who always presented themselves as if they were bigshot high-rollers, a result of watching too many rap videos. Just because they walked around with a few thousand dollars in their pockets, they felt like they could objectify the girls like they were all whores who could be bought with a little cash. Then there were the stick-up guys who only came in to splurge after a particularly good score. They were good tippers and sometimes fun to hang out with, but they were usually lowlifes who would get drunk and brag about their latest criminal exploits. Then there were the professional athletes who tossed money around like it grew on trees. They usually came in when their girlfriends and wives failed to meet their sexual needs. After a few drinks, they became inflated with self-worth and acted like the girls should fall at their feet. And she couldn't forget the married businessmen whose wives thought they were attending important meetings, when in fact they were there at the club drinking and soliciting the "working girls" to have sex with them at a nearby motel. But the list of sleazeballs didn't stop there. She couldn't forget the upper-class perverts—the crooked cops, narcissistic politicians, alcoholic judges, and corrupt city officials. The list went on and on. They all treated the girls like they were nothing but sexual play toys for hire. The club's owner, Sal Finazzo, always gave these men special VIP treatment because they were men who could dole out favors.

Of course, the club's most common patrons were simple blue-collar factory workers who came in every payday to get drunk and spend all their money on lap dances before going home drunk and broke to their angry wives. But she could deal with such men. They were relatively harmless, and the bouncers handled them when they got out of line. She had even learned to enjoy and appreciate their attention.

There was, however, one group of patrons who made her nervous. No, they made her more than nervous. They downright scared her. The Italian Mafiosi. The wiseguys. She knew from the grapevine that the club was owned by Italian mobsters, an enigmatic lot of men who came in from time to time. Mysterious men in dark tailored suits. Dangerous-looking men who always posted a couple of intimidating bodyguards by the bar and front door. They had money but never flaunted it. They usually sat in one of the VIP booths and talked in hushed tones as they ate dinner. They rarely got lap dances from the girls, who were given explicit instructions to never, ever approach them during their informal dinner meetings. It hadn't taken her long to learn the who's who of their pecking order. Sal, the club's owner, often made himself seen when they were around. And he always made sure to treat the ones with rank like literal royalty, though they rarely seemed impressed by his efforts. In fact, they sometimes acted like they were the ones who actually owned the place, using Sal's basement office when they wanted a more private setting or a place to play high-stakes poker games. They did solicit the services of working girls from time to time, but never once had they propositioned her. Somehow they knew she was one of the rare few who wasn't for hire. Occasionally she'd dance for one of them, and they would tip her generously, but they always made her nervous. She knew they were bad men. Dangerous men. Maybe she had watched too many movies, but she wanted nothing to do with mobsters. Twice she had been asked out by one of them, and though they had been handsome and very respectful, she wanted nothing to do with such men. Even though she didn't really have a steady boyfriend, she had broken the cardinal rule of stripping by telling them she was in a serious relationship. She came to work to make her money and go home, not look for a boyfriend. Stripping was just a way to pay the bills until she finished school and launched her own business.

Unfortunately, tonight she was working, which meant she couldn't just ignore the dangerous-looking man now beckoning her over to his table, even if he gave her the heebie-jeebies. Sure he was handsome, well-dressed, and had certain mystique about him. But she knew from eavesdropping on his conversation with Joe that he was some kind of Mafioso fresh out of prison. From the way Joe had treated him, he obviously had status. Because Joe almost never fussed over the wiseguys who frequented the club. In fact, tonight was the first time she had ever seen him come out of the kitchen to pay homage to one of them. He had acted as if this ominous brute of a man had once been some sort of boss, which she found surprising since he was relatively young. It was almost always the older ones who received such gestures of respect. She wished she could just ignore him and go back to working the blue-collar drunkards who worshiped her like she was a goddess. But he was waving her over, staring at her with those scary black eyes, so all she could do was play it cool and hope that he would lose interest in her. After all, the working girls were always eager to entertain a man like him. Because the last thing she needed in her life was some mobster fresh out of prison obsessing over her.

"Would you like a dance?" she asked playfully, morphing into her flirty work persona as she stepped up to his table.

He chuckled and shook his head. "Why do I feel like we've had this conversation before?"

"Deja vu?" she quipped, forcing a smile. "So… is there another reason you called me over?"

"Is that a proposition?" he asked, grinning salaciously.

"No, it isn't," she said, unable to suppress an amused giggle. "But you called me over. I didn't want to seem rude."

"I still owe you a drink."

"I'm not thirsty."

He pointed at the empty booth across the table. "Sit."

She remained standing and folded her arms across her chest. "Wow, is that an order?"

"Please sit?" he amended, trying to disarm her with a smile. "Is that better?"

"A little," she admitted, grinning slightly, finding his charm nearly impossible to resist.

He flagged down a passing waitress. "My friend here would like a...?" He looked at her and waited for her to fill in the blank.

63

"A Diet Coke, Pam. No ice."

The waitress gave King an eager-to-please look. "And for you, Mr. Falcone?"

"A Corona and lime," he said, having had enough Players Punch.

"Right away, Mr. Falcone," said the waitress, scurrying off toward the bar.

The petite brunette stood there with her eyes narrowed on him curiously. "So… *'Mr. Falcone,* who exactly are you?" she asked, exaggerating the pronunciation of his name.

He studied the contours of her face for a moment, never letting his eyes drop below her chin. Maybe it was the alcohol, but she seemed even more attractive. Very unique looking. Bordering on beautiful. Like a little porcelain China doll. Big, innocent doe eyes. But why did she seem so standoffish? Most strippers were much more aggressive.

"What's your name, bella?" he finally asked.

"I asked you a question first," she countered defiantly.

"I'll tell you after you tell me your name."

"Paige," she said with little conviction.

He raised an eyebrow. "Paige?"

"Yes, Paige."

"I meant your real name."

The first rule of exotic dancing was never divulge your real name to a patron, and she had never broken it before. "What makes you think Paige isn't my real name?" she asked, trying to avoid those probing dark eyes.

"Oh," he shrugged, "let's just say I have a knack for knowing when people are lying to me."

The look he was giving her made her giggle. For some reason he made her feel giddy, which was odd since she never got giddy around guys, especially customers. "Fine," she acquiesced, "I shouldn't tell you but my real name is Madonna. But if I said that first, you wouldn't have believed that either."

"No, probably not," he admitted, unconsciously glancing at her bare navel. "So, Madonna, are you going to sit and at least have a drink with me?"

Her conviction wavering, she slid into the booth across from him. "One Diet Coke. But then I have to get back to my paying customers."

"Madonna," he said, almost to himself, rolling the name over in his mind. "I like it. A bit ironic, but I like it."

"Ironic?" she asked with a confused look. "What do you mean ironic?"

"Well, the name Madonna evokes thoughts of the Virgin Mary. And, no offense, but you being a stripper is a bit of a contradiction."

She took a moment to decide she wasn't offended by that. "Huh, I can't believe I never thought of that."

He slowly examined her features for a moment. "So, Madonna, may I ask your nationality?"

"Why?"

He shrugged. "I was just wondering if you might be Italian."

"I'm French, actually," she said proudly. "Can't you tell from my looks and my pudgy nose?"

He glanced at her nose. "It's a cute nose."

She leaned back in the booth and began to blush. "You men are all the same. You all tell us what you think we want to hear. But you don't have to lie. I know my nose is too pudgy."

"I have to disagree. I like it. I think it fits you perfectly. You're a doll. I'm sure guys tell you that all the time."

She narrowed her eyes at him, trying to discern if he was just running more of his playboy game. Guys were always running their sycophantic bullshit on her. Especially here at work. The men who came in night after night were almost always the same. Sleazy. Horny. Eyes burning with lust. No matter who they were, their attempts to impress her were universal—flaunting their money, always claiming she was the

65

most beautiful girl in the club. It became trite and redundant. But the money was good, so she always played along.

"Sure, guys run their game on me all the time," she said with a meek shrug, trying her best to maintain eye contact. "But I know they're full of shit. You, though? You're good. When you say it, you almost sound like you mean it. You're obviously a player."

He furled an eyebrow, a bit surprised that such an attractive girl was so insecure. "I assure you, sweetie, I'm no player."

She was ready to challenge this when the waitress returned and set their drinks on the table. But when King tried to pay for them, the waitress refused to take his money.

"Sorry, Mr. Falcone. I can't take your money. Jerry said your dinner and drinks are on the house."

"Then take this for yourself," he said, thrusting a $20 at her.

Again she refused, holding up both hands as if in surrender. "Thank you, Mr. Falcone, but you're a house guest. I can't take your money. House rules."

As she scurried off, a slight frown appeared on his face, for he didn't appreciate being calling mister. It made him feel old. He had to remind himself that he was no longer a young man, but in fact a grown man wearing a $3,000 suit. Forcing away such thoughts, he took a sip of his Corona and returned his attention to Madonna.

"So where were we?"

"You were trying to convince me you weren't a player," she said, grinning, slowly taking a sip of her Diet Coke through a curly straw. "And I was about to say you're full of shit like every guy who comes through these doors."

His eyes bored into her. "That's awfully cynical for such a young girl. And dead wrong. Like I said, I'm not a player. It's not my style. If you knew me you'd know this. I just call it how I see it. You're a beautiful girl. It's not hard to see. That's no line. No bullshit. It's simple fact."

She suddenly felt flushed and uncomfortable, even embarrassed. There was something about this large and dangerous-looking man. He had originally shunned her up at the bar, but now he seemed to have cast a spell on her. A spell that was somehow overriding her usually astute sense of better judgment. Why did she feel so drawn to him? He was older, but by no means old. Probably early thirties. Yet he carried himself like that of a much older man. More mature, with the swagger and confidence of a man who came from a background of pedigree and prestige. But he wasn't overbearing. So many men with his looks and charm were arrogant to the point of cocky, but not this one. Yet based on his looks alone, he had reason to be cocky. Whatever it was, he now had her feeling like a teenage schoolgirl. She didn't like it. Not one bit. Sure, he was strikingly handsome and charming, but her gut told her he was a bad man. A dangerous man. And her gut had never led her wrong before. It was time to forget she ever met him and get back to work.

"Well, Mr. Falcone, it's been nice talking to you," she said, offering him a polite smile as she slid to the edge of the booth and prepared to leave. "And thank you for the Coke. But it's still early, and I need to make some money. Gotta pay the bills."

He gently grasped her hand, motioning her to remain seated. "At least finish your drink," he said, a softer look in his eyes. "And do me a favor, call me King. Just King. The whole 'mister' thing makes me feel old."

His touch was electric, sending a surge of heat through her body. She suddenly had goose bumps and felt light-headed. His hand was so large and strong, callused and rough the way a man's hand should feel. She wanted to get up and run, but she was paralyzed, unable to move a muscle. Why did he have to be so damn good-looking? And those eyes! Why did she feel as if they were reading her every thought? It took her a moment, but she regained herself and settled back into the booth, deciding he wasn't going to let her leave even if she wanted to. Which, she now realized, she didn't.

"King?" she chuckled. "And you had the nerve to question my name?"

"My real name is Omnio. It's a derivative of an old Latin word that means King. Sort of a regional word used in Sicily where my family is from."

She studied the countenance of his face. "So, *King*... how old are you?"

"Thirty-two. How old are you?"

"Twenty-three."

He nodded and shot a quick look around the busy club. "Well, bella, I understand you want to get back to work and make some money. But would you at least stay and finish your drink with me?"

"Why?" she asked, her eyes locked on his. "If you haven't noticed, the other girls in here are drooling over you. Most of them are way prettier than me and they all know you're some kind of..." She let the words trail off and glanced around nervously.

"Some kind of what?" he prompted, casually taking a sip of his Corona, his eyes again boring into her.

She leaned forward and whispered conspiratorially. "I know what you are. Jerry doesn't give just anyone the platinum treatment. Not even the athletes get it. Only wiseguys. And only ones who have status. So that means you must be a someone."

He leaned back in his booth, his hand clutching the sweaty Corona bottle. "You know..." he said, then took a sip and tipped the bottle to her. "From the moment I saw you something told me you were more than just a pretty face." He surveyed the loud, smoky room. "But as to who I am... Well, I'm nobody special. I barely even know Sal Finazzo. And I never met your manager before tonight. I know Joe from back in the day, but I haven't seen him in years."

"But you *are* Italian?" she asked, clearly sensing he was downplaying who he was.

"Sure," he shrugged. "I'm half-Sicilian. Is there anything else you'd like to know?"

She thought for a moment. "Nope. That tells me enough. I might be just a stripper, but I'm not stupid. I know what goes on in here. I know what Sal does and who he really works for, and I also know there is a lot more to you than you're letting on. You're just selling me a canard."

"A what?" he asked, confused.

"*Vendre des canards a moitie*," she said in perfectly enunciated French.

He raised an eyebrow. "What is that, French?"

"Yes. It means to half-sell the ducks. English translation: You're half full of shit. I told you, Mr. Falcone, or King, or whoever you are, I'm not stupid. I heard you and Joe. You just got out of prison, and that's why you said you haven't been in the company of a woman for so long."

"I said I haven't been in the company of a *beautiful* woman," he corrected, flashing her a smile.

She rolled her eyes. "You just don't give up, do you? I know I'm not beautiful? Cute, sure, but far from beautiful. I'm too short and chubby to be beautiful. Beautiful girls are tall and skinny."

He slowly took in her curves. "Beauty is in the eye of the beholder," he said, sipping his Corona. "Some guys like girls with nice curves."

"Yeah, right!" she scoffed. "Find me a guy who prefers short girls to tall ones, and I'll find you a girl that prefers fat old men to guys who look like you."

"That's easy. You're looking at one. I've always preferred short girls to tall ones. I don't like bony girls. I'm Sicilian. We like our women to eat and have curves. It means they're healthy and fertile."

He then stared at her for a long moment without saying another word. There was something very different about her, something he had not expected. A high level of intelligence. It was in her eyes, but also in how she talked. She was articulate and well-spoken. Not just for a stripper, but for any woman her age. Clearly, her job here was just a theatrical performance she used to put food on the table. But he sensed there was much more to her. He found himself very intrigued and suddenly wanted to get to know her better.

"Madonna," he finally said, "Do you mind if I ask you a personal question?"

"Depends what it is."

"Do you like working as an exotic dancer?"

She eyed him suspiciously. "You mean do I like being a stripper?"

"If that's what you prefer to call it."

"It pays the bills," she shrugged, a touch of shame in her eyes.

"That's not what I asked."

She suddenly became very defensive. "I know it sounds cliché, but I'm only doing it to put myself through school. I'm studying to be a certified public accountant. You know, a CPA. When I graduate I'll help people do their taxes, balance their bills, consolidate debt, give investment advice, stuff like that. My goal is to start my own accounting firm. I was thinking maybe even on-line. The Internet gives me access to millions of potential clients."

King nodded, impressed. Just as he suspected, she was indeed more than just a stripper with a cute face. She had a head on her shoulders, and from the sound of it, one with a pretty good brain in it. Seeing her in a whole new light, an idea began forming in his head, the gears of his mind clicking away.

"So what do you think of Mr. Finazzo?" he asked, studying her reaction.

She narrowed her eyes on him. "That's a loaded question. He's your friend."

He shook his head. "I assure you, Salvatore Finazzo is no friend of mine. I told you, I barely know the man. To be honest, I always thought he was a bit of a slimeball."

At that she expelled a melodic giggle. "Hey, great minds really do think alike."

"So, are you with someone?" he asked, studying her face for any telltale signs of deception.

"Are you asking if I have a boyfriend?"

He nodded. "Yes."

Of course, she always told customers that she was single and available. It was part of the job, one of the cardinal rules of stripping. Men always spent more money on lap dances when they thought they actually had a chance. To them, it always came down to their wallets. Though she played along and always pretended to be impressed by their money, it was simply a ruse to encourage them to keep spending it on her. The truth was that she was not impressed by money. She wasn't looking for a sugar daddy. She made her own money. Quite a lot of it, actually, and she was entirely self-reliant. Unlike so many of the other girls she worked with, she would never depend on a man to take care of her. The fact that she didn't have a boyfriend made it all that much easier to dupe men into thinking they had a shot with her. But she would never date a guy from the club. Especially not one who tried to impress her with money and hollow promises of material gifts. She found such men to be repugnant and pathetic.

But this mysterious Adonis hadn't tried to impress her with money, even though from the way he was dressed it appeared he had some. He also didn't seem to be putting on an act for her, pretending he was someone he wasn't. In fact, he called himself a nobody. She knew that was a lie. She was certain, just from the way he carried himself, that he was indeed somebody. Or at last had been before he was sent to prison.

"No," she answered honestly. "I don't have a boyfriend. Haven't had one since I started working here almost a year ago.

Guys are just too insecure about it. But it's no big deal. I don't have time anyway. I go to school full-time at Wayne State. I work here six nights a week. I've got my own place, bills, a cat. Plus, I'm saving for grad school. Who needs a man? They're too clingy and jealous. Nah, I'm good. I don't have time to be bothered."

He nodded pensively and glanced at her diet Coke. "So let me get this straight: You don't drink. You're going to college. You got your own place. No boyfriend. And you're saving for grad school. Wow, if that doesn't break the stripper mold I don't know what does."

She burst into full-out laughter. "Huh, I never thought of it that way. But don't tell anyone. You'll ruin my bad-girl image. And if you're wondering why I don't drink, it's because I'm allergic to alcohol."

"Seriously?" he asked, eyes wide with surprise. "I've never heard of anyone being allergic to alcohol. What happens if you drink it?"

She gave him a deadpan look. "Oh, I have a terribly adverse reaction. Trust me, you don't ever want to see it."

He leaned forward with his elbows on the table. "Seriously, what happens?"

"I get drunk," she said matter-of-factly. "It ain't pretty."

This caused him to expel a thunderclap of laughter that reverberated throughout the entire club, attracting the attention of everyone within. That was the icing on the cake. Not only was she cute and smart, but she was also witty and funny. Right then and there he decided he had found his good girl—and quite possibly more.

"Madonna, do you have a car?" he asked.

"Of course, why?"

"Would you take me somewhere?"

"When?"

"Now."

"But I'm working."

"So what?" he shrugged. "You said it yourself, Jerry thinks I'm a someone. I'll just ask him if you can take the night off."

She glanced around the crowded club. "It's Friday night. Look how packed we are. He'll never let me leave."

"Just let me handle it," he said, a dangerous glint in his eyes. "I'm sure I can persuade him to let you take the rest of the night off."

"But I..." she began, but it was too late. He was already on his feet, heading for her manager, Jerry, who was posted by the bar. All she could do was sit and watch while he had a hushed exchange with her boss. As she discreetly watched them talk, she couldn't help being amused by how he towered over Jerry, both in height and sheer size, and how Jerry almost seemed to cower in his presence. After several head-nods from Jerry, they shook hands and he returned to her table with a triumphant smile on his face.

"Go get changed," he said, gesturing toward the dressing room. "Jerry said you're free to go."

She could feel Jerry watching them from across the room, but she was scared to even look in his direction. "What did you tell him?" she asked nervously.

"You quit," he said matter-of-factly. "That you're done stripping." Again he motioned toward the dressing room. "Now go get dressed. I want to—"

"You *WHAT*???" she exclaimed, cutting him off, causing everyone within earshot to look their way.

He shrugged insouciantly. "I told him you decided it was time for a change of occupation, and that you're coming to work for me. As my accountant."

She was suddenly flushed with anger, her head spinning, a ringing in her ears. She couldn't remember the last time she felt this angry. It had taken her months of auditioning to get this job, and she had to work the shitty day shift for nearly a year before she was allowed to work the far more profitable night shifts.

73

"Are you crazy?" she yelled, barely able to hold it together. "Do you know how hard it was for me to get this job? Do you even realize how much money I make? This is *the* top club on the eastside. Dozens of girls audition here every week. It took me a year to finally get on nights! Sometimes I make over a thousand a night! And..." She glared at him. "You don't even know me!!"

He couldn't help being amused by her sudden outrage. "Relax, sweetie," he said, flashing her his most charming smile. "It's going to be okay. I'm looking for some help. Good help. And you seem like you have a head on your shoulders. Don't worry, you'll make more money working for me, and you won't have to take your clothes off to do it." He grinned down at her breasts. "Well, unless you want to. But don't expect a bonus."

She glared up at him. "You *ARE* crazy!"

He shook his head. "Honey, I may be a lot of things, but crazy isn't one of them. Now, why don't you go get dressed? We'll talk more as you drive."

She continued glaring at him, angry but somehow intrigued at the same time. His confidence and casual disposition was somehow deflating her anger. Maybe he was crazy. Maybe he was a bad man. But something about him fascinated her. As angry as she was, she now realized that she wanted to know more about him. So, after a long moment of ambivalence, she decided there was no turning back now, because he clearly wasn't taking no for an answer. All she could do was head for the dressing room and change into her "street clothes."

Ten minutes later she emerged from the dressing room looking like a completely different person. Her hair was pulled back. She had removed most of her makeup, and was now wearing plain blue jeans, sneakers, and a white sweatshirt under a black windbreaker. But when she noticed King quietly conversing with Jerry and Joe the cook by the bar, she decided to wait for him at the front door, wanting to avoid any words with her boss.

After King had reiterated to Joe and Jerry that he wanted his arrival back in town to be kept between them for the time being, he turned and strode over to the front door where she was waiting. "All set, shorty?" he asked, flashing her a smile.

"No," she answered, still looking annoyed. "I can't believe you told Jerry I quit. I hope you know what the hell you're doing, Mr. Bigshot."

"What did I tell you about calling me mister?"

"Whatever," she grumbled, pushing the door open to lead him outside. As soon as the valet attendant saw her, he quickly ran off to retrieve her white Cadillac Escalade.

"Thank you, Brian," she said to the attendant, handing him a five-dollar bill. Then, still trying to look annoyed, she turned to King. "You drive. I hate driving."

"*That's* your car?" he asked, pointing at the Escalade as the valet pulled it up.

"Sure. You like?"

He gave the big SUV a quick once-over. Pearl white. Chrome rims. Tinted windows. A beautiful Cadillac. Expensive for sure. Impressive for a young girl, and an interesting choice for someone who was so diminutive. But the truth was that he also hated driving. He didn't even have a valid license. In fact, he'd never had one. Before going to prison, he always had a driver or his *protettore* to drive him around.

"Yes, it's very nice," he said, opening the passenger door, sliding onto the front passenger seat. "But I'd prefer you drive. I've had a few drinks and you don't want me crashing, do you?"

After climbing into the driver's seat, she gave him the slightest grin. "Crashing my car is the last thing I'm worried about. I'm still not sure if you're some kind of psycho or serial killer."

He flashed her a smile. "Well, I'm definitely not a serial killer."

"That's not funny."

"Am I really that scary?" he laughed.

"Yes," she answered, partially serious and partially joking.

"Well, you have nothing to worry about," he assured her, noticing how small she looked behind the wheel, wondering why such a tiny woman would drive such a massive SUV. "I'm not planning to chop you up." He grinned salaciously at her thighs. "Although, eating you might be nice."

"Funny," she said, rolling her eyes before pulling the big Cadillac out onto east-bound 8 Mile Road. "So, where are we going?"

"Just drive east toward the water," he answered, pointing straight ahead.

For the next ten minutes, as they drove, he tried to ease her anxiety and nervous apprehension by engaging is some basic small talk, trying to learn a more about her.

"So where are you from, Madonna?" he asked, genuinely interested to know.

"Canada. And you can just call me Donna. Only my parents call me Madonna."

"Canada, eh? Well, that narrows it right down, doesn't it?"

She giggled and punched him playfully on the arm. "Smart ass. I was born and raised in Toronto."

"So where do you live now?"

"Why?"

He shrugged. "Just curious."

She was beginning to sense that he was indeed harmless. At least to her. So she tried to relax and not think about the money she could be making. And, strangely, she soon found that she was actually enjoying herself.

"I have a little apartment in Mt. Clemens."

He nodded pensively. "Have you ever seen Grosse Pointe's Lakeshore Drive?"

"No, but isn't that where all the rich people live?"

"It is. And it's only a few minutes from here. I'd like to show it to you."

"Why?"

76

"Oh…" he shrugged. "Let's call it inspiration. For both of us. Just keep driving until 8 Mile until turns into Vernier. When you get to Lakeshore Drive, make a right."

Several minutes later, when they reached Jefferson Avenue, she turned right and was struck silent by what she saw. Situated on the shores of Lake St. Clair were the types of homes that she never knew existed in Michigan. Mansions. Huge pretentious estates with gated drives and elegantly manicured landscapes illuminated by floodlights. Never in her life had she seen such ostentatious displays of wealth. Some of the homes were breathtaking, resembling castles, including homes owned by the furniture mogul Art Van Elslander, and the estate once owned by Edsel and Eleanor Ford. As far as the eye could see were huge palatial estates overlooking the water.

Though King was amused by the awestruck look on her face, he was not nearly as impressed. He'd seen this stretch of lakefront real estate many times. Thousands of times. Despite what he had surreptitiously led her to believe, he had not asked her to take him there for inspiration. Nor was he there to appreciate the area's grandeur and opulence. He was window shopping. He was looking for a new home.

"Slow down," he said, almost forcefully, pointing at one particularly impressive mansion. "That's the one."

She slowed down and followed his gaze to a massive, a Greek Revival style mansion at the end of a private cul-de-sac. Nestled deep in some trees, far back from the road, the home was enormous with huge, white Ionic columns supporting a gigantic front porch. A wrought iron gate bore a family crest and gave access to a long expanse of cobblestone drive that meandered through a perfectly manicured landscape. The entire property was illuminated by a series of powerful, strategically-positioned floodlights that accentuated the home's magnificence. In the center of its circular drive was a massive bronze statue of Atlas, the Greek Titan who was forever condemned to carry the weight of the world on his back. Parked in front of the home's

77

huge eight-car garage was a black Mercedes-Benz and some kind of sleek European sports car.

"My God," she mused, never having seen anything so excessive, yet so elegant and beautiful. "That house is incredible!"

"I'm going to buy it," he said matter-of-factly

"Are you now?" she chuckled sarcastically. "Well, I don't mean to burst your bubble, big guy, but don't you think that's..." She paused to find the right words. "Oh, a bit optimistic for a guy who just got out of prison yesterday?"

By now the house was out of sight, but he continued staring back in its direction. "Maybe," he said, finally turning to face her. "But I have a plan, bella mia."

"Belly mia?" she echoed with a confused look. "What does that mean?"

"*Bella* mia," he laughed. "Not belly. It means my beauty."

"Oh," she said, blushing. Even though she was used to receiving compliments like this every night at work, she loved the way it sounded in Italian. Especially coming from him. She wanted to hear him say it again, for it gave her a hot, tingly sensation down below. But, of course, she didn't want to fish for compliments. She knew that would only make her seem desperate and insecure.

"So, big-timer, tell me about this plan of yours," she asked instead. "I mean, it better be a good one, because that house probably cost a couple million bucks."

"Closer to ten million."

"Yeah, well, we all have dreams," she said, not even considering he might actually be serious. "Speaking of, I worked at Players to pay for school. And now, thanks to you, Mr. Day Dream Believer, I might not have a job to go back to. I'm going to have to kiss Jerry's ass just to get back on days, and I would've made at least $500 tonight."

He removed a wad of cash from the inside pocket of his suit jacket. "You work for me now," he said, peeling off ten $100's and holding them out to her.

She glared at the money as if it was toxic waste. "Hey, I don't want your money, asshole," she barked, the offense in her voice audible. "I'm *NOT* a hooker. You can get out of my car right now if that's what you think this is!"

"I know you're not a hooker," he said, thinking she was a feisty little spitfire. "Consider the money an advance. Soon I'll be in need of an assistant, someone to keep track of my finances and business affairs; someone to oversee collections, investments, banking; someone to make calls and schedule my appointments. Sort of a secretary slash accountant slash assistant. Stuff like that." He held the money out to her again. "Take it. It's a small advance."

She looked at the money. "A small advance?" she parroted.

"Yes. To cover what you would've earned tonight."

Again she glanced at the money. "Where did you get that? I mean, didn't you just get out of prison yesterday?"

"It was a gift from a friend I was in prison with. Tomorrow I'll go see more friends to get the money I'll need to start my business back up."

She considered this for a moment. "So you were serious back there? You actually think you're going to have the money to buy that house?"

"Yes," he answered without even batting an eye. "In order to achieve greatness, you must first believe in yourself." He motioned a hand toward the passing waterfront real estate. "The people who own these homes, they didn't become successful by accident. They had a plan. They believed in that plan. They were determined and worked hard. I know it's cliché, but all things are possible if you just believe. Every great accomplishment started with a dream. A dream is really just a plan never put in motion. Once you achieve it, it's no longer a dream. It's reality. If you can envision it in your mind, you can accomplish it. You just have to have a solid plan and then implement it. I've known some very powerful and wealthy men who started with nothing but a plan. That's how I know it can be done."

She nodded, both amused and impressed. "Wow, that's quite the maxim you have there. Where did you get it, Confucius?"

His eyes suddenly went from pensive to stern and cold. "No," he answered tersely. "It was the philosophy of a great man."

"Yeah? And who was this great man?"

"My grandfather."

"Oh yeah?" she asked, flashing him a goading smile. "Does he happen to live in one of these big houses?"

"No," he said, his eyes glazing over with a sad, distant look. "But he did before he died. We passed it about a mile back."

From the sullen, nostalgic look in his eyes, she realized he was serious and that his grandfather had meant a great deal to him. So rather than push the issue, she decided to not add anything and just allow him a moment of reverence.

With his grandfather's words echoing in his head, he stared out the passenger window, subconsciously crumbling the wad of cash in his hand, lost in his inner thoughts. He had so many fond memories of his grandfather, and not a day went by that he didn't miss him.

Meanwhile, as they drove in silence, her mind began to dissect the strange night she was having. It was like she was in a dream. She felt as if this handsome and mysterious man had somehow cast a spell on her. It was a bit unnerving, even scary, for she had never been under such a spell. He was certainly unlike any man she had ever met, so arcane and confident. Yet he was surprisingly humble, especially considering his physical looks. He was beyond handsome. He was beautiful, like the Greek gods she had envisioned in her mind while studying Greek Myth in high school. But there was something else. His eyes. Never had she seen such unique eyes. It was almost as if he didn't have irises. Just giant pupils. Pitch black. Intelligent and full of life but calculating and dangerous. Almost hypnotic. And they seemed to bore directly into her soul every time he looked at her. Since the moment he had locked them on her back at the club, she felt like she was drifting through some kind of sublime dream. There was much behind those dangerous eyes, and she suddenly wanted to know what it was.

"King," she said, finally breaking the silence. "Would you like to come home with me?"

He turned from the window and looked at her as if he had forgotten she was there. "Huh?"

"I said would you like to come home with me?" she repeated, looking dead ahead at the road, purposely avoiding those eyes.

"Are you asking me to spend the night with you?" he asked, a bit surprised by her forwardness.

"Yes," she answered softly, daring to gently put her hand on his. "I want to spend the night with you."

Her touch sent a surge of excitement coursing through his veins, and suddenly he felt hot and flush all over. "Who do you live with?" he asked, his heart racing in his chest.

She gave him a coquettish grin. "Just my cat. Do you want to meet my kitty?"

Her look and tone told him all he needed to know. He glanced down at the swell of her breasts and instantly felt an erection growing in his pants. He wanted her. No, he needed her. Badly!

"Yes, I definitely want to meet your kitty," he said salaciously, knowing quite well that she was not referring to her cat.

# CHAPTER 3

Madonna stepped into the room and stared down at the man sleeping in her bed. He was lying on his stomach, face down, completely naked. He was the most beautiful man she'd ever seen, real life or otherwise. A solid mass of corded muscle, with the dark Mediterranean looks that most women find irresistible. His skin was smooth and without blemish. He even seemed to have a tan. *How'd he get a tan in prison*? she wondered, having no idea the prison he was released from was in southern Georgia.

They had spent most of the previous night making love. Or at least that's what it had felt like to her. She'd been surprised by his gentleness. At times he had acted as if he might break her. The majority of men she dated tended to be rough with her. They usually liked to manhandle her. She figured it was some kind of fantasy for men to toss around a little woman in bed. Made them feel bigger. More manly. But not this one. No, this beautiful Adonis was surprisingly gentle. Even though he'd been celibate for many years, he had taken his time to please her, attentively paying attention to how her body reacted to his every touch. It was as if he'd made love to her, rather than simply had sex with her. Lovemaking. It was a foreign notion. She hadn't felt it in a very long time. He had kissed her passionately and held her tightly after each round–and there were several. Of course, the first one hadn't lasted long. No more than more a few seconds, which was to be expected from a man who had been locked up for eight years. But after he released that initial explosion of pressure, he slowed down and maintained a pace that made her climax over and over.

Now, as she watched the rhythmic motion of his breathing, her knees felt weak, and she found herself becoming aroused, her thoughts drifting back to the previous night. No man had ever made her feel that way. She knew it wasn't love, of course, but it was definitely something new. She wondered if a man like him was even capable of love. If he was, she knew she could never be the one to win his heart. A man like him would never fall in love with a lowly stripper. But he was there now, sleeping in her bed, so she decided to enjoy him while she still could.

"Wake up, sleeping beauty," she whispered in his ear, climbing onto his back, straddling him, gently brushing her erect nipples against the knotted muscles of his upper back.

He popped awake with a smile on his face. "Good morning, doll," he breathed sleepily, rolling over so he could get a better look at her.

She straddled him and slipped her silk negligee over her head. "Good morning, you," she cooed, leaning down to softly kiss his chest.

He stared down at her, taking in her body. Her breasts were full, and her nipples looked hard enough to cut diamonds. "My, my, is someone feeling frisky this morning?"

"I'm not the only one," she teased, wrapping a hand around his rock-hard penis.

"You seem to have that effect on me," he said, sliding his hands up her stomach until he wrapped them around her breasts.

As she watched him begin to lick and tease her nipples with his tongue, she stiffened, and her heart began racing with excitement. Never had she felt so aroused by a man. His hands were so large and strong. His movements were gentle, yet somehow forceful. Within seconds she felt her body nearly shaking with anticipation. She'd already had enough foreplay. She wanted him inside of her. No, she *needed* him inside her.

Barely able to contain herself, she raked her fingers through his hair and clawed at his back, pressing his head into her breasts, watching him lick and tease her anxious body.

He was very much enjoying playing with her wanton body, prolonging the inevitable, but when she began begging "I want you inside me," he could hold out no longer. With her still on top of him, he forcefully slid himself inside her, causing her to release a high-pitched moan. He began thrusting himself upward into her. Slow at first, but then faster and faster as he sat up and clasped her firmly by the neck with one hand and her buttocks with the other. Matching his rhythm, she began thrusting hard against him, crying out, clawing at his neck and back.

Driving her pelvis into him, taking his full length inside her, she felt an impending orgasm building. She tried holding it back, but it was impossible. She was powerless to him. "Omnio, I can't hold it," she whimpered into his ear.

Without warning, he rolled her over and pinned her arms over her head. She opened her legs wide to accommodate him, and he began driving himself into her with slow, deep thrusts, causing her to cry out and moan. After several seconds, he could no longer hold back. With one final thrust, he let out a guttural grunt and exploded inside her, both of them climaxing at the same instant.

For a moment he just lay there atop of her, trying to catch his breath. After nearly a minute he propped himself up on both elbows and peered down at her, watching the rise and fall of her chest, the jiggling of her breasts as she gasped for air. She was so short and compact that her head barely reached his chest. She wasn't even half his size. Her muscular little legs were sticking out from under him, but the rest of her was almost completely concealed by his mass. He was sure he could wrap both hands around her entire waist if he tried. Looking down at her, he hoped that he hadn't hurt her. Then he saw her face. Her eyes were closed and she was breathing deeply, but she was smiling.

"Service with a smile?" he said.

Her dilated eyes opened to mere slits, and she began caressing his glistening chest. "Mmmmmm..." she half moaned, running her fingers from his chest to the curves of his buttocks. He was still planted inside her, but she could feel him softening. She wished he could stay hard and do it again.

"I didn't hurt you, did I?" he asked, backing out of her, looking down at her, captivated by her compact and curvaceous body.

She expelled a satisfied sigh and rolled out from under him. "I might be little but I'm tough," she boasted proudly, slipping on her negligee. "Although, I'll admit I am a little sore." She glanced at his now flaccid member. "You're definitely well proportioned;"

He sat up in bed and examined her body through the sheer satin of her negligee. "As are you, little lady," he said, pulling her to him, giving her a quick peck on the lips.

She smiled blissfully. "Are you hungry?"

"I'm starved."

"Good, because I already made breakfast. It's why I came in here to wake you up. I figured it was the least I could do after all the energy you spent on me last night. But then I saw you laying there naked and... Well, guess I got a little excited."

"I'm not complaining," he said, pulling her to him, sliding his hands down her back until the came to rest on her behind. "I can think of no better way for a man to wake up." He stood, stretched, and nodded toward the adjacent bathroom. "But right now I need a shower. Give me ten and I'll meet you in the kitchen."


After a long hot shower, he stepped into the kitchen and found her laboring away, preparing him a breakfast feast. "Smells delicious," he said, sidling up behind her in a towel, wrapping his arms around her, kissing the back of her neck.

85

"Sit," she ordered, playfully brushing him away. "I have to warm everything back up since you took all day in the shower."

He plopped down at the kitchen table and took in the room. Again he was surprised by how nice her apartment was. It looked like something out of Better Homes and Gardens. Everything was designer, beautifully decorated, and sparkling clean. In fact, it appeared she was a compulsive neat freak. It was obvious she took pride in her little apartment. For a stripper, she really seemed to have herself together.

She tended to him like a nurturing mother. With a fervent pep in her step, she glided around the kitchen in her see-through negligee, serving him homemade pancakes, bacon, fried eggs, toast, and orange juice. As he silently devoured the food, he decided that it tasted that much better because it had been cooked by the nurturing hands of a woman. Since the moment he met her, she had exceeded his expectations in every way.

"How was it?" she asked, walking over to the sink to start on the dishes.

"Amazing," he declared, soaking up some egg yolk with his fourth piece of toast. "I haven't had a meal like that in years. My mom used to make me breakfasts like this when I was a kid. I almost forgot what it was like to have a woman cook for me. I guess food always tastes better when it's cooked with love."

She was washing the dishes with her back to him, but she hadn't failed to notice his choice of words. He said "love." She had only been in love once, or at least that's what she thought it was. Maybe it had been puppy love. Or infatuation. Whatever it was, it hadn't lasted long. It had been her high school sweetheart, and he'd broken her heart when he cheated on her with one of her best friends. Until last night she thought she would never meet another man who stirred such carnal feelings in her. But King Falcone was unlike any man she'd ever met. And as she now scrubbed the dishes, she decided she could definitely fall in love with him, though she was certain the feeling was not mutual. It would take a very special woman to win the heart of a man like King Falcone. But it didn't stop her from dreaming and wanting to know more about him.

"Speaking of your mother…" she began, her back still to him as she scrubbed a frying pan. "Where is she?"

His eyes glazed over with sadness. "She died while was in prison," he answered, sounding solemn and pained. "Ovarian cancer."

"Oh, I'm sorry," she said, turning from the sink to face him. "I didn't mean to—"

"Don't worry," he said, holding up a hand. "It was probably for the best. She'd been sick most of her life. She was suffering, physically and mentally. She never got over the death of my father. She's in a better place now."

"Your dad is dead, too?" she asked, her eyes tearing up with genuine sadness.

"Yes," he shrugged. "He died the year I was born. I have no real memory of him. I've seen pictures, but that's it. My mom never got over him, though. I think it broke her heart. And her spirit. She spent…" He choked up and looked away.

She wiped her hands dry and walked over to sit on his lap. "Oh, I'm so sorry, baby," she whispered, wrapping her arms around his neck. "So do you have any other family?"

"I have some cousins, aunts, and uncles."

"Do you talk to them?"

He shook his head. "No."

"Why?"

"Long story."

"So you're all alone in this world?"

"Pretty much," he shrugged.

She leaned in and kissed him on the lips. "Well, you have me now. I'll be your momma and take good care of you."

"I bet you will," he said, gently brushing his knuckles over her nipples.

She had never been the sexually aggressive type, but for some reason this morning she felt more sexually charged than ever in her life. It was almost as if she had no control of herself. Before she even realized it, she slipped a hand under his towel and found he was already completely erect. So, eager to please, she yanked the towel off, straddled him, and slid his swollen shaft inside her.

"I need you!" she blurted, looking him in the eye. "And don't be gentle. I want you to own me!"

That's all he needed to hear. Thoughts of his dead mother were instantly replaced with burning lust. He rolled her over and took her right there on the kitchen table, driving himself into her slow, deep, and hard. Within a minute she began moaning to the rhythm of his movements as her orgasm began to crescendo. Clamping her hands around his buttock, she spread her legs wide, cried out his name and climaxed. Unable to stop himself, with one final thrust he drove himself deep and again exploded inside her.

"Ahhhh...." he whispered, still atop her, his member still inside her. "That was nice..." He gently kissed her shoulder and brushed several locks of hair from her face. "But as much as I'd love to keep this up all day, I have some things I need to get done."

"Like what?" she asked, running a finger down the side of his face, dedicating every inch of it to memory.

He backed out of her and stretched. "Well, for starters, I need to buy some new clothes. All I have is that suit."

"Do you have money?" she asked, slipping back into her negligee.

"Some," he answered, his mind carefully calculating who he needed to go see first.

"Well, if you need more I have some. I've been saving for over a year now."

"I appreciate that, doll, but I would never take your money.

"Well, if you need it you're welcome to it."

"But you barely even know me."

"That's true," she shrugged. "But you said I work for you now. You'll make it up to me. After last night, I feel like I owe you something."

"Huh," he chuckled. "I was thinking I owe *you* something, especially after that breakfast. Dessert wasn't bad either."

She punched him playfully. "You were hard! I didn't want to waste it."

"No, it's not good to be wasteful," he quipped. "Let me guess, you recycle too?"

"Jerkoff," she said, playfully slapping his arm.

"You're right, though," he said, now looking serious. "You do work for me now, and I'll make it up to you. But right now I need you to go get showered and dressed. Wear something nice but casual. We're gonna go see a few old friends of mine."


Thirty minutes later, King was waiting in the living room, clad in his Brioni suit, when she emerged from her bedroom wearing a blue, loose-fitting Marc Jacobs dress that perfectly accentuated her skin tone and curvy figure. It was a casual spring dress, but it made her look elegant and beautiful, although he was a bit surprised that she owned a dress that surely cost well over $500.

"Wow," he whistled, impressed. "Nice dress. You look beautiful."

She sashayed into a pirouette. "You like?" she asked, striking a seductive pose.

"Very much. You're rockin' that dress, girl."

"What, this old thing?" she joked, striking another pose. "I picked it up at Macy's in New York last winter. I've been waiting for a nice day to wear it. And since it's supposed to get up to seventy degrees, I figured today was as good as any."

"Well, if you're trying to impress me, mission accomplished. I've never met a stripper who shopped at Macy's in New York.

You look sexy as hell in that dress. I'm looking forward to taking it off you."

She giggled and eyed him seductively. "No time like the present, big boy. I think I can spare a few minutes."

He was very tempted to toss her on the bed, rip that dress off, and have his way with her again. But he needed to stay focused. "Later," he said before he changed his mind. "Right now I have work to do."

"All work and no play," she pouted. "Fine, let's go see these friends of yours."


Ten minutes later they stepped out into a sunny, cloudless afternoon. The air was warm and smelled of springtime—flowers, lawnmowers, and freshly cut grass. King looked around and inhaled deeply. "Ahhhhh, freedom…" he mused, feeling like a new man. He hadn't realized just how badly he needed last night until now. "It's good to be alive," he added, smiling down at his beautiful companion.

He had Madonna drive him to Eastland Mall, a large shopping complex on Detroit's eastside. Once inside, he headed straight for Van Dykes, a high-end designer clothing store that he had frequented regularly before going to prison. Back then the store had been managed by an animated old black man named Jimmy Smith, a slick eastside hustler who always reminded King of the singer James Brown. King had often spent hundreds, sometimes thousands of dollars with Jimmy, on everything from new suits and Italian leather shoes, to dress shirts and designer boxer shorts. He loved buying these things for his friends and relatives. He'd always been generous like that. His grandfather had taught him that it was a show of respect to give gifts to those who did you favors. Whenever he shopped at Van Dykes for such gifts, Jimmy Smith always made himself available to offer his expertise and preferred customer discount.

King now smiled inwardly as he remembered one such shopping excursion. He had been haggling with a salesperson over the price of several Pelle Pelle leather jackets when Jimmy Smith, or in his mind "James Brown," asked to meet him in the mall's food court for lunch. Curious as to why, King agreed. As they ate, Jimmy asked him if he was interested in buying some custom-tailored Armani suits, priced at less than half of retail. It seemed Jimmy had figured out a way to make suits disappear from inventory by using an associate who worked in the company's corporate warehouse. King told Jimmy he would take all the suits he could get. It worked out to be a great arrangement. Jimmy even asked for the proper measurements so each suit could be custom-tailored to fit its intended wearer. From that day on King set a dress code for himself and his crew. They were to wear suits whenever they were conducting business with other members of the *borgata*, and it was Jimmy Smith who outfitted them all.

In the ensuing years, King had developed a genuine friendship with Jimmy "James Brown" Smith. They had a very symbiotic business partnership that was mutually beneficial. King ended up buying hundreds of Versace, Armani, Louis Vuitton, Gucci, and Perry Ellis suits from him, each of them hand-tailored. He also bought designer dress clothes, Italian shoes, alligator skin belts, leather jackets, and many other items that he flipped on the black market for large profits. He would buy $2,500 suits for $750, and then sell them to business associates for $1,500. All he had to do was call Jimmy and place an order. A few days later he would pick up the order at Jimmy's house. It was one of King's many hustles as a teenager, one that always earned him a few thousand extra each month. He had all his cousins, uncles, and entire crew decked out in the finest designer apparel. Thanks to Jimmy, he and his men were dressed to impress at all times. Not because they wanted to show off or act like something they weren't, but because King knew that people always showed a little more respect to a man wearing a nice suit. Even a young man.

As King now approached the entrance of Van Dykes Designer Apparel, he could only hope that his old friend still worked there. Stepping into the busy store with Madonna hovering closely by his side, he took a quick look around. The store itself had changed. It was much larger than he remembered, and it now carried designer women's clothing, whereas in the past it had only carried men's. The place was packed. Saturday afternoon shoppers were out in droves, milling about the store, browsing the designer names. But Jimmy was nowhere in sight.

Wondering if he was wasting his time, he headed over to a saleswoman wearing a professional Christian Dior blazer and skirt. "Excuse me, Miss," he said, getting her attention. "I had a friend who used be manager here about eight years ego. I was wondering if he might still work here."

The saleswoman, an attractive black woman in her early thirties, offered him a flirtatious smile. "What was your friend's name?" she asked, examining his suit with a trained eye.

"Jimmy Smith."

Recognition registered on her face immediately, and she again smiled up at him flirtatiously. "Mr. Smith is no longer a manager here. He's the owner."

"You're kidding?" he asked, unable to contain an excited grin.

"Not at all," she answered, motioning toward the back stock room. "He's in his office right now. Just got in a few minutes ago. Would you like me to get him for you?"

"Yes. That would be great."

"And you are?"

"King Falcone."

Grinning seductively, she slowly looked him over, examining him from head to toe, appreciating his broad shoulders and brooding good looks. "That's a very unique name," she said, smiling at him invitingly, overtly thrusting her chest out, pleased that he immediately took notice.

Madonna had enough of the woman's flirting, so she tucked an arm under his arm and gave her a cold look. "He's a very unique man. Now if you don't mind, could you please go get your boss? We're very busy."

The saleswomen narrowed her eyes on her and seemed to bite back the words she really wanted to say. "Yes, of course," she said with a forced smile. "I'll send him right out."

When the saleswoman was gone, King smiled down at Madonna. "Do I detect a touch of jealousy?" he asked, looking amused.

She glared up at him. "That bitch was flirting with you!"

"Soooo… you *are* jealous?"

"No, but she was being disrespectful. She saw me. For all she knew I could be your girlfriend."

King chuckled inwardly. She was obviously jealous, but he wasn't going to call her on it. It was sort of cute, although he hoped that she wasn't becoming emotionally attached. Not after one night. He didn't need a clingy woman in his life. At least not right now.

"Respect is important," he said dogmatically. "You're right, it was disrespectful of her to just ignore you. But I have a feeling that she was actually jealous of *you*. Look around. Every guy in here is staring at you. You in that dress. *Minchia madonn*! There isn't a guy in here who hasn't undressed you with his eyes. Women are catty sometimes. That chick probably didn't you like stealing all her thunder. She feels threatened by other attractive women. But if you're going to work me you'll have to learn how to ignore people like her. Some people are just assholes. And sometimes the assholes are the most important people. It doesn't matter if you like them. What matters is that they *think* you like them. That way you can manipulate them and bend them to your will. It's how you gain an advantage over them without them ever—"

"King!" a voice boomed from behind them, stopping him mid-sentence. "My main man, King Falcone! Where the hell you been? I ain't seen you in years."

King turned and saw Jimmy "James Brown" Smith strutting toward him with his arms held out. The man looked exactly the same. Same ridiculous hair. Same loud suit. Same baritone voice. Same friendly smile. Only a few locks of gray indicated that he was subject to Father Time like everyone else.

"Jimmy!" King said, embracing him in a hug. "How are you, old friend?"

"Pretty damn good," Jimmy answered, taking a step back to look him over. "My God, you've grown into quite a man. What happened to you? It's been years."

King shot a quick look at Madonna. "Well, Jimmy, I was away for a while. But I'm back now."

Jimmy was not stupid. He remembered King very well, including the types of people he hung around. An abrupt disappearance and then sudden reappearance with an extra fifty pounds of muscle could only mean one thing. Prison. Even back when he was a mere teenager, a young King Falcone had come into the store with his pockets stuffed with cash, looking to spend it on the latest designer apparel. Jimmy always liked him because even as a young man King had talked to him as an equal.

"And who's this little angel?" Jimmy asked, smiling at Madonna, who blushed and returned a bashful smile.

"Donna," King answered, glancing down at her. "A friend of mine."

Jimmy remembered how King had often come into the store with another such beautiful girl. Same height. Same dark hair. Same curvy figure. But this girl was definitely not her. No, the girl he remembered had a strong Italian accent and was remarkably beautiful.

"Pleasure to meet you, Miss Donna," he said, offering her a hand, nodding toward King. "Your friend here used to be one of my best customers."

She shook his hand timidly. "Yes, that's what I hear," she said, looking up at King. "He told me all about you."

Jimmy returned his attention to King. "What a blast from the past. You look great. Nice suit, too. Could use a little loosening around the neck and shoulders, but very nice."

"Thank you, Jimmy," King said, glancing around the busy store. "You also look great. Haven't aged a day. But I hear you own the place now. Looks like you're doing pretty good. Business is booming."

"I'm doing alright for an old street hustler," Jimmy said, offering him a wink. "But enough about me. Something tells me you didn't stop in just to say hello to an old friend. Let me guess, you're looking for something?"

"You're very perceptive," King nodded. "Some things never change."

"Yes, well, I've always made it a habit of getting to know my best customers. Tell me, what exactly are you looking for?"

"Depends," King said, glancing around the store. "You still offer the same discount?"

"Oh, I think we can work something out," Jimmy replied, flashing him a conspiratorial grin. "Why don't we step into my office? I'll need your measurements. You got a neck like a damn bull these days."

"I hope you don't have a problem with me opening a line of credit," King said, pulling out the remainder of his cash. "I'm a little strapped at the moment, but I should be in the black by the end of the week."

Jimmy had no problem with offering him a line of credit, but since taking over ownership of the store, he'd given up offering "back door" discounts. But he did still maintain a relationship with his warehouse connection, which he occasionally used for special customers. And since King had at one time been a very special customer, he decided to do him this favor. After all, they were old friends, and a friend like King Falcone was a good friend to have. He was a man who knew how to return a favor.

After a half hour of haggling, King stood, shook Jimmy's hand, and handed him $1,200 in cash, a deposit for his $5,000 order: three Armani suits, seven Prada dress shirts, four Perry Ellis slacks, two pair of Salvatore Ferragamo loafers, two Gucci belts, four ties, and an assortment of socks and silk boxer shorts. Some of it—socks, boxer shorts, and a few casual outfits—he took from the store. The rest he would pick up at Jimmy's house in a few days.

After thanking Jimmy one last time, King led Madonna to the mall's food court for lunch. He opted for a Greek gyro. She went for Chinese.

"So, your friend Jimmy was awfully trusting," she said, picking at her food. "I mean, I'm curious as to how you plan to pay him for all those clothes?"

"We go way back," he answered, taking a huge bite of his gyro. "He knows I'm good for it."

"For a guy so young, you sure have a lot of old friends. And all of them seem eager to kiss your ass."

"Must be my charming personality," he quipped, taking another bite of his lamb sandwich.

She eyed him suspiciously. "Something tells me it's more than your charm. I think people are just scared of you."

"Scared of me?" he chuckled. "What makes you say that?"

"I just do. I don't know what it is but there's something scary about you."

He shrugged and took a sip of soda. "The only people who should be scared of me are people who cross me. I'm a nice guy to everyone else."

She shrugged and let it go, but as they made small talk over lunch, she found herself studying his every mannerism, analyzing his every word. No matter what he said, or how much he downplayed himself, he still frightened her. She knew there

96

was a dangerous man lurking just below the surface of his charm and good looks. Yet she felt safe with him. She wondered if she had made a serious mistake by letting herself become so captivated by him. But at this point, it was out of her control. She was powerless to those eyes and his magnetic charm. She felt drawn to him by some unseen force. He was a complete mystery to her, an enigma, and certainly not the type of man she needed, or wanted, in her life. But she was under his spell completely, and now there was nothing she could do but ride the wave and see where it took her.

After lunch King had her drive him to see an old associate named Joseph "Diamonds" DeMaglio, a high-end jeweler he'd done business with before going to prison. As soon as he stepped into the elegant jewelry store, Joey, a stocky Italian in his forties, looked at him like he saw a ghost.

"I'll be damned!" Joey exclaimed, stepping from behind the counter to embrace him and kiss his cheek. "So the rumors were true. They really let you out of that fuckin' place."

The man seemed genuinely excited to see him, but as Madonna watched them interact she sensed Joey was nervous and uncomfortable by King's sudden appearance. At some point they began speaking in Italian and King asked her to wait in the showroom while they stepped into a back office to have a private conversation. Twenty minutes later he emerged from the office wearing a brand-new platinum Omega watch, a diamond pinky ring, and Cartier sunglasses. And he hadn't given the jeweler a dime for any of it. In fact, before they left, Joey Diamonds even insisted on giving King a stack of cash as a welcome home gift. All of it made her wonder who King Falcone really was, and how she had allowed herself to get involved with such a man.

# CHAPTER 4

After his short but productive shopping excursion, King took Madonna on a guided tour of his old neighborhood, an area of Detroit's upper eastside built by immigrant Italian stonemasons back in the 1920's. Situated along the uppermost reaches of the Detroit River and adjacent to the affluent suburb of Grosse Pointe, it had once been one of the most sought after neighborhoods in the city, inhabited by mostly first-generation Italian and Greek immigrants. As he now showed her his old haunts, he explained how the neighborhood had once been a very ethnic enclave of the city, one that prided itself on old-world culture and values. But that had all changed. Due to the crime and drugs of encroaching neighborhoods, these middle-class families had long since relocated to the city's outlying metropolitan suburbs, where it was much safer to raise a family. Today, his once-beloved neighborhood was a slum, predominantly inhabited by lower-class blacks.

But there were a few Italian families still scattered throughout the neighborhood, and King made a point of stopping to see the parents of several friends from his youth. He even dropped by several local businesses, restaurants and liquor stores to pay respects to their owners. Wherever he went, he was received with warm hugs and smiles. The instant people saw him, they shouted his name and embraced him affectionately, as if he was their long-lost son or brother. He seemed to know everyone, and they all seemed genuinely thrilled to see him, offering him food and gifts. One particular old

Italian man who owned a produce market insisted he take a huge box of fresh fruit and vegetables. Several people even offered him money as welcome home gifts, but he always refused such offers of generosity.

Madonna felt like she was in the Twilight Zone. As he stopped to see all of his old friends and acquaintances, he would respectfully introduce her as a good friend. Everyone was extremely nice and seemed genuinely excited to meet her. Some of the older Italian men, and even women, gave her hugs and kisses on the cheeks. It was a new experience for her. She had only seen people greeted like this in the movies. Mafia movies. And observing how people received King, how they did everything short of kiss his pinky ring, it made her feel like she was on the set of one such movie. But this was no movie. This was real. He was real. And with each passing moment, she realized that she knew almost nothing about this mysterious man named Omino "King" Falcone. All she knew is that he had touched her very soul while making love to her last night.


After showing Madonna some of his childhood hangouts, he took her to one of his old favorites, "Nick's & Cuts," a neighborhood barbershop that was owned by a fatherly old Italian named Niccolo Moceri. Located only a few blocks from his childhood home, the shop was directly next door to another of his old favorites, "Mr. Q's Billiards & Arcade," where he and his neighborhood cronies had spent countless days hanging out, hustling and flirting with neighborhood girls. He was surprised to see that both buildings were still intact. It fact, they looked exactly the same. Most of the neighborhood had changed, but not this little corner where he'd spent so much of his youth. As they now parked and stepped onto the sidewalk out front, he couldn't help but smile at the burned-out old sign above the shop's front door. "Nick's & Cuts." Even as a child the pun wasn't lost on him.

When he snatched open the front door, a pair of bells jingled melodically, announcing their arrival. Nick was cutting the hair of a balding older man when he looked up expecting to see just another customer. But when he saw King smiling at him, he froze in shock.

"*La mio bella figlioccio!*" Nick said in Italian. His beautiful godson.

Madonna saw excitement in the old man's eyes, but she also noted something else. He didn't look all that surprised. In fact, he almost looked like he was expecting him. Unlike all the others they had visited today, this old man had no fear in his eyes. There was nothing but genuine excitement, even love in his eyes, and he expressed it by dropping his clippers onto the counter and embracing King in a long hug.

"Omnio..." the old barber stammered, his throat constricting, his eyes welling with tears. "*Mio bambino, sei a casa*, you're finally home!"

A heavy-set, matronly woman with thick black hair that was graying at the temples appeared from a door leading into the back of the shop. She took one look at King and charged over to steal him away from her husband. "Omnio, *mio bambino!*" she wailed, pulling his face down to hers. "You're home! I can't believe it. Your nonno said he would find a way but..." She let her words trail off, knowing how much his grandfather had meant to him.

"Yes, I'm home, Vicky," King said with a loving smile, bending down to hug her affectionately. "Grandpa always had his ways."

Growing up, Niccolo and his wife, Victoria, had been godparents to King. Nick had been a friend of his father's, and Victoria had often babysat him when his mother was too sick to take care of him. He had spent countless days under their watch at the barbershop, which was a neighborhood landmark. All of his friends, cousins, and uncles had gotten their hair cut there. In fact, the entire neighborhood got their hair cut at Nick's & Cuts. It was a place where everyone went to catch up on the latest neighborhood gossip. It was tradition to drop in at least once a month for a cut and to catch up on all the recent happenings in the neighborhood. Everyone trusted them. Getting your hair cut by them had an almost therapeutic effect. For some reason, when people lounged back in the old leather barber chairs, they became relaxed and often felt inclined to divulge intimate details of their lives. Of course, Nick and Vicky never spread bad news or malicious gossip, but their shop acted as the neighborhood grapevine. If anyone from the old neighborhood wanted to get a message to someone, or find out what a person was up to, all they had to do was drop by the shop. By the time they were finished getting their hair cut, they would be caught up on all the latest neighborhood gossip.

Nick quickly finished trimming the old man's hair and then sat King in his chair for a "full service" trim and shave. Meanwhile, Madonna sat and listened quietly as Nick and Vicky caught King up on all the latest news, including the whereabouts of several old friends and acquaintances. She saw the sadness in his eyes when they told him how several people had passed away. Most died of natural causes, but a few had tragically died young from car crashes, drug overdoses, even murder. This seemed to sadden him greatly. But not all the news was bad. They also relayed how many of his old acquaintances had succeeded in life and moved out of the neighborhood. There were many marriages, new families and lots of young children, all of which seemed to make him very happy. Over and over he expressed how excited he was about the prospect of seeing this person or that person. He laughed and recounted stories about his old friends and relatives from the neighborhood. He truly seemed in his element, and his usually dark and ominous eyes were beaming with genuine joy.

They shared many stories, but what Madonna found most entertaining were the ones involving King and his group of neighborhood ruffians. She was very much enjoying listening to these humorous anecdotes from his past, but she was an instinctively perceptive person and sensed that Nick and Vicky were holding back, as if there was something they wanted to tell him in private. She also found it peculiar that neither of them brought up the subject of King's family. Or at least not his immediate family. They spoke of his cousins, even a few aunts and uncles, but there was no mention of his mother, father, or siblings. She also found it interesting that Vicky mentioned in passing that they'd already heard he was home. How was that even possible? She distinctly remembered him telling her that no one knew he was out. Including his family. News couldn't travel *that* fast. Or could it? Whatever the case, she knew she was missing part of the story.

After Nick finished giving King the full-service treatment, he invited him back into his office for a private tete-a-tete, leaving Vicky to run the shop and entertain Madonna. Once in his office, Nick dropped into a creaky old swivel chair behind his desk.

"Have a seat, *giovane amico*," he said, gesturing toward a lone leather chair in front of his desk. "It's so good to see you. It seems like so long. You look like a million bucks. That's a nice suit for a guy who just got out the Big House two days ago."

King chuckled and sat in the chair, casually flattening the lapels of his suit. "Yes, well, Grandpa always stressed the importance of appearance. People respect a well-dressed man."

"Sure," Nick nodded. "In your case that's true. But most men need more than a fancy suit to command respect."

"That's true," King agreed. "Clothes never make the man. It's the man who makes the clothes."

"So… the girl," Nick said, no longer able to avoid the subject. "Who is she?"

"Just a new friend. Why?"

Nick shrugged. "Just wondering. She's cute. Sort of reminds me of Contessa at that age."

King hadn't heard that name in many years, and just the mere mention of it sent a wave of suppressed emotion surging through him. "Like I said, she's just a friend," he said coldly, clearly uncomfortable with the subject.

"Sorry, Omnio," Nick said, realizing he had touched a nerve. "I didn't mean to—"

"I know, Nick," King interrupted, holding up a hand. "But the past is the past. My grandfather always said let sleeping dogs lie."

Nick offered him a fatherly smile. "Yes, of course, bambino. Your grandfather was always smarter than me. I suppose that's why he was so successful and I'm just a lowly barber."

"So, Niccolo..." King said, leaning back in his chair, looking him in the eye. "What's on your mind? I can tell you have something to tell me."

Nick shifted uncomfortably in his chair and seemed to gather his thoughts. "It's your cousin Dino," he began slowly, nervously. "He was here, just this morning, waiting for us when we opened the shop. He wanted to know if you'd been in yet."

"I figured as much," King said, nodding pensively. "That's how you knew I was home. I was at one of Vito Vitale's places last night. I'm sure someone passed it along to Sal Finazzo, who reported it to Anthony. So what else did Dino say?"

"He knew you would be coming in for a cut. You know, to catch up on what's been happening in the neighborhood."

"That it?" King asked, knowing there was more.

"No," Nick answered, looking twitchy and apprehensive. "He wanted me to give you a message."

"A message?"

"Yes. He said your Uncle Leo wants you to go see him at one of his night clubs. His new place. I think it's called Atlantis. Up in Marine City. Or is it New Baltimore? I can't remember. But it's somewhere out that way."

King studied the old barber, who had always been like a father to him. He was a master at reading people, especially people he knew well, and he sensed that Nick was definitely holding something back.

103

"That all Dino said?" he asked.

Nick took a deep breath, stood and walked over to an old metal filing cabinet, from which he removed two shot glasses and a dusty old bottle of grappa, Sicilian moonshine. After pouring each of them a shot, he set one on the desk in front of King.

"Here, paisan, drink," he said, returning to his seat. "You're a grown man now. We can all use a stiff drink once in a while."

King glanced at the glass but didn't move. "A stiff drink often precedes bad news," he said dogmatically. "Tell me, Nick, what else did Dino say?"

Nick pointed at the shot glass. "Drink first," he insisted.

Mildly annoyed, King gulped down the shot and set the glass back on the desk. He hadn't drunk in many years, and the effects were almost instant, the strong alcohol immediately warming his chest and stomach. Within seconds he felt the mild rush of euphoria that Nick thought would calm him before the bad news. It didn't.

Nick drained his glass like a seasoned drinker and expelled a satisfied sigh. "Dino is a cocky little bastard," he declared, a bit more confidence in his voice. "You know I never liked him or Anthony. They were always trouble. And now Dino is just Anthony's errand boy."

King furled his brows in annoyance. "Nick, just spit it out. Tell me what Dino said. Have you ever known me to shoot the messenger?"

"No, paisan," Nick answered, looking relieved, pouring himself another shot. "You've always been a good boy. Very respectful. Nothing like those cousins of yours. They have no respect for anyone."

Nick's sun-spotted old hand shook as he poured the moonshine, which made the muscles of King's jaw flex and quiver as he bit back his anger. Whatever Dino had said or done, it clearly had the old barber shaken. But King did not overtly show his anger. He simply flashed Nick a warm smile

104

"Nick," he began, leaning forward in his seat, "I have several more stops I need to make today, and I know you have customers to get back to, so no more beating around the bush. Just tell me what Dino said."

Nick drained his second shot of grappa, the alcohol finally giving him the courage to come right out and say what he had to say. But first, he removed an envelope from his desk and set it between them. "He gave me this," he said, staring at the envelope like it was toxic.

King opened the envelope and saw it contained twenty $100 bills. "What's it for?" he asked, setting the envelope back on the desk.

"Information," Nick answered matter-of-factly. "He wants me to call him if I hear anything about what you're up to. He also wanted me to give you a warning. You can't do anything without Anthony's permission. He told me to tell you that things have changed since you've been gone."

King's eyes suddenly looked cold and menacing, his face hardened with anger. "Well, next time you see Dino, you tell that little fuckin' *canooda* I said to go fuck himself. I don't need Anthony's permission for anything. He's not my boss. Never has been. Never will be. I work for myself. If he has a problem with that, tell him to take it up with Gino Salestro in New York."

Nick held up his hands as if warding off a blow. "Hey, you said you wouldn't shoot the messenger. I'm just relaying what he told me. You've always been like a son to me. Vicky feels the same way. Don Falcone was always good to us. He helped us open this shop over thirty-five years ago, and he always made sure we were protected. I cut your daddy's hair before you were even born. Vicky went to school with your mother." He pointed at the envelope of money. "I don't want that. I'm not going to tell that little weasel shit. Your business is your business, Omnio. If I hear anything, you know I would never repeat a word of it. Not to him or anyone else."

"Yes, I know this, Nick," King said, genuine affection in his eyes. "I trust you completely."

A look of relief appeared on Nick's face. "Thank you for saying that, Omnio. It means a lot to me. I'm too old to get involved in this type of shit. I'm just an old man who runs a crummy old barbershop. I've never worked for your family. I run a legitimate business. Your uncles, cousins, they've tried many times to get me to run numbers out of here. Or host poker and dice games in the basement. But I never wanted any part of that. I know it pissed them off, but they left me alone because I was friends with your grandfather, God rest his soul. Now that your grandfather is gone, the only reason Leoni doesn't bother me is..." He gestured toward the window behind him. "Look out there. The neighborhood has gone to shit. Nobody cares anymore. The *melanzani* don't take care of their homes. They steal anything that isn't bolted down. They sell drugs right on the streets. They kill each other over pennies. Druggies walk around the neighborhood like zombies. And the cops don't do shit. Your grandfather would've never let this happen. He loved this neighborhood. But Leoni? Anthony? They don't give a shit. They say there's no money left down here, so they let the blacks turn it into a wasteland like the rest of the city. That's why everyone left. All the old families are gone. Five years ago, when we sold our house, we barely made enough to put a down payment on a little ranch out in St. Clair Shores. Now we have a big mortgage we can barely afford. But at least we don't need bars on our windows or have to worry about waking up to find our car stolen."

He paused to take a deep breath and force down his rising anger. He was tempted to pour himself another shot but decided two was enough. "Anyway..." he continued, forcing away thoughts of his dying neighborhood. "What was I supposed to do? I know Anthony sent Dino. If I didn't take the money and agree to help, I'd come to work tomorrow and find my shop burned to the ground. I mean, I know this place isn't much, but it's all I got. A few more years and we'll have our house paid off. Then we'll retire and maybe buy one of those fancy motor home deals. You know, the kind we can live in." He grinned as he pictured his lifelong dream. "We want to drive around the country, see the sites, enjoy our old age, do what retired people are supposed to do."

Feeling a deep sense of love and affection for the old barber, King stepped around the desk and embraced him in a hug. "Paisan, I'm sorry for snapping at you. You and Vicky were always good to my mother and me. Let me get on my feet and I will see what I can do to help."

Nick gave him a firm embrace and stepped back to look him in the eye. "I won't tell Dino anything, Omnio. I swear it on the Blessed Mary."

"I know you won't," King said, setting a reassuring hand on his shoulder. "Next time you see him, just tell him I dropped by to get a cut and catch up on the neighborhood gossip."

"I will," Nick said, then thought of King's nefarious uncle. "But will you go see Leo?"

"Eventually. He'll want to know what my plans are. Not that I'll need to tell him, since I'm sure he'll have his guys watching every move I make."

Nick looked at him nervously. "I hear that he's not well, Omnio. I hear some of the others in the community are not happy with him."

"Yes, I've also heard that. But he has orders to leave me alone."

"Will he?"

"I doubt it."

Nick snatched the envelope off the desk and held it out to him. "Take this. I don't want it."

King pushed the envelope back to him. "Keep it. Use it toward your mortgage. Take your grandkids to Disneyland. Whatever. It's yours."

107

Nick thrust the envelope back at him, switching to Italian for emphasis, a habit that many Italians did when upset. "Take the money, Omnio! I know you need it. For Christ's sake, you just got out of prison. Suck up your pride for once and take the money. If you need more, you come see me. By no means am I a rich man, but I have a few dollars in the bank. What's mine is yours. We may not be *sangue*, but you have always been like a son to me and Vicky. We were devastated when you went away. We're thrilled to have you home. You'll always be part of our family."

King could tell the alcohol was making the old barber emotional, but he also knew that Nick would be offended if he didn't take the money. So, reluctantly, he took the envelope and slid it into his inside pocket. "Thank you, Niccolo," he said, also switching to Italian. "You're a good man and a good friend."

Nick beamed with genuine love and affection. "And you are a good man, Omnio. Which reminds me, have you gone to see Giovanni yet?"

King grinned at the thought of his faithful protettore. "Actually, he's next on my list of stops."

"Does he even know you're home?"

"I doubt it," King shrugged. "They don't keep him in the loop. Anthony never liked him because of me."

"And because of Pamela," Nick added with a chuckle.

"Yes," King nodded, also chuckling. "And Pamela."

"Well, that explains why they got him peddling *puttane* from that dive he runs…"

After a few more minutes of casual banter, they returned to the front of the shop to find Vicky cutting the hair of a young woman while finishing up what must have been a particularly funny story, because Madonna was listening with rapt attention and a broad smile on her face.

"What's so funny?" King asked.

Madonna winked at Vicky. "Oh, she was just telling me how you once hung your cousin's bike in the tree out front. That wasn't very nice of you."

King grinned, remembering the day quite well. He was no more than twelve. A hot summer day. He and his crew of neighborhood ruffians had been hanging out at the billiards hall next door all afternoon. After a few hours of video games, they stepped outside to sit on the front stoop and wisecrack on random passersby while munching on penny candy from old man Gus' liquor store across the street. They were enjoying the mid-summer weather, lounging in the sun, laughing and having a good old time when his younger cousin, Anthony Gianolla, showed up on a new bicycle, bragging about how it was better than everybody else's bike. This irked King, because even at a young age he hated a braggart. So when Anthony ran inside Gus' store to buy some candy and ice cream, King decided to play a little joke on him. It wasn't easy, but with much effort he hauled Anthony's bike up into the old Dutch elm out front. About twenty feet up he hung it on a limb so it dangled precariously over the street. When Anthony came out and noticed his bike was missing, he broke into a panicked fit of tears, even dropping his ice cream on the ground. King and his crew roared with laughter and thought it was hilarious. They laughed even harder when Anthony began demanding they tell him who stole his bike. They howled with laughter until King finally ended the ruse by pointing up in the tree. Anthony was furious and promised to tell his father. King thought nothing of it at the time, but the incident ended up being the beginning of a rift in their relationship that would escalate in the years to come. At the time, it was just a silly adolescent prank, but he now remembered how his grandfather had scolded him for it in front of his uncle Leoni, Anthony's father, but then later pulled him aside and told him Anthony had it coming for bragging about his bike.

Knowing he had a few hours to burn before he could make his final stop of the day, King decided to treat Madonna to a nice dinner. So after a final hug from Nick and Vicky, he had her drive him to one of his favorite restaurants in the city, an obscure little steakhouse on Gratiot Avenue called Capers, where steak was sold by the ounce. He knew the old couple who owned the place, and asked for them upon being seated. Just as he expected, they were both there and delighted to see him. Like everyone else, they refused to take his money, insisting his bill was on the house.

Madonna had no inhibitions when it came to eating. She was small, but loved to eat. So she ordered a 16-ounce sirloin with a baked potato that turned out to be the biggest potato she had ever seen. In fact, everything seemed bigger at Capers. Even the glasses were twice the normal size. She was utterly amazed by the amount of food King was able to eat. He devoured a 48-ounce porterhouse, which was by far the biggest steak she had ever seen. He even had a salad, breadsticks, two massive glasses of milk, and a piece of pecan pie for dessert. She decided it must be all those muscles that needed so much fuel. Either that or he had a tapeworm.

It was after 7:00 PM by the time they finished dinner, so King decided it was time to make his final stop of the day— Duchess Gentlemen's Club, a seedy strip joint located on the corner or Duchess Street and 7 Mile Road. But when they got there, the valet booth was empty and looked as if it hadn't been used in years. Yet the parking lot was surprisingly full. He had Madonna park in an empty space reserved for handicapped drivers, and when he stepped from the car he noted several expensive sports cars and luxury sedans parked in the dark alley behind the building. They looked oddly out of place in this rough neighborhood, and one of them in particular caught his attention. A brand-new Cadillac CTS. Black. Tinted windows. Sparkling clean and polished to mirrored perfection. He knew exactly who it belonged to.

As they made their way to the front door, Madonna glanced around nervously. Though she worked in Detroit, she'd never been in a real ghetto. Not like this. The building directly next door was boarded up and covered with graffiti. The building next to that was completely burned down. A stray dog was wandering aimlessly around in its overgrown parking lot, sniffing at piles of garbage. Standing on a corner across the street were what could only be a pair of professional prostitutes. A gang of boisterous black teenage boys walked by shouting derogatory expletives at the hookers, who returned a series of rapid-fire expletives of their own.

"Nice neighborhood," she joked, easing up closer to him.

"Yeah, real highfalutin," he quipped, holding the front door open for her. As soon as they stepped into the entry foyer, they were met by a large black bouncer wearing a tight black T-shirt that read "SECURITY" in bold white letters.

"I.D.," the bouncer said stoically, sizing King up.

King tried to disarm him with an amiable smile. "I'm looking for Giovanni."

Again the bouncer scrutinized him suspiciously. "You a cop?"

"No," King chuckled, amused by the irony of the question. "I'm definitely not a cop."

The bouncer narrowed his eyes at him. "Vonni ain't here."

King remembered the CTS parked in the back alley. He had given Vonni his first car, a black Cadillac CTS, and Vonni had driven one ever since, buying a new one every year. It was his trademark. "Are you sure?" he asked, looking the bouncer in the eye.

"Yeah, I'm sure," the bouncer replied smugly.

King glanced up at a security camera on the wall. It was trained right on them. "Why don't you check and make sure. I saw his car parked out back."

111

The bouncer folded his arms over his chest. "I told you, man, he ain't here. So if you're coming in, I need to see some I.D."

King's eyes went from patient and amiable, to cold and menacing. "I don't have any I.D.," he said, motioning up toward the camera. "But if you tell Vonni I'm here, I'm sure he'll vouch for me."

The bouncer's hardline conviction suddenly began to waver. There was something he didn't like about this guy. It was his eyes. They meant business. They screamed danger. They guy could be a detective. Or worse, a close friend of Vonni's. And it was never good to piss off the boss, or his friends. So, reluctantly, he stepped into an adjacent coat-check closet and snatched a house phone off the wall.

Giovanni "Vonni" Battaglia, a lithe and muscular man with an intrinsically bad temper, was in his basement office, barely an hour into his regular Saturday night poker game when he heard his phone trilling on his desk. As the game's host, it was his job to make sure that everyone was happy and things ran smoothly. For over an hour he'd been intently watching his five players, each of them seated at a felt-covered octagon poker table, stacks of cash and chips piled in front of them. Cuban cigars smoldered in ashtrays, filling the air with pungent gray smoke. A scantily clad cocktail waitress scurried about, serving them complimentary drinks. Each player was completely focused on their cards, their expressions blankly indifferent as they donned their best poker faces.

When the phone continued trilling, Vonni felt his anger rising. His staff knew better than to interrupt him during these weekly games. They had been instructed to never interrupt his games unless the building itself was on fire. He had good reason for not wanting to be interrupted. Sometimes his games would last all night, and on a good night they would net him upwards of $10,000 in profit. Even though tonight's players were by no means high rollers, they had money to lose. One of them was a gambling addict who owned several local businesses. Two were mid-level drug dealers. One was an executive at Chrysler. And one was a particularly adept safe-cracker who had just hit a major score.

Vonni hosted such games three Saturdays a month for his boss Anthony, but this was his personal game, which he hosted every third Saturday of the month. It was his bread and butter, when he earned nearly half his monthly income. And he needed tonight's players to start betting big if he was going hit his $10,000 goal. But some of the players were already getting frustrated. The businessman was catching all the cards. Barely an hour into the game and he was already up $40,000.

Annoyed by the interruption, Vonni finally snatched the phone off his desk. "How come I don't smell smoke?" he growled into the phone. "Because I thought I told you never to bother me unless the place is on fire."

"There's some guy up here asking for you," the doorman replied.

"Really, Nate? This is why you interrupt me? There's a guy at the door asking for me? Who the hell is he? The fuckin' president?"

"Didn't say. But if you ask me he looks like a cop. Big guy. About your age. Nice suit. He's got some little white chick with him."

"Well, I don't give a shit who he is. I'm not expecting anyone so get rid of him. Tell him I'm out of town or something. If he's a cop, give him our best booth and comp his first drink. And..."

He was about to give the doorman a stern warning about not interrupting him again, when a sudden thought occurred to him. He had security cameras monitoring the whole place, including the entry foyer. When he turned and looked at the bank of security monitors behind his desk, he saw the guy his bouncer was referring to. The footage was grainy, and at first he didn't recognize him, but then he focused on the little monitor and was barely able to believe who he was looking at.

113

"Unbelievable," he mumbled under his breath.

"What's that, boss?" the doorman asked, confused.

"That's goddamn King Falcone!" Vonni blurted.

"Who?" asked the doorman, not recognizing the name.

Vonni ignored the question and began barking out orders. "Take him up to the bar. Comp him anything wants. Then wait five minutes and send him down with Bruno."

"Down to your office?" the doorman asked, even more confused. "Don't you got a game going on down there?"

Nothing infuriated Vonni more than having his subordinates question his orders. "What the fuck did I tell you?" he boomed into the phone. "Get it done. Give me five minutes and send him down."

"Yeah, I got you, boss. Five minutes. I'll send him down."

With a distant look in his eyes, Vonni set the phone down and stepped over to the poker table. "Gentlemen, I'm sorry, but this will be your last hand of the night. Something's come up that requires my immediate attention."

One of the drug dealers, a heavyset black named Devon, jumped to his feet. "That's bullshit, Vonni," he spat angrily. "I don't care what came up, you gotta give me a chance to win my money back."

Vonni gave him a genuinely apologetic look. "Devon, I'm sorry but these things happen. You'll just have to win it back next time."

Devon glanced at the businessman, who had nearly $20,000 of his money stacked in front of him. "Fuck that shit, man. I ain't leavin' till I get a chance to win my cake back!"

Vonni made a discrete motion toward the two massive sentries posted by the door, both of whom immediately stepped behind the disgruntled card player. "I'm sorry, Devon," he said, offering him a threatening glare. "This is my game and I make the rules. I decide when the game is over. And tonight's game is over. But if you all agree, we'll resume this game next Saturday night?"

The players looked up at the two behemoth sentries, both of whom were wearing shoulder-holstered automatics. They knew Vonni was not the type of guy to play with. He said what he meant and meant what he said. The continuance of the game was not up for debate. So all of them but Devon agreed to come back next Saturday.

"So, Devon…" Vonni said, offering him a forced smile. "Will you be joining us next Saturday?"

Devon glanced back at the two armed sentries and knew he had no choice. The only people permitted to carry weapons in Vonni's club were Vonni's men. Period. Everyone else was subject to a hand-held metal detector at the front door. Also, attendees of his poker games were thoroughly frisked before being allowed to sit at the table. At least two armed bouncers remained posted by the door at all times, and tonight's two bouncers were currently staring down at him with cold malice in their eyes.

"This is bullshit, Vonni," Devon grumbled, a defeated look on his face, snatching his leather jacket off the back of his chair. "I'm down almost twenty fuckin' grand and you kick me out?"

Vonni splayed his hands apologetically. "I'm sorry, Devon. I really am. But this isn't a casino. This is my game. I make the rules. Sometimes these things hap—" The door to the office swung open, interrupting him mid-sentence, and he could barely believe who he was looking at. "Gentlemen, again, I apologize for cutting tonight's game short. Please come back next week and we'll resume where we left off. As a consolation, I won't cut the first ten pots."

Having no choice, the frustrated players donned their coats, gathered their cash and chips, and began making their way from the office. But as they went, they glanced at the new arrival, wondering who he was, knowing he was surely the reason their game had ended so abruptly.

When the players were all gone, Vonni locked eyes with King and knew his life was about to change forever. *"Benvenuti a casa, fratello*," he said in Italian, holding his arms out. "They said it couldn't be done but the don still had a few tricks up his sleeve, eh?"

As they held each other in a long embrace, Madonna noticed that both of them had tears in their eyes, and both were so choked up they could barely speak.

# CHAPTER 5

## SEVENTEEN YEARS EARLIER, BROOKLYN, NY

Giovanni Battaglia, known to his friends and associates simply as "Vonni," had grown up in Brooklyn, New York, where his Bay Ridge neighborhood was predominantly middle-class Italians. His mother, a 3rd grade teacher, was of Jewish descent. His father, an iron worker at the Brooklyn Navy Yard, was a second-generation Italian American. People generally liked the Battaglia family, who were known in their community as hard working, God fearing people with old-world values. Their home was a cozy brownstone on 83rd Street, just off 3rd Avenue, the main thoroughfare in their section of Brooklyn.

From the outside looking in, the Battaglia family appeared to be living the American dream. But this was not always the case for Vonni and his two siblings when they were growing up. Being that their mother was Jewish, they were often looked upon with contempt by certain neighborhood kids who took great pride in being thoroughbred Italians. In school, they were often ostracized because of their mixed lineage. But like all kids, they adapted and eventually found friends who accepted them as they were. Ann Marie, the eldest of the three siblings, had it the easiest. By the time she entered high school she was already a beautiful young woman and talented singer who was loved by everyone, especially the boys in the neighborhood. The second oldest, Noah, also grew into his own upon reaching his teens. A gifted athlete with multiple soccer scholarship offers by the time he was a sophomore in high school, he was handsome, popular, and a bit of a lady's man. He and his older sister were their parents' pride and joy.

Then there was their younger brother, Giovanni. Though he was a bit short and skinny as a teenager, he was exceptionally handsome and genetically muscular. And like his brother, he was a natural athlete. But he chose to use his physical prowess for things other than sports. Growing up in the shadows of his older siblings, he had developed a case of low self-esteem and often acted out for attention. His outlet was fighting. He loved to fight, and he was good at it. He liked that people feared him because of it. Growing up, he was suspended dozens of times for fighting. By age 14 he had already been arrested several times for fighting and disorderly conduct. The majority of his fights always stemmed from school bullies teasing him for his mixed lineage. Before he earned himself a reputation for being a fierce fighter, the bigger kids in the neighborhood had tormented him, calling him everything from a "kike" to "Jesus-killer." Usually, he let these insults roll off his shoulders with a grain of salt. But when they were aimed at his defenseless sister, he would defend her with ferocity, fists flying with no regard for the consequences. Even though he knew his brother and sister considered him a bit of a loose cannon, he loved them dearly, more than anything in the world. He looked up to Noah and felt the need to protect Ann Marie. They were very different from him in personality, but his blood connection to them ran deep.

At age 14, the summer before he was set to begin his freshman year at Fort Hamilton High School, Vonni was arrested for breaking into Brooklyn's Cherry Hill Textile plant. He and his friends had been stealing thousands of dollars' worth of fabrics to sell in Manhattan's garment district for pennies on the dollar. Using a broken window as a point of entry, they managed to steal hundreds of yards of fabrics before finally being caught. That's when his parents knew they had to do something about his behavior before he got himself into real trouble. Sensing things would only get worse, they decided it would be best for him to spend the rest of the summer far away from their neighborhood, where trouble found him more and more often. His mother had a sister who lived in Detroit, and that is where they sent him to spend the summer.

Vonni arrived in the Motor City on a hot June afternoon. His Aunt Sarah and cousin Jack were waiting at the Greyhound Terminal when he stepped off the bus. He didn't want to be there, but he had no choice. All he wanted was to be back home with his friends, running the streets, shooting dice, and causing mischief with his neighborhood buddies. The last place he wanted to be was Detroit, where he knew nobody and nobody knew him. He was going to miss his neighborhood, his friends, and his brother and sister. Especially his brother, who he looked up to and practically idolized. Sure they fought and argued like any other brothers, but Noah was his best friend and hero. He envied his brother's inherent wit and charisma. He tried to emulate him in almost every way. He got much of his character from his older brother. Even though it would only be a few short months, he was going to miss him.

Vonni had been to Detroit only twice before. The first time was to celebrate the birth of his younger cousin, Erika, when he was very young. The second time, when he was ten, was to accompany his mother on a weekend trip there to celebrate Hanukkah with his Aunt Sarah. He always found it odd that his parents practiced two different religions. His mother still practiced Judaism, while his father was a devout Catholic. It was the source of many heated arguments between them. Yet they always compromised by leaving the other to their own faith and religious practices.

One thing that made Detroit slightly bearable was his cousins, Jack and Erika. He and Jack were the same age, while Erika was a year younger than them. Both shared the same Jewish blood of this mother, but their affinities ended there.

119

Erika was a popular cheerleader who was passionate about art, particularly painting. Jack was a bit of a misfit, a skateboarder with long hair and grunge clothes. Vonni and Jack were both handsome in their own respective ways, but Jack was a tall, skinny, gangly kid, while Vonni was shorter, stocky, and muscular. They couldn't have differed more in personality. Vonni was hyper, athletic, extroverted and outspoken. He liked to fight and cause mischief. Jack, on the other hand, was quiet, reserved, and introverted. While Vonni loved to play sports like baseball, basketball, and football, the only physical activity Jack engaged in was skateboarding. He had never even played an organized sport, which struck Vonni as very odd since he had played organized sports all his life. Back in Brooklyn, everyone played organized team sports. Even girls. But Vonni had to admit the stunts Jack did on his skateboard were quite impressive. Back in Brooklyn, nobody skateboarded like his cousin Jack. There were plenty of skateboarders, sure, and even a few BMX tricksters, but none could do the ridiculous stunts that Jack did so easily.

Though they were very different in background and personality, Vonni did genuinely like Jack, who was smart, well-grounded and harbored dreams of someday being a doctor, which was exactly why Vonni's parents had sent him to Detroit in the first place. They hoped that some of Jack's sensibilities and good attributes would rub off on Vonni. Unfortunately, things didn't work out that way. They underestimated the power of their son's personality. As it turned out, by the end of the summer, Vonni rubbed off on Jack.

Immediately upon arriving in Detroit, Jack began showing Vonni around his neighborhood and introducing him to his friends, all of who Vonni thought talked funny. Everything—the people, the houses, the layout of the streets—it all seemed so different from what he was used to. But it wasn't long before he found himself intrigued by the neighborhood. Much like his own Brooklyn neighborhood, it was a tight-knit community made mostly of first and second generation Italians. Also like his neighborhood back home, most of the businesses were family-owned and operated. Everything was right there, within a several block radius. A grocery store, a couple of bakeries, an auto repair shop, a butcher shop, a delicatessen, a laundromat, a liquor store, several restaurants, and many more. All owned by Italians and a smattering of Greeks who lived in the neighborhood. It was no different than Brooklyn.

As the summer wore on, Vonni and Jack became more than two cousins who barely knew each other. They became genuine friends and did everything together. They snuck through a hole in the fence to get into Grosse Pointe's affluent Windmill Point Park, where they would swim in the park's huge pool and flirt with all the rich girls. They attended local high school parties in the neighborhood. They fished in the Detroit River at Angel Park. They played arcade games at the local billiards hall. Jack even taught Vonni how to do a few tricks on his skateboard.

But as much as Vonni was enjoying Jack and his time there in Detroit, he still missed home. He missed Brooklyn. He missed his friends and family. Back home, everyone knew him. There in Detroit, nobody knew him. Even though he did get along with Jack well, Jack's group of oddball skater friends were not overly friendly with him. He just didn't have anything in common with them. Like all kids their age, they had their own unique clique and social pecking order, which he didn't seem to fit into. He was an outsider and was treated as such. His only consolation was that most of the girls they hung around seemed to like him. They were always trying to get him to talk. At first he thought they were making fun of him, but he soon realized they just liked hearing his Brooklyn accent. There was even one girl he had his eye on. A short, busty Italian girl named Angelina. He'd seen her around the neighborhood a few times, but when he voiced his interest in her to Jack, he was given a stern warning not to even look in her direction. When he asked why, Jack explained that she had two very protective older brothers who were neighborhood tough guys. But more importantly, it was rumored that her father was in the Mafia.

It was this day that Jack told Vonni about the presence of the Mafia in the neighborhood. But Vonni wasn't stupid. He already knew the Mafia had a strong presence there. He saw how certain men, women, and even kids received extra respect from various local business owners. It was no different back in Brooklyn. He'd grown up seeing this his whole life. The Mafiosi were easy to spot. They lived in the nicest homes. They drove the nicest cars. They wore the nicest clothes. Their kids were spoiled to an almost ridiculous degree. Everyone was always extra respectful when dealing with them. Back in Brooklyn, people wanted to be friends with the local "wiseguys." Well, not everyone. His father detested them. He was 100% Italian and believed the "mob" gave all Italians a bad name. He called them a bunch of thugs and criminals. But Vonni always wondered why his father harbored so much contempt for them. They seemed like regular people, albeit people who had the best of everything. He also wondered why his father constantly warned him to stay away from kids connected to these mob families, calling them "young thugs in training."

There was, however, something that nobody knew about Vonni, something that bubbled up from the innermost reaches of his psyche. Not even his friends or brother knew about it. From a very young age, the Mafia had intrigued him. His favorite movies were *The Godfather, Goodfellas,* and *A Bronx Tale.* He had watched them dozens of times. The esoteric world of the Mafia seemed to call out to him. Its presence was much more obvious back in New York, but even there in Detroit he could feel it all around him.

Several weeks into his summer in Detroit, Vonni had his first brush with the local Mafia. It was a particularly hot day, so he and Jack decided to walk up to the local party store for a couple of cold Faygo sodas. They often made this trip to the store out of sheer boredom, but on this day Jack had an ulterior motive—Jackie Reed, a neighborhood girl he had a crush on. A shortcut down an alley behind the store would take them right behind her house. Fueled by boiling teenage hormones, he was hoping that she and her friends would be sunbathing by her pool like they so often did. With high hopes of catching a glimpse of her in a bikini, he led Vonni down the alley.

Without a care in the world, they made their way down the trash-laden alleyway, where garbage overflowed from dumpsters and feral cats battled rats in an age-old turf war for trash supremacy. They were casually ditty-bopping along, arguing over which city had bigger rats, New York or Detroit, when then came upon a garage with an open back door leading into the alley. The interior of the garage was cluttered with dozens of bikes and various bike parts, and kneeling in the middle of it all were four teenage guys. From the piles of cash strewn on the floor in front of them, it was obvious they were shooting dice. All of them were dark-haired, clearly Italian, and tough looking. When they noticed Jack and Vonni walking by, they stopped shooting dice and stared up at them with a combination of curiosity and contempt.

Jack suddenly looked nervous and motioned for Vonni to pick up the pace. As they did, the four guys in the garage stepped out into the alley and continued to stare at them. When Vonni turned back and noticed the indignant, caustic looks on their faces, he wondered what their problem was. He even locked eyes with the biggest one, a tall kid with dark eyes, broad shoulders and an athletic build. For a moment they seemed to size each other up.

"Who are they?" Vonni asked, finally breaking eye contact.

Jack waited a few more steps before answering, ensuring they were completely out of earshot. "King Falcone and his cousins."

"Which one was he?"

123

"The big one. They call themselves *'La Quattro Duchi*. It means—"

"The four dukes," Vonni finished, perfectly fluent in Italian from growing up in an almost exclusively Italian neighborhood. "I know what it means. But why do they call themselves that?"

"I have no idea," Jack shrugged. "But I know their family is the mob. People say King's grandpa is the boss of it all. I don't really know any of them, though. My parents say they're trouble, but none of them ever mess with me. They don't even talk to me. They pretty much stick to themselves. I heard it's some kind of Mafia code. If you're not part of their family, they see you as an outsider."

Vonni glanced back down the alley to see they had all gone back into the garage. "So how do you know all this?" he asked curiously.

"Everyone knows. They own everything in the neighborhood. All the stores, restaurants, bakeries, gas stations, party stores... they own it all. That was King's garage back there, but the rest of them live across Alter Road in Grosse Pointe. They come down here to hang out because there's more to do and less cops. Plus they have a ton of family in the neighborhood. They get free shit from everyone. The store owners kiss their ass. They can walk in any store and take whatever they want without anyone saying shit about it. If they're not hanging out back there in King's garage, they're up at Mr. Q's shooting pool. You saw all those bikes in his garage?"

"Yeah, what's up with that?"

"You didn't hear it from me but word is that King runs a bike chop shop out of there. My buddy Mike bought a badass Haro Master from him a while back for only a hundred bucks! Thing was tricked out, too. All new frame stands, axle pegs, Verde rims. Had to be worth a thousand bucks. I figure King has his crew steal the bikes in Grosse Pointe and bring them back to his garage to strip down and turn into new bikes. I was thinking about seeing if he could get me a GT Pro Performer."

"Sounds a lot like my neighborhood back in Brooklyn," Vonni said, taking a swig of his cream soda. "There's lots of mob kids, and my parents say the same thing as yours. They're always telling me to stay away from them."

Jack hurled his empty soda bottle at a rat that scampered across the alley. The bottle shattered mere inches from the emboldened rodent, which stopped and glanced back at him for a moment before disappearing under a dumpster.

"Damn," he said, popping a piece of bubble gum in his mouth. "Did you see how that thing looked at me?"

Vonni chuckled. "Yeah, the same way them dudes in the garage looked at us."

Jack shrugged. "King don't talk to me no more, but I've known him all my life. We were friends when we were little. King was real cool back then. But now he only hangs with other mob kids. Even the girls they hang around are mob daughters. Whenever I walk by, they stare at me but never mess with me. I think it's probably 'cause I used to be friends with King. Plus Tony Gianolla has a thing for my sister. He was the little one back there in the garage, the one with the slicked hair. Erika says he's cute, but my mom forbids her from even talking to him."

"Sounds like my parents," Vonni said, taking another casual swig from his soda. "My sister had a crush on a mob kid named Joe Grimaldi, but my dad wouldn't even let him call our house."

Jack picked up a rock and launched it at a rat that was perched atop a bag of garbage. "King Falcone," he mused, narrowly missing the unsuspecting rat. "Would you believe he's like us? Half Jewish. Growing up he was always the toughest kid in school. I've seen him fight. It ain't pretty. Last year I watched him kick the shit out of a kid just for grabbing Pamela Gianolla's ass. It was at a football game. He waited until the game was over and caught the kid in the parking lot. Broke his jaw with one punch. Knocked him out cold! Kid's head hit the ground like a bag of bricks. Split right open. Blood all over the place. I actually

125

felt bad for him. He had no idea Pam was King's little cousin. And that wasn't even the end of it. A few weeks later the guy's older brother showed up looking for King at one of our basketball games. Walked right into our school with a couple of his boys, thinking they were gonna jump King. Bad move. King and his crew ended up beating the shit out of them. Right in front of everyone. On the fuckin' basketball court during halftime. I mean really stomped them! There was blood all over the place. A couple of them got taken away in an ambulance. The whole school saw it, even our teachers and principal. But they didn't say shit about it. Not a word. They knew better than to get the cops involved. They didn't want any smoke from King's people. Even they know who his family is."

As they walked back to Jack's house, Jack changed the subject and they chatted about girls and music and nothing in particular. But Vonni was still thinking about the four guys in garage. The look they had given them was clearly a warning. It was their way of saying don't walk back there again. It was enough to make him decide he would avoid that alley for the rest of his time there in Detroit. He knew kids like them back in Brooklyn. They didn't take kindly to strangers, and the last thing he needed was trouble with some local Mafia kids. After all, the reason his parents had sent him there in the first place was to keep him out of such trouble.

But Vonni and Jack did cross paths with the *Quattro Duchi* several more times that summer. Usually it was at the billiards hall where all the neighborhood kids played video games, shot pool, and hung out. Occasionally it was at Angel Park, where Jack and his cronies did their skateboard stunts. The *Quattro Duchi* even showed up at a few of the backyard parties Jack took Vonni to. But wherever it was, King and his cousins were always accompanied by an entourage of tough-looking Italian guys. A bevy of the cutest girls in the neighborhood flocked around them like they were celebrities. They always seemed to be having the best time, laughing and joking amongst each other without a care in the world. And the menacing King Falcone seemed to be their nucleus, the center of attention, always calm and in control of everyone around him. Vonni was impressed that someone so young had such a powerful presence. It reminded him of how people treated his brother Noah.

Vonni was relieved that the *Quattro Duchi* never bothered him or Jack. A few times, when Vonni tried talking to one of the girls they hung around, they shot him mildly annoyed looks, but usually they ignored him whenever they crossed paths. That is, until the incident in Jackie Reed's backyard.

It was a hot August afternoon and Vonni was with Jack, the two of them splashing around in Jackie's pool, enjoying her and all of her bikini-clad friends. Vonni was doing his best to impress them by jumping off her garage into the pool, when suddenly Frankie Bommarito and King Falcone came racing up the driveway on their Honda Helix scooters. Frankie, a rotund fifteen-year-old with no neck and a bullish face, was one of the *Quattro Duchi*. He also happened to have a thing for Jackie. The instant he saw Jack, who he knew also had a crush on Jackie, he jumped off his scooter and began bullying him, threatening to "kick his ass" if he didn't leave. Jack was skinny and by no means a tough guy, so Vonni decided he had no choice but to stand up for him. Jumping out of the pool he got right up in Frankie's face, telling him to leave or he would kick *his* ass.

For a moment, Frankie looked dumbfounded, unable to believe that Jack's cocky cousin from New York would be so brazen. But then he remembered Jackie was watching. As one of the biggest kids in the neighborhood, he prided himself on being one of its toughest. And in the event he needed help, which was unlikely, he had King with him. King *was* the toughest kid in the neighborhood. So, without hesitation, he proceeded to punch "Johnny New York" in his smart mouth, expecting him to go down. But to his surprise, Vonni took the punch like a champ and sent a hard right hook crashing into his nose. A heated battle ensued.

For nearly five minutes the two of them rolled around on the grass, punching, and wrestling until Frankie finally overpowered Vonni and began pummeling him savagely. That's when King stepped in and broke it up. For a fleeting moment, Vonni, who was bleeding badly from a gash over his eye, thought King was about to jump in and finish him off. He was tough but not *that* tough. He knew he'd be no match for the likes of King Falcone, who was twice his size and all muscle. Frankie was still yelling and trying to fight, but to Vonni's surprise, King shoved him back and gave him a stern warning to settle down.

Once King had them separated and calmed down, he turned to Jackie. "Go get these idiots some ice and bandages," he ordered, and then stepped over to examine the gash above Vonni's eye.

"I don't need no fuckin' bandages," Vonni spat defiantly.

But King ignored him and stepped even closer to look at the gash. "Shit, that might need a couple stitches," he said, unfazed by the blood leaking from the cut. He pointed at the pool. "Wash your face in there. Then go home and tell Jack's parents you fell off his skateboard. And do yourself a favor, don't come back here no more. Because next time I might not be here to pull Frankie off you..."

Later that afternoon, when Vonni's aunt and uncle saw his face, they knew he had been in a fight. But he stuck to the story and insisted he'd fallen off Jack's skateboard. Of course they knew better. Based on the condition of his face and knuckles, it was obvious that he'd been in a serious fight. Yet no matter how hard they pressed him about what *really* happened, he claimed that he had fallen off Jack's skateboard.

Throughout the remainder of the summer, Vonni and Jack ran into King and Frankie Bommarito several more times, but to Vonni's surprise they never bothered him. Frankie would shoot him dirty looks, even cold stares, but nothing else came of the fight they had in Jackie's backyard. It was almost as if King had ordered Frankie to let it go, and Vonni couldn't help but wonder why.


Vonni finally returned home to New York in early September, and he was surprised that he almost immediately missed Detroit. There was something he liked about it. People seemed more genuine. They didn't try to be anyone other than themselves, which was rare in his Brooklyn neighborhood. Though he was happy to be back home with his family and old friends, they didn't seem all that happy to have him back. In fact, they seemed to have barely even noticed he was gone. In Detroit, people took notice of him. His accent, his mysterious background, his New York swagger, it all made him stand out. But back in Brooklyn, he was just another half-breed Italian kid running around Bay Ridge, one of thousands.

Strangely, after his summer in Detroit, Brooklyn no longer felt like home to Vonni. Everyone seemed different. Good friends no longer seem like good friends. Even his brother had changed. Now sixteen-years-old, Noah had begun dating a girl named Lisa Fratianno, who only wanted to smoke pot, get drunk, and hang out in her basement. Vonni found her to be repugnant. Other than having a decent figure, there was nothing even attractive about her. But she seemed to have cast a spell on his brother.

Even Ann Marie, his beloved sister, seemed different. She had just turned eighteen and spent most of the summer attending a voice camp in Manhattan. While there, she had met several agents, producers, and record label executives who claimed to be interested in her talent. Vonni knew she was a talented singer, even gifted, but he also knew the recording industry was full of shady characters who often exploited young girls like her. He feared that some old record label pervert would try to sell her a dream just to get in her pants. But when he voiced this to her she called him a stupid kid and told him to stay out of her business.

Over the summer his parents also seemed to have changed. His father had gotten laid off from his job and began hanging out at neighborhood pubs, drinking until the wee hours of the morning. When Vonni came home from school each day, his parents would barely even acknowledge him. Usually because they were too busy fighting. Sometimes it was over their difference in religion. Other times it was over money or bills. But most often it was over his father's late night drinking benders. His mother also suspected that his father was cheating on her. Vonni wondered how things had changed so dramatically over the course of only one summer. Nothing seemed the same. By the middle of his freshman year in high school, he was beginning to wish he were back in Detroit.

As the weeks grew into months, Vonni found himself falling into a depressive funk. He began to loathe his old friends and often found his thoughts on Detroit, particularly King Falcone and the *Quattro Duchi*, the young heirs to Detroit's Mafia families. The Mafia. It was always there, a secret society of alleged criminals who laughed in the face of authority. He'd seen all the Hollywood films but knew almost nothing about the real Mafia. He wondered who they were and what they really did. Maybe it was the Italian half of his blood, but for some reason he was intrigued by them, and even felt a strange connection to them. They were a powerful presence in his Brooklyn neighborhood. Like back in Jack's Detroit neighborhood, Mafiosi owned nearly every store and shop for blocks. He wanted to learn more about them, how they worked and operated. He wanted to be one of them. He wanted to be feared and respected like the neighborhood wiseguys. But of course he kept such thoughts to himself, because if his parents ever learned that he harbored thoughts of someday being a gangster, they would no doubt ship him off to boarding school.

The next two years of Vonni's life saw things change drastically. His parents got divorced and his father moved to New Jersey. Noah dropped out of school and moved in with his girlfriend, who supported them by stripping at a Bronx strip club. His sister forewent college to spend all of her time in a recording studio working on her demo. But Vonni plugged along like the soldier he was, ditching most of his old friends to be a lone wolf. Even though he had a bad temper and liked to fight, he was also very intelligent and enjoyed school. By day he went to school, and by night he made money working at a local grocery store. One of the reasons he liked working at the store was that it was owned by an old Italian named Pepe D'Arco, whose brother, "Big Al," was a local wiseguy who hung around the store all day. Al was a huge, fat, mountain of a man whose associates made regular stops at the store to see him. Pepe always sent them on their way with boxes of meats, fruits, and vegetables. Big Al liked Vonni and soon began introducing him to his associates as "Young Johnny Batts." They considered him a good kid and often tipped him handsomely for carrying boxes of meat and produce to their cars. One of them, a guy named Tony "The Teacher" Ciulla, even tried to set him up on a date with his daughter. But Vonni knew her from school. She was fat and had an abrasive personality, so he politely lied and told him he had a girlfriend.

As the months wore on, Vonni felt less and less connected to his family, and more and more connected to the wiseguys who came into his work each night. He found it easier to talk to them, and they seemed to accept him without prejudice. They didn't care about his mixed lineage. To them, he was just "Young Johnny Batts from Bay Ridge." Everyone showed them respect. Everyone looked up to them and treated them like celebrities. He wanted to be like them, but figured he never could because he wasn't born into one of their families. That is, until he witnessed something that gave him hope.

131

One day while cleaning the alley behind the store, something peculiar caught his eye. He was sweeping behind a dumpster when he looked down the alley and noticed a guy from his neighborhood engaged in a hushed conversation with a highly-ranked Mafioso. The guy from his neighborhood was Tony Scagliano. Vonni only recognized him because he sometimes hung around his brother, Noah. Scagliano wasn't affiliated with any of the local Mafia crews, but he was known around the neighborhood as a sleazy character, a thief, swindler, and drug dealer. Rumor had it that he even got caught breaking into his own grandmother's house to steal her safe. Vonni often wondered why his brother would hang around such a shady character.

After a brief conversation, the Mafioso popped open his trunk and handed Scagliano a large duffle bag that appeared to be stuffed full of something. Later that night, when Vonni called his brother and asked him what Scagliano was doing for the Mafioso, Noah got angry and snapped at him. "Mind your fuckin' business, Giovonnni!" he yelled into the phone.

But seeing Tony Scagliano doing business with a high ranked Mafioso gave Vonni hope that he, too, may someday be able to work his way into the good graces of a big Mafioso. He figured if a slimeball like Scagliano could get a job working for the Mafia, so could he. Unfortunately, a week after he saw Tony Scagliano in the alley, Noah's body washed up on the shores of Staten Island. He'd been shot twice in the head.

The murder of his brother changed Vonni. His heart became cold and filled with rage. Consumed with thoughts of revenge, he bought a .357 Smith & Wesson revolver and vowed to hunt down his brother's killer. Unfortunately, before he could even begin the hunt, his mother found the pistol while cleaning his room.

Scared that she would lose yet another son to the streets, she put him on a bus to Detroit. He would never again return to live in New York.

# CHAPTER 6

Vonni arrived back in Detroit while on winter break, but his return to Motown wasn't quite what he expected. For starters, he wasn't prepared for the weather. Back in New York it had been had been cold but not nearly as cold as it was in Detroit, especially compared to the summer he had spent there two years previously, when the weather had been so warm, sunny and pleasant. The second thing that came as a surprise was the neighborhood itself. Now that it was the dead of winter, everything seemed deserted, desolate and devoid of life. The last time he was there, kids were playing in the streets. The parks were always bustling. People had been out mowing lawns, walking down sidewalks, washing cars, and working on their homes. The neighborhood had been alive with activity. But now it seemed the city's brutal winter had forced everyone into hibernation.

Then there was Jack, who had clearly changed for the worse. His hair was long. He had grown a shaggy beard, and he'd gained weight. A lot of it. In fact, he had gotten downright fat. All he wanted to do these days was hang out with his pothead friends, smoke weed, eat junk food and play video games in his basement. Vonni had smoked pot several times but never liked it. It made him lazy and paranoid. He also didn't care much for alcohol. It made him belligerent and prone to fighting. He was smart enough to refrain from both. If he needed something to occupy his time, he lifted weights or played sports. The contrast in his and Jack's personalities had grown exponentially over the past two years.

Vonni was not overly excited to be back in Detroit, particularly because he was still haunted by the murder of his brother. Anger, rage, remorse, revenge—it still consumed him, and being away from home only made things worse. He was supposed to be back in Brooklyn avenging his brother's murder. He was supposed to be hunting down his brother's killers. Instead, he was stuck in Detroit, against his will. Like his first time there, all he could do was suck it up and deal with it. If there was one upside to his circumstances, it was being away from his parents. He was happy that he no longer had to deal with their incessant lecturing and trying to impose their plans for his future on him. It was his life and he would do what he wanted with it.

A week after arriving back in Detroit, Vonni began the second half of his junior year of high school. As he settled into his new life, the painful memory of his brother's murder finally began to subside. But adjusting to a new school was not easy. At age 16, with hormones running wild, it was a difficult time to make such a dramatic transition. Though his aunt and uncle seemed to genuinely care about him, he couldn't help but wonder if they considered him a burden. After all, he was another mouth to feed, another kid to worry about. A kid with a troubled history. He knew if it weren't for his aunt's love for his mother, he would never be there. He even sensed that Jack didn't particularly care to have him there. Most of the time Jack was distant and barely spoke to him, especially at school where as the "new kid," Vonni often felt like a pariah. Perhaps, he thought, it was his own fault. He knew he sometimes alienated himself from people. He had become a bit of an introvert, rarely sociable with his classmates. He missed his old friends, his old neighborhood, his old life. And he was still grieved by his brother's death. It was hard to picture a future without his beloved brother, the person he had always tried to emulate, the person who had molded his very character. Though he knew his mother intended for him to stay there and finish high school in Detroit, he vowed that he would someday return to Brooklyn and avenge his brother's murder.

Another thing he didn't care for was his new school. By Detroit standards it was a large school, yet it was barely half the size of Fort Hamilton High, his school back in Brooklyn. The ethnic makeup was far different, too. Back home, the majority of the student body was almost exclusively Italian, Jewish, or Hispanic. But there in Detroit, the student body was more than half black, the rest an eclectic mix of differing ethnicities that varied from neighborhood to neighborhood. And with the exception of a handful of Jack's friends, none of them even knew Vonni existed. The few who did know of him only knew that he was Jack's cousin from New York, which is how he earned the nickname "Johnny New York." Changing schools at any age is difficult, but in high school where the social pecking order is firmly established, it can be extremely unpleasant. Which was proving to be the case for Vonni, who found himself existing outside of any social clique or pecking order. Back home, at least he was respected as a known tough guy. There in Detroit, however, he had no reputation and no real friends. He was the epitome of a nobody.

Jack drove them to school each morning in his beat up old 4-cylinder Mustang, which leaked oil and often needed a manual push to start. Vonni was embarrassed to be even seen in it. He wondered why his cousin was so lazy. The least he could do was get off his ass and get a job so he could buy a better car. After all, his parents were by no means well-off. His mother only worked part-time as a secretary for a seasonal cement company. His father was a maintenance custodian at Wayne State University. Their combined income was less than $40,000. Though they budgeted well and appeared to live a fairly comfortable life, it was obvious they struggled to make ends meet. And yet Jack did nothing to help. He was a lazy, freeloading bum who contributed nothing to their family. He didn't even seem to care about his appearance. His clothes were tattered, dirty and old. His hair was long, greasy and scraggly. His shoes smelled atrocious, and his car made him the laughingstock of the school.

Vonni knew that back home in Brooklyn very few people even owned a car. Between the subway and bus systems, there was no need for a car. Cars drank expensive gas, and it was almost impossible to find a parking space for them. With traffic the way it was in New York, it was usually faster to just take the subway or bus. But this was not an option in Detroit. Lacking an effective mass-transit system, a car was a necessity. To Vonni, there seemed to be millions of them. Everyone from senior citizens to teenagers had a car. But cars in Detroit were more than just transportation. They were also a sort of status symbol. Especially amongst young people. The best-looking girls at school seemed to only date guys who drove nice cars, and guys were constantly trying to outdo each other by embellishing their cars with fancy rims, custom paint, televisions and elaborate sound systems. It didn't take long for him to realize that he was going to need a nice car if he wanted to be noticed at his new school. Especially noticed by the girls.

As Vonni settled into his new life, he sometimes found himself wondering about *La Quattro Duchi*—The Four Dukes. He never saw them around the neighborhood. Nor did he see any of them at school. He was tempted to ask Jack about them, but decided that would be a waste of time. Jack was so stoned most of the time that he barely even knew where he was, let alone the whereabouts of someone else. Plus the *Quattro Duchi* were part of a very secretive clique, one that Jack was by no means part of. Vonni always kept an eye out for them, but they seemed to have vanished from the neighborhood. He especially wondered what happened to the foreboding King Falcone, the young Mafia prodigy. The Mafia. Even though he was now 16, he had not grown out of his fascination with them. But of course, he did not want to make any waves by inquiring about them. The memory of Frankie Bommarito pummeling him in Jackie Reed's backyard was still fresh.

By his second week in school, Vonni already had his eye on a girl. She wasn't in any of his classes, but he saw her in the halls from time to time. She was short, no more than 5'3", with a very curvaceous figure. He liked girls with curves. Most Italian guys did. But on top of being beautiful, this girl was very poised and elegant. Almost regal. He'd heard her talking with friends, and she was very articulate. She dressed surprisingly conservative compared to other girls in school, and she carried herself with an air of gentility. He had known plenty of cute Italian girls back in Brooklyn, but none of them had ever captivated him like this one. In the past, he had always been confident and sure of himself when approaching girls. He knew they liked his quick wit and sense of humor. In fact, they were usually the ones chasing him. But something about this girl intimidated him. Just the sight of her in the halls made his body flushed with excitement. He had been studying her from afar for over two weeks now, and she didn't appear to have a boyfriend. At least not there at school. He was tempted to ask about her, but he didn't know who to ask. The only people he knew were Jack and his troupe of skateboard pot-heads.

Eventually, he decided he was being ridiculous. After all, he had nothing to lose from just introducing himself. He knew her daily routine, so one day after school he made his move. He waited until his final class let out and he followed her out to the student parking lot, where he met Jack every day at his crappy old Mustang.

"Hello, shorty," he said, sidling up next her, flashing her a smile. "What's your name?"

She continued to walk but studied him for a moment. "Are you making fun of me?" she finally asked.

"What?" he asked, feigning ignorance. "Of course not. I would never make fun of you. I just meant... Well, where I come from we call cute girls shorties."

A slight grin appeared on her face. "Where you come from?" she asked, trying to decipher his accent. "And where might that be? Boston? New Jersey?"

"Close," he said, his chest swelling proudly. "Brooklyn."

She gave him an incredulous look. "And in Brooklyn they call girls shorties?"

"Sure, but only cute ones."

"Huh," she said, smiling, stopping at the curb, casting a furtive glance around the crowded parking lot, apparently looking for someone. "What did you say your name was?"

"I didn't. But it's Giovanni. Most people just call me Vonni."

She batted her big brown eyes at him. "Well, Vonni, that was very sweet of you."

He peered into the parking lot, wondering who she might be looking for. But all he saw was an incongruous mass of bodies and cars vying for position. People were yelling back and forth. A dissonance of music poured from dozens of stereo systems. The air reeked of marijuana. But nobody seemed to be paying any attention to them.

"Yes, well, I'm a pretty sweet guy," he said, grinning down at her. "At least my mom thinks so."

"Yeah?" she chuckled melodically. "Hitler's mom probably thought the same thing."

"Really?" he said, looking offended. "Hitler? You're comparing me to Hitler?"

"Kidding," she giggled. "You know I'm kidding."

"Oh, you got jokes? Cute *and* funny. You're the total package. Except you still haven't told me your name, shorty."

"Shorty," she mused, glancing nervously into the sea of cars. "That's funny. Nobody has ever called me that before. And I thought only my boyfriend liked short girls."

"So you have a boyfriend?" he asked, looking like he just got punched in the stomach.

"I do," she confirmed, waving over a black Cadillac CTS with tinted windows. "And here he comes now. But thank you for the compliment. Your mother was right. You are a sweet boy."

The blacked-out Cadillac pulled up and stopped a few feet in front of them. Inside it was a driver and passenger. The driver, a hulking brute who had to be in his mid-twenties, immediately stepped out and glared at Vonni while he held the back door open for her. As she slid into the back seat, she cast him a barely perceptible smile. Then the driver shut the door, shot him another cold look, and returned to the driver's seat. A moment later they drove off.

Dejected, all Vonni could do was make his way through the crowded lot toward Jack's old junker Mustang. But as he went, he watched the ominous black Cadillac park in the back of the parking lot, away from all the other cars. He was almost to Jack's car when the Cadillac's passenger window powered down, revealing its passenger, who was looking right at him. Even from over a hundred feet, with dozens of kids milling about between them, Vonni immediately recognized who was staring back at him. It was none other than King Falcone. They locked eyes for a long moment before several guys stepped over to the Cadillac and began talking to King through the passenger window.

As usual, Jack was running late, presumed to be somewhere in the parking lot smoking pot with his pot-head friends. So all Vonni could do was lean against Jack's car and wait for him to show up. But his eyes were drawn to the black Cadillac. Two guys were now standing next to it talking to King, both of them very well dressed and clearly Italian. Vonni was not surprised when one of them removed a large knot of cash from his pocket and discreetly handed it to King through the window. He did, however, find it surprising how everyone else in the parking lot seemed to be ignoring them like they weren't even there.

Ten minutes later, as the parking lot finally began to clear out, Jack came sauntering up, red-eyed and reeking of pot. Mildly annoyed at having to wait, Vonni sat back in the dirty old Mustang, looking forward to getting the hell out of there, the sting of disappointment still lingering. But just as Jack put his car in drive and began to pull out, the shiny black Cadillac rolled to a stop in front of them, blocking them in. The passenger window powered down, and Vonni found himself face to face with King Falcone, who looked even more menacing than he remembered.

"What the fuck?" Jack mumbled, wondering what was going on.

But as fast as it appeared, the Cadillac pulled off.

"What the hell was that all about?" Jack asked, finally able to pull out.

"That was King Falcone, right?" Vonni asked, already knowing the answer.

"Yeah, but why the hell was he looking at us like that?"

"I think he was looking at me," Vonni said matter-of-factly.

"What?" Jack said, giving him a confused look. "Why would he be looking at you?"

"Does he have a girlfriend?"

"Yeah, sure, a couple of them. Why?"

"One of them a short chick built like a gymnast with big tits?"

Jack's eyes went wide with trepidation. "Shit, man, that's King's main girl, Mary Licavoli! What'd you do? Tell me you weren't hitting on her?"

Vonni couldn't help but chuckle at the look on his cousin's face. "Actually, yeah, I was just mackin' on her. I walked her out of school. But I didn't know she was King's girl."

"Shit, man," Jack said, shaking his head. "Are you crazy?"

Vonni flashed him a smile. "Define crazy."

"This shit ain't funny, Vonni!" Jack blurted, clearly not amused. "You're going to get us both fucked up. Of all the girls in school, you had to hit on King's? I told you he ain't to be played with."

Vonni rolled his eyes. "Relax, man. All I did was tell her she was cute. I never saw her talking to guys, so I figured she didn't have a boyfriend."

"Duh! Guys don't talk to her because she's King's girl! She's been with him for a while now. Which is why you never see guys messing with her. Everyone knows she's off-limits."

Vonni flashed him another smile. "But she liked me. I could tell."

"Stop playing, Vonni!" Jack spat, glaring at him. "You think this is a joke, but you don't realize who you're fucking with. That was King's way of warning you. This is the second time you pissed him off. You don't mess with a guy like him. Especially not with his girl. I'm telling you, Vonni, you're just asking to get fucked up."

Vonni gave him an annoyed look. "Man, Jack, sometimes you sound like such a pussy. Why are you so scared of him?"

"Because I know him," Jack scoffed. "You don't."

"What do you even know about him?"

"I know him and his boys are into all kinds of shit."

"His boys? You mean *La Quattro Duchi*?"

"No. Those are his cousins, and they all go to Grosse Pointe South. He's the only one who still lives down here. And he dropped out of school last year."

"He dropped out?" Vonni asked, surprised. "Why?"

"I don't know. I heard his mom got sick and he needed to take care of her. Something like that. But he still has boys who go to our school. Most of them are Italian, but I've been seeing him kickin' it a lot lately with some Mexicans who live down off Conner. Some of the Serbians, too. I think he's got them working for him."

"Working?" Vonni asked curiously. "Doing what?"

"All kinds of shit," Jack said matter-of-factly, pulling out of the parking lot and heading for home. "They sell weed, chop cars, run numbers, loan money, run after-hours clubs. You name it and they've got their hands in it. I heard they'd even fuck someone up for the right money, and King is their boss. He runs everything. I get my weed from Joey Lombardo, one of King's main guys. They've been boys ever since grade school. Joey acts like he works for himself, but I'm not stupid. I know he answers to King. They all do. That Caddy? It's King's, but he never drives it. The big dude driving it was Dean D'Anatto. He's King's bodyguard and a 'roided-out maniac. I heard he almost killed some dude in a bar fight a few years ago."

Vonni considered all this for a moment. "So, have you ever thought about working for King? I mean, you said you guys were good friends back when you were little. And God knows you could use the money. Your parents are broke as shit, and this car is pathetic. You should see if King will give you a job. You could save some money and get rid of this bucket."

"Fuck that!" Jack exclaimed. "I don't want any part of them guys, and they would never deal with me anyway. They only deal with each other. You know, all their Italian mob codes and shit."

"But you just said King has Serbians and Mexicans working for him. You guys go way back. How do you know he wouldn't give you a job?"

"He just wouldn't," Jack snapped. "He would never deal with me."

Vonni wanted to ask him why but already knew the answer. It was obvious. King was a go-getter, a hustler, and born leader. Naturally, he only associated with other such people. Jack was anything but a leader, and certainly not a go-getter. Once upon a time, before he became addicted to pot and video games, he had harbored big dreams of someday becoming a doctor. Now he was nothing but a loser who was at best destined for mediocrity. Vonni, however, was nothing like his cousin Jack. Indeed he was a go-getter, a born leader, a hustler. So he decided it was time he started paying closer attention to King Falcone and his infamous crew of go-getters. After all, they were of like minds.

# CHAPTER 7

The next several months seemed to crawl by for Vonni. He and his cousin occasionally hung out, but with nothing in common they were becoming more and more distant. While Jack showed no interest in his future, Vonni was constantly thinking of ways to become successful, wealthy, and most importantly—respected. In his mind he was slowly beginning to formulate a plan, and it did not include his lazy doper cousin. Part of his plan was to make some new friends, and he began doing just that. One of these new friends was a neighborhood tough guy named Tommy "Guns" Moceri, a stocky Italian kid with disproportionately large arms, which was how he earned the moniker "Guns." They'd seen each other around school but never had spoken until the day Vonni hustled him out of $20 bucks in a game of pool. Both were seventeen, Italian, and intrinsic tough guys who loved sports, lifting weights, and fighting. With so much in common they immediately hit it off and became nearly inseparable. They played basketball at Angel Park, shot pool at Mr. Q's, and lifted weights at Muscles Gym, a hardcore gym where Vonni even got himself a part-time job after school.

Vonni also began dating a petite little Italian girl named Katie Vitale, who had a bubbly disposition and a hyperactive sex drive. She wasn't beautiful but she was cute and able to satisfy his youthful sexual needs. One day while at school he had approached her, poured on his New York charm, and within a week she was his girlfriend. He liked her, and considered her a nice girl, but the truth was that he sometimes found her annoying. He could only take her in small doses, usually no more than an hour or two at a time. But it wasn't just her. He found most girls to be boring, witless, superficial clones who tried to be whatever they thought guys wanted them to be. They annoyed him with their incessant gossiping and chatter about people he knew nothing about. He was nice to Katie, always treating her respectfully, flirting and making her laugh with his antics, but he intentionally kept her at a distance so she wouldn't get too attached. The last thing he wanted was for her to fall in love with him, although he was beginning to think she already had.

Vonni was relieved when spring finally arrived. The Michigan winter had been long and even colder than the ones back in New York. But when spring finally made its appearance in mid-April, the city seemed to awaken from its slumber. Slowly but surely people began to emerge—walking dogs, washing cars, working on homes, and sitting on porches. Once again kids could be seen playing in the streets and playgrounds. Music poured from open windows. The smells of spring foliage and barbecue grills filled the air. It appeared that he wasn't the only one excited about the fact that summer was just around the corner.

As summer vacation grew near, he began to make a few more friends at school. Most were Italian, since he naturally felt a connection to them, but for the most part he hung with Tommy Guns Moceri. Both were quick-witted ruffians who loved to laugh and joke, and it wasn't long before they were the best of friends, sharing even the most intimate details of their lives with each other. So, one day after school, while Tommy was driving him to work at the gym, Vonni decided to ask him something that had been on his mind for quite some time.

"Tommy," he said, looking him in the eye. "What do you know about King Falcone?"

Tommy was curious as to why his new friend would want to know about the likes of King Falcone, a young Mafioso, but he told him everything he knew. Which really wasn't much. Only bits and pieces of rumors he'd heard over the years. King's family supposedly sat atop the local Mafia hierarchy. Tommy had no idea in what capacity King worked for his family, but he did share with Vonni what he knew about King's various business endeavors. They were numerous, all of them illicit street rackets, everything from gambling and drugs to extortion and stolen merchandise. Tommy also told him to keep such inquisitions to himself in the future, warning him that he would have a serious problem on his hands if King ever learned that he was inquiring about him.

Vonni took Tommy's advice and never asked about King Falcone again. He simply went about his life—school by day and work at the gym by night. The gym's owner, an old Italian bodybuilder named Sonny "Sonny D" DeAugustino, had grown fond of him and began trusting him to manage the place in his absence, giving him free rein, including free protein shakes, free workout apparel, and discounted memberships for any of his friends. Sonny even told him that he could even comp his close friends and family free memberships, a perk he had yet to take advantage of. Until one Sunday morning.

Sunday mornings were always quiet and slow, which was why he was seated behind the gym's counter doing homework when he heard the front door open. When he looked up, he was surprised to see King Falcone and his hulking bodyguard coming toward him. He'd rarely seen any of King's crew over the long winter, and almost never saw King himself. Only on rare occasions had he caught a fleeting glimpse of the shiny black Cadillac drive by, or idling in the student parking lot after school. When he did see him, King always stared at him, sometimes even offering him a barely perceptible nod. But they had never spoken. Not once. And Vonni now felt his body tense up as the imposing young Mafioso stepped up to the counter and pierced him with those portentous black eyes.

"What's up, Johnny New York?" King said cordially. "I didn't know you worked here."

"No offense, but my name is Giovanni," Vonni replied, looking him in the eye, hoping he didn't sound too abrasive. "People just call me Vonni."

"Huh," King said, looking almost amused. "I sort of like Johnny New York. Think I'll stick with it."

"Suit yourself," Vonni shrugged, not wanting to get on his bad side. "So what brings you guys in this morning? You lookin' to get memberships?"

King glanced around the quiet gym. "Actually, Johnny New York, we are. The Powerhouse on Van Dyke is too far away, and Bally's on 8 Mile has too many finooks. So we were thinking about coming here. What's the ticket on a monthly membership?"

Vonni considered this for a moment and glanced at the computer. "I'll tell you what, how about I just comp you guys a couple of free year memberships?"

King frowned incredulously. "Comp us memberships?" he said, eyes gleaming with suspicion. "And why would you do that, Johnny New York?"

Vonni shrugged. "My boss said I can comp my close friends and family."

King chuckled and glanced at his bodyguard, Big Dean. "But we're not close friends or family."

"No, but you seem like the kind of guy who appreciates a favor. And who knows, maybe someday I'll need a favor from you."

King nodded, grinning slightly. "A favor for a favor, eh?"

"Yeah," Vonni said, grinning back. "A guy never knows when he might need a favor."

King's eyes seemed to light up. "That's true, Vonni. It's good to have favors on the books."

146

Vonni noted how he had not called him Johnny New York. "Like I said, I pegged you for a guy who appreciates a favor."

"I am, paisan," King said, taking on a philosophical tone. "My grandfather says favors are like money in the bank. The more people owe you, the richer you are."

"Makes sense to me," Vonni said, grinning, pleased with himself. "Now let me hook you guys up so I can put a little money in the bank."

From that day on King and his omnipresent bodyguard became regulars at the gym, coming in several times a week to pump iron. And though King was still a bit standoffish, he always made sure to stop at the front desk and say, "What's up, Vonni?" He never engaged him in conversation but always addressed him as Vonni, no longer Johnny New York. Vonni knew it was a show of respect—one that never went unnoticed.

King had an impressive physique to begin with, but Vonni was surprised by how seriously King took his workouts. He and Big Dean would barely say a word as they put themselves through grueling, high-intensity workouts that often lasted over two hours. People occasionally called the gym looking for him while he was there, but he always left Vonni with explicit orders to never interrupt his workouts. Sometimes he would get calls from people claiming that it was an emergency, that they needed to speak to him immediately, but King didn't care. He would simply tell Vonni to write their names down. The only time he ever stopped in the middle of his workout for a call was if the call came through on his cell phone, which he always left at the counter with Vonni. At times Vonni felt like his personal secretary.

When school finally let out for the summer, Vonni was left with plenty of spare time and nothing to do with it. His only real friend, Tommy Guns, began working full-time at his father's construction company. Katie got a job at her mother's nail salon for the summer. So, bored, friendless and without a car, Vonni took up running as a hobby. He found it meditative, and it allowed him to put a finger on the pulse of the neighborhood. As he jogged up and down every block, he familiarized himself with the neighborhood's most subtle nuances, marking popular businesses, their owners, and how people addressed them. He noted the various cliques of young people, their regular hangouts, and who they associated with. But no matter where he went, he always saw guys who were somehow connected to King Falcone. He even observed some of them having hushed conversations in the back of Mr. Q's Billiards Hall, one of their favorite hangouts.

Before long he began to have a pretty good idea of who the upper echelons of King's crew were, and how they operated under a distinct chain of command. But he learned the most from observing King at the gym. After King finished his workouts, he would often meet various members of his crew across the street at the local Dairy Queen. They seemed to have some sort of system. As soon as he arrived at the gym, he would leave his cell phone with Vonni at the counter, with instructions to bring it to him when it rang. When it did, King would answer it and tell the caller to meet him across the street at a specific time. After he finished his workout, he would shower, change, order a protein shake, and have Big Dean drive him across the street. A few minutes later a car would pull up and park next to them. In these cars, there were almost always two guys. Vonni figured one was a bodyguard. They all seemed to have a bodyguard or "driver." The passengers, whom Vonni assumed were King's top guys, would step out and, often with little or no discretion, hand something to King through his passenger window. Sometimes it was an envelope. Other times it was a brown paper bag. A few times it was a duffle bag. Then, while the drivers waited in their respective cars, King and the passenger would go inside the Dairy Queen and sit in a booth by the front window, away from everyone else, and have a hushed conversation over a burger or ice cream. When they were finished, King would always leave first, while the other guy would wait about ten minutes before leaving. It was always the exact same routine. Vonni witnessed it almost daily.

With each passing day, Vonni found himself more and more intrigued by King Falcone. He was perplexed as to how someone so young had attained such status. He knew King and his crew were making a lot of money. It was obvious. They all drove expensive cars, dressed in tailored suits, wore expensive jewelry, and surrounded themselves with beautiful young girls. It was impressive how King, a mere eighteen-year-old, was so driven, so business savvy, and so feared. It was also impressive how he had been able to amass such a large group of faithful followers, some of whom were much older than him. Back in Brooklyn, Vonni had known a number of young mob prodigies. But none had the presence or influence of King Falcone.

After seeing how King and his crew had the best of everything, Vonni decided he wanted what they had. He was tired of being broke. He was tired of not having a car. He was tired of being a nobody. He wanted to dress in custom suits and Italian calfskin   shoes. He wanted a nice car to impress the girls. He yearned to have the finer things in life. Working at the gym wasn't cutting it. He'd been working there for several months now, making a paltry $8.25 an hour, and even with his pool hustle he'd barely been able to save a thousand bucks. He needed to find a way to start making more money, and he decided King Falcone might be able to help him find it. After all, the young Mafioso owed him a favor. Unfortunately, the only time he ever saw King was at the gym, and King never discussed business at the gym. So all Vonni could do was bide his time and wait for an opportunity to present itself. Or make one.

With Jack always busy smoking dope and Tommy always working, Vonni once again became a bit of a loner. His aunt and uncle thought his antisocial behavior was just his way of acclimating to his new surroundings, but the simple truth was that he was bored. So one hot summer afternoon, after a long run through the neighborhood, he took it upon himself to do something about it. Parched and sweating, he headed up to old man Gus' party store for a cold soda. But on the way there he purposely made a detour that took him directly past King's house, where he sometimes saw King and his crew hanging out. Most of the time they were in King's garage, which King had apparently converted into a makeshift lounge of some sort. But as Vonni now walked by, he was disheartened to see the garage's bay door was shut tight, with no sign of King or his crew anywhere. He did, however, notice a car in the driveway with two guys seated in it. He figured they were some kind of lookouts or sentries, since they stared at him threateningly as he made his way past on the opposite sidewalk.

But he was not ready to give up. After cooling down with a Faygo soda and a couple of games of pool at Mr. Q's, he decided to take an alternate route home, cutting down the alley behind King's house, the same alley he had first encountered *La Quattro Duchi* two summers previous. It looked exactly the same. Overflowing dumpsters and garbage cans. Rats and cats. The smell of rotten garbage. There were no people in sight, and other than a distant police siren and some barking dogs the afternoon was eerily quiet. But as he approached the back of King's garage, he noticed the back door was shut. He considered walking up and just knocking on the garage door, but there were several cars parked in the alley. He immediately recognized them all. One was King's black Cadillac, but the rest belonged to his top lieutenants. Vonni suddenly realized that he had almost walked in on King hosting a meeting with his top chieftains. This definitely was not the plan. He had hoped to catch King alone, or at the very worst with one or two of his guys. All he wanted to do was to ask him for a job, a chance to make some extra cash. A small part of him still wanted to walk right up to the garage and knock—a very small part—but he just

150

wasn't that bold. Nor was he that stupid. He knew to do so would only anger King. So, in the end, all he could do was walk on by, never knowing that he had in fact accomplished exactly what he had set out to do.


Don Falcone originally had five children: one son and four daughters. But his only son had been murdered nearly two decades previous. Now all he had left were his beloved daughters, three of whom had married various *capi* in the "Detroit Partnership," which in recent years had come to be known as the Syndicate. From these daughters, he had a total of seven grandsons, but none of them possessed the Falcone family name. His eldest daughter, Patricia, had married Leoni Gianolla, a ruthless *capo* who had landed himself at the top of the Syndicate's hierarchy via a combination of street savvy, brute force, and dumb luck. By marrying the Boss' daughter, he had instantly put himself in line for the throne. He wasn't the don's first choice to take over the Family, but with no male heir— at least none the Commission would sanction to take over the Family—Leoni was his only choice. If he wanted to begin easing himself into a life of semi-retirement while still retaining a semblance of control, it had to be Leoni. But first, he needed to start testing his son-in-law, giving him more responsibilities, introducing him to his many friends and associates in the government. Leoni was a feared and respected *capodecina*, and he was good at managing his various operations, but he was still relatively young and inexperienced. He needed to be pruned and trained if he wanted to someday become the Syndicate's top boss. The Commission still considered Don Falcone to be Detroit's "*Capo di Tutti Capi*," Boss of all Bosses, but they were aware of his interest in a sanctioned retirement. And since he'd maintained a tight ship for nearly four decades, a vote had been taken. The Council agreed to let him hand the reins of his Family over to his son-in-law, Leoni Gianolla.

Leoni, knowing he would soon be the Syndicate's top boss, was already beginning to introduce his two sons, Anthony and Dino, to the family business, preparing them to take their rightful positions within what he already considered his Family. In time, Anthony would become his underboss. Dino would be his street boss and liaison to the Syndicate's other *capi*. But never for a second did he consider his nephew for a position within the Family. He'd always felt a deep-seated contempt for Omnio, who was the product of a Jewish woman that nobody, including Don Falcone, had ever cared for. Yet Leoni knew that Omnio was still the don's favorite grandson, which irritated him to no end. But what irked him even more was the fact that, even though Omnio's mixed blood would keep him from ever becoming a Made Man, the don still had dreams of seeing him someday take over the Family.

It was true. Don Falcone did harbor dreams of seeing King someday attain enough power and influence to give the Commission no choice but to overlook his mixed blood and make him a Made Man, maybe even let him take over the Family. Or at the very least become a *capo* over one of the Family's crews. But he knew the only way this could ever happen was if King made himself so invaluable that they had no choice. And in order to do so, he would have to start young, work his way up fast, and make the other *capi* fear him. Most importantly, though, he would have to learn from those who had experience. And nobody had more experience than Don Falcone, who had fought his way to the top of the Syndicate and remained there for nearly four decades. He knew if King wanted to have even the slightest chance at earning the favor of the Commission, he would have to adhere to the old decrees they lived by. King was intelligent enough, with just the right combination of street savvy, cunning, and ruthlessness to pull it off. But it was going to be a long road. The odds were firmly stacked against him. Even his own blood was working against him.

King spent most mornings at his grandparent's beautiful waterfront home in Grosse Pointe. While his grandmother cooked breakfast, he and his grandfather would sit on the back veranda sipping espresso and discussing everything from politics to women. It was during these regular morning palavers that Don Falcone tutored King on the sacred codes that governed his world, the obscure and dangerous world of *Cosa Nostra*. King always listened with rapt attention, hanging on his grandfather's every word, absorbing everything and missing nothing. He loved listening to his grandfather's lectures and tutorials. He could sit and listen to him all day, for the don was his greatest hero.

Lately, the don had been lecturing him on the importance of expanding his various enterprises into legitimate arenas that would help him launder his illicit proceeds. The most recent topic of discussion was how King had pooled his monies with various members of his crew to purchase a floundering pub whose owner was down on his luck. In other words, the owner had fallen deeply in debt with one of the Family's bookies. King had already taken possession of the building and planned to reopen it as a modern nightclub, but there was a problem—the liquor license. The original owner of the license was not willing to sell it. Usually, it was not that difficult for the Family to get a liquor license. They had many friends, including highly ranked city officials. A bribe here, a favor there, and a liquor license would suddenly become available. Unfortunately for King, another of the Syndicate's upper echelon *capi* operated a series of nightclubs in the same district, and he was stonewalling him by manipulating the license holder. It was a slimy, underhanded move but King understood it was just business.

Though he was the don's favorite grandson, King was still a *dragoncello difetto*, a disparaging term used to describe someone not of pure Sicilian blood, literally meaning "one born with a birth defect." Because King was a difetto, he had been forced to operate semi-autonomously from the Syndicate, which

153

included operating outside of his grandfather's umbrella of influence. The frustrating part was that he still had to kick a significant portion of his proceeds up to all the Family's *capi* when he operated in their territories, which was a source of much animus, for he knew most of them looked down on him with contempt. But kicking up a portion of his profits was a show of respect, and because of it, he received the Syndicate's local police protection.

The Commission may have advised Don Falcone to only help King in a consulting capacity, but much to the chagrin of the Syndicate's other *capi* he often did much more than that, calling in favors, using his influence whenever King needed help. He even backed him financially and provided him with trusted men for some of his larger operations. The other *capi* knew of this but never dared confront him about it. The don was getting older, yes, but by no means was he weak or feeble. His mind was sharp as ever, and he still had a small army of faithful soldiers who would give their life for him without question. The Syndicate's other *capi* knew the aging don's days were numbered, but they also knew it was never good to upset the infamous Butcher. So, as much as they resented him for helping King, all they could do was bite their tongues and keep an eye on his maverick *difetto* grandson.


One day after returning home from having breakfast with his grandfather, King gathered his top four lieutenants in his garage to discuss the liquor license situation. He always held such meetings in his garage because he didn't want to upset his ailing mother. Nor did he want her knowing his business. His garage was basically his office, complete with couches, tables, chairs, and even a bar. It was the one place he felt safe to discuss business freely.

It was well into the afternoon, and they were currently discussing a banker who was going to setup a legitimate LLC that would allow them to own the club without raising any IRS and FBI red flags. They had already remodeled the club's interior, furnished it, and even installed a new $20,000 sound system. Located in Saint Clair Shores, a middle-class suburb outside of Detroit, they knew the club would turn a considerable legitimate profit. More importantly, though, it would be used to launder much of their illicit proceeds. Most of the nightclubs in the area were owned or controlled by various Syndicate *capi*, all of whom were not going to be happy about having their racket infringed upon. But despite the Commission's orders to remain neutral when it came to King's operations, Don Falcone had made it clear to the other *capi* that King was to be allowed to run his club with impunity. He even made sure that he received the Syndicate's local police protection. This meant that the other *capi* could not encourage the cops to harass his patrons, which was often the case when someone from outside the Syndicate tried to open a club in one of their territories.

King now explained to his crew that everything was coming together as planned, but they were still faced with one major problem: the liquor license. Obtaining it was proving to be much harder than expected. The City of Saint Clair Shores was not the problem. Don Falcone assured him that his connections in City Hall would approve his purchase of the liquor license and necessary operating permits. The problem was that each city only issued so many liquor licenses per zoned district. And the licenses in the district they needed were accounted for, grandfathered in and purchased many years ago by individuals who held onto them like they were gold mines, essentially monopolizing the liquor licenses in the district. Occasionally one of these individuals would sell their establishment and include the liquor license, but more often than not they would simply lease the license to the new proprietor, a slick way of retaining control of it. King had tried his best to get the city to issue him a new one, but the district already had five more licenses than it was supposed to, a result of various Syndicate *capi* threatening

155

and/or bribing certain city officials into issuing them licenses. His only options were to (A) lease a license or (B) purchase one. But he didn't like the idea of leasing one because the owner could, and surely would, lord it over him. No, he wanted to own the license outright, and fortunately for him, he was in luck. With some help from the don's connections in City Hall, he learned that an older gentleman had recently closed the doors of his Irish pub because he wanted to retire. The pub, including liquor license, was up for sale. Unfortunately, the owner considered the pub to be his retirement plan and was asking an exorbitant $250,000 for the license alone, far more than King was willing to pay. There was much debate on what they should do. The don wanted them to at least try to refrain from anything illicit. But King was beginning to lose his patience.

Tony "Taps" Tappio was a slick and effervescent character who ran a string of after-hours clubs in Detroit, making him one of King's top earners. He was also extremely ambitious and loyal, following orders without question, which was how he had earned the rank of King's unofficial street boss. And he now had the floor, pacing the garage, pondering what they should do. He was about to make a suggestion when he noticed a shadow pass by the window.

"Yo, who the fuck is out in the alley?" he asked, pointing at the window.

Billy Profaci, King's second cousin and an adept car thief, stepped to the window and peered out. "Ain't that Jack Russo's cousin, Johnny New York?"

King looked out the window and saw Vonni walking down the alley. "Yeah, that's Vonni. But what the hell is he doing in my alley?"

"Vonni?" Billy asked, confused. "I thought his name is Johnny New York?"

King looked at him and shook his head. Billy was a master at re-tagging stolen cars, and he ran a crew of car thieves who brought in tons of money, but he was a bit of a dolt at times. His

156

pronounced lazy eye made him look even dumber than he was. But King knew he was loyal and completely committed to him, and because of this, he loved him like a brother.

"Billy," King said, switching to Italian, "you speak Italian, yes?

Billy shrugged and answered in Italian. "Sure. Why?"

"Then tell me, cousin, how do you say Johnny in Italian?"

Billy thought for a moment. "Oh, yeah," he said, looking ashamed that he hadn't made the connection. "Duh! Giovanni."

"Yes," King nodded. "Vonni is just short for Giovanni. He doesn't like to be called Johnny New York."

Paulie "Pal" Palazzolo, King's resident larcenist, raised an eyebrow. "And how the hell you know that?"

"Because he told me," King answered matter-of-factly. "He works at my gym. I see him there all the time."

Billy dropped down on a couch in front of an oscillating fan, grinning up at King derisively. "So what's up, cousin, you and Johnny New York some kind of goombas now?"

Everyone, including King, chuckled their amusement.

"No, jerkoff," King said, shaking his head. "We're not goombas. But the kid seems solid. He even gave me and Dean free memberships."

Joey Lombardo, King's second-in-command, reclined back in his chair with a pensive look. "His cousin buys weed from one of my guys every day," he said, picturing Jack and his crew of torpid potheads. "For a bunch of broke ass stoners, those skateboarders can smoke some weed. You wouldn't believe how much they smoke."

For a minute they returned to discussing their liquor license dilemma, but Tony Taps noticed the intense look in King's eyes. "What's up, paisan?" he asked, wondering what the look was about. "What's on your mind?"

King slowly turned toward Joey. "You say your guy sells weed to Jack Russo?"

"Yeah, sure," Joey nodded. "Why?"

157

"You ever see Johnny New York get high?"

Joey thought for a moment and shrugged. "Nope, can't say I have. Come to think of it I never see him with Jack and them skateboard wasteoids. He doesn't seem like their type. He actually seems like he's got his shit together."

"He hangs out at Mr. Q's a lot," said Gino Mianchetti, the overseer of King's loan shark operation. "Him and Tom Moceri. I've played nine-ball with him a few times. Kid's good. Real good. Fucker hustled me out a hundred real quick. A few weeks back he hustled a couple bikers who got pissed and tried to jump his ass. But he's a cocky little fucker. Went at them with a pool stick. Ran them right out the place. I'll give it to him, he's got heart."

"Yeah, he's definitely got heart," King concurred. "A few years ago he got in a scrap with my cousin Frankie. Frankie got the best of him, but the kid held his own. It was the only time I ever saw Frankie even come close to losing a fight."

"Frankie almost lost a fight to Johnny New York?" Paulie asked, looking shocked.

"Yeah," King answered, and then thought for a moment. "Listen, Tony, do me a favor and keep an eye on him."

"Why?" Tony asked, curious. "What's up with him?"

"Nothing," King shrugged. "I just have a feeling there's more to him than we think."

"What's to know?" Billy asked. "He's a cocky little punk from New York."

King shot him a look. "Enough of about Johnny New York," he said, deciding it was time they get back to business. "We need to figure out what we're gonna do about this liquor license. We sank all that money into our place and now we can't even open it."

Billy lit a cigarette and took a puff. "I say fuck it," he declared, exhaling a thick cloud of gray smoke, casually blowing a series of rings. "We'll just open the place without a license.

Give the cops a little taste. Them greedy fucks are always looking to squeeze us for some extra cash."

King shook his head, frustrated. "Billy, what aren't you understanding? We've been through this a thousand times. We need a legitimate place to clean our money. What good is making all this money if we can't even spend it without the feds or IRS on our ass? And don't forget the place will turn a nice profit. The location is perfect. Big spenders will come from Grosse Pointe. It could be the hottest new club in town. But it needs to be legit. We can't afford to have the feds crawling up our ass. This club is our baby. It's not connected to the *borgata* so we won't have any Fed protection. My grandpa used his pull to keep us protected by the locals, but the other *capi* are already pissed about it. And…" He shot a cold look at each of them. "I'm not supposed to tell you this, but the Feds are fucking with him again. Something about the Frontier and Stardust skims in Vegas. Old shit from way back. He's not sure why, but his Fed contacts here in Detroit say his name keeps popping up again. So we really need to be on our toes. And that means operating our club with a legitimate liquor license."

"I say we just squeeze that old Mick into selling us the license," Tony Taps suggested again. "That little pub of his? We'll just threaten to burn it down if he don't sell us the license at a reasonable price."

King considered this for a long moment. "You're right, Taps," he finally agreed, knowing they were running out of options. "Go see him. Bring Gino and one of his guys. Offer him another ten grand. Tell him it's our final offer. If he still wants to play hardball, send a couple of our guys to torch the place. And make sure it looks like arson. If the insurance company suspects he burned the place down to collect a payout, they'll conduct a thorough investigation that could take months. They might even refuse to pay the asshole. That ought to motivate him to sell us the license. But make sure he knows that if he goes to the cops, we know where he lives."

159

When King finally adjourned the meeting, he dismissed everyone but Joey, the smartest and oldest member of his crew. "Joe, do me a favor and stick around for a minute. I want to talk to you about something."

"What's up, boss?" Joey asked when everyone else was gone.

King sat down and rubbed his chin pensively. "You say Jack Russo and his boys buy a lot of weed from your guy?"

"Yeah, sure. Why?"

"About how much do they buy?"

Joey thought for a moment and shrugged. "Well, in the grand scheme of things not that much. They're just a bunch of smokers. Maybe a few ounces a week. Quarter pound at most. Why? What's up?"

Again King appeared in deep thought. "I want you to go talk to his cousin, Johnny New York. Ask him if he's interested in moving a little weed for you. He can sell to them skateboarders."

"Why?" Joey asked, confused. "My guy takes care of them."

"Because I want to test him. If he passes, I might have something else for him to do. You know Jose, right?"

"The stocky Puerto Rican kid? Always hangs with Big-Nose Tony and Fat Robby?"

"Yeah. He's actually half-Mexican and has family back in Mexico who sends him boxes of steroids. So I was thinking we could have Johnny New York push them at that gym he works at. There's tons of juice-heads in there, and there's huge money in 'roids. My cousin Dino goes down to Tijuana and picks up $500 worth and then comes back here and sells them for ten times that. Since I started working out at that gym, I've probably had twenty guys ask me if I could get them 'roids. Johnny New York and that gym could open up a whole new racket for us. It may be time we put him to work. I like how he carries himself. Doesn't take no shit. Seems like a natural hustler. Go see him tomorrow. Talk to him about the weed. If he wants in we'll put him to work and feel him out for a while, see if he can handle his business. If he can, we'll go from there."

Joey nodded subserviently. "You got it, boss. I'll go see him tomorrow."

# CHAPTER 8

As soon as school let out for the summer, Vonni began working full-time at the gym. Monday through Friday he showed up at noon and often stayed late to help close the place. He didn't mind working there, but by the end of the week he'd had enough of looking at sweaty men. So when weekends came around all he wanted to do was relax and have fun. And one of his favorite ways to have fun was playing basketball with Tommy at Angel Park, a small riverfront park a few blocks from his house. He especially enjoyed playing there because groups of girls always gathered in the bleachers to watch the games. He was good at basketball. Very good. Two-on-two is what he played. He and Tommy took on all comers. Tommy was his muscle in the paint and he was the shooter. They rarely lost, and if the right opportunity presented itself, they would even wager a few dollars on games.

On this Saturday evening, Tommy picked Vonni up in his new Camaro and they headed up to Angel Park for a few games of two-on-two basketball. It was a hot, humid day and the park was alive with activity. Gathered around picnic tables and parked cars were groups of teenagers—all of them laughing, joking, drinking, smoking, and just enjoying the beautiful weather. Music echoed throughout the park. The smells of marijuana and barbecue created a sweet, calmative ambrosia that hung in the air. Half a dozen anglers were fishing in the Detroit River from the park's boardwalk. Some of the older guys were playing tackle football on the grass by the river's edge.

Others were playing a game of "21" on the basketball court. And just as Vonni had hoped, the basketball bleachers were packed with girls.

Feeling cocky, Vonni walked over to the basketball court and sounded a universal challenge to all comers. "Twenty bucks says me and my boy can school any two of you," he challenged, nodding toward Tommy.

An hour later they were up a hundred dollars, a perfect ending to their day. With the sun beginning to set, the park's occupants were slowly dispersing—and for good reason. It was common knowledge that the park could be a dangerous place after dark. Nevertheless, dark was still nearly an hour away. Plenty of people were still milling about, standing around cars, gathered at picnic tables, drinking beer, smoking pot, listening to music and socializing. A few families were still barbecuing on smoldering grills. On the boardwalk, several committed fishermen were not quite ready to call it a day. Over by the park's restrooms, Jack and his posse of skateboard vagabonds were smoking pot and jumping their skateboards off steps and benches. With their greasy long hair and tattered clothes, they looked strangely out of place. But people generally ignored them unless they had a particularly hard fall, in which case onlookers would have a good laugh at their expense.

Hot, sweaty, and tired from an hour of doing battle on the basketball court, Vonni decided it was time to take a break and cool down. There was an old Italian man named Antonio who ran a gelato stand in the park, so he and Tommy jogged over to the stand and ordered a couple of raspberry gelatos before "Tony Gelato" closed down for the night. The fruity Italian ice cream was the perfect way to counter the evening's oppressive heat. Vonni even admitted that it was as good as any gelato he had back in New York. Maybe even better. He even claimed that Antonio used some kind of secret ingredient to make it so delicious, a compliment that made the old man beam with pride.

163

Gelatos in hand, Vonni and Tommy perched atop a lone picnic table to cool down and appreciate a group of cute teenage girls walking by. Tommy was commenting on the pert breasts of one particularly buxom girl when a black Range Rover with tinted windows pulled up and parked not fifty feet away.

"Ain't that Joey Lombardo?" Vonni asked, scooping a bite of the delicious gelato into his mouth with a wooden spoon.

"Yeah," Tommy answered, also recognizing it. "But why's he looking over here?"

Before Vonni could speculate, Joey's bodyguard, a massive brute named Nick "The Neck" Peppitone, stepped out of the Range Rover and walked right up to Vonni. "Joe wants a word with you," Nick said stolidly, staring down at him.

"With me?" Vonni asked, glancing at the Range Rover. "What for?"

"That's between you and Joe," Nick answered tersely, still staring down at him.

Vonni felt a sense of trepidation as he looked over at the Range Rover and saw Joey staring back at him through the SUV's tinted windshield. He wondered if he had done something to piss someone off. Maybe his inquisitions about King had somehow gotten back to him, for it was common knowledge that Joey Lombardo was one of King's top guys. Joey was older, in his mid-twenties, and looked like a stereotypical Hollywood Mafioso: dark-haired and handsome with a perfectly tailored suit, hair always slicked just so, a big gold watch and a diamond pinky ring. But he was no Hollywood Mafioso. He was the real thing, and he carried himself with an air of certitude that came with being feared and respected by those who knew him. Word on the street was that he ran a crew of professional larcenists and "box men," AKA safe-crackers. He also had his hands in the local pot market. Like most of King's crew, he lived somewhere out in the affluent suburb of Grosse Pointe, which was why he was rarely seen at Angel Park. Especially at this time of day, when the park was beginning to make its nightly transformation.

By day it was safe, its patrons mostly families barbecuing, fishermen, and young people hanging out. By night, however, its inhabitants became mostly drug dealers and addicts, pimps and prostitutes, and the occasional stickup kid looking for victims to rob.

Vonni now wondered why Joey Lombardo, a known wiseguy who was part of the King Falcone crew, wanted a word with him. So, trying not to show any outward apprehension, he set his gelato down and walked over to the Range Rover's passenger window, where he saw Joey smiling back at him from the driver's seat.

"Get in, paisan," Joey said, gesturing toward the passenger seat. "I need to have a word with you."

When Vonni opened the door and slid onto the soft leather seat, he was met with a welcome rush of cool air-conditioned air. "What's up?" he said, trying to sound indifferent.

"Pleasure to meet you, Vonni," Joey said, holding a hand out to him. "I'm not sure if you know who I am but my name is Joey Lombardo."

Vonni gave him a firm handshake. "I know who you are," he said, and then gave him a skeptical look. "But how do you know me?"

Joey flashed him one of his trademark smiles. "Oh, let's just say I keep my ears to the streets. This is my old neighborhood. I grew up only a few blocks from here. I know everyone." He nodded toward Jack and his crew of skateboarders, who were now doing tricks on the handicap ramp leading into the restrooms. "I know your cousin, Jack. We do business from time to time."

Vonni glanced at his cousin, having no idea Jack did business with anyone, let alone with the likes of Joey Lombardo. "Business with Jack?" he asked, even more perplexed. "What kind of business?"

Joey's Hollywood smile vanished and his face became a mask of seriousness. "Well, paisan, that's why I'm here. As I'm

165

sure you know, Jack and his friends smoke a lot of pot. But what you might not know is that they actually get it from me. Well, from one of my guys. I have the best weed in town. 'Northern Lights.' Straight from Canada. But my guy who sells it to them… well, I need him for something else. So I was thinking that maybe you could take over for him. The money is good and I'll set you up with everything you need."

This was the opportunity Vonni had been waiting for, but he couldn't believe it was just falling in his lap like this. "So let me get this straight," he said, a contemplative look on his face. "You want me to start selling weed for you?"

"Yes," Joey said matter-of-factly. "I need a guy here in the neighborhood to take over some of my guy's clientele. You would be doing me a favor, and you'd make yourself some good money in the process. It's not hard. I'll give you the product and when someone calls your cell, all you'd do is call them back and ask how much they want. It's that simple."

"Calls me? But I don't even have a phone."

Joey removed a Nokia cellphone from his inside pocket. "I got you covered, paisan. It's paid for and yours if you want the job."

Vonni took the phone and studied it for a moment. "So I can make some decent money?" he asked, not wanting to seem overly eager.

"Yes," Joey answered, offering him a grin, knowing he had him right where he wanted. "A lot more than you're making at that gym."

Vonni eyed him suspiciously, wondering how he knew so much about him. They did have one common denominator: King. Vonni saw King at the gym almost every day, and now wondered if King had something to do with this unexpected business proposition. It was conceivable, he thought, but unlikely. After all, they barely spoke at the gym. King knew nothing about him other than the fact that he was Jack's cousin from New York.

"So why me?" Vonni asked curiously. "I mean, why not just have Jack sell for you?"

Joey nodded thoughtfully. "That's a good question, but I think you already know the answer. Jack's a good guy but he's no hustler. He doesn't have it in him. I mean, let's be honest here, Vonni, he'd smoke all my profits with his boys." He paused and looked him in the eye. "But you're not like your cousin, are you? Word on the street is that you're a stand-up guy."

Vonni raised an eyebrow. "Word on the street?"

"Yes, word on the street."

Vonni wondered where he was getting his information, but decided it didn't matter. Joey was right. Jack was a screw-up who could never be trusted with any kind of serious business venture, especially one involving pot. All he would do is sit around and smoke it all up with his friends. Though Vonni had no idea where Joey heard "word on the street" that he was a stand-up guy, he did indeed consider himself to be a stand-up guy.

"So how much money are we talking about?" he asked, visions of a new car flashing through his head.

Joey considered this for a moment. "Well, I was thinking—that is, if you accept my offer—starting you off with a pound. Nothing major. My guy will pass along your pager number so you can take over his clientele, which will include your cousin and his crew. If you get overloaded, you can branch out and have a couple of guys sell for you." He glanced at Tommy, who was still seated at the picnic table with Nick "The Neck. "I know your paisan, Tommy. He's also a stand-up guy. Maybe you could partner up with him? I'll charge you a flat one-thousand per pound. Bag it up into quarters, eighths, and halves, and you should more than double your money. If you hustle hard, you could easily work your way up to a pound a week. Maybe more."

Vonni was good at math and quickly crunched the numbers. A smile appeared on his face as he considered the prospect of making a $1,000 plus per week. With that kind of money coming in it wouldn't take him long to save enough to buy a sweet new car to impress the girls. "So if I agree, when would I start?" he asked, unable to mask his excitement.

"I could have my guy drop off your first batch of product tomorrow morning," Joey answered. "That is, if you agree."

Vonni thought for a moment and nodded. "Okay, I'm in. But have your guy drop it off around 9:30 tomorrow morning. My aunt and uncle go out to breakfast at 9:00 AM sharp."

"Perfect," said Joey, handing him a stack of blank business cards. "Take these and pass them out to your customers. Give each of them a personal code. Have them text it to you before they call. That way, you know who they are. Keep a log of the codes until you memorize them. If you get called by a number and don't recognize, don't answer. And make sure nobody ever asks for anything via text. Texting leaves a digital record. You always need to be careful of the cops. They can be tricky bastards."

"So this is the number to the phone?" he asked, studying the cards intently. They were completely nondescript, with nothing on them but a seven-digit number and a blank space for a name or code.

"Yes," Joey answered. "Pass those out to only people you know. And I'd refrain from doing any business at your house. You don't want your aunt and uncle knowing what you're up to. Plus your neighbors will wonder about a sudden spike in traffic. It's best to deliver to your customers. When they page you, call them back and have them meet you somewhere nearby. Somewhere like Gus' party store or Mr. Q's. Even here at the park is good. But never, and I mean never, do business with anyone you don't know. No outsiders. People get busted when they deal with people they don't know. If you, Tommy, or Jack don't know them, don't fuck with them. Period. This includes women—no matter what they look like. Women can be cops, too. We definitely don't want any trouble with the local narcos." He gave him a cold look of warning. "And whatever you do, paisan, never use my name. Ever. With anyone! If the cops ever trip you up, just keep your mouth shut and hang tight. We have friends and lawyers who can clean these things up. But, in case of such an event, I shouldn't have to tell you what would happen if you were to ever mention my name."

Vonni nodded, the warning perfectly clear. "No worries, man. I know how it works."

"Good," Joey said, satisfied, offering him a hand to solidify the agreement. "Expect my guy at your house around 9:30 AM tomorrow morning. His name is Brian. Brian Pfeifer. Solid dude. You'll like him. He'll be your regular go-between."

Vonni shook his hand and stepped back out into the hot evening air. "I appreciate this, Joe. I've been lookin' for a way to make some extra cash. I won't let you down."

"I know you won't, paisan," Joey replied, dismissing him with a wave of a hand. "If I didn't think you'd do well with this I wouldn't be here."

Feeling a great sense of excitement, Vonni shut the door and returned to the picnic table where Tommy was still waiting patiently with Nick "The Neck," who immediately returned to the Range Rover.

"Yo, what the fuck was that all about?" Tommy asked, watching the black Range Rover disappear into the night.

Vonni sat down on the picnic table next to him, a distant look in his eyes. "Do you know anyone who might be interested in buying some weed?" he asked.

Tommy gave him a confused look. "Do I know anyone who wants to buy some weed?" he echoed, wondering what the hell he was talking about.

"Yes, weed. Good weed."

Tommy thought for a moment and shrugged. "Sure, I know all kinds of people who smoke weed. My brother is always asking me if I know where he can get some good weed. Him and his boys smoke joints like cigarettes. Why?"

169

Vonni flashed him a smile. "Because I'm about to go into the weed business."

"With Joe Lombardo?" Tommy asked, glancing at where the Range Rover had just been parked.

"*For* Joey Lombardo," Vonni clarified. "He said he's already got a guy who sells to Jack and the rest of the neighborhood, but I guess he needs him for something else. So he wants me to take over for him. He's gonna front me a pound tomorrow. I was thinking I'd just split it with you so we can both make some cash. I mean, that is, if you're up for it."

"Holy shit, bro!" Tommy exclaimed, his eyes alight with excitement. "Are you kidding? Fuck yeah I'm up for it! I can finally quit humpin' concrete for my dad. That shit's been killin' me!"

Vonni grinned excitedly. "Joey says his weed is the best in town."

Tommy punched him playfully on the arm. "Then we are about to get paid, kid!"


The following morning, at precisely 9:30 AM, a guy named Brian showed up at Vonni's house to deliver exactly one pound of high-grade marijuana, a digital scale to weigh it on, and a box of small plastic baggies. As soon as the guy was gone, Vonni began weighing the pungent green buds into eighth-ounce, quarter-ounce, and half-ounce bags. When he was finished, he called Tommy over and split it with him.

On just his first day alone, Vonni managed to sell over an ounce to Jack and his crew of skateboard stoners. And from that day on his business grew exponentially. With such a premium product, word quickly spread throughout the neighborhood that he and Tommy were selling some of the best weed in town. Before long they were selling over a quarter pound a day, their pagers beeping ceaselessly. And they didn't discriminate when it came to customers. They sold to workers from the nearby automotive plants. They sold to groups of black kids who come up from the ghetto to score the good stuff. They sold to the pimps and prostitutes who frequented Angel Park after dark. They even sold to a couple of neighborhood housewives who liked to unwind with a nice joint as they went about their daily housekeeping.

With their clientele constantly expanding, it wasn't long before the money was pouring in. It took Vonni barely a month to save over $4,000. At the end of each day, when he sat down to count his profits, he felt as if he had hit the lottery. He still had no idea why Joey had picked him for this job, but he was happy that he had. And not just because of the money. No, it was more than just the money. For the first time in his life, people were showing him respect. Genuine respect. Whether it was because he was working for Joey, a known wiseguy in the neighborhood, or because he had the best weed around, it didn't matter. Respect was respect. People now looked at him differently, addressed him differently, and treated him differently. It was a new experience, and he loved it. He'd been waiting his whole life to be respected, to be taken seriously, to be seen as a someone. Even though he was only selling relatively small quantities of pot, he felt like a kingpin. Walking around with his pockets stuffed with cash gave him a sense of satisfaction and empowerment that he'd never known. He became addicted to from day one, which was exactly what King intended.


Vonni stayed in regular contact with Joey, but they rarely met in person. His only face-to-face dealings were with Pfeifer, who Vonni found to be quite an interesting character. Pfeifer was extremely hyper and often rambled about nothing in particular. He chewed his nails incessantly and always seemed to be in a hurry. One thing that Vonni found peculiar about him was that he almost always made his deliveries in a different car, which Pfeifer always claimed were his. Joey later explained that

171

Pfeifer's day job was stealing cars for King's cousin Billy, and the cars he drove were all re-tagged. Which, of course, piqued Vonni's interest since he would soon be in the market for a new car. Even a re-tagged one.

With all the money coming in from his new business endeavor, Vonni wanted to quit his job but Joey advised against it, explaining that the job would help keep his aunt and uncle from becoming suspicious about how he was making all the money. So, following his advice, Vonni kept his job at the gym and had Tommy handle his customers when he was working. Several weeks passed and this arrangement was working perfectly. Then one day while he was at work he received an unexpected call from Joey, requesting a dinner meeting with him at *"Mangiare Grande,"* an elegant little Italian restaurant whose name literally meant "Great Eating." The place was known for serving the best Italian food in town. It was rumored that its owner had recruited the chef from a famous restaurant in Naples, Italy. Vonni had been there only once on a dinner date with Katie, and the food had been amazing, every bit as good as his grandmother's back in Brooklyn. But he wondered why Joey wanted to meet him there, of all places.

Though Vonni and Tommy were business partners, it was clear who was in charge of their operation. Vonni handled the money, major distribution, and all dealings with Joey and Pfeifer. Tommy was dedicated and loyal, but he didn't possess Vonni's brains or natural business acumen. So he began to settle into the role of Vonni's unofficial bodyguard, driver, and ears to the street. He was perfectly fine with this role. It was a natural fit for his personality. He knew everyone in the neighborhood, and made sure Vonni knew who he should and shouldn't deal with. He introduced Vonni to all the local business owners, ensuring that Vonni knew which ones were connected to the Syndicate and which ones weren't. He considered himself to be Vonni's personal *"conamore consigliere,"* his devoted advisor. He even began calling Vonni "boss." So when Joey summoned Vonni to a

172

dinner meeting at *Mangiare Grande*, Tommy donned his best outfit and picked his boss up in his shiny new Camaro.

As advised, the arrived at the exclusive little restaurant at precisely 7:00 PM. After valeting Tommy's car, they stepped into an entry foyer and were immediately met by a beautiful young hostess who was clearly expecting them. Without saying a word, she motioned for them to follow her through the main dining room and into an adjacent VIP dining room, which was completely devoid of patrons except for only four people. Posted next to the door was Joey's bodyguard, Nick "The Neck." Seated at a table in the back of the room were Joey two guys Vonni had never seen before.

Joey thanked the hostess and handed her a $20 before dismissing her with a smile. When she was gone, he embraced Vonni in an affectionate hug and gave Tommy a firm handshake.

Vonni glanced around and took in the ambiance. Italian mandolin music was playing from some hidden speakers in the walls. The table's centerpiece of fresh flowers had a scented candle burning in the middle of it. On the walls were original oil portraits by Italian artists Piero Manzoni and Bruno Munari. Two bottles of red wine and a basket of fresh bread were on the table. The smell of gourmet Italian cuisine wafted from the kitchen.

"Place is jumpin'," Vonni joked, wondering why they were the only ones in the room.

Joey chuckled and pulled out a pair of chairs for them. "Yes, well, I wanted us to have some privacy so I reserved the entire dining room," he said, nodding toward the other two guys at the table. "Now sit. I want you to meet my associates, Robby and Jose."

Vonni and Tommy extended hands to them before sitting, surprised by how young they were. Neither appeared more than twenty. Nor did they appear Italian. Robby was a fat white guy with a shaved head. Jose was a muscular guy that Vonni pegged as some kind of Latino. Neither wore suits, but both were well dressed in button-up shirts and slacks.

Joey opened a bottle of wine and poured each of them a glass. "Drink up, gentlemen," he said, winking at Vonni, knowing he wasn't old enough to drink. "This *vino* comes straight from the mountains of Tuscany. Some say it's the best wine in the world." He pointed at their menus. "And order whatever you like. Dinner's on me. I'm not sure if you've ever been here, but the food's amazing. Best Italian in Detroit. It's the only place my grandmother will eat outside her own kitchen. And the owner happens to be a personal friend of mine."

Tommy glanced at the door to the kitchen, where the hostess had disappeared a moment ago. "Could you hook me up with that hot ass hostess? I'd love to tap *that* ass!"

For a brief moment Joey stared at him, looking almost offended, but then he expelled an amused chuckle. "Sorry, paisan," he said, slowly waving a finger at him. "Gina is off limits. The only person I'm trying to hook her up with is me. And so far, I haven't had much luck. Her dad owns this place and he guards her virtue like it's the crown jewels. I wouldn't be surprised if she's wearing a chastity belt."

Everyone had a good laugh and then began studying their menus as Joey broke into some casual conversation about how his Tigers had beaten Vonni's Yankees earlier in the afternoon. Unfazed by this jestful goading, Vonni simply shot him a mildly annoyed look and continued to study his menu. A few minutes later a matronly old Italian woman stepped over to their table and asked for their orders. Vonni ordered a simple meal of spaghetti pomodoro with Sicilian breaded sirloin cooked medium-rare, grilled artichoke, eggplant parmigiana, and chini d'bibi soup.

As they waited for their food, they sipped wine and prattled extraneously about nothing in particular. Though it was a relaxing setting, there was still a little voice inside Vonni's head that kept asking, *Why am I here? And who are these other two guys at the table?* He knew Joey had to have a reason for inviting him to this extravagant dinner. He also knew there had to be a reason for the other two guys being there. But until Joey was ready to make him privy to both, all he could do was sit back and try to enjoy himself, which wasn't hard. He had to admit, Joey knew how to make statement. Not only had he selected the nicest restaurant in town for this meeting, but he also reserved the entire VIP dining room for their small party. This alone was a testament to his clout with the owner, which was especially impressive considering he was a mere 24-years-old. Vonni was also impressed by how well-spoken and articulate Joey was as he controlled the tempo of their conversation. The guy was clearly used to being the center of attention, yet he didn't come across as cocky or overbearing. In fact, he was surprisingly humble, even making himself the butt of his jokes. He obviously appreciated the finer things in life, for tonight he was wearing a flawlessly tailored Armani suit, a massive gold Rolex, and a pinky ring that had to have at least three carats of diamonds in it. On top of all that, he was currently running up a bill that would push a thousand dollars by the time they were finished.

But as they waited for their meals, sipping wine and engaging in casual conversation, Tommy was tense and clearly not in his element. Being the son of a construction worker, he was rough around the edges and not at all eloquent in word. He definitely was not used to rubbing elbows with well-spoken, sophisticated wiseguys like Joey Lombardo. Vonni, on the other hand, was perfectly comfortable in this setting, joking and engaging Joey in conversation like they were old friends. After a couple of glasses of wine he even loosened up enough to share a few humorous anecdotes from his childhood in Brooklyn, which Joey listened to with rapt attention.

An hour later, after they finished their meals and polished off a few bottles of expensive Tuscan wine, Joey suddenly turned to Tommy with a serious look. "Tom, would you mind giving me a few minutes alone with Vonni?" he asked politely, but Tommy knew it was not up for debate.

"Uh, sure, Joe," Tommy replied, looking nervously at Vonni. "I need to take a piss anyway."

When Tommy disappeared into the restroom, Joey turned to Vonni and spoke in Italian in order to keep his other two associates from understanding. "Giovanni, when I asked you to meet with me here tonight, did I mention anything about bringing your paisan, Tommy?"

"No," Vonni answered in Italian, wondering why he looked so annoyed.

Joey pierced him with a glare. "That's because this was supposed to be a business meeting between you, myself, and my two associates here. Not Tommy."

Emboldened by the alcohol, Vonni sat up and met his glare with a glare of his own. "Listen, Joe," he said, jerking a thumb toward the restrooms. "Tommy is more than just my paisan. He's my partner, my advisor, and my driver."

"Your driver?" Joey asked, his look of annoyance morphing into one of amusement.

"Yeah," Vonni answered, mildly ashamed. "I don't have a car and I never got my driver's license back in New York."

Joey considered this for a moment. "Do you trust him?"

"I do," Vonni said without hesitation. "I know he's got my back."

Again Joey considered this for a long moment. "Okay," he said with a shrug, switching back to English. "I wanted this to be only between just us here at this table, but I respect your loyalty. If you trust Tommy as your partner and *conamore consigliere*, then he should be part of it."

Vonni relaxed back into his seat. "Part of what?" he asked, casting a curious look at Joey's two associates.

Joey removed a small velvet box from his jacket pocket. "This is our first order of business," he said, sliding the box across the table to him.

176

Vonni opened it and was surprised to find a platinum Patek Philippe watch inside. "What's this?" he asked, staring at the beautiful designer watch.

"A gift. I have a jeweler friend who does a bit of fencing on the side. He owed me a favor so when he came across that Patek, he thought I might like it. But I want you to have it. Consider it a show of my appreciation for doing such a great job with our little arrangement. Try it on, see how it fits."

Vonni slipped the watch onto his wrist. It was almost a perfect fit, although it was much heavier than it looked. He'd heard of Patek Phillippe watches. Or rather he'd seen them for sale in Manhattan's diamond district while window shopping there with his mother. They were some of the most expensive designer watches in the world, even more expensive than Rolex. But he had no idea that the one now on his wrist was a special edition that had originally cost over $25,000.

"Thanks, Joe," he said, a bit overwhelmed to have been given such an extravagant gift, especially considering he had only been working for him less than six weeks. "I don't know what to say. I've never had a watch like this." He held it up and examined it proudly in the candlelight. "Thing must be worth a couple grand."

Joey chuckled at his naïveté. "Oh, it's worth a bit more than that, paisan. But enough about the watch. It's time we get down to the real reason we're all here…"

Just then Tommy returned from the restroom. "What's up?" he asked, looking nervously at Joey. "Everything good? You guys need more time?"

"No," Joey answered, offering him a smile. "We're all set here, paisan. In fact, you're right on time. Sit down. We're about to get down to why we're all here tonight." He nodded toward his two associates. "I've recently gone into the steroid business with my friends here. Jose's family lives in Mexico. They ship the stuff up by the case. Robby helps us sell it, but our distribution network is limited. That's where you two come in. We're hoping

177

you can help expand our distribution network. Tommy, you lift at the Powerhouse on Van Dyke. Vonni, you work at Muscles Gym. So my question to you both is this: Would you be interested in helping us find some new buyers for our products? There's a lot of money to be made in steroids. For all of us."

"It's true," Robby chimed in. "We can wire a thousand bucks down to Jose's people in Tijuana and they'll mail us back a package that we can flip up here for five times that. Sometimes more. Our only problem is distribution. We need more buyers. We just don't have any plugs at the local gyms."

"This is something that can significantly increase your income," Joey added. "Vonni, with all those 'roiders at your gym… Well, we're hoping you can setup a distribution network there and maybe at some of the other local gyms. With a little hustle you should have no problem moving twenty, maybe even thirty grand a month. Your cut would be 20% of whatever you sell. Not bad for a little extra work." He looked him in the eye, a message passing between them. "And you would be doing my associates and me a big favor."

Vonni was calculating his potential profits when a disturbing thought occurred to him. "What about my boss? I mean, we're cool, but he'd probably call the cops on my ass if he found out I was pushin' roids at his gym."

Joey flashed him a conspiratorial grin. "I wouldn't worry about him, paisan. He and I have some mutual friends. Word on the street is that he also sells a few 'roids on the side. He might end up being your best customer."

Vonni pictured his boss, a huge bodybuilder named Sonny, who was constantly talking about steroids with his cronies at the gym. And they weren't the only ones. It seemed like half the gym was either on steroids or trying to find some. There were dozens of high school football players who worked out at the gym, and they were constantly asking Vonni if he could get them steroids. There were tons of bodybuilders, power lifters, and regular everyday guys looking to bulk up or impress the ladies. There were even several professional athletes from the Detroit Red Wings, Tigers, and Lions who lived in nearby Grosse Pointe and trained there on their off-seasons. Indeed there was a lot of money to be made selling steroids at the gym.

"But I don't know anything about steroids," Vonni admitted.

"We'll teach you everything you need to know," Jose assured him. "There's lots of different kinds and they all do different shit, but we have a book called *The Anabolic Reference Guide*. It has everything there is to know about 'roids. Honestly, though, most guys already know which drugs they want. All you'll have to do is tell them what we have available in our inventory. Then take their orders and I'll fill them for you. It's really that simple."

Vonni looked at Joey, wondering where he fit into all this. "So what's your cut?"

Joey took a sip of wine and gestured toward Jose and Robby. "Oh, don't worry about me. I'll take my cut from these two."

Vonni turned to Tommy. "What do you think?"

"I say we do it!" Tommy answered enthusiastically. "I know a shitload of guys looking for 'roids. My cousin Dom just asked me if I could get him some. And he lives out in Bloomfield with the big money. Him and his boys are all a bunch musclehead 'roid freaks. Shit, we can make a killing off them alone."

Everyone was silent while Vonni considered the business proposition for a long moment. "Fuck it," he finally said, looking at Joey. "I'm in. When do we start?"

"When do you work next?" Joey asked.

"Tomorrow, noon to eight."

"And will you see guys who might be interested in some Mexican steroids?"

"All day long."

"Then you start tomorrow."

Jose handed Vonni a list of their current inventory. "Take this with you. Show it around. Write down any orders. At the end of the week, I'll fill them for you. It's that easy."

Joey stood and poured each of them a glass of wine. "To new friends and new money!" he said, hoisting his glass in the air for a toast. "*Salute!*"

Vonni raised his glass and drank to their new business endeavor, not even realizing that he had just taken one step further into the obscure world of La Cosa Nostra.

# CHAPTER 9

When Vonni went to work the next day, he began subtly hinting to guys that he had access to both pharmaceutical and veterinary grade steroids. He was surprised by how many of them were interested in purchasing a several-week supply, known simply as a "cycle." By the end of that first week alone, he took nearly $5,000 in orders. High school football players wanting to bulk up cashed in their savings to score a cycle. Older guys looking to reverse the effects of aging tapped into their bank accounts for a quick boost of youthful hormones. Skinny guys wanting to buff-up to impress the ladies forked out hundreds, sometimes thousands of dollars for a cycle. Power-lifters bought androgenic steroids to boost their strength. Bodybuilders bought anabolic steroids to increase their muscle mass. A runner training for a marathon wanted some to boost his endurance. Even a woman fitness model wanted a little anabolic assistance to give her an edge in her next competition. There were no limits to the types of people who wanted a shortcut to a better body. It didn't matter if they were old, fat, skinny, or young, they knew steroids were the fastest way to achieve their fitness goals. But Vonni himself had good genetics and a naturally muscular frame, so taking drugs to better his body never even crossed his mind.

By his second week in business, everyone at the gym knew he was the new go-to guy for steroids. Everything was going smoothly until one day his boss, Sonny, asked him into his office for a private word. Figuring Sonny had somehow gotten wind of what he was doing, he thought he was about to get fired. But to his surprise, Sonny only told him to stop doing the actual transactions there at the gym.

"I can't have any trouble with the cops," Sonny explained. "I'll lose my business license."

But what Sonny did next really shocked Vonni. After telling him to stop selling steroids there at the gym, he called one of his associates into his office, a stocky Italian bodybuilder named Vito DeMaglio, a local jewelry store owner who sold steroids on the side. It turned out that Sonny and Vito were partners in the steroid business, and they were indeed looking for a new supplier. So they worked out an arrangement with that would be advantageous for all. Vonni would consign them large quantities of steroids, which they would advance to their own network of distributors throughout the metropolitan Detroit area.

From that day on, when someone there at the gym inquired about steroids, Vonni would simply refer them to Sonny or Vito, who in turn would refer them to one of their distributors outside the gym. This new arrangement proved to be very lucrative, but it wasn't long before Sonny and Vito were ordering more steroids than Vonni could provide. It seemed the steroid market was much, much bigger than they anticipated.

With a gap between supply and demand, Joey ended up sending Jose and Robby down to Mexico to arrange for several pharmacists and veterinarians to send even larger packages of the drugs back up to Detroit. Inside these large packages—boxes often the size of washing machines—were hundreds, even thousands of bottles of varying types of steroids. They arrived each week like clockwork, the drugs inside already bought and paid for by waiting customers at a dozen metropolitan gyms. Vonni couldn't believe how fast he was selling the stuff. Nor could he believe how much money he was making. In one particularly busy week alone he made over $4,000 in profit, not including what he made from his pot sales.

With all of this new money pouring in, Vonni decided it was time he and Tommy celebrate their good fortune by doing a little splurging. They began buying new clothes, jewelry, custom suits, and pretty much anything else that met their fancy. With money coming in faster than they could spend it, daily shopping excursions became part of their regular routine. One day when returning from one of these shopping excursions, they passed a local motorcycle shop and Vonni suddenly thought of King Falcone. The young Mafioso and his entire crew drove café-style race bikes, known as "crotch rockets." They could be heard coming from blocks away, and often seen blazing through the neighborhood at breakneck speeds, weaving in and out of traffic with no regard for the law. Vonni thought the bikes were the coolest things he had ever seen, and King's bike was the coolest of them all—a black-and-chrome Kawasaki Ninja ZX 900, which he often drove to the gym. Sometimes, while King was working out, Vonni would slip outside to admire the bike up close, fantasizing about having one just like it.

"Pull in there!" he blurted, pointing at the motorcycle shop. "I'm gonna buy me a bike!"

"Buy a bike?" Tommy asked, looking at him like he was crazy. "What the fuck are you talking about? I thought you were saving for a car?"

By now they had passed the shop, but Vonni continued to stare back at it. "Man, it's summer. Fuck a car. I want a badass bike. You should get one, too. We have the money. Let's do it!"

Tommy thought for a moment, and then a broad grin appeared on his face. "Fuck it, let's do it," he said, and did a quick U-turn.

An hour later, after filling out the paperwork and paying cash, they were the proud new owners of a pair of Kawasaki Ninjas. But when Vonni got home, his aunt and uncle were not happy. Not only were they concerned about the danger of driving a motorcycle, but they wanted to know where he had gotten the money to buy one. He told them that he had financed it on a payment plan, but they suspected he was lying and even conveyed this to his parents back in New York.


By no means were Vonni and King friends, but King slowly began warming to him at the gym. Vonni suspected he knew why. King had to know what he was doing for Joey Lombardo. That meant some of the money he was helping Joey make was finding its way into King's pockets. So, in a sense, Vonni was now an extension of King's crew. A distant extension, sure, but an extension nonetheless. A few days after he bought his new Ninja, he was working at the gym when King and Big Dean pulled up on their bikes and parked out front. But before they came inside, Vonni saw them stop for a moment to look over his bike.

"That your ZX-9 out there?" King asked, setting his phone and keys on the counter.

"Yep," Vonni answered proudly. "Just got it a couple days ago."

"First bike?"

"Yep."

"Nice. But can you ride it?"

Vonni raised an eyebrow. "Well, that would be a matter of opinion. I'm still getting used to it."

King chuckled, appreciating the candor. "Don't feel bad, paisan. It took me all of last summer to get used to mine. You just gotta strap your nuts on, twist the throttle, and let her rip. You should come ride with us one of these days. On the weekends we like to cruise Gratiot for a while before heading down to French Road to do a little racing."

"I'm in," Vonni said, setting King's keys and phone in a drawer. "Me and Tommy will roll with you guys anytime. I've never been out on Gratiot but I hear there's tons of girls."

"There are," King confirmed with a grin, picturing the hordes of young girls who cruised the avenue looking for guys. "And they all want a ride on the bikes… I'll tell you what, swing by my house Friday after work and we'll head out there. We'll see what kind of skills you got on that bike."

Later that night while Vonni lay in bed, he found himself thinking about the money he was making, how it was a pittance compared to what King and his crew were making. He thought about the respect people now gave him, how it was nothing compared to the respect people gave King and his crew. Everyone, from young to old, knew and feared the infamous King Falcone crew. They were treated like celebrities in the neighborhood. And as Vonni now stared at the ceiling, contemplating his new life, he dreamed of someday being like them, with real money, real power, and real respect. He still had a long way to go, but he was on his way. And, for now, that was enough.


With the beginning of his senior year only a few weeks away, Vonni found himself dreading going back to school. Life was good and getting better by the day. He'd even gone cruising with King several times. They never actually spent any real time together outside these occasional cruises, but they were still seen together. And people took notice. They began treating him differently. Even being acquainted with King elevated his social status in their neighborhood. And when some of the more sought-after girls began asking Tommy about him, he knew it was only because of his new association with King, reinforcing his view that King was indeed the king of their little neighborhood.

The last Friday before school was set to begin, Vonni and Tommy decided to enjoy the evening with a cruise on their bikes. After making their regular circuit through downtown, they headed back to Angel Park, their favorite hangout. They were well-known there, as it was no secret that they now dealt some of the best pot in town. As soon as they came racing into the park on their bikes, people began approaching them to buy bags. Within twenty minutes they were sold out.

With their weed sold and the onset of nightfall only minutes away, they decided to relax and enjoy the sunset from a boardwalk bench overlooking the river. The evening was warm and comfortable, the park tranquil and quiet, the last vestiges of the sun's amber rays reflecting off the river. A massive freighter sounded its air horn as it made its way downstream for destinations unknown. Several fishing boats were far out in the river, slowly trolling against the swift currents. But with the exception of a few groups of kids hanging out in the parking lot, the park itself was nearly empty. There were no lovers sprawled on blankets under the willow trees. No families were gathered around picnic tables. Not a single angler fished from the boardwalk. The basketball courts and bleachers were empty. Even Jack and his crew of skateboarders were nowhere to be seen.

Summer was nearly over, and an almost somber ambiance hung in the air. But Vonni and Tommy didn't seem to notice. Life was great. And as they now sat there on a bench overlooking the river, they reminisced on the success of their summer exploits, laughing and joking without a care in the world. Just a few short months ago they were relative nobodies. But now they were somebodies, making more money than they had ever dreamed of. They had their new bikes, designer clothes, jewelry, and pockets stuffed with cash. More importantly, they had new social status. And of course, what always came with improved social status was girls. Both were handsome and athletic, but never had so many girls been interested in them. It was like they were real wiseguys. They weren't even a blip on the radar of real Mafiosi, but whispers on the street were that they were connected to King and his infamous crew. This alone gave them new status in the neighborhood.

Excited as they were about their new life, however, they dreaded going back to school. With each of them making nearly

$10,000 a month, far more than the average white-collar professional, they saw school as a frivolous waste of time. Vonni even considered dropping out but decided against it when he thought of his parents back in New York. Before shipping him off to Detroit, they'd made him promise to stay in school until he graduated. This was a big deal to them, particularly because neither of them had graduated high school, which his father claimed was the reason he couldn't find a decent-paying job. Though Vonni had his issues with his parents, he still loved them dearly. He didn't want to disappoint them, so he had decided to stay in school one more year until he graduated. Tommy, on the other hand, didn't care what his parents thought. He didn't get along with them and wanted to drop out so he could get his own apartment. He'd had enough of them bossing him around and dictating his life. He had his own money and no longer needed them. But most of all, he hated school, having barely skated through it most of his life. The only reason he hadn't already dropped out was girls. He loved girls, and the best place to find them was at school. But now, with his new money and new social status, he had more girls than he could handle. There was no reason left to stay in school.

Vonni was in the middle of trying to talk him out of it when he looked up and noticed two older black guys walking toward them on the boardwalk. Even though it was nearly dark, he could see they had a certain purpose in their stride. Two things immediately warned that they might be trouble. The first was that he had never seen them before. The second was that one of them was carrying a crowbar tucked against his side. An alarm went off in his head, but before he could react, it was too late.

"Run your pockets and them chains, motherfuckers!" one of them ordered, brandishing the crowbar.

Tommy, a thoroughbred tough guy, looked almost amused. "Who the fuck you think you're talking to, asshole?" he spat defiantly, jumping to his feet. "How'd you like it if I ram that fuckin' crowbar up your--"

187

CRACK!!! The thug smashed the crowbar across the side of Tommy's head.

There was a terrible cracking sound as Tommy went crashing to the boardwalk with a sickening thud. Vonni instantly leaped to his feet, ready for battle, but found himself looking down the barrel of a large semi-automatic pistol.

"Don't move, motherfucker!" the other thug snarled menacingly, pointing the pistol at his face. "It ain't worth your life. Just run your shit and you live to see another day."

Vonni had a bad habit of carrying large amounts of cash on him. He thought it made him look like a someone, mostly because he'd seen real wiseguys in the neighborhood pull out large knots of cash when they paid for things. But he wasn't a real wiseguy. He was only a small-time pot and steroid dealer. And as he now looked down the barrel of a pistol, he suddenly realized that he'd made himself a target by being so pretentious and flashy with his money.

"You're making a big mistake," he said calmly, slowly slipping his heavy gold chain over his head. "You're fucking up, my man. You're fucking up real bad!"

"Shut the fuck up!" the thug barked, cocking the pistol's hammer. "Now give me that watch and empty your pockets."

Vonni removed $4,000 in cash from his pocket. "I know you think you're making a score here," he said, handing him the money. "But I'm telling you you're making a big mistake."

"And the watch!" ordered the thug, snatching the wad of cash from him.

Vonni looked him dead in the eye. "I'm keeping the watch," he stated boldly. "You got my money. You got my chain. But I'm keeping my—"

"Shoot the motherfucker!" yelled the thug with the crowbar. "We'll dump 'em both in the river."

The one with the gun suddenly looked twitchy and apprehensive, glancing nervously around the deserted park. "Just give me the fuckin' watch, white boy!" he ordered, spittle

188

flying from his mouth. "Don't make me pop your punk ass! Just give me the fuckin' watch!"

Vonni hesitated for a moment but knew it was time to acquiesce. The watch meant a lot to him, but it wasn't worth dying for. Reluctantly, he slid it off his wrist and handed it over. The two thugs then pocketed their score and ran off into the night, leaving him standing there, staring in the direction they had disappeared. Never had he felt such a sense of pure, unadulterated rage. But after a moment he blinked away his anger and looked down at Tommy, who was unconscious and bleeding from a gash on the side of his head. Trembling with indignation, all he could do was pull out his cell phone and call for an ambulance.

Tommy spent three days in the hospital with swelling around his brain, but besides a nasty scar on his head he would eventually make a full recovery. Unfortunately, the events of that night left Vonni with a mental scar that would last a lifetime. The last vestiges of his youth had vanished when he stared down the barrel of that gun. Even back in Brooklyn, when he'd bought a pistol with intentions of avenging his murdered brother, he hadn't been sure if he could actually pull the trigger. But he now knew with complete certainty that he could kill, and he vowed to do just that if he ever caught up with the two thugs who robbed him and Tommy at the park that night.

Joey was extremely upset when he learned what happened. It was almost as if it had been a personal attack on himself. He even promised Vonni to do everything within his power to find the thugs who did it. In the meantime, he referred Vonni to an associate who dealt in stolen guns. The very next day, Vonni purchased a pair of 9mm Berettas and vowed to never again to be caught off guard.

# CHAPTER 10

The Monday following the incident in the park, Vonni began his senior year of high school. He had even been able to convince Tommy to stay in school one more year until he graduated. Within days they were back to business as usual, and school opened up an enormous new market for their pot business. During the summer their clientele had been made up mostly of people in their immediate neighborhood, and maybe a few guys from the gym. But once word spread around school that they were selling the best weed in town, their sales nearly doubled overnight. Vonni continued working at the gym to keep his aunt and uncle happy, but by now Sonny and Vito were handling almost all of his steroid distribution. Their sales were growing exponentially, to the point that he was barely able to keep up with their orders. In fact, Joey was so impressed by his performance in both the pot and steroid business, he ended up inviting him to the grand opening of a new club that one of his "associates" was opening. But Vonni wasn't stupid. He'd heard through the grapevine that the club, "Vanzetti's," was owned by none other than King Falcone.

Vonni and Tommy arrived at the club around 10:00 PM, both of them dressed to the nines in new suits. And right away they were impressed by what they saw. It was much bigger than they expected—a modern two-story building the size of a small warehouse. A series of huge windows offered people waiting in line a glimpse of the party taking place inside. The parking lot was already packed to near capacity with cars. Several stretch limousines were parked on the side of the building, but valet attendants were parking the nicest cars in a roped-off VIP parking area directly in front of the club. Already there were a couple of beautiful red Ferraris, several Corvettes, a Viper, a couple of Porsches, a Bentley convertible, and at least a dozen Jaguars, Cadillacs, and Mercedes. But with a long line of cars waiting to be valeted, Tommy just parked in the alley behind the club. It wasn't the grandest entrance, but nobody was going to be impressed by them pulling up in a five-year-old Camaro.

After parking in the alley, they walked back out front, bypassed the line, and stepped up to a large Italian bouncer checking IDs and collecting cover charges. "We're friends of Joey Lombardo," Vonni declared proudly. "He said we'd be on some kind of list."

The bouncer eyed them incredulously and removed a black booklet from his back pocket. Inside it was a list of VIP invitees. Vonni and Tommy were not on it. "Sorry, fellas," he said, not looking at all apologetic. "You ain't on the list. Back of the line. "

But when Vonni insisted that Joey Lombardo had personally invited them there, the bouncer decided he better at least check to see if they might be telling the truth. Using a small walkie-talkie, he conveyed the situation to someone inside. A moment later a voice crackled over the radio: "Send them up to VIP." The bouncer immediately held the red velvet rope aside and allowed them to enter the club without asking for the $20 cover charge or identification.

The instant they stepped inside, they were met with the cacophony of thumping dance music and hundreds of people shouting to be heard over it. The air was hot and thick with cigarette smoke. Even though the place was incredibly loud and packed to near capacity, everyone seemed to be having a great time doing what they came there to do—dance, drink, mingle, and be seen.

191

They were less than ten steps into the club when another bouncer walked over and told them to follow him. After threading their way through the mass of party revelers, they came to a staircase at the back of the club. Blocking access to it was yet another bouncer, a Goliath wearing a black tuxedo.

"Joe's expecting them," their escort said to the reticent giant, who confirmed this using his radio before stepping aside to allow them access.

Joey was waiting at the top of the stairs. "Vonni!" he yelled excitedly, embracing him in an affectionate hug before offering Tommy a hand, cringing at the fresh pink scar on the side of Tommy's head. "Tom, how's that big head of yours?"

Tommy shook his hand firmly. "Sore," he said, half-jokingly. "But I'll live. My mom always said I had a hard head."

"Well thank God for that, paisan," Joey said, and then motioned for them to follow him into a VIP lounge that encompassed nearly the entire second floor. "Come on, Vonni, I have some friends I'd like you to meet."

As they followed him, Vonni took in his surroundings. The lounge was plush and actually made up of several small private VIP lounges encompassing a larger a central lounge in the middle of the room, each of them complete with leather couches, recliners, and glass coffee tables. The central lounge was huge and even had its own bar that boasted a full complement of bartenders and waitresses. Everyone up there was much more formally dressed than the people downstairs. Almost every guy was wearing a suit. Almost every girl was wearing a dress. But Vonni barely noticed the beautiful girls all around him. His eyes were too focused on the six guys seated around a large glass coffee table at the center of the main lounge. He recognized them immediately.

Joey led them right up to King Falcone's top lieutenants and spoke to them in Italian. "Gentlemen, I'd like you to meet my good friend, Giovanni Battaglia. He and his partner here were the ones who had that little run-in with the eggplants at the park

192

a few weeks back." He turned to Vonni and gestured to the six young Mafiosi. "Vonni, these are my good friends Billy Profaci, Gino Mianchetti, Victor Aquiano, Paul Palazzolo, Georgio Corado, and Tony Tappio. They're the hosts of tonight's little soiree."

Each of them stood and respectfully offered a hand to Vonni and Tommy, but it was clear that their focus was on Vonni. Tony Tappio, who Vonni sensed was the highest ranked amongst them, put a hand on his shoulder and led him over to the balcony.

"So, Giovanni, what do you think of our new place?" Tony asked, studying him intently as he removed a cigar from his inside pocket.

Vonni peered over the balcony at the sea of people below. The dance floor was a solid mass of sweaty bodies that seemed to be synchronically swaying and bouncing to the club's massive sound system. Hanging from the ceiling were what could only be described as gigantic birdcages filled with dancing girls wearing nothing but body-paint bikinis. Beautiful young waitresses threaded their way through the crowds carrying trays of drinks and racks of shots in plastic tubes. The club's epicenter was a huge circular bar, where half a dozen bartenders were currently flipping bottles and putting on a show as they served throngs of thirsty patrons. Vonni had been to a few teen clubs in Canada with Tommy, but he had never seen anything like this. Back home he'd heard of such clubs in Manhattan, but he never expected to see one here in Detroit.

"Place is amazing," he finally answered, staring down at the scene below.

"I'm glad you like it, paisan," Tony said, lighting his cigar. "You're a welcome guest here anytime. Now come join us for a drink."

Vonni hadn't planned on drinking, but refusing would be taken as an insult. So, trying to seem indifferent, he and Tommy sat down to join Joey and his associates for a drink. Tony snapped a finger at a passing waitress, and a minute later she returned with two bottles of chilled Louis Roederer Rose Cristal champagne. Glasses were filled and raised to salute the success of the grand opening. As Vonni tasted champagne for the first time in his life, he could barely believe he was amongst them, sharing a toast with the actual club's hosts. The seven young men now sipping champagne with him and Tommy were all somebodies, young wiseguys, all of them known and respected throughout the area. And for reasons beyond him, he had been invited to celebrate this most special of nights with them. He felt honored to be sharing a drink with them, but surprisingly, he didn't feel out of place. They seemed to sense that, because they immediately began engaging him like he was an old friend. When Joey told them that he was from New York, they all wanted to hear about what it was like growing up in the Big Apple. As he recounted tales of his youth for these seven young Mafioso, for the first time in his life he felt like he was exactly where he was supposed to be.

Eventually, Joey and his associates headed off to mingle with their other guests, leaving Vonni and Tommy to fend for themselves. After securing one of the smaller VIP lounges, Vonni ordered another glass of champagne and took the people all around him, noting names and faces, logging in his memory how Joey and his associates spoke to various individuals. There were girls dancing in the lounge, and everyone was drinking heavily, but Vonni soon realized that being a VIP was really just a social statement. Anyone who was anyone was invited up from the main club to enjoy the perks of the VIP lounge, where the girl-to-guy ratio was nearly 5-to-1. Even though Vonni and Tommy were only seventeen and looked far too young to be there, they were having a great time. Tommy was especially enjoying himself, drinking and flirting with every girl that walked by.

Around 11:00 PM Vonni noticed a number of older Italian men being trickling into the lounge. Dressed in expensive suits, they usually arrived in groups of twos, each of them eagerly congratulating Joey and the rest of King's crew on the success of their grand opening. It wasn't hard for Vonni to discern who were the real Mafiosi. There were lots of street level wiseguys in the room—soldiers and associates—but the real Mafiosi stood out in their perfectly-tailored suits and omnipresent bodyguards always hovering close by. They had a certain swagger that announced who they were. But the most obvious indicator was how people received them. Joey and his associates shook their hands excitedly, even kissing them on each cheek. These real Mafiosi were catered to like royalty, offered the best liquors, champagnes, and even cigars. Some of them were surprisingly young, no older than mid-twenties, but most were in their thirties, forties, and fifties. A few were even in their sixties, making them look extremely out of place in a modern nightclub filled with young people.

Vonni was an intrinsic people watcher who always studied the manner and body language of people around him. And as he now watched Joey's associates greet these upper-echelon Mafiosi, he began to notice something peculiar. There seemed to be an almost tangible tension between them. Though they were being cordial to Joey and his associates, their smiles and congratulatory handshakes seemed forced. There were many hushed conversations in the shadows, accompanied by oblique stares that seemed to carry contempt, even malevolence. Vonni couldn't help wondering what he was missing. But he was most confused about the whereabouts of King. The club was filled with wiseguys from all over the city, but the guy rumored to own it was nowhere to be seen.

At precisely midnight, a low murmur of whispers changed the pitch of the room. When Vonni looked up, he saw a small crowd gathering at the back of the lounge near an emergency fire exit. In the middle of this crowd was King Falcone. But King was not alone. Standing next to him was a handsome older man with a barrel chest and broad shoulders. The man's white-gray hair was slicked back, and his dark eyes seemed to be scanning every face in the room. His simple ensemble of slacks, shirt, and tie were unable to cloak his air of nobility. Within seconds every Mafioso in the lounge began making their way over to shake his hand and kiss his cheek. He graciously offered each of them smiles and friendly handshakes, but the hard features of his face and his piercing dark eyes warned that he was a dangerous man. And if this wasn't a clear enough warning, his four bodyguards were never more than a few feet away.

"Yo, who the fuck is that?" Vonni whispered to Tommy, who was on the couch next to him, flirting with a buxom blond who was surely ten years his senior.

Tommy studied the crowd of men clambering to pay respects to the old man. "I have no idea, but he's definitely a boss," he said, then returned his attention to the girl.

While a stream of Detroit's mid-level Mafiosi paid homage to Don Falcone, King led Joey and his other six lieutenants into an adjacent office for a quick report on the progress of the evening. Ten minutes later they returned to the party looking more than pleased. King then walked over to his grandfather and whispered a few words into his ear before walking him out the same way he arrived, through the rear fire exit.

From a couch in one of the smaller private lounges, Vonni watched King begin greeting his guests, his face beaming, clearly proud that his grandfather had come to support him on this special night. But the don's appearance was more than a show of love and support. There were representatives from every Syndicate crew there in the lounge, sent there to reconnoiter their new competitor in the nightclub business. But Don Falcone's brief appearance was his way of warning them that he was backing his grandson, and that he would not tolerate any interference from them.

As Vonni sat there wondering who the old man was, again he took in his surroundings and felt oddly out of place. He seemed so much younger than everyone. He was a nobody, an outsider. The lounge was filled with shot-callers from all over the city. Including real Mafioso, men ranked far higher up the Syndicate ladder than even King and his crew, who were really nothing more than a bunch of low-level street hustlers. Some of the Mafiosi in attendance were no doubt top Syndicate players, lieutenants and enforcers for King's grandfather and other Syndicate bosses. There were things taking place in the lounge that were far beyond Vonni's realm of comprehension, real Mafia politics and tactical displays of power he could never understand. It all made him wonder why he'd been invited to witness it.

With these thoughts running through his head, Vonni watched King make his rounds through the crowded lounge, shaking hands with various wiseguys, flirting with the beautiful girls vying for his attention. Everyone was eager to steal him away for a few moments of private conversation. Some of the older Mafioso hugged him affectionately, kissing him on the cheek like he was a son or young brother. It was impressive to watch someone so young command such respect, even from men of their status. Wherever he was, he emanated a certain air of power and pedigree, but tonight he stood out like a beacon of light on a dark night. Tonight his name was perfectly fitting. He looked like a king amongst commoners.

Vonni was sitting the couch with Tommy, sipping champagne and entertaining a group of girls, when he noticed King walking toward him. "Johnny New York!" King said, extending a hand to him. "I'm surprised to see you here."

"Here in your club?" Vonni asked, standing to shake his hand. "Or here in the VIP lounge?"

"Both," King answered. "You're only seventeen, right? You're not even old enough to be in here."

"Neither are you," Vonni countered, grinning.

"Touché, paisan," King chuckled, tipping his drink to him. "Lucky for me I know the owner."

197

"So is this your nice way of telling me I have to leave?" Vonni asked, half-jokingly.

"Of course not. Stay as long as you like. Enjoy yourself. You're welcome in my club anytime. If you need anything, let me know." He flagged down a passing waitress and pointed to Vonni. "Emily, this is my good friend, Giovanni. His money is no good here. Anything he wants, charge it to my personal account."

After a few more polite words, King shook his hand and sauntered off to resume mingling with his guests, leaving Vonni to the small bevy of girls Tommy had gathered on the couch. Never in his life had he felt more like a someone, which was exactly why King had made sure to invite him there.

By the end of the night, both Vonni and Tommy were far too drunk to drive so Joey ordered a limousine to take them and several girls to a suite of rooms in the downtown Marriott, where Vonni ended up in bed with a pair of brunettes who took full advantage of his youthful sexual vigor. Once again, without him even realizing it, King had nudged him one step further into the Machiavellian world of La Cosa Nostra.

# CHAPTER 11

The hotel phone trilled on the nightstand, jolting Vonni awake. Blinking away the cobwebs of last night, he snatched it up. "Yo…" he croaked groggily. "Who's this?"

"Sorry if I woke you, Mr. Battaglia," a woman at the front desk answered. "But there's a gentleman named Nick down here asking for you. He says you're expecting him."

Groggy and hung-over, he set the phone down. It was 12:05 in the afternoon, but he felt like he'd fallen asleep only minutes ago. His mouth was dry and parched. There was a dull throbbing in his head. He wanted nothing more than to go back to sleep for a few more hours, but Nick in the lobby could only mean one thing: Joey wanted to see him. So, reluctantly, he dragged himself out of bed. But as he began dressing, he grinned at the two naked girls still sleeping blissfully, his mind drifting back to the things that they had done to him the previous night.

After waking Tommy, they headed down to the lobby and found Nick "The Neck" impatiently waiting to drive them back to Club Vanzetti's. Twenty minutes later, Nick parked in front of the club and looked to Vonni. "Joe's in a meeting," he said in his usual monotone. "Go upstairs and wait."

While Tommy went to reclaim his car from the back alley, Vonni headed inside, wondering why he was being summoned. Compared to the previous night, the interior of the club was bright, empty, and eerily quiet. The only sounds were coming from a small crew of custodians who were busy vacuuming and cleaning the aftermath of the grand opening. The smell of cigarette smoke and booze still lingered, but compared to the previous night the air seemed pristine.

After making his way up to the VIP lounge, he plopped down on a couch to wait. As he sat there silently waiting, his thoughts drifted back to the night before, particularly all the wiseguys and the odd tension there seemed to be between some of them. But mostly he found himself thinking of the intimidating old man who had arrived with King. He still wondered who the man was and why everyone had treated him like a celebrity.

But thoughts of last night vanished when he heard what sounded like a heated argument coming from inside an adjacent office. Suddenly he felt nervous and wondered if he'd done something wrong. After all, he had gotten pretty drunk the previous night. He'd never been one to hold his liquor well, which was the reason he rarely drank. He hoped that he hadn't offended someone without realizing it. *Maybe I asked the wrong person about that old man*? For a moment, he sat there rubbing his temples, trying to remember who he had spoken to. Unfortunately, most of the night was a blur.

Finally, after what felt like an eternity, but was, in fact, less than ten minutes, Joey stepped from the office. He was wearing a freshly pressed suit, and his straight black hair was slicked back with pomade, every strand perfectly in place. Vonni couldn't help wondering how the guy always looked as he had just walked off the set of a GQ cover shoot.

"Goombadi Giovanni!" Joey practically yelled, his face alight with excitement as he stepped over to shake his hand. "Sorry to keep you waiting. I was in a meeting with my partners."

"No problem, Joe," Vonni said, standing to shake his hand, feeling a little self-conscious about his rough condition. "I've only been here a few minutes."

Joey looked him over with a touch of amusement. "I take it you haven't been home yet?"

"No," Vonni answered, subconsciously trying to flatten the wrinkles in his shirt. "Not yet. I was still in bed when Nick came to get us."

"So..." Joey said, flashing him a knowing grin. "I take it my friends Amy and Lori took good care of you last night?"

Vonni grinned as images of the girls flashed through his head. "Yeah, they took good care of me alright," he said, slightly blushing. "I never had two at once like that."

Joey sat on one of the couches and removed a pack of Marlboros from his inside pocket. "Good," he said, casually lighting a cigarette, a pensive look on his face. "I'm glad you enjoyed yourself. It was a pleasure having you as a guest on opening night. You're welcome to drop by anytime."

"I appreciate that, Joe," Vonni said, taking a seat on the couch directly opposite him. "I'm sure I'll be taking you up on that..." He paused for a moment, trying to gather his words, a nervous look on his face. "But can I ask you a question?"

"Of course, paisan," Joey said, puffing on his cigarette. "What's on your mind?"

"That old man last night. The one with King. Who was he?"

Joey considered the question for a long moment. "That was King's grandfather, Don Falcone," he finally answered, looking him dead in the eye, exhaling a thick cloud of smoke. "Why? Is there something in particular you'd like to know about him?"

"No," Vonni answered, the message perfectly clear. This subject was obviously not to be pursued. But things suddenly made sense. The reason King was so feared was because his grandfather was indeed a boss, a *capo*. And not just any *capo*, but a don, a title given to only the highest ranking Mafiosi. Vonni suddenly felt stupid for not making the connection.

"So..." Joey said, studying him as he took another long pull from his cigarette. "I suppose you're wondering why I sent Nick to get you?" he asked, purposely changing the subject.

"Yeah, actually I am," Vonni answered. "I figured we'd just catch a cab back here and grab Tommy's car. But now, with the way you're looking at me, I'm wondering if I did something wrong last night."

"You did nothing wrong, paisan," Joey chuckled. "In fact, I was impressed by how well you carried yourself. And so were my partners. They liked you. I mean, being only seventeen I'm sure you probably felt a bit out of place amongst the type of people who were here last night. But you handled yourself well. You were confident but not cocky. I like that about you, Vonni. I like that you have a little swag but aren't too cocky. That's a rare attribute these days. I think you have a lot of potential. Which is one of the reasons I wanted to see you this morning."

He walked over to the bar and removed two bottles of water. "Paisan," he continued, tossing a bottle to him, "I have a new assignment for you. I'm putting you in charge of a couple guys. Younger guys not much older than yourself. They specialize in, for lack of a better word, thievery. They were working for one of my associates but they work for me now. I'm putting you in charge of them."

"Me?" Vonni asked, both surprised and confused. "Why me? I mean, no offense, Joe, but I ain't no thief."

Joey flashed him one of his Hollywood smiles. "No, of course you're not. But that doesn't mean you can't be in charge of a couple guys who are. These guys are professionals. They are very good at what they do. And I've recently acquired an inside connection at a major alarm company. An installation technician. For a small fee, he has agreed to provide me the deactivation codes for certain, oh, sophisticated alarm systems. So, from time to time I'll be giving you addresses and deactivation codes. Your job will be to relay them our professional larcenists, who will, in turn, use them to ply their craft. Your only other job will be to see that each score is delivered to a small warehouse downtown near the Eastern Market. Once the scores are there, you'll inventory each item and determine its value. Our friends will keep half of the total value. You and I will split the rest."

202

Vonni considered this for a moment. "So we're talking about residential homes?"

"Some, sure, but mostly commercial businesses and an occasional warehouse. But leave the jobs up to me. All I need you to do is relay the codes and addresses, and then inventory the swag. That's it."

"Sounds easy enough," Vonni said, grinning, excited to be taking on more responsibilities.

"It will be. And don't worry, the guys I'm putting you in charge of are pros. They've already done jobs for me and my associates. They've never let us down. But I also want you to start thinking about putting together a crew of your own. Expand your operations. Recruit some guys to start selling more weed for you. Front them a little and see how they work out. Same with the 'roids. Recruit a few guys from the gym. Send them into other gyms to find new customers. Also, if you know of any guys at school who specialize in things like safe-cracking, shoplifting, stealing cars, breaking into homes, shit like that, let them know you'll pay a fair price for any good merchandise. Cash them out and bring the goods to the warehouse. I've got people who will take it off our hands at a decent profit. And if you think of anything else that could make us some money, don't be afraid to run it by me. My partners and I are always looking to expand our operations. But be careful about who you deal with. Stick to only guys you know and trust. Standup guys. I usually just deal with Italians from the community." He looked him directly in the eye, sending him a message. "*Our community.* They know who we are and what we do. That means they know what will happen if they fuck us around. But whatever you do, never, *ever,* do business with junkies. They can't be trusted…"

He took a pull from his cigarette and thought for a moment. "Honestly, Giovanni," he continued, pointing the cigarette at him, "I'd prefer you also just stick with Italians from the neighborhood. Guys Tommy can vouch for. Pay them well and treat them right. That way they'll always be loyal. But whoever you recruit, make

203

sure they know how to keep their mouths shut. Remember, loose lips sink ships. Really, the fewer people you deal with directly, the better. In fact, since Tommy has turned out to be more muscle than partner, why don't you just let him deal with the guys you recruit? Give him a little responsibility. Wet his beak. Pay him a cut from each score. He's not the smartest guy around, but he is loyal and fearless, which are two traits in short supply these days. But if anyone gives you guys more trouble than you can handle, let me know and we'll handle it together. *Capisce?*"

Vonni grinned inwardly, knowing he was finally being invited to be more than just a mere low-level associate. Putting his own crew together would mean that he was, in fact, an extension of Joey's own crew, which was really just an extension of King Falcone's crew. A few minutes ago he had been worried if he had done something wrong, but now he was being told he had done everything right. So right, in fact, that it was time he becomes an official part of Joey's crew. The sense of honor he felt was nearly overwhelming.

"Yeah, I understand," he said, his chest swelling with pride. "I'll handle it. I've already been thinking about branching out. And it's funny that you've got a fence for stolen goods, because guys are always trying to trade me shit for weed. But I've been strictly cash-and-carry. I haven't had a need for car stereos, computers, guns, jewelry, rims, shit like that. I didn't want to get stuck with it. But if you got a fence for it I'll start grabbing it up for pennies on the dollar."

"Yes!" Joey said excitedly. "Buy it up. That's exactly the type of stuff we're looking for. Get the word out to your customers that you're interested in buying that kind of merchandise. We can make some good money on it. But I shouldn't have to remind you, Vonni, never use my name. Ever. Not to anyone. This is strictly between us."

"Come on, Joe," Vonni said, looking genuinely offended. "I'm insulted you'd even say that. I may only be half-Italian, but I know how *Omerta* works. You never have to worry about me. I know the risks involved with what I do, and am prepared to face the consequences if I ever get knocked."

Joey jammed the butt of his cigarette into an ashtray on the coffee table between them. "Good," he said, looking satisfied, removing a piece of notepaper from his inside pocket. "Now that we have that out of the way, I want to give you this."

Vonni reached across the table and took the small piece of paper. "What is it?" he asked, reading what appeared to be an address.

"A gift," Joey answered, his face twisting into a conspiratorial grin. "It's where you can find those *melanzani* who robbed you and Tommy at the park. Didn't I tell you they'd turn up? I had my guys ask around. Turns out, there was a hooker working the park that night and she told Mickey LaFatta she saw what happened. Said she knows the guys who got you. I guess they robbed her once at a trap house on Conner where they sell dope. Took her money and wouldn't give her the dope. One of them drives an old red Cutlass with gold spoked rims. The other drives a black Suburban with chrome rims. If their cars are there, you know they're there..." His conspiratorial grin became almost maniacal. "So, paisan, now that you know where they are, what are you going to do about it?"

Vonni stared down at the piece of paper and felt a hot rush of rage course through his veins. "I'm gonna make the fuckers pay," he said menacingly, the rage visible in his eyes.

"Vonni," Joey said, sounding almost fatherly. "Settle down, paisan. You have to take your time with these things. Plan it out. Consider every scenario. Cover every angle. Guys who do these things on impulse are the ones who get caught. Prisons are full of them. Don't be one of them. You're a smart kid, Giovanni. These punks aren't going nowhere, so take your time and do it right."

"I plan to," Vonni said, an almost trancelike look in his eyes as he subconsciously ran a hand over the pistol tucked in his waistline. "I got a surprise for them motherfuckin' eggplants!"

Joey studied him for a moment, strangely unnerved by the look in his eyes. "Yes, well, remember what I said. Plan it out and make sure to cover your tracks. You're a good man. I don't want to lose you over a couple of punk *melanzani*. So let me give you some advice. The cops. They change shifts three times a day: midnight, eight in the morning and four in the afternoon. Right after these shift changes, most of the new shift is still in the precinct loading up on coffee and donuts, swapping out cars, playing grab ass with their partners. That leaves a small window of opportunity, usually about thirty minutes, when there are almost no cops on the streets. This is when you want to handle your business. You'll need a police scanner. And a decoy. And a..."

Joey spent the next fifteen minutes giving him a tutorial on how to handle the two thugs. When he was finished, he shook Vonni's hand and sent him on his way. But as Vonni made his way downstairs and headed for the exit, the front door opened and three guys stepped into the empty club. He recognized them immediately. They were three of the original *Quattro Duchi*—King's cousins Frankie Bommarito and the Gianolla brothers, Anthony and Dino. None of them said a word as they brushed passed him and headed for the back staircase. But Frankie's face registered both recognition and malevolence. Obviously, he hadn't forgotten about their fight in Jackie Reed's backyard. Just as Vonni was about to step from the club, he glanced back and saw King staring down at them from the VIP balcony. He did not look happy to see them, and Vonni wondered why.


For a few small bags of weed, Vonni began renting his cousin's old clunker Mustang so he could case out the house that the two thugs supposedly sold their drugs from. Located in a predominantly black ghetto known for drugs and crime, the house was a dilapidated mess that had likely been abandoned at one point, only to be resurrected as an illegal drug bazaar. Every day after school Vonni and Tommy would cruise past the house several times in an attempt to establish the thugs' nightly routine. Usually, during the day and early evenings, just one of their cars were parked in the street out front. But both cars were almost always there throughout the night, when the streets came alive with addicts looking to score a fix.

Several times, late at night, Vonni had snuck down the alley behind the house and crouched in the overgrown weeds next to the garage, watching zombified junkies slink up to the back door and buy drugs. Some of them even came up the alley and walked within feet of him hiding in the weeds, their minds too muddled by drugs to even notice him.

While reconnoitering the house and surrounding neighborhood, he began formulating various strike scenarios. One was to dress up like a cop and burst in like he was part of a drug raid. But he was too young to be a cop, and they would probably recognize him anyway. He contemplated firebombing the house, but that might not achieve the desired effect. He considered the possibility of contracting someone to do his dirty work for him, but this posed two problems. First, it would leave a connection to him. Second, it wasn't nearly personal enough. No, he wanted to look them in the eye as he exacted his revenge, which meant he would have to do it himself.

After a week of careful consideration, he decided on a plan of attack. It was bold and straightforward, but it was time to prove his mettle. After getting Joey's approval to move forward, he purchased the tools he'd need: a stolen Pontiac Grand Am, a police scanner, and a semi-automatic 12-gauge shotgun with a sawed-off barrel.

That Saturday night, while his aunt and uncle thought he was with Tommy at a concert at the Fox Theater, he and Tommy drove past the house several times in the stolen Grand Am, making sure both thugs were there. When they saw both cars, they knew this was the night. Vonni had gone over every detail of his plan with Tommy a dozen times, and after one final rundown he had Tommy pull to a stop at the mouth of the alley that ran behind the dope house.

"Make the call and get back here ASAP," Vonni said, glancing at his watch, seeing the time was five minutes to midnight. "Then shut the lights off and back into the alley. Leave the car running. Be ready when you see me coming." With that, he stepped out of the car and disappeared into the penumbral shadows of the overgrown alley.

Tommy drove to a liquor store two miles away, on the corner of Harper Avenue & Outer Drive, where he used a pay phone to dial 911 and report an armed robbery in progress at a B.P. gas station across the street. He then hung up and listened to the police scanner as he drove back to the alley and parked in the shadows. As planned, a dispatcher began routing all available squad cars in the vicinity to the B.P. gas station on the corner of Harper Avenue and Outer Drive, where a "211" was in progress.

Clad in a black jogging suit, black boots, and black gloves, Vonni made his way down the defunct alley, through a bramble of overgrown weeds and piles of discarded garbage. The night was cool and quiet. A half-moon cast just enough light to navigate the alley in complete stealth. Every few minutes an occasional car sped down the street out front. Police sirens echoed from somewhere far off in the distance. Several unseen dogs barked throughout the neighborhood, as if talking to each other in some kind of coded canine language. Somewhere farther down the alley, a pair of cats screamed in the heat of battle. But none of it affected Vonni, for he was completely focused on revenge.

Moving with the precision of a Special Forces Commando, he blended into the shadows. In a heightened state of awareness, his eyes adjusted to the darkness, his ears tuned to every sound, his body taut with anticipation. The weight of the compact shotgun in his hands gave him a sense of power and invincibility he'd never experienced before. And as he now crept up behind the house, he forced himself to recall the memories of that night in the park. The barrel of the gun pointed at his face. The threatening tone of the thug's voice. The contemptuous look in thug's eyes. The metallic clang of the crowbar slamming into Tommy's head. The rage he felt standing over Tommy's unconscious body. And the vow of revenge he swore to himself.

Trying to determine how many people were in the house, he crept around the side, staying tight to the shadows, peering in several windows. The interior was gutted and filthy. Only a single room at the back of the house had light coming from it. Vonni assumed it had once been a family room before the house became abandoned. Loud music coming from inside it muffled several voices. When he slowly peered in one of the room's windows, he saw them. Right there, mere feet away. The two thugs who robbed him and Tommy. They were sitting on a tattered old couch, playing a video game, appearing without a care in the world. But they weren't alone. Two women were also in the room. Vonni recognized them as hookers from Angel Park. He'd seen them there several times. One had even propositioned him. Currently, they were taking turns smoking crack from a glass pipe while dancing rhythmically to the rap music that was blaring from a cheap boom box on the floor. A makeshift coffee table of plywood and milk crates was covered with empty 40-ounce beer bottles, dime bags of cheap pot, cigar blunts, and some greasy Church's Chicken wrappers. Amongst this clutter was a plastic bag filled with small rocks of crack cocaine and a black automatic pistol.

Seeing the two women, Vonni was tempted to abort the mission and try again another night. But the sight of that pistol, the very same pistol that had been pointed at his face, reminded him of the vow he made. The rage instantly came flooding back. He glanced around one last time to make sure nobody was

209

around. When he saw no one, he took a deep breath, aimed the shotgun at one of the thugs through the window, and pulled the trigger. *KABOOM!* There was a tremendous concussion, and the blast of buckshot blew a hole in the window the size of a basketball. The thug was thrown backward and then collapsed in a bloody heap, dead before he hit the floor. For a brief moment, everyone else in the room froze in shock and confusion. But, seeing his partner on the floor twitching in death throes, the second thug leaped to his feet and made a break for it. Vonni trained the shotgun on him and again pulled the trigger. *KABOOM!* The thug stumbled and fell into an adjacent hallway, blood splattering onto the wall and ceiling behind him.

With the two hookers frozen in shock and terror, Vonni charged up the back porch, kicked in the back door, and burst into the room with murder in his eyes. The two women immediately began pleading for their lives, but he knew what he had to do. If he recognized them, they could recognize him. With Joey's words ringing in his head, "Leave no witnesses," he raised the shotgun and pulled the trigger twice, both head shots at point blank range, splattering skull fragments and gray matter across the floor.

The room fell eerily still, the metallic stench of blood and the acrid smell of spent gunpowder hanging in the air. With the barrel of his shotgun still smoking and rap music still blaring from the boom box, he began making his way around the room, confirming they were all dead. But when he came to the second thug, he was surprised to find him still alive, writhing around on the floor in the hallway, softly moaning and clutching at several buckshot holes in the side of his chest. But he was even more surprised to see his Patek Philippe watch on the thug's wrist.

Vonni knelt down and looked him in the eye. "You remember me, motherfucker?" he growled maniacally, poking him in the face with the barrel of the shotgun. "Yeah, you remember me, don't you? I warned you. I told you that you were fucking up. You should've killed me when you had a chance, you piece of shit!"

The thug mumbled something unintelligible that could have been an expletive, so Vonni put the barrel of the shotgun against his forehead and pulled the trigger, blowing a larger chunk of his head across the floor. He then casually reclaimed his watch and strode from the house like he was heading out for a leisurely stroll, disappearing into the shadows of the alley, where he found Tommy waiting several houses down with the lights turned off and car running.

"I heard the shots," Tommy whispered, putting the car in gear. "What happened?"

"It's done," Vonni said, sliding onto the passenger seat next to him. "Now go! And drive cool."

They drove the next several minutes in silence, quietly listening to the police scanner. There was only one call reporting the sounds of gunfire in the neighborhood, but the caller was unable to determine where the shots originated. Being that it was a drug-infested ghetto where gunshots were a common occurrence, the local cops probably wouldn't even send a squad car to investigate. It would be at least several hours before someone stumbled upon the gruesome murder scene. And by then, Vonni and Tommy would be fast asleep in their beds, all evidence destroyed, tickets to the concert on their nightstands.

Tommy drove the stolen Grand Am downtown, where his car was stashed in the alley behind an abandoned warehouse. There Vonni quickly changed clothes and tossed the black jogging suit, boots, and gloves into the backseat of the Grand Am. Tommy then doused it with gasoline and set it ablaze. From there they drove to Angel Park, where Vonni dumped the shotgun in the river. Finally, after letting their nerves calm down a bit, they headed to Club Vanzetti's to create alibis by making themselves seen.

When they arrived at the club just before 1:00 AM in the morning, the main floor was packed to capacity with hundreds of people drinking and dancing. But Vonni and Tommy headed straight up to the VIP lounge, where Joey and his partners were entertaining a large party of friends. When Joey saw them coming, he immediately excused himself and motioned Vonni into the adjacent office.

"I want details," Joey said, shutting the door behind them, stepping over to a small dry bar to pour them double shots of whiskey.

Vonni drained his glass in one long gulp and immediately felt the calmative effects of the alcohol. "Fuckers still had my watch..." he said, proudly holding up his wrist to display the watch like it was a spoil of war. He then spent the next twenty minutes relaying every detail of what transpired.

"Good," Joey said, sounding like a proud father, pouring him another shot of whiskey. "You did everything right. Maybe the next pair of *melanzani* will think twice before trying to rob you, eh? For now, you and Tommy just relax and act normal. Have a good time. Mingle with the girls. Make yourself seen. If anyone asks, you got here at eleven, right after the concert let out."

After a few more calming words, Joey sent him back into the lounge to mingle and drink with the rest of the party. Surprisingly, Vonni felt his nervous anxiety quickly melt away. He knew he had covered his tracks, left no witnesses, and done everything right. His plan had gone down without a single hitch. And as he now sipped a cold beer in the boisterous lounge, he felt a great sense of satisfaction knowing that he had made the thugs pay the ultimate price for what they had done to him and Tommy.

Later that night, as he lay in bed, Vonni thought about what he'd done and felt surprisingly little remorse. The two women were unfortunate collateral damage, in the wrong place at the wrong time, but they were drug-addicted hookers, not upstanding members of society. The two thugs were just that—

212

thugs. Not only did they sell destructive hard drugs like crack and heroin to their own community, but they robbed and hurt people. After what they'd done to him and Tommy, they got exactly what they had coming.

But Vonni fell asleep that night never knowing that it was, in fact, King Falcone who sent the two thugs to rob him in the park. King had wanted to teach him a lesson about being flamboyant and flashy with his money. More importantly, though, he wanted to see how Vonni would react when given a chance to exact revenge on someone who had so blatantly disrespected him. A simple test. And once again, Vonni passed it with flying colors.

# CHAPTER 12

Following Joey's suggestion, Vonni immediately began expanding his operations, recruiting new guys from the neighborhood. Tommy, eager to take on more responsibility, even helped him organize a small crew of petty thieves to work with Joey's two professional larcenists, Jimmy Milioto and Carlo Specatelli, a pair of young hoods from the neighborhood.

Joey's connection at the alarm company, a computer programmer who handled software programming for the company's mainframe computer, turned out to be an incredibly valuable asset. But his services hadn't come easy. A middle-aged family man, he was a straight shooter who had never broken a law in his life. So when he refused a sizeable bribe, Joey and his partners resorted to good old-fashioned extortion, threatening his family unless he provided them with what they wanted. And what they wanted was nothing short of a key to the vault. Concerned for the welfare of his wife and children, not only did he begin providing them with the deactivation codes for the company's sophisticated alarm systems, but he also provided them with the addresses of certain residential homes and businesses suspected of having large caches of cash and valuable merchandise in them. Joey would relay these codes and addresses to Vonni, who would then pass them along to Jimmy and Carlo, who were indeed very good at what they did. Sometimes they would case out a potential job for days, even weeks, waiting for the right time to deactivate the alarm and make their illicit entry.

But Jimmy and Carlo did more for Vonni than just break into the buildings. They also began training his new recruits in the art of larceny—disarming alarms, casing out potential jobs, lock-picking, stealth entry, safe-cracking, even high-end shoplifting and cashing stolen checks. Working under their tutelage, Vonni's crew of young larcenists began breaking into nearby suburban homes, commercial warehouses, retail stores, cars, and pretty much anywhere else that might have something worth stealing. And after each successful job, they would deliver the score to Vonni, who would then deliver it to a small unmarked warehouse and inventory each item in a coded ledger. It was a very efficient arrangement, and within a month the warehouse was already cluttered with high-end audio equipment, big-screen televisions, DVD players, home theater systems, video cameras, computers, guns, fur coats, entire collections of compact discs, even expensive pieces of art. But these items were only icing on the proverbial cake. What Joey and his partners wanted was cash and jewelry, and there was plenty of it. The warehouse had a small office with an old safe built in the floor. This is where Vonni deposited the cash and jewelry from each score. In the first month alone he deposited over $100,000 in cash and nearly double that in jewelry. For overseeing the operation, he was allowed to keep a small portion of the cash, some of which was used to pay his network of young larcenists, including Jimmy and Carlo. But about half of every score went to Joey and his nameless "partners," who Vonni knew were really just King Falcone and his inner circle of lieutenants.

The stolen goods racket turned out to be a great new source of revenue for Joey and his partners, but fencing so much stolen merchandise was much more difficult than they anticipated. Originally their plan was to sell everything from a pawnshop they opened in Detroit, but they soon realized they couldn't just fill the shelves with locally stolen items. Because if they did, sooner or later someone would walk in and recognize their property sitting on a shelf. Of course, they also had to worry about the local cops, who had special detectives that periodically audited the merchandise of local pawnshops, particularly pawnshops suspected of selling stolen goods. But Joey and his partners came up with an ingenious solution. Some of their affiliates in Chicago were in a similar predicament, having a hard time moving stolen merchandise through their own pawnshop. So Joey and his partners made arrangements to swap their stolen Detroit merchandise for stolen Chicago merchandise. This kept the cops off their back and people from potentially walking in and seeing their property on the shelves. Problem solved.

"Operation Swag Swap," as they jokingly called it, worked out perfectly. While their affiliates in Chicago began selling Detroit merchandise from their pawnshop, Joey and his partners began selling Chicago merchandise from their own pawnshop, which they named "The Exchange" as an inside joke. The arrangement turned out to be extremely lucrative for all parties, including Vonni and his new crew.

With all of his various endeavors thriving, Vonni began making considerable money, sometimes taking in well over $4,000 a week. But he'd learned his lesson about being flashy. He was done drawing attention to himself. Instead, he maintained a low profile and conducted his business well under the radar. In fact, other than Tommy, nobody even knew what he was doing for Joey. But of course there were rumors, whispers on the streets that he was somehow connected to King Falcone and his notorious crew. He saw the looks people gave at school, heard their hushed conversations as he passed them in the hallway. He'd been seen around the neighborhood with Joey Lombardo, and other times cruising the streets on his motorcycle with King himself. Because of this, people addressed him with a little more respect, almost as if they were scared of him. Girls at school seemed nervous around him. Even his teachers addressed him differently. And he basked in it all. He was becoming who he always wanted to be. A somebody. A wiseguy.

When winter break arrived, Vonni made arrangements to fly home and spend Christmas with his family in New York. He wanted to share with them the success he was having in Detroit, but of course, that wasn't an option. As far as they were concerned, he was a good kid, maintaining a solid 3.0 GPA, staying out of trouble while making a little money on the side working at a local gym. They were proud of him, and he wanted to keep it that way.

His flight to New York was scheduled for Monday morning, the day before Christmas, only two days away, but he still needed to buy some gifts for his family. So, Sunday morning, he decided to hit the mall with Tommy to do a little last-minute Christmas shopping. But first, he needed to stop at "Nicks & Cuts" for a haircut. After all, he wanted to look his best for his family. Normally, the barbershop was closed on Sundays, but because of the holiday Vonni knew Nick would be opening early for business. Wanting to beat the morning rush, he had Tommy drive him there first thing in the morning, hoping they would get there just as Nick opened up at 9:00 AM.

When they stepped inside, Nick and Vicky greeted them with warm smiles and pleasant salutations, but it seemed they weren't the only ones trying to beat the morning rush. It was only 9:05 and already an old man was seated in Nick's chair, getting a trim and shave. Since Vonni preferred Nick's barbering skills to Vicky's, he politely suggested Tommy get his hair cut first while he waited for Nick.

As Vicky went to work on Tommy's thick mane of coarse black hair, Vonni sat in one of the shop's weathered old chairs and began flipping through an issue of Sports Illustrated. But as he scanned the pages, something caught his attention from the corner of his eye. Something that didn't sit right. The front of the shop was a series of plate glass windows that of offered a clear view of the street and surrounding neighborhood. Given that it was early Sunday morning, both were deserted and devoid of activity. So when he saw the same blue minivan drive past the shop three times in less than ten minutes, he noticed it right away. But he became even more curious when the van drove past a fourth time and parked across the street, just down the block. From his angle in the barber shop, he could make out two guys sitting in the front seats, both of them scanning the streets as if they were looking for someone. He wasn't sure why, but something about them didn't feel right. They seemed out of place just parked there, the two of them looking around as a light snow began to fall. As he continued flipping through the Sports Illustrated, he found himself periodically glancing up at them, wondering who they were and what they were doing.

Twenty minutes later, after the old man paid Nick and stepped out of the shop, Vonni was climbing into Nick's chair when he noticed a tinted black Cadillac CTS pull up out front. He could just make out King Falcone in the passenger seat, casually talking on his cell phone. A moment later, King's driver, "Big Dean" Diangelo D'Annato, stepped from the car and walked into the barber shop.

"Hey, Niccolo," Dean said, acknowledging Tommy and Vonni with a curt nod. "King will be here in a minute. He's across the street getting somethin' to drink."

"Great," Nick said with one of his amiable smiles. "And will you be getting a trim today, Diangelo?"

"No," Dean replied tersely, a pained look on his face, patting his belly. "I think I got food poisoning or something. My stomach has been messin' with me all morning. Think I can use your john?"

"Of course," Nick chuckled, gesturing toward the back of the shop. "You know where it is. Just don't make a mess in there, eh?"

Dean indeed looked pale faced and sick as he headed back to the bathroom without saying a word. But Vonni barely seemed to notice, for his eyes were locked on the idling minivan. Something definitely was amiss. As Nick wrapped a smock around his shoulders, he watched King step from the Cadillac and head across the street to old man Gus' liquor store. The instant King walked through the door, the two guys in the minivan stepped out onto the sidewalk and made a beeline straight for the store, both of them moving with a distinct purpose in their step. They appeared to be older, maybe mid-thirties, and both were wearing baseball caps, leather gloves, and dark sunglasses. As they hurried up the block toward the store, they looked nervous and anxious, their heads swiveling back and forth as if they were scanning the streets for potential witnesses.

Vonni immediately recognized the intent in their stride, for it was the same stride that the two thugs had that night in the park. He didn't hesitate. The instant they stepped into the store, he tore the smock off and sprinted across the street. When he got to the door, he stepped inside with his pistol tucked against his side.

Like always, Gus was seated behind the counter, watching an old 13" black-and-white TV. He was about to wish Vonni a good morning when Vonni held a finger to his lips and motioned toward the back of the store with his gun. Confused, Gus glanced up at the parabolic mirror he used to keep an eye on would-be shoplifters. It offered a distorted view of the entire store, and when Vonni looked up at it, he saw the two guys from the minivan creeping down an aisle toward King, who was at the back of the store scanning the coolers for something cold to drink. Ducking low, he peered around the corner of the aisle and saw that they were both carrying pistols. Just as he thought—assassins! King was partially obscured by the corner of the aisle and completely oblivious to their presence.

Without hesitation, Vonni aimed his pistol and opened fire. *POP-POP-POP-POP* "King!" he yelled, pulling the trigger as fast as he could, his gun booming like thunder in the quiet store. "Look out!" *POP-POP-POP-POP-POP*

Chaos ensued. As everyone opened fire at once, the store turned into a hailstorm of gunfire. One of the assassins raised his pistol and fired at King. Vonni opened fire on him. The other assassin spun and fired at Vonni. King dove around the corner, drew his own pistol, and returned fire. In what seemed like slow motion, Vonni charged down the aisle, pulling the trigger over and over, aiming on pure instinct until his gun finally clicked empty.

Then, as fast as it began, it was over, an eerie silence falling over the store, the air filled with smoke and the acrid smell of spent gunpowder. One of the assassins was clearly dead, blood pouring from a gaping exit wound in the back of his head. But the other assassin was still alive, writhing around on the floor, clutching his throat where a bullet had smashed through his larynx, creating a sickening gurgle as he choked on his own blood. Vonni felt a wave of relief when King casually stepped into the aisle and looked down at the two assassins, his coal black eyes burning with rage. A bullet had struck his upper left arm and blood was already seeping through his gray Fila jacket.

"You okay?" King asked, calmly loading a fresh magazine into his pistol.

"You're hit," Vonni said, ignoring the question, pointing at his arm.

"It didn't hit the bone," King said, wincing as he slowly tested his arm. "At least I don't think so. What about you? You good?"

Vonni seemed to snap out of a trance. "Yeah, I think so," he said, looking himself over. "Nothing hurts."

King pointed at Vonni's pistol, which had a small tendril of smoke rising from its barrel. "You got another mag for that thing?"

"Yeah," Vonni nodded. "I always keep an extra in my sock."

"Then load up. There might be more waiting outside."

Vonni didn't think there were more assassins waiting outside, since only the two had pulled up in the minivan. Nevertheless, he listened and quickly loaded the spare magazine into the pistol.

Gus stood at the front of the aisle, his face pale with shock. "Omnio..." he mumbled, staring down at the carnage.

King pointed at the door. "Lock up and put the closed sign in the window," he ordered the old store owner, his tone calm and pragmatic. He then turned to Vonni. "Go stand by the door. Tell me if anyone pulls up."

Vonni quickly posted himself by the door and scanned the street. Nothing was moving but he could see Tommy, Nick, and Vicky looking at him through the windows of the barber shop across the street, all of them surely wondering what was happening. There was a chance that they had heard all the gunfire, but he figured they probably hadn't.

While Vonni maintained a vigilant eye on the street out front, King began speaking in rapid-fire Italian to Gus, who was still in a bewildered state of shock, unable to say a word as he stared down at the gruesome scene on the floor of his store. When King asked if there were any security tapes, all Gus could do was shake his head and mumble no. King then stepped right up to his face and looked the old man in the eye.

"Gus, you tell the cops that a pair of black teenagers did this. They robbed and shot the two men on the floor. Understand me?"

Gus nodded his understanding but said nothing. The message was very clear. He knew what he had to do.

King then kneeled down and pointed his pistol at the face of the one assassin who was still alive. "Who sent you?" he demanded. "Who do you work for?"

But when the assassin responded with only a choking gurgle, King shot him in the head and began rifling through his pockets. When he had both assassins' wallets, he stood and again looked Gus in the eye.

"Gus, you're going to be fine," he said, setting a reassuring hand on his shoulder. "Just remember what I said. Vonni and me were never here. It was a couple of young *melanzani*. That's all you saw. Now wait five minutes and call the cops. *Capisce*?"

"I understand, Omnio," Gus answered nervously, his voice trembling with fear.

With that, King beckoned Vonni to follow him out a door in the back. In the deserted alley behind the store, he pulled Vonni next to a dumpster and said something that caught Vonni completely off guard.

"You're coming with me," he said, tucking his pistol into his waistline. "I need you to get my back. If Dean reaches for his gun, or even looks like he's reaching for it, pop the motherfucker."

"What?" Vonni whispered, confused, glancing up and down the alley nervously. "Why? What did Dean do?"

King motioned toward the store. "Those were professional hitters. They must've got antsy and jumped the gun when they saw me go in the store. Dean set me up. He's the only one who knew I'd be here this morning. Fuckin' Judas! Now come on, we don't have time to stand around and bullshit. He probably still thinks the hit is supposed to go down while I get my hair cut..." He paused and looked him in the eye. "Now I need to know, Vonni, can I trust you? Because if Dean thinks I'm onto him, he might try to do me himself. And I don't want to kill that fuckin' Judas until I find out who paid him to set me up."

Vonni could barely believe what was happening. It felt surreal, like some kind of bad dream or movie. But it was real. A thousand questions flashed through his head, but he met his eyes and nodded. "Yeah, I got your back," he said, knowing he really had no choice at this point.

"Good," King said, looking relieved. "Now come on. Follow me and don't say a word. Just sit in the back of the car and keep an eye on him. If he makes any sudden moves, pop his ass in the back of the head."

Then, without adding another word, he led them around the building and back to the barber shop, both of them moving at a casual pace, making sure not to draw any attention to themselves. The street was clear and there was an eerie silence, the only sound coming from the minivan still idling by the curb down the block. But when they stepped into the barber shop, Dean was nowhere in sight.

"Where's Dean?" King asked, his fury masked under a facade of calm.

Nick motioned toward the back. "Using the john," he said, and then noticed King's bloodstained sleeve. "What happened to you?"

"Some hitters just tried to get me in Gus' store," King answered matter-of-factly, staring at the door leading to the back of the shop.

"Oh my God, baby!" Vicky exclaimed, stepping over to look at his arm. "Are you alright?"

Dean suddenly stepped out from the back and froze in his tracks. "Yo what the fuck happened to your arm?"

"Two hitters just tried to whack me across the street," King answered, his tone completely indifferent. "Now come on, we need to get the hell outta here before the cops show up." He turned to Nick and Vicky. "None of us were here. The cops are gonna come over and ask if you saw anything. Tell them you saw a couple of teenage *melanzani* run out of Gus' store about five minutes ago."

Vonni looked at Tommy, who was wide-eyed with confusion. "I'm going with King, but you stay here and back their story about the two black kids. Then go home and wait for me to call."

"Omnio, you have to go to a hospital!" Vicky pleaded.

"I will," King said, offering her a reassuring smile. "But right now we have to go."

223

With that, he motioned Dean and Vonni to follow him out to his parked Cadillac. Just as Dean put the car in gear, the sounds of distant police sirens could be heard racing toward their location.

"Where we going?" Dean asked, concentrating on driving casually through the snowy back streets, trying not to draw any unwanted attention to themselves.

"My grandpa's warehouse," King answered, and then used his cell phone to call his grandfather.

Meanwhile, Vonni sat in the car's back seat, pistol in hand, prepared to shoot Dean if he made any sudden moves. But after King hung up the phone, Dean dove into an earnest apology for not being there when the assassins showed up. King responded by patting him on the shoulder reassuringly, telling him not to worry, that it wasn't his fault.

As they sped down Jefferson Avenue toward downtown, King studied the contents of the two assassins' wallets. Each contained a few hundred dollars in Canadian cash and a Canadian driver's license that was surely counterfeit. He figured they must have been contracted from across the river in Windsor, where contract killers were often recruited when assassins with no ties to the Syndicate were needed. This was a clear indicator that whoever hired them had wanted there to be no connection to anyone in the Syndicate.

Ten minutes after leaving the barber shop, Dean turned down a deserted alleyway that ran between two long rows of warehouses in the Eastern Market. The fresh snowfall squeaked under the tires as he eased the car to a stop in front of a nondescript metal door. As they stepped from the car, a flock of pigeons burst into the air from behind a dumpster, causing the three of them to flinch nervously. Vonni immediately noted the stench of death and decay in the air, as the bay doors directly across the alley belonged to the largest slaughterhouse in the city.

King glanced up and down the alley before keying open the squeaky metal door to the warehouse. Inside was cool, dark, and smelled of fresh produce. Leaving the lights off, he led them through a labyrinth of wood pallets stacked with crates of fresh fruits and vegetables. When he came to a large, industrial-style elevator, they stepped inside and he cranked a brass hand-lever that lowered them down to the basement. When the elevator came to a jarring halt, he flipped on a light switch and a series of dim bulbs illuminated a cool dank room that was cluttered with wooden vegetable crates. Inside the crates were accounting ledgers. Thousands of them.

At the back of the basement, King keyed open the door to a spartan little office that had a concrete floor and rafter ceiling. Besides a pair of metal filing cabinets, the only furnishings in the office were a small desk, a pair of metal folding chairs in front of it, and a tattered old couch.

"Everyone sit and chill while I think for a minute," King said, gingerly taking off his jacket to examine his wound.

While Dean dropped onto the couch and lit a cigarette, Vonni remained standing with one hand inside his jacket pocket, where it remained gripped tightly around his pistol. "What is this place?" he asked, taking in the room but alert to Dean's every move.

"My grandma's office," King answered, grimacing in pain as he removed a first aid kit from one of the filing cabinets. "She balances all the sports books down here. My grandpa has over fifty bookies working for him. All those books you saw out there? That's what they were. Bets and vig. She's the Family accountant."

"Oh," Vonni said, still discreetly watching Dean's every move. "I was wondering what those were."

King said nothing more as he cleaned and bandaged his wound. Fortunately, the bullet had indeed missed the bone and made a clean pass through his upper bicep muscle. Because the hot bullet had partially cauterized the wound, there was

225

surprisingly little bleeding. Once he finished bandaging it with gauze and surgical tape, he put his track suit jacket back on and began rummaging through the office until he found a dusty old bottle of Johnny Walker Red. After taking several long swigs straight from the bottle to calm his nerves and dull the pain, he decided it was time to get down to business. Without warning, he drew his pistol and pointed it at Dean's face.

"Don't even blink, you Judas motherfucker!" he growled menacingly. "Vonni, get his gun."

"What the fuck is this?" Dean demanded as Vonni relieved him of the .357 tucked in his shoulder holster.

"You didn't think I would figure it out?" King asked icily.

Vonni tucked the big .357 in his waist and stood off to the side with his 9mm Beretta trained on him.

"Figure what out?" he asked, the look on his face a combination of confusion and outrage.

King slowly shook his head. "Paisan, do you take me for a fool?" he asked, his eyes burning with malevolence. "I've known you all my life. We went to Sunday school together. Our mothers are goomadi. Why—"

"This is bullshit, King!" Dean snapped, cutting him off. "I had nothing to do with this shit. I can't believe you'd even suggest I did. Like you said, our moms are *migliori di amici*."

King leaned against the edge of the desk and silently studied him. "You know something?" he said, taking on an almost philosophical tone. "My grandpa always tells me to be careful of the people I trust the most, because they're the ones that can hurt me the most. Now, why don't you make this easy on yourself and tell me who paid you to set me up."

Dean looked up at him like he had truly lost his mind. "Omnio, you're talking crazy! I don't know what the hell you're talking about. You should know I'd never—"

*CRACK!* King shot him in the knee, causing Vonni to flinch and nearly drop his pistol.

226

"What the fuck!" Dean wailed, a searing white-hot pain shooting through his leg. "Are you crazy? I would never set you up!"

King aimed at his other knee. "Who?" he asked calmly. "And what did they pay you?"

"Omnio, calm down," Dean pleaded, holding his hands up. "I'm sorry I wasn't there when those fuckin' hitters showed up. I get it, I fucked up! But that doesn't mean I set you up. For Christ's sake, man, think about it. Your own grandfather commissioned me to be your *protettore*. We've been like brothers ever since."

Losing his patience, King slid one of the folding chairs over and sat directly in front of him. "You must really think I'm stupid," he said, looking him deadpan in the eye. "Besides my mom, you were the only one who knew I'd be at the barbershop getting my hair cut this morning. And I'm pretty sure she didn't set me up. So that leaves you. You asked me twice yesterday if I'd be getting a cut this morning. Why would you ask me twice? Stupid. That was your first mistake. Your second was hiding in the bathroom while the hitters were supposed to show up."

"King, that's crazy! Just coincidence."

King studied him incredulously. "Then why would you ask me twice to confirm where we would be at a specific time this morning?"

"I... I don't know," Dean choked out, the throbbing pain in his knee growing more and more intense by the second. "I guess because I haven't done any Christmas shopping. I wanted to know if we were gonna have time to hit the mall today."

King considered this for a moment, nodded his understanding, and then shot him in the other knee. "Was it Anthony?" he asked, aiming the pistol at Dean's face.

Dean wailed in agony. "No, wait, King, please don't!" he pleaded, tears streaming down his face, knowing the ruse was up. "It wasn't Anthony. It was the Scroi brothers. They said you were cutting into their business."

227

King lowered the pistol, a disgusted look on his face. "How much did they pay you?" he asked, fighting to control himself.

"They... they..." Dean stammered, choking on his words, his eyes pleading for mercy. "They promised me Vanzetti's."

King reeled back and laughed maniacally. "My club? They told you they would give you my club? And you believed them?"

Dean dropped his head in shame. "I had no choice, King," he groveled pitifully, finally breaking down. "When I told them to go fuck themselves, they threatened to kill my kid brother, Mikey. He's only fuckin' twelve! What could I do?"

"Really, you fuckin' coward?" King scoffed, staring down at him with complete abhorrence. "You could have come to me. Do you really think my grandfather would have let them kill an innocent kid?"

Dean shrugged pathetically, tears of guilt streaming down his face. "I don't know. You said it yourself the don is retiring. Leoni and the others are taking over his territories. The Scrois are Made guys. They got a lot of pull with the other Bosses."

King suddenly looked more offended than disgusted. "So you're saying you fear the Scrois more than my grandfather?"

"I'm sorry, Omnio," Dean whimpered. "I had to protect my kid brother."

"And my club was just going to be an added bonus?"

"Fuck your club!" Dean yelled, spittle flying from his mouth. "I was protecting my kid brother. I'm not you. I don't have the goddamn Boss of Bosses protecting me."

"What does that have to do you and me? Haven't I always taken care of you? Haven't I always been a friend to you? Hasn't my grandfather treated you like one of his own?"

"Fuck you, King!" Dean spat defiantly. "You're a goddamn *dragoni difetto!* You'll never be Made. You'll never be a *capo* or take over the Family. I had to think about myself and my own future. What the fuck did you think? I was gonna spend the rest of my life driving you around? The others think you're just a punk ass kid who hides behind Don Falcone. But you can't hide forever. Your grandpa is being muscled out and new guys are taking over. Guys like the Scrois. They don't give a shit about you or your grandpa. They're Made guys. They were gonna kill my kid brother if I didn't help them do it."

King nodded his understanding. "Yes, well, now your little brother will never know you gave your life to save his."

Just as Dean registered the meaning this, King raised his pistol and fired one shot. The bullet struck him in the forehead, sending a geyser of blood and brains splattering onto the wall behind him.

In that instant, Vonni's life changed forever.

# CHAPTER 13

Vonni stood paralyzed. He'd almost been convinced that Dean had nothing to do with the two assassins. But King knew all along. Dean's half-hearted confession had been the equivalent of signing his own death warrant. Without even batting an eye, King killed him in cold blood. Although it was a ruthless act of violence, it gave Vonni a whole new respect for him. Such betrayal warranted nothing short of death.

"It had to be done," King said, seeing the look on Vonni's face. "You heard him. Fucker sold me out. Backstabbing Judas! He could have come to me... if he would've just told me what the Scrois were planning..." His features seemed to soften as he realized the finality of what he'd done. "Big dumb bastard. We could've hit the Scrois first."

Vonni forced himself to look away from Dean's bloody corpse. "But I heard him say they were Made. I mean, I don't know how these things work, but I thought you can't just go around killing Made guys."

"I would've gotten permission," King said confidently, setting his pistol on the desk. "Retired or not, my grandfather is still the Boss in this town. Nobody can just put a contract on me because my club is taking away too much of their business. My grandfather would've had a sit-down with the other Bosses. They'd have given us the green light to hit them fuckin' Scrois first..." He was quiet for a moment, wondering if Dean had told him everything. He knew there were others who would like to see him dead, including some members of his own family.

"Either way, it's on now! Greedy fuckers. When my grandpa hears about this, he'il want their heads. They tried to hit the wrong *difetto*."

"The other Bosses?" Vonni asked, confused. "Who are they?"

"Never mind that," King said, looking him in the eye. "Right now I want to thank you for risking your life to save mine. That means more to me than you'll ever know. You're a rare breed, Johnny New York. A true *soldato*. I told Joey you were solid and today you proved it. I'm forever in your debt."

Vonni suddenly had goose bumps and felt a great sense of pride knowing the likes of King Falcone was indebted to him. "So what now?" he asked, not knowing what else to say.

King looked down at Dean's lifeless body, blood still oozing from the gaping hole in the back of his head. "First thing we have to do is get rid of this piece of shit, and I know exactly where to do it. My grandpa's paisan owns the slaughterhouse across the alley. He turns all the animal scraps into pig feed with a giant meat grinder. Makes everything into a weird paste." He grinned conspiratorially at Vonni, and then looked down at Dean, whose eyes were wide open and staring blankly at the ceiling. "We're gonna turn the Judas fucker into some premium pig feed. They'll eat his ass and shit him out like the piece of shit he is."

King then placed two phone calls. The first one was to his grandfather, who in turn called the owner of the slaughterhouse and explained the situation. The second call was to his top lieutenant, Tony Tappio.

Thirty minutes later, Tony arrived at the warehouse with his driver, Onofrio. When they stepped into the office, Tony set a duffle bag filled with jogging suits on the desk. "Fuckin' scumbag," he growled, staring down at Dean's corpse. "You should have tortured his ass for a while before you popped him."

King stepped out into the warehouse with Tony for a private word. "My arm is starting to hurt," he admitted when they were alone. "I'm pretty sure the bullet didn't hit the bone, but it's still

231

throbbing. My grandpa has a doctor meeting me at his house. I need to go."

"Want Onofrio to drive you?"

"No," King answered, shaking his head. "I can drive myself. I need you guys to stay here and get this mess cleaned up. Don't leave a trace. Nothing, *capisce*? Use bleach and scrub everything. I want it spotless. Remember, Tony, my grandma works down here."

"And Dean?" Tony asked, nodding his understanding.

"Dominic is on his way. He knows what to do. This won't be his first rodeo."

"And the kid?" Tony asked, motioning a thumb toward the office. "You leaving him with me?"

"He's not a kid, Tony. He's the same age as me, and he saved my ass today. Give him some credit. He's one of us now, so treat him like it, eh? And yeah, I'm leaving him with you. He can help you clean up. When you're finished, bring him to my grandparents' house. I'll be there waiting."

"You want me to bring him to Don Falcone's?" Tony asked, surprised.

"Yeah, my grandpa wants to meet him."

"No shit?"

"Yeah," King said tersely, gesturing a hand toward the office. "Now get this place cleaned up. There's rags, mops, cleaning supplies in the closet upstairs. When you're done, burn everything in that old wood furnace back there. When Dominic gets here, let him take the lead. He knows what to do."

"And the Scroi brothers?"

"They'll get theirs," King said, his ebony eyes suddenly glinting with malice. "They're probably sitting by a phone right now waiting for Dean to call and confirm the hit was a success. But by tonight when he doesn't call they'll know something went wrong. When he doesn't turn up at all, they'll figure he told me who put him up to it. But don't worry, my grandpa will handle them. For now, you just get this place cleaned up and bring Vonni to my grandpa's when you're done."

Tony glanced at King's bloody arm. "You want Ono for a few days? He's solid as they come."

King considered this for a moment but shook his head. "No, Onofrio is your guy," he declined, having someone else in mind. "But send the Campisi brothers, Vitor and Luigi, to my grandpa's in a few hours. They can look after me until I find a new driver."

"Done," Tony said confidently. "Now go get that arm fixed up before you bleed to death, eh?"

King offered him a brotherly smile. "Don't worry, paisan," he said, glancing at his arm. "It'll take more than this scratch to take me out." He then gave him a hug, turned and made his exit.

Back in the office, Tony found Vonni pale-faced and staring down at Dean's lifeless body. "You alright, *amico mia*?" he asked, removing a pack of cigarettes from his pocket.

"Yeah," Vonni answered, blinking his eyes as if snapping from a trance. "Why?"

"You look a little out of it," Tony shrugged, offering him a cigarette.

"I don't smoke."

"Suit yourself," Tony said, lighting a cigarette as he stared down at Dean with a mixture of pity and disgust.

"So where did King go?" Vonni asked.

"To get his arm looked at," Tony answered, exhaling a cloud of smoke that seemed to hang in the air like some kind of apparition.

Vonni pointed at Dean. "What about him?"

"No worries, *amico*," Tony said, offering him the slightest grin. "A friend is on the way to help." He pointed at the bottle of Johnny Walker on the desk. "In the meantime, why don't you have a drink? It'll help calm your nerves."

"No thanks," Vonni politely declined, his stomach in no mood for whiskey. "My nerves are fine."

233

Fifteen long and uncomfortable minutes later, the owner of the slaughterhouse, a stoic old Greek named Dominic Katranis, stepped into the office. In one hand he carried a bucket of rags and cleaning supplies. In the other, a roll of canvas tarpaulin. He seemed unaffected by the gruesome scene on the floor, and after surveying the office for a moment he began barking out orders. First, he had them wrap Dean's body into the tarp. Then he had them carry Dean out the warehouse, across the alley, and into the back door of his slaughterhouse. The instant they stepped inside, they were met with the fetid stench of death, blood, and animal feces, causing Vonni to retch with disgust. The sight of Dean's brains and blood leaking on the floor had had little effect on him. But the putrid smell of the slaughterhouse made him gag and choke down vomit.

After stripping Dean's body naked, they slid him down a stainless steel chute that led to a series of high-speed tungsten steel blades that churned livestock carcasses into a fine paste. The massive meat grinder made little work of Dean's body. Within seconds his entire body—bones, teeth, hair and all— were churned into a paste the consistency of tomato puree. Fifty-pound bags of cornmeal and ground soybeans were then added to the mix, creating a high-protein, high-calorie pig feed. When this emulsion process was finished, the thickened paste was pumped into a pair of plastic 50-gallon drums. After the drums were capped and sealed, Dominic used a hand-dolly to deposit them into a refrigerated storage locker filled with dozens of such drums. By next week, local pig farmers would be feeding Dean to their pigs, all evidence of his existence ceasing to exist. Vonni thought it was a fitting end for a guy who sold out his own boss and lifelong friend.

After thanking Dominic for his help, Tony sent him on his way and led Vonni and Onofrio back to the warehouse to begin the daunting task of cleaning up the basement office. King had given them explicit orders to make sure the office was cleaned and sanitized thoroughly, because it was where his grandmother handled all the accounting for Don Falcone. She could never know that a brutal murder had taken place in her office. Unfortunately, King had dispatched Dean with a head shot, which had left a terrible mess. There was a huge pool of congealed blood on the floor. Brain matter and skull fragments were splattered against the wall. It was a gruesome, macabre scene, but after nearly two hours of mopping and scrubbing they were able to remove all traces of it.

The warehouse had been built in the late 1800s and was originally heated by a coal furnace in the basement. Many years ago, however, Don Falcone had converted the old furnace into an indoor barbecue grill. Grilling was one of his favorite pastimes, and the indoor grill was his pride and joy. He often got boxes of freshly cut meats from Dominic across the alley, and then barbecue all of it on his huge grill. When he was finished cooking, he'd set up a table in front of his warehouse and invite his many friends from the market over to partake in the feast. His basement barbecue pit was famous throughout the market, but today it came in handy for disposing all of the blood-soiled towels and mops. They also burned their clothes after changing into the jogging suits Tony had brought in the duffle bag.

When they finally finished, Tony slowly surveyed the office. "Look's good to me," he said, casually lighting a cigarette. "What do you think, *amico mia*?"

Vonni glanced at his watch. "I think I need to get home," he answered matter-of-factly. "I'm leaving for New York in the morning and I still have to do some Christmas shopping."

"Really?" Tony asked, exhaling a cloud of smoke. "After everything you've been through this morning you're worried about Christmas shopping?"

"Yeah," Vonni shrugged. "I ain't gonna lose no sleep over this." He glanced at the spot where Dean's body had been. "Fucker was a Judas. He got what he had coming."

"Yeah, he did," Tony agreed, taking another pull from his cigarette, narrowing his eyes on him. "You really showed your

235

stripes today, kid. I got to admit, I'm impressed. So was King. I got a feeling you're about to get a new job."

"What kind of new job?"

Tony snubbed his cigarette out in an ashtray. "Let's just say King isn't the kind of guy who will forget what you did. In fact, it's time to go. He wants me to bring you to see him right now."

"Where?"

"His grandfather's house."

"But I thought he went to get his arm looked at?"

"He did. His grandfather had a doctor meet him there. He couldn't just go to a hospital. They report all gunshot wounds to the cops, and that would've raised questions we can't have. Now let's go. I got orders to bring you straight there when we're finished. And as far as I'm concerned, we're finished."

Thirty minutes later, Tony's driver, Onofrio, turned down a long driveway that led to a sprawling Mediterranean style home with white stucco exterior and red-tiled roof on the shores of Lake Saint Clair. Parked out front, in a circular turn-around, were several luxury sedans, all of them tinted and sparkling clean. The home's five-car attached garage was open, so Onofrio pulled into a vacant space next to King's black Cadillac. Before they were even out of the car, an old woman stepped from the doorway leading into the house. She kissed Tony on his cheek and then turned to Vonni.

"Is he the one who saved Omnio?" she asked Tony in Italian, her eyes filled with tears.

"Yes," Tony answered in English. "His name is Giovanni but he likes to be called Vonni."

She stepped over and stood directly in front of Vonni. "Thank you, *bel giovanotto*," she said softly, calling him a handsome young man, gently pulling his face down to kiss his cheek.

Vonni stood rigid, not expecting such a welcome. She was a tiny woman, barely five feet tall, and smelled of garlic. The spaghetti sauce smeared on her apron told him why. From her thick accent it was obvious that she was from the Old Country. She reminded him of his own grandmother back in Brooklyn.

"You're welcome, Signora Falcone," he said in perfectly enunciated Italian.

She smiled up at him, impressed by his command of her native tongue. "So, tell me, *bambino*..." she began, but paused and studied him curiously. "They told me you aren't from around here. Why would you risk your life to save my Omnio?"

He glanced at Tony, who gave him a barely perceptible nod. "King and I are friends," he answered in Italian, if just to make her more comfortable. "Not great friends, but still friends. I'm sure he would have done the same for me."

"Yes, I'm sure he would have," she said, gesturing toward the house. "Please come inside. My husband is waiting to meet you. The doctor just left." She made the sign of the cross over her heart. "Thank the Blessed Mary, Omnio's arm is going to be fine. He just needs to rest it for a few weeks."

As she led him inside, Vonni discreetly took in his surroundings. The interior of the house was much bigger than it appeared from the outside. Its decor was a cross between modern contemporary and Old World Tuscan. The marble floors were covered with ornate woven rugs. On the walls were paintings brushed by Italian artists. The furniture was plush yet practical. But what really got Vonni's attention was the smell. Signora Falcone was obviously cooking dinner, and the heavenly ambrosia emanating from the kitchen was an instant reminder that he hadn't eaten all day.

Signora Falcone brought them to a parlor at the back of the house, where King and Don Falcone were seated on a small leather sofa. Opposite them on a matching sectional couch were three men Vonni had never seen before. But from the looks on their faces it was obvious they were discussing a serious matter when he stepped into the room.

"Dinner will be ready in a half hour," Signora Falcone announced, and then offered Vonni one last smile before retreating back to the kitchen.

King, with his bandaged arm in a sling, stood and walked over to Tony. "You and Onofio can go," he said, and then lowered his voice to a whisper so only Tony could hear. "Gather up the guys and meet me at the club in a few hours. Stay on high alert."

As Tony turned and led his bodyguard from the room, Vonni stood there motionless while everyone else stared at him like he was a stage performer who had forgotten his lines.

After seeing Tony off, King walked over and set a comforting hand on Vonni's shoulder. "Giovanni," he said, gesturing toward Don Falcone. "I'd like you to meet my grandfather."

Don Falcone stood and seemed to glide over to him with the ease of a much younger man. "Giovanni," he said in a fatherly tone, embracing him in a powerful hug. "You did my family a great service today. We are forever in your debt."

"King would have done the same for me," Vonni said bashfully, not knowing what else to say.

"Of course he would have," said Don Falcone, motioning the other three men to stand. "Giovanni, I want you to meet Omnio's uncles. They also want to thank you for what you did this morning."

These three men were not King's blood uncles, but rather uncles by marriage, having married three of his four aunts. The first two, Paul Zirello and Giocoma Toccio, were near clones of each other. Both were of average height, with thinning gray hair and amiable dispositions. They shook Vonni's hand and offered him a friendly smile. But the third man, King's Uncle Leoni Gianolla, was much more imposing and far less amiable. In his mid-forties, he was a tall brute of a man with a face like a bulldog and shoulders like an NFL lineman. As he gave Vonni a slack handshake, he did not seem impressed.

238

"Our family is grateful," Leoni said curtly, his tone lacking both conviction and sincerity.

Vonni found himself unnerved by this hulk of a man, so he simply nodded and gave him a firm handshake.

Don Falcone sauntered over to a small dry bar in the corner of the room. "I know you're too young to drink, Giovanni," he said, pouring wine into a glass, "but you've had a long day. One glass of vino won't hurt. It'll settle your nerves and prime your stomach for dinner."

King nodded his approval. "It's okay, Vonni. Relax, have a glass of wine. Everything is being handled. Give us a few more minutes here, and then you can join us for dinner. My grandfather wants to hear about what it was like growing up in New York."

He then led Vonni into an adjacent anteroom and told him to wait there while he finished speaking with his grandfather and uncles. In the anteroom were several bodyguards who barely acknowledged Vonni as he dropped into a recliner and took a sip of his wine. The anteroom was separated from the sitting room by an arched doorway some thirty feet away, and from where he was sitting he could still see King, Don Falcone, and the three uncles. He couldn't hear what they were saying, but they appeared to be engaged in a heated discussion of some kind. He assumed it had to do with what happened this morning. He wondered if they were debating on how to handle the Scroi brothers, the men who had contracted the assassins to kill King.

Sitting there in the quiet anteroom, sipping his wine while the reticent bodyguards flipped through a stack of old newspapers, Vonni began to wonder if he was somehow being tested. The don, King's uncles, none of them had even mentioned Dean or the actual events of this morning. They simply thanked him and dismissed him to the anteroom while they finished their meeting. A sudden wave of fear washed over him. Could they be discussing him? Was he a liability? Would they kill him to eliminate the only witness to Dean's murder? He was suddenly aware of the bodyguards scrutinizing him. When he glanced back in the sitting room, he saw Don Falcone was now on his feet, his face flushed with anger. Several times he jammed a finger at King's uncle Leoni, who suddenly looked nervous and submissive. In fact, all three of the uncles seemed to shrink and cower as the old don addressed them individually.

As the minutes wore on, Vonni's sense of trepidation grew exponentially. While Don Falcone paced the sitting room, controlling the conversation in rapid-fire Italian, King's uncle Leoni shot him several contemptuous looks. In fact, Leoni barely seemed to be listening to the don's haranguing. Though he was clearly trying to appear as if he was listening, it was obvious he wanted to be anywhere but there.

Eventually, Signora Falcone returned and announced that dinner was ready. And with this announcement, the meeting was officially adjourned. Don Falcone dismissed his sons-in-law and beckoned Vonni to join them in the dining room, where the don seated himself at the head of a long antique table made of hand-carved oak. King sat at his right hand, with Vonni to his left. Don Falcone poured more wine. Signora Falcone set steaming bowls of rigatoni in front of them, then scooped ladles of chunky meat sauce over each bowl. When everyone was served, she seated herself at the end of the table, opposite Don Falcone, and bowed her head to receive grace. King and Vonni immediately did the same.

Don Falcone steepled his hands together on the table and bowed his head. "Heavenly Father," he began, "we come to You this afternoon to ask for Your divine grace, that You bless us with health and protect us from our enemies. Today you sent an angel in the form of Giovanni to save my grandson from sure death. For that we are forever grateful. We thank You for our health, our friends, and most importantly our *Famiglia*. We pray that You continue to bless us with Your unwavering mercy. And lastly, we ask that You bless this wonderful meal momma has prepared for us. Let it sustain us and nourish our bodies. We pray this in the name of The Father, the Son, and the Holy Ghost. Amen!"

Everyone echoed "amen" and then turned their attention to their bowls of pasta. A dish of freshly-ground Parmesan was passed around. Liberal amounts were spooned atop each bowl. While they enjoyed Signora Falcone's delicious appetizer, Don Falcone began bantering about nothing in particular, as if today had been no different than any other. Vonni felt like he was in some kind of bizarre dream. The morning's events still hadn't fully sunken in yet, and now he was having dinner with Don Falcone, the Syndicate's Boss of Bosses. He couldn't help wondering why he was there. It seemed like a strange place to be after everything that had happened. Even stranger was their casual indifference, as if this morning's events never even taken place. But all he could do was play along and try to enjoy his pasta, which he had to admit was delicious.

After they warmed up with bowls of pasta and meat sauce, breaded steaks, grilled artichokes, and a three-bean salad were set on the table. "*Mangia!*" Eat! Signora Falcone commanded. And so they did.

The food was simple but cooked to perfection. Vonni devoured every bite with the fervor of a young man who hadn't eaten all day, which of course made Signora Falcone very happy. As he ate, Don Falcone began asking him a series of very personal questions about his family and mixed lineage. He asked if he missed New York and liked living there in Detroit. He asked about his parents and siblings. He asked what he wanted to do with his life. The don's soothing cadence was very disarming, and it wasn't long before Vonni found himself feeling totally at ease, his trepidation melting away like frost in the morning sun. Trying to maintain an air of calm composure, he answered the don's every question with the utmost confidence. That seemed to impress the don, who expressed genuine interest in everything he said.

After dinner, Signora Falcone served homemade cannoli for dessert. As they washed it down with small cups of espresso, the don leaned back in his chair and regarded Vonni inquisitively. "Giovoanni..." he began, but stopped, as if a sudden thought occurred to him. "What are you doing for Christmas?"

"Going home to Brooklyn," Vonni answered, taking a bite of his cannoli.

"Oh..." said the don, clearly disappointed. "That's too bad. I was hoping you might join us for dinner. My whole family will be here and we'd love to have you join us."

Vonni couldn't believe he was being personally invited to have Christmas dinner with Don Falcone and his family. There was no higher honor. Unfortunately, he already had plans to spend the holiday with his own family.

"I'd be honored, Don Falcone," he said respectfully. "But it would break my mother's heart if I didn't come home."

Don Falcone nodded his understanding. "Yes, of course, you must go home to see your family. In fact, I'm glad to hear you say that. Family should always come first. But after what you did this morning, I feel like you're now part of my own family. So what about New Year's? I host a small party here every year. Just immediate family. *Famiglia.* We gather to celebrate the coming of a new year." He looked at King lovingly. "And thanks to you, Giovanni, we have much to celebrate. Will you be back from New York by then?"

Vonni perked up with excitement. "Yeah, actually I will be," he said, glancing at King, who grinned and nodded his approval. "I'd be honored to celebrate the New Year with you and your family, Don Falcone."

"Great!" Don Falcone boomed, clapping his hands together triumphantly. "Then it's settled. You can pick up Omnio and bring him here early. That way, you can relax with us and watch the Rose Bowl while momma and my girls finish cooking."

242

Vonni suddenly looked embarrassed and ashamed. "Well, to be honest Don Falcone, I don't have a car."

Don Falcone looked at King. "No car?" he said, confused. "Why doesn't he have a car?"

"He's been saving for one," King answered.

The don looked at Vonni as if the notion of not owning a car was inconceivable. "Well, you need to get a car, my friend. This isn't New York. Here in Detroit, we don't have cabs and subways on every corner. You need a car in this town. But until you get one, King will just pick you up."


Later that evening, while Vonni sat in his basement playing PlayStation with his cousin Jack, he overheard his aunt tell his uncle about the robbery and double murder that took place at Gus' liquor store. She then dove into a diatribe about how the neighborhood was going downhill, and that they should start thinking about moving north to a safer suburb. Vonni shook his head at her naiveté. These things could happen anywhere. Because no matter where they went, La Cosa Nostra would be there, operating in society's shadows. The Mafia was everywhere.

Late that night as he lay in bed, Vonni recounted the day's events and again felt like it was all a strange dream. A vivid montage played over and over in his mind: The barber shop. The assassins. The terror on Gus' face. The ride to the warehouse. Dean's confession. King shooting Dean in the face. The rancid smell of the slaughterhouse. Dean's body being churned into pig feed. Don Falcone's palatial home. The looks from King's Uncle Leoni. The don's invitation to the New Year's party. It was all so surreal. He knew his life was about to change because of it.

# CHAPTER 14

Vonni's parents were happy to have him home for the holiday, and expressed how happy they were that he was staying out of trouble, but the truth was that their approval meant very little to him. Strangely, they no longer felt like family. Nor did Brooklyn feel like home. He had spent virtually his entire life growing up in Brooklyn, yet it now seemed oddly foreign. But it wasn't Brooklyn that had changed. It was him who had changed. At one time he had thought Brooklyn was the center of the universe. Now he realized it was nothing but another speck on the map.

It wasn't just Brooklyn that seemed foreign to him. His old friends also seemed different than he remembered. All they did was gossip, drink, smoke pot and play video games. They acted so adolescent and immature compared to his new friends in Detroit. He'd seen and done things they could never imagine. In Brooklyn, his old friends treated him like he was a nobody, just another half-breed "Jewtalian" *difetto* like thousands of others. But back in Detroit, his new friends treated him like he was a someone, an up-and-coming young wiseguy, a known associate of the infamous King Falcone crew. He even had a small crew of his own. People showed him respect. His old friends there in Brooklyn had no idea who he really was, who he had become. Part of him wished he could share with them his recent exploits, he knew this was out of the question. Even if he did tell them, they would never believe him anyway. Of course, there were a few up-and-coming young wiseguys there in Brooklyn who might be able to relate, but even they probably wouldn't take him seriously. Most of the New York Families naively considered the Detroit Family to be nothing more than a bunch of hoodlums, strong-arm street toughs and racketeers, which was anything but the truth. In fact, the FBI's Organized Crime Division had recently published a manifesto declaring the Detroit faction of La Cosa Nostra to be the most efficient and profitable Mafia faction in the entire country, stating: "They are so efficient because—unlike the East Coast factions who like to see their names in the papers—they operate completely sub rosa. They work very hard to make sure you never even know they're there."

Even though by his second day home he was already missing Detroit, Vonni was happy to spend some time with his mother and sister. Seeing them in person was a reminder of just how much they meant to him. His father, on the other hand, was a different story. Christmas dinner had been at his grandparent's house, and his father hadn't even bothered to show up. In fact, his father seemed to want nothing to do with any of them. It broke his mother's heart, and nothing hurt Vonni more than seeing his mother upset. It was bad enough that she was still dealing with his brother's death, which was another thing that made his homecoming bittersweet. The memory of his brother's murder still haunted him. He missed his brother dearly. Not a day went by that he didn't think about him, and being back in the neighborhood only rekindled the pain of his loss. He knew there was nothing he could do about it, that life goes on, yet for some reason he still felt compelled to ask around, to see if anyone had information about what happened to his brother. Unfortunately, just as before, nobody knew anything. Or if they did, they weren't talking. But he was not ready to give up. He would never give up. Sooner or later he would learn who killed his brother. And when he did, he would make them pay.

By his third day home, Vonni was bored with Brooklyn and anxious to get back to Detroit. Thoughts of that fateful morning in Gus' store consumed him. Did the cops know anything? If so, were he and King suspects? Were there any witnesses they didn't know about? Could Nick and Vicky be trusted? Did Gus stick to the cover story? Twice he had phoned Joey, and Joey had assured him that everything was being taken care of. But he knew Joey would never say anything potentially incriminating over the phone, an unspoken rule they strictly adhered to. So, until he returned to Detroit, all he could do was try to enjoy what little time he had left with his mother and sister. But the truth was that all he could think about was Don Falcone's impending New Year's Eve party.

Four days after returning home to Brooklyn, Vonni boarded a Northwest Airlines plane bound for Detroit. During the short flight, he quietly reflected on his new life, on how much it had changed since moving to Detroit. It seemed like a lifetime ago since he first set foot in the Motor City. He'd grown so much. More mentally than physically. He'd matured into a man. Detroit had changed him. No longer did he feel like an outcast. No longer did he lack a social identity. Detroit had helped him realize who he was destined to be. And what happened that morning in Gus' liquor store would end up being pivotal to the outcome of that destiny.

His plane arrived at Detroit's Metro Airport just before noon, and when he stepped out through the gate, he found Tommy waiting anxiously in the terminal.

"Paisan!" Tommy boomed excitedly, pulling him into a powerful hug. "Welcome home!"

Vonni found his choice of words ironic, for he did indeed feel like he was home. "Thanks, Tom. It's good to be back."

As they made their way onto I-94 from the airport, Tommy relieved Vonni's concerns by telling him that the police had no leads on what happened in Gus' store. Detectives were looking for a pair of black teenagers. It seemed King had adequately covered their tracks. Nobody but Gus, Nick and Vicky knew the truth, and they would never cooperate even if the police did suspect they were hiding something. They knew better. So did anyone else in the neighborhood who may have heard or seen something. They knew that informing on anyone tied to the Mafia could have fatal consequences.

During the ride home, Tommy also caught him up to speed on the state of their various business endeavors. Things had been going well, which Tommy confirmed by handing him his cut of the week's take—$5,300. In fact, things had been going so well that Tommy suggested they add a few more guys to their crew. The pot and steroid rackets were booming. The stolen merchandise racket was doing even better. If they wanted to keep up with demand, they would have to expand their ranks. Vonni was happy to hear this, and promised to bring it up with Joey. But in the back of his mind he could hear Tony's words: *"I have a feeling you're about to get a new job."*


The next morning, Joey summoned Vonni to Club Vanzetti's for a private meeting. Tommy drove, and when they got there they found Joey and his driver Nick waiting upstairs in the VIP lounge. Joey welcomed Vonni home with a quick handshake and then led him into the office for a private tete-a-tete, leaving Tommy and Nick to wait in the lounge.

As Vonni stepped into the office, he discreetly studied Joey. As usual, the guy was an impressive sight, with his perfect hair and tailored designer suit, looking like he'd jumped straight off the pages of a men's fashion magazine. The knot in his tie was flawless. His hair was slicked with pomade and combed to perfection. His cologne was just subtle enough to be pleasant but not overwhelming. His olive skin had a healthy tan, as if he had just returned from a vacation in the tropics. Every time Vonni saw him, he thought the guy could take a shot at modeling if his life of crime didn't work out.

"So, Vonni," Joey said, leaning back against King's heavy mahogany desk, "how was your trip home?"

"Good," Vonni answered, casually dropping onto a plush suede sofa. "Brooklyn is Brooklyn. It never changes. People are clones. Sheep."

"And your parents? "How they doing?"

"They're alright," Vonni shrugged, picturing the dead look in his mother's eyes. "My mom's still pretty broke up about my brother. And my dad ain't helpin'. He lives in Jersey with some skank half his age. It's messed up what he's putting my mom through when she needs him most."

"Yes, that is messed up, paisan," Joey agreed. "But these things happen. Hopefully your mother will find someone new and move on."

Vonni frowned. The thought of his mother with someone other than his father made the hair on the back of his neck stand up. It didn't seem natural. But this was not a subject he wanted to discuss with Joey, so he simply nodded and kept his mouth shut.

"So did Tommy handle things well while you were gone?" Joey asked, taking a seat behind the desk, looking every bit like a young executive.

"Yeah," Vonni answered, relieved by the change of subject. "He did good, actually."

"I'm glad to hear that, Vonni," Joey said, a cryptic grin on his face. "I was hoping he'd be able to handle things in your absence."

"Why?" Vonni asked, wondering why he was grinning at him like that.

"Because he's about to take over your operations."

Vonni jumped to his feet. "What's that supposed to mean?" he demanded, his face raging with anger. "Why would Tommy be taking over my operations?"

"Settle down, Giovanni," Joey chuckled, holding up a hand. "I'm about to lose you, and that leaves Tommy to take over most of your operations."

"Lose me?" Vonni asked, his anger suddenly replaced with trepidation. "Why would you lose me?"

"Relax," Joey said, gesturing for him to sit. "This is a good thing. There was a sit-down. You've been promoted. From now on you'll be working for King. He likes you. And he trusts you. He wants you more involved in what we do. But that's for him to explain. For now..." He snatched a set of car keys off the desk and tossed them to him. "He wanted me to give you these."

Vonni snatched the keys from the air. "What are these?" he asked, confused.

"Keys to your new car," Joey said matter-of-factly. "Well, not brand-new. It's a year old, but I'm sure you won't mind. Oh, and that reminds me. Don't forget to check the trunk. There's a couple new suits in there. Armani. Silk. Very nice. If they need tailoring, take them up to Van Dykes in Eastland Mall. Ask for Jimmy Smith. Tell him you work for King. He'll fix you right up."

Vonni continued to stare at the keys. "What kind of car?" he asked, wondering if this was some sort of joke.

Joey pointed at the keys. "Well, what does it say there on the key chain?"

"Cadillac?" Vonni mused, suddenly recognizing the emblem on the key chain.

"They're keys to King's CTS. He wanted you to have it. It's yours now. Beautiful car. Fully loaded. Detroit luxury at its finest. Actually, I've been thinking about getting one myself."

Vonni gave him an incredulous look. "He just wants to give me his car?"

"No," Joey answered, shaking his head. "He already gave you his car. It's a done deal. All you have to do is transfer the title at the Secretary of State. You did get your license, didn't you?"

"Sure," Vonni said, his face suddenly beaming with excitement. "I had to get one for my motorcycle." He looked down at the keys. "So no strings attached? He's just gonna give me his forty thousand dollar car?"

249

"Sure," Joey shrugged, leaning back in his chair with languid indifference. "He said it's the least he can do after what you did for him the other day. Such an act of loyalty should never go unrewarded. And there's more. From now you'll be reporting to him directly. Which is why I'm losing you."

Vonni spent a moment absorbing this. "So..." he began, and then thought of his best friend." My operations... will Tommy still be working with me?"

"Yes and no," Joey shrugged. "You'll still be in charge of your operations. You'll still get your due cut, but he'll now be reporting to me or one of my guys."

"But he's my driver."

"You don't need a driver."

"Why not?"

"Well, for starters you have a car now. And, well... I was gonna let him tell you, but your new job is going to be King's driver."

"King's new driver?" Vonni blurted, trying to grasp the magnitude of this.

"Yeah. I was going to let him tell you, but since I could see you weren't gonna let it go.... well, there's no point in keeping it from you. Congratulations, paisan. You're moving up. King really thinks highly of you. You've proven your loyalty to him and he trusts you."

"But he barely even knows me."

"He knows enough."

"But I'm still in school," Vonni said, remembering the promise he made his mother to stay in school until he graduated. "How can I be his driver if I'm still in school?"

"That's for you guys to work out. I'm just here to relay the news. King may not be a Made guy, and he may never be one, but I don't give a fuck. He's still my boss and the smartest cat I know. I trust his judgment completely. And if he trusts you to be his new *autista*, then I do, too. Shit, I've been telling him for months that you need more responsibilities."

"So when do I start?" Vonni asked, grinning.

"When he gets home from Miami. He's down there on business with his grandfather, but he'll be home by New Year's Eve. Which reminds me, he wants you to pick him up New Year's Day at noon. Don't be late. If there is one thing you'll learn from being his driver, he hates being late." He flashed him one of his trademark smiles. "Unless it's fashionable."

"He wants me to pick him up in his car?"

"It's *your* car, "Giovanni. Get it through your head. Which also reminds me, you need to come up with a good bullshit story to tell your aunt and uncle."

"Yeah, no shit," Vonni said, imagining what they were going to think when he came home with a new Cadillac. "What the hell am I going to tell them?"

Joey pondered several options for a moment. "I got it!" he finally said, snapping his fingers. "King's uncle Sal owns a used car lot up on 8 Mile. Every once in a while he raffles off a car. You know, as a promotion to bring people in. Just tell them you dropped a few bucks on a long shot. You never thought you'd actually win. I'll call King's uncle and give him a heads-up. He can print up some *fugazi* paperwork. Baddah-boom, baddah-bing, problem solved."

It was the perfect cover story, and Vonni was impressed that Joey had come up with it off the cuff so easily. But now that he had a viable story to tell his aunt and uncle, all he wanted to do was take a ride in his new car. After all, he had never owned a car, let alone a Cadillac, the American symbol of success and prestige.

"So where is it?" he asked, unable to mask his excitement.

"In the alley out back," Joey said, jerking a thumb over his shoulder. "I had Nick take her to get washed and waxed. Go take her for a spin. Send Tommy in here on your way out. I need to talk to him about filling your shoes."

Unable to contain his excitement, Vonni practically ran out the room and blurted something to Tommy about Joey wanting

251

to see him. After dashing downstairs and out the back door, he found King's gleaming black Cadillac parked in the alley. For a moment he just stared at it, appreciating its sleek beauty. He couldn't believe it was actually his. *If only my boys back in Brooklyn could see me no*w, he thought to himself as he deactivated the alarm and slid into the driver's seat.

It was a gloomy day, with gray skies and a light snow falling. But he felt anything but glum. He was riding a euphoric high he had never experienced before. He couldn't believe his good fortune. Not only did he now have a beautiful new car, but he also was about to be King Falcone's personal driver. Life was good.

Feeling like the king of the world, he spent the next two hours driving around the neighborhood, dropping by his favorite haunts, showing off his new ride. When he parked in front Mr. Q's Billiards Hall, everyone inside stared at him, obviously having expected King and Big Dean to step out, not Johnny New York. But as he continued cruising the snowy streets, he began to wonder if the rest of King's crew would accept him. Or would they resent him for how he became King's new driver? After all, they barely even knew him. As far as they were concerned, he was just "Johnny New York," the new kid in the neighborhood who had been working for Joey Lombardo the last several months. Would they trust him? Might they think he was too young or unseasoned to be King's driver? Even though King himself was very young, the rest of his crew was older, most of them in their mid-twenties. And they'd known King all their lives. Some had no doubt been hand-selected by Don Falcone himself. Vonni knew they still considered him an outsider, and he really couldn't blame them. After all, they knew very little about him. The only thing they knew was that he was a good earner for Joey, and that he had saved King's life. All he could do was hope that this was enough to earn their respect.

Vonni spent most of the next two days helping Tommy transition his new position as overseer of their various operations. Pfeifer, their pot supplier, would now deal with Tommy directly. Jose and Robby would deliver the shipments of Mexican steroids straight to Tommy. Their crew of young larcenists would now be led by Jimmy and Carlo, who would deliver their stolen goods straight to Tommy. Although Tommy would now be getting a significantly larger cut of their profits, the largest cut would still go to Vonni. But Vonni would now have to kick a significant portion of his cut up to King. This was the way it worked. Everyone had to kick up to the boss.

Vonni ushered in the New Year at Club Vanzetti's, which was packed to capacity with hundreds of New Year's Eve revelers. Everyone was dressed to impress and drinking heavily. And, as always, the VIP lounge was the party's epicenter, where beautiful young women outnumbered guys 3-to-1. Tables were covered with premium drinks and bottles of champagne. Anyone who was anyone was in the lounge. Even a few players from the Detroit Lions had shown up to usher in the new year at Club Vanzetti's. Like everyone else, they all wanted to been seen rubbing elbows with the party's hosts—a group of young wiseguys who were quickly earning a name for themselves throughout the city.

As much as Vonni was enjoying the festive ambiance, he knew he had a big day ahead of him tomorrow, so he kept his alcohol intake to a single glass of champagne. He actually preferred being sober anyway. He didn't need alcohol to feel confident. And tonight, unlike his first time at Club Vanzetti's, he felt very confident. He even found himself mingling with some of the wiseguys from other crews, laughing and joking with them like they were old friends. Though nobody outside King's innermost circle knew he was about to be King's new driver, the preferential treatment he was receiving from King's top chieftains clearly denoted he was a someone of importance. Beautiful women, some of them ten years his senior, gathered around him, flirting, hanging on his every word. Low-level wiseguys and various Syndicate associates made a point of introducing themselves. And he reveled in it all.

But there was one thing he found disconcerting. King's entire crew was there, from his top lieutenants down to his many associates, yet King himself was nowhere to be seen. Was he worried about the Scroi brothers trying another attempt on his life? Was he in hiding? Would he make a grand entrance like he'd done the night of the grand opening? Whatever the case, the party seemed incomplete without him.

In King's absence, however, there was no question who was in charge. Tony "Taps" Tappio took on the role of host and acting boss. He looked the part in this tailored three-piece suit, sitting in the lounge surrounded by people of importance. Scads of beautiful young woman flitted around him, vying for his attention. Wiseguys from all over town dropped by to shake his hand. And when someone of significant importance stopped by to pay him homage, he made a point of introducing Vonni to them, which was his way of telling them Vonni was now part of the Falcone crew. By the end of the night, there wasn't a single person in the lounge that didn't know Johnny New York was someone to remember.


The following morning, Vonni's aunt stepped into his room and tried to wake him for breakfast, but he simply rolled over and went back to sleep. Lately she'd become concerned about him, about where he went and what he did every day. She and her husband were honest, hard-working, God-fearing people. Their lives revolved around their family and they treated Vonni like he was part of it. But he had become so secretive and standoffish. Whenever they inquired about his private life, he'd become defensive. They had given him a midnight curfew, but he rarely adhered to it. He was respectful enough, and was maintaining good grades in school, but he acted like certain rules didn't apply to him. Like attending nightly dinners with the family, for example. He refused to sit and have dinner with them, which really bothered his aunt. But what really bothered her was that he seemed to have far too much money. He only worked part-time at a local gym, yet he had a brand-new motorcycle and was constantly going shopping, buying new clothes, shoes, and jewelry. Unlike other kids his age, he always wore expensive suits or a shirt and tie. It was the exact opposite of her son, Jack, who dressed like a slob and never seemed to care about his appearance. But what now had her more concerned than anything was his car. A nearly new Cadillac! When he had come home with it two days ago, she knew something was seriously wrong. He claimed to have won it in some sort of raffle, but she wasn't sure if she believed him. When she asked Jack about it, he claimed to know nothing more than she did. But of course, she knew her son wasn't a total dummy. Vonni was always buying him things. No doubt hush money. He wasn't about to bite the hand that fed him. So whenever she asked about Vonni's doings, he simply feigned ignorance.

Vonni had a feeling it was going to be an interesting day, and he wanted to be well rested, so rather than have breakfast with his surrogate family, he chose to sleep in. Eventually, around 10:00 AM, he rolled out of bed and took a quick shower. After drying off, he donned one of his new suits, sprayed on some cologne, and snapped on his coveted Patek Philippe watch. For his feet, a new pair of Ferragamo brogues. Around his neck a silk Gucci tie. For several minutes he just stared at himself in his bedroom mirror, barely able to believe he was the person looking back at him. He looked so much older than his friends back home. He felt older, too. But he did wonder if he was perhaps overdressed. After all, it was only a New Year's party. Then again, King had made a point of leaving the new suits in the trunk of his car. He must have wanted him to wear one.

On his way out the door, he grabbed the final piece of his ensemble off the coat rack—an $800 full-length wool trench coat with chinchilla collar. Looking at himself in a mirror behind the door, he had to admit he was an impressive sight. But he was so enraptured by his own reflection that he failed to notice his aunt sidle up behind him.

"Honey," she said, snapping him from his self-reverence, "where are you going all dressed up like that?"

"To a friend's," he answered, still looking at himself in the mirror. "He's having a New Year's party."

"A friend?" she asked, narrowing her eyes at him suspiciously. "And who is this friend?"

"You probably don't know him," he answered, tightening the coat's belt around his waist.

"Is he from around here?" she asked, feigning casual curiosity.

A wave of guilt washed over him when he turned and saw the look on her face. It was the look of a worried mother. And he did love her like a mother. She was very good to him and treated him like one of her own. He hated being so abstruse and always lying to her. But she would never understand who he really was.

"Yeah," he said tersely.

"Oh," she said, offering him a forced smile. "Who is he? Sometimes you're so cryptic, Giovanni."

He hesitated for a moment but didn't have the heart to lie. "King Falcone," he answered.

The look of worry and concern on her face instantly turned to that of dread, as if her deepest fears had come true. She knew exactly who King Falcone was. She had seen him in the neighborhood over the years—a big, tall, menacing Italian boy with scary dark eyes. She'd heard rumors about his family, including that his mother was crazy and his grandfather was in the Mafia. That was later confirmed when a local newspaper ran an article about how the FBI believed his grandfather was the boss of the entire Detroit mob and had knowledge about the disappearance of Jimmy Hoffa.

"Honey, I didn't know you were friends with that boy," she said, wondering how she hadn't seen this coming. "How do you know him? Jack said he dropped out of school last year."

"I met him at the gym," he lied, looking away uncomfortably. "We've been working out together. It's not like we're best friends."

She looked at him incredulously. "But you're good enough friends that he would invite you to his family New Year's party?"

"Aunt Sara, I have to go," he said, and then moved toward the door.

But she gently grabbed his arm. "Giovanni, I hope you aren't getting involved with those people. His grandfather—"

"I know who his grandfather is," he interrupted. "I love you, Aunt Sara, but don't worry about my friends. You don't know King."

"Honey..." she said, her shoulders slumping in defeat, a pleading look in her eyes. "Please don't get involved with those people. You're a good boy. You're so smart. You can be anything you want to be. But if you hang around those kinds of people you'll just end up in trouble. Or worse."

"Aunt Sara..." he began, his eyes suddenly growing cold and obdurate. "You and Uncle Mike have been good to me. And I do appreciate that. But you don't know me. I'm not who you think I am... but I am who I am."

With that, he turned and walked out the door without saying another word.


King lived with his mother in a large brick home several blocks from Vonni. But the house was nothing special. Just another Italian-style home built in the 1920s, nearly identical to dozens of others in the neighborhood. The only thing that made it stand out was its state of disrepair. The gutters were stained and sagging. The wood trimming was warped and cracked. The paint was fading and chipped. The shrubbery was a tangled, overgrown mess. The old wood porch sagged to one side and looked like it might collapse at any moment. As Vonni pulled up and parked in the driveway, he couldn't help but wonder why King Falcone, grandson of an obviously very wealthy mob boss, would live in such a squalid old house. Especially considering how much money King himself was making from his various business endeavors.

For a moment, Vonni just sat there parked in the driveway, wondering if he should knock on the door or just blow the horn. He was hoping King had heard him pull up and was on his way out. But after several minutes, when King failed to appear, he stepped up onto the rickety old porch and knocked on the door. He heard several approaching footsteps and a heavyset woman cracked the door open and gave him a puzzled look. Her frizzy dark hair was graying at the temples, and she was wearing a baggy summer dress covered in a pattern of bright flowers. He found that odd considering it was the middle of winter.

"Hello," he said politely, flashing her a smile. "I'm here to pick up King."

She examined him for a moment, only opening the door as far as the security chain would allow. "Who are you?" she asked, her words slow, almost lethargic, as if she were under the influence of some kind drug.

"My name is Giovanni," he answered, offering her another smile. "I'm supposed to be driving King to his grandparents' house."

She peered around him as if looking for someone. "Where's Diangelo? Why isn't he driving him?"

King suddenly appeared behind her. "Let him in, Mom," he said, unlatching the chain and opening the door. "Vonni is my new driver."

"Pleasure to meet you, ma'am," Vonni said, offering her a hand.

But she simply mumbled something and walked off.

"Sorry about that, bro," King said, gesturing for him to come inside. "She gets nervous around strangers. I think it's her meds." He turned and began walking up an old wooden staircase behind him. "Come on up. I need to finish getting ready. We got in late last night and I ended up oversleeping. Fuckin' storm had our flight delayed fourteen hours! That's why I wasn't at the club last night. But I heard you were there."

"Yeah, it was packed," Vonni said, following him up the creaky old stairs. "I was wondering where you were. Joey said you were in Florida, but he didn't say anything about a storm."

"Yeah, it was *pazzo*," King said, stepping into his bedroom. "The whole coast was a mess." He chuckled and looked around his messy room. "Shit, it looks like a freakin' storm hit in here! I need to get a maid. A hot Spanish one who doesn't speak English."

Vonni chuckled. "I hear Asian women really know how to clean a house, if you know what I mean?"

King flashed him a conspiratorial grin. "Well, I don't know if they can clean a house, but they sure know how to give a good massage… if you know what *I* mean?"

"Yeah, I think I do," Vonni laughed, knowing exactly what he meant.

"So how was your trip home?" King asked, buttoning up a white oxford dress shirt, his slow, labored movements indicating his arm was still tender where he'd been shot.

"It was good," Vonni answered, but his tone lacked conviction. "It was nice to see my mom and sister."

King slid a black-and-red tie under his collar. "Well, I'm happy to hear that," he said, tying a perfect Windsor knot. "But I'm glad you're back." He slipped his suit vest on and then turned to look him in the eye. "So you're cool with your new job as my driver?"

"Yeah, sure, but I wanted to talk to you about a few things," Vonni said, his nervousness almost audible.

259

"Relax, paisan," King said, offering him a disarming smile. "You don't have to do it if you don't want to. Although I'm hoping you will. You're a good man and I know I can trust you. But if you're not interested..." He shrugged. "Well, I guess I'll have to find someone else. Just think about it. You can give me your answer by the end of the day. For now, no more business. My grandpa always tells me I'm too young to worry about business. Today is a day of celebration. It's a new year, and we have much to celebrate. I have big plans for us this year."

Vonni decided he was right. Indeed they were too young to always be concerned with business. So, while King finished getting ready, he sat back and took in his surroundings. He'd always wondered what King's room might look like. Surprisingly, it wasn't much different than any other guy's room his age. On the walls were posters of bikini-clad girls, exotic sports cars, and his favorite athletes. Above his bed was a framed poster of Al Pacino in Scarface. A small wood desk was cluttered with weight-lifting magazines and a laptop computer that looked like it hadn't been used in months. A small shelving unit displayed several baseball trophies. A bulletin board had a couple dozen pictures of friends and girls tacked to it. A dresser was covered with colognes, hair products, and lotions. A boom-box on a night stand was playing Tupac's "All Eyez On Me." Clothes were strewn haphazardly on the floor. A fat scruffy cat was sleeping lazily under an old heat radiator. Except for the fact that the closet was filled with designer suits and Italian leather shoes, the room was no different than any other eighteen year-old's room.

"So how are you liking the car?" King asked, examining himself in the dresser mirror.

"I love it!" Vonni blurted enthusiastically. "But I can't believe you just gave it to me.... I mean, don't get me wrong, I ain't complaining. I just wasn't expecting it."

"I'm glad you like it," King said, slipping on his suit jacket. "It was my grandpa's idea to give it you, so I guess you have him to thank. He told me it was the least I could do after what you did for me the other day."

"Can I ask you somethin'?" Vonni said, studying him. "Why do you want me to be your new driver?"

"Because I trust you," King said matter-of-factly.

"But I'm still in school," Vonni said, looking torn. "And I promised my mom I'd finish out the year."

"Relax, paisan," King said, setting a hand on his shoulder. "I told you, no more business until later. Everything will be fine. After today all your questions will be answered. Now come on, let's roll. My grandma makes a feast for New Year's and I'm starving."

# CHAPTER 15

As Vonni drove, King began talking about how much money he stood to make off the various New Year's Day bowl games, but Vonni was barely listening. He was too distracted by his surroundings. He'd often heard people speak of the affluent suburb of Grosse Pointe, but this was only his second time seeing it for himself. The first time had been after the incident in Gus' store, when he'd still been in a semi-state of shock. Now that he was able to actually take it all in with a clear head, he found himself awed by what he was looking at. As far as the eye could see, Lake Shore Drive was lined with huge mansions. One after another they seemed to go on for miles. Many were still were illuminated by elaborate displays of Christmas lights. There were entire nativity scenes, Santas and reindeer, even a thirty-foot tall giant snowman. Some were intricately detailed, made of hundreds of thousands of tiny twinkling lights. He had never seen anything like it, and he was having a hard time keeping an eye on the road as he drove.

Ten minutes after leaving King's house, Vonni pulled through the wrought iron gates that marked the entrance to Don Falcone's waterfront estate. As he approached the grand home from the long driveway, he quickly became unnerved by what he saw. The don had said the party would be "an intimate gathering of just immediate family." Vonni anticipated maybe ten, twelve people at the most. But apparently he had misjudged the size of the don's immediate family, for the entire driveway was lined with parked cars. Nearly two dozen of them!

King directed him to park in front of the garage, where a group of little kids were playing in the snow, all of them bundled up in mittens and winter parkas. Four little girls were working on a snowman while five little boys bombarded them with snowballs.

"My cousins," King said, gesturing toward the tiny snow warriors. "Hope you like kids, because we're about to get bum-rushed. For some reason, they always follow me around like I'm the friggin' Pied Piper."

"I didn't realize there'd be so many people here," Vonni said, staring at all the parked cars.

"Relax," King chuckled, setting a comforting hand on his shoulder. "You're my personal guest. Have fun. Enjoy yourself. Eat. I'm the oldest grandson so I got to pick the meal. Ever have spiedini?"

Vonni raised an eyebrow. "You're joking, right? It's one of my favorites."

"Mine, too!" King said excitedly. "Now come on, I'm starving."

The instant they stepped from the car, the troop of young boys stopped tormenting the girls, cried out King's name, and began bombarding him with snowballs.

"You'll never take me alive!" King yelled, playfully lobbing snowballs back at them.

A tiny little girl cloaked in a hooded pink parka charged up to him and wrapped her arms around his legs. "Omnio, will you dance with me?" she asked, adoring doe eyes staring up at him.

"Of course I will dance with you, *bella mia*," he said, kneeling down to kiss her. "You can get the first dance."

She shrieked gleefully and began jumping up and down, clapping her hands with felicity. But before he could say anything else, a particularly tough-looking little dark-haired boy hurled a snowball at him and yelled, "Get Omnio!"

Dodging a barrage of snowballs, King led Vonni through the front door and into a marble foyer. The instant they shut the door behind them, the mirthful shrills of little kids were replaced by the melodic sounds of Italian mandolin music coming from somewhere deep within the house. After wiping the snow from their shoes, they hung up their coats in a coatroom and made their way to the kitchen, where Signora Falcone and three of her four daughters were putting the finishing touches on dinner.

King's grandmother greeted him with a loving kiss and hug. His three aunts immediately did the same. But just as he was about to introduce Vonni, his Aunt Grace stepped into the kitchen and lit up with excitement. Not only was she King's favorite aunt, but she was also the don's only daughter who had married outside the Family. Usually daughters of a *capo* were expected to marry high-ranking Mafiosi from within the *borgata*, or "community," a strategic maneuver used to strengthen the Syndicate as a whole and thwart outsiders from infiltrating the Family. All but one of the don's daughters had done so. Only King's Aunt Grace had chosen to marry outside the community. After her only brother, King's father, was murdered the year he was born, she wanted nothing to do with the family business—or anyone even remotely tied to it. That was why she ended up marrying a Swedish lab technician who had no ties to the Syndicate. King shared a special bond with her. Not just because she was exceptionally kind and loving toward him, or because she had often looked after him when his mother was sick, but because she had been ostracized by much of her family for not marrying an Italian man from their community. He knew what it felt like to be ostracized by family for reasons beyond his control, and because of it he had a special place in his heart for her.

"There you are, baby," she said, giving him a hug and kiss. "Where have you been? I was beginning to worry about you."

"Happy New Year, Aunt Grace," King said, leaning down to kiss her lovingly. "I overslept. Grandpa and I didn't get in till late last night."

"Oh, yes, the storm," she said, and then stepped over to Vonni and introduced herself with a kiss on his cheek. "And you must be the boy from New York?"

Vonni smiled down at her. Like all of Don Falcone's daughters, she was short—barely five feet, and curvaceous like most Italian women. She was a pretty woman for her age, which he estimated to be mid-forties. He figured she had probably been quite beautiful in her youth. Even now she was still very attractive, and there was no doubt that she was a thoroughbred Falcone, for her irises were black as onyx.

"Pleasure to meet you, ma'am," he said politely.

"The pleasure is all mine," she said, and then seemed to examine him for a moment. "Wow, you boys look so handsome in your suits."

"Why thank you, m' lady," King said with an exaggerated British accent, trying to sound knightly and chivalrous. "And you're looking beautiful as always."

She rolled her eyes and actually seemed to blush. "Oh, Omnio, always the charmer. Your father was exactly the same at your age." She turned and looked at her mother, who was standing by the stove, stirring a huge pot of pasta sauce. "*Madre*, are we ready to eat? Because these boys look hungry."

Signora Falcone opened the oven and studied its contents for a moment. "Ten minutes," she answered in Italian. "Go tell Poppa to start bringing everyone to the dining room."

King's Aunt Grace flashed him a motherly smile. "Honey, would you be a sweetheart and round up the babies? And while you're at it, tell Nonno that dinner is just about ready."

There were children of all ages running around the house. Some in their teens, others mere toddlers. They seemed to be everywhere. But no matter how old they were, they all greeted King with excited hugs and kisses. Of course he was equally excited to see them, but since he hadn't eaten all day he wasted no time herding them into a huge dining room. Once all the young children were gathered in the dining room, he set off to find his grandfather, who he found with the rest of the men in the home's expansive formal living room. All of his uncles and adult cousins were lounging around, smoking cigars, drinking wine, laughing and joking, clearly in a festive mood.

"Look what the cat dragged in!" Don Falcone boomed, stepping over to embrace him. "We were starting to worry about you, Omnio. It's not like you to be late."

"I overslept, grandpa," King admitted, kissing his beloved grandfather the cheek. "But don't blame me, blame Mother Nature and her little thunderstorm."

As nearly a dozen of King's uncles, great uncles, and cousins welcomed him with enthusiastic hugs and kisses, Vonni stood off to the side, feeling awkward and out of place. A few of them introduced themselves, but from the looks on their faces they were clearly wondering who he was and what he was doing there. Some of them almost looked offended that King would bring an outsider to such an intimate family gathering. Especially the hulking Leoni, who looked at him like he was a parasite.

"So you boys ready to eat?" Don Falcone asked. "Momma should be about ready for us."

"Actually, she is," King said, gesturing toward Vonni. "We just rounded up the rug rats. They're waiting in the dining room, which is where we need to be. Because I'm starving!"

Don Falcone chuckled. "Well, Momma made your favorite. Don't you ever get tired of spiedini?"

"Nope," King said, grinning.

"Me neither," Don Falcone chuckled, and then turned to address the rest of the room. "Gentlemen, to the dining room. Momma says it is time."

The dining room was a sprawling expanse of open space that resembled a small banquet hall. There was an impressive seven-tiered crystal chandelier hanging from a cathedral-style ceiling. In the center of the room were a pair of massive, authentic Victorian era dining tables—one for the grandchildren, the other for the adults—that were draped in fine linen and set with sterling silver utensils, fine porcelain dinnerware, crystal glasses, and embroidered napkins. On the center of each table were beautiful centerpieces made of fresh flowers and an effigy of the Virgin Mary.

At almost eighteen years old, King could have chosen to sit with the adults. But he chose instead to sit with his younger cousins, whom he found to be far more entertaining. Much to the chagrin of his cousin Anthony, King was the eldest grandson, which naturally afforded him the seat at the head of the table. Vonni, being his personal guest, was given a seat to his immediate left. But as Vonni seated himself, he noticed how the adult's table had some sort of unspoken seating arrangement. Yet for the life of him he couldn't figure out what dictated the order. It definitely wasn't age, because to the don's immediate right was his second youngest daughter, Patricia, and her husband, the bullish Leoni. If the order were indeed dictated by age, these seats of distinction would have been given to the don's eldest daughter, Grace, and her husband George.

The seating order at the children's table, however, was indeed chronological. To King's right was his cousin Frankie, who was only a few months his junior. Seated next to Frankie was Anthony, who was younger by only a month. Then there was Dino, who was a year younger than Anthony. Then Vincenzo, Bruno, Big Paulie, Vito, Billy, Salvatore, Peter, Johnny, Georgio, Little Paulie, and finally Joey Jr., who was the youngest grandson at age 4. But no matter how old they were, they all had one thing in common: except for King, they were all sons of Don Falcone's four daughters. Directly across from them, beginning at Vonni's right, were all of King's female cousins, starting with the eldest, Pamela, who was 15, down to the youngest, Gina, who was about to turn 3.

As everyone found their respective seats and waited for dinner to be served, the room became incredibly loud and chaotic. It seemed everyone was talking at once. The children were especially loud, yelling back and forth, with little boys harassing the little girls, kicking and pinching them under the table. But the adults weren't much better, chattering away boisterously in Italian, the men arguing over who was going to win the Rose Bowl, the women boasting about the extravagant gifts their husbands had lavished them with for Christmas. Taking it all in, Vonni felt like he had been transported into a scene from The Godfather. The beautiful mansion. The Italian mandolin music playing in the background. The smells of authentic, home-cooked Italian food. The handsome little children in their suits and dresses. The enigmatic old don surrounded by his adoring family. It was surreal, and it made Vonni feel honored to be there.

Once everyone was finally seated and settled in, Signora Falcone and her daughters began serving the standard Sicilian appetizer of pasta and meat sauce. Vonni found it amusing how the room, which had been so chaotic only seconds ago, almost instantly came to order once the food was served. Even the kids stopped horse playing. But the room fell completely silent when Don Falcone bowed his head and began a prayer. Not even the youngest babies dared make a sound while the family patriarch communed with God. Vonni did, however, happen to look up and notice how several of King's male cousins, particularly three of the original *Quattro Duchi*, were staring at him with a combination of curiosity and contempt.

When the don finally concluded his prayer, he made the sign of the cross, spread his hands wide, and commanded everyone to *"Mangia!"* Eat! Once again the room erupted into chaos as everyone began devouring their bowls of pasta and meat sauce. As the adults ate, they poured glasses of wine and engaged in idle chitchat, prattling about everything from politics to sports while maintaining a semblance of order and table manners. The children, on the other hand, ate with little regard for table etiquette, laughing and joking, talking with their mouths full, burping and horse playing without recourse.

Meanwhile, Vonni ate in silence. His father had come from a much smaller Italian family, and they never gathered as a family unit like this clan of stentorian Sicilians, so this was all new to him. Everyone was talking at once, many of them with their mouths full. But their lack of table etiquette came as no surprise. He knew from his own family that table manners were not a prescribed part of Italian social convention. Some of the men sounded almost animalistic as they wolfed down their food. Little boys burped and slurped their glasses of soda. A few of the children were hurling verbal jabs back and forth, but there was no shortage of jestful parlance at the adult table either. Many of the men were goading and "ball busting" like young fraternity brothers. Vonni found it all to be quite entertaining.

When everyone finished their bowls of pasta, the women cleared the tables to make room for sterling silver platters piled high with fried eggplant, grilled artichokes, and steamed asparagus. But these were merely side dishes. The main entrees were fried squid, baked lasagna, meatballs, sausage, breaded steaks and, of course King's favorite, spiedini—breaded veal cutlets wrapped around a mélange of thinly-sliced parmesan cheese, prosciutto ham, salami, onion, black olives, and provolone cheese—skewered and grilled over an open flame.

Like King, Vonni loved spiedini. Even though it was expensive and time-consuming to make, his grandmother had made it from time to time on special occasions. So he had no reservations as he now piled several of them on his plate, adding a few artichokes, sausage and meatballs. As he began savoring every delicious bite, he listened to the various conversations taking place all around him. King was talking to his cousin Vincent, who was asking about the big storm in Florida. Several of the teenage girls were chatting about cheerleading and boys. A couple of the young boys were talking about a new video game. And of course, the teenage boys were talking about football.

Vonni did add a few words when spoken to, but he still felt awkward and out of place. Dining with such a large group of strangers just felt odd. Especially considering how he and King weren't even close friends. And there was something else. Maybe it was his imagination, but there seemed to be a certain tension in the air between King and several of his cousins. It wasn't that noticeable, but Vonni was very perceptive. Some of them, particularly the brothers Anthony and Dino, seemed frigid, even curt with King, barely even acknowledging him. Their distaste for Vonni was also obvious from how they looked at him. Yet some of King's other cousins were quite friendly with him, even goading him about the Lions' recent victory over the New York Jets.

Dessert was a collection of tiramisu, cannoli, biscotti, and bowls of fresh fruit smothered in homemade cream. Glasses of milk were poured at the children's table, while espresso and more wine were poured at the adult table. Eventually, after everyone ate their fill, the party began to disperse, the children down to the basement game room, the men to the main living room to smoke after-dinner cigars, leaving the women to clean up the aftermath. But King and Vonni lingered in the dining room, too stuffed to move.

"You eat enough, paisan?" King asked, rubbing his belly, grinning as he watched two of his little cousins fight over the last cannoli.

"I'm frickin' stuffed!" Vonni declared, leaning back in his chair, also rubbing his own belly as he stifled a belch with a fist over his mouth. "Your grandma can cook! Wish my Aunt Sara could cook like that."

"Probably a good thing she can't. You'd be fatter than my cousin Georgio."

"Good point. With the way I like to eat, I'd end up looking like Dom DeLuise. Although, would that really be so bad? I mean, in some cultures fat is a symbol of success."

King chuckled. "I've read that," he said, trying to sound scholarly. "Maybe we should have my grandma bring us out another plate of cannoli? I mean, we do want to look successful, don't we?"

Vonni raised an eyebrow. "I might puke if I take another bite."

King flashed him a grin. "At least you'd have room for more cannoli."

"True," Vonni nodded, watching the two little boys agree to split the last cannoli.

The little girl from outside suddenly scampered up to King and grabbed his hand. "Omnio!" she shrieked, trying to yank him from his chair. "Come downstairs and dance with me!"

"Dance with you?" he said, snatching her up onto his lap, tickling her while he kissed her face. "I'd rather just kiss your little face!"

"Stop!" she shrilled, giggling, trying to wriggle from his grip. "Come dance with me! You promised!"

"I'll be down in a minute," he assured her, gently setting her down. "You just go get your feet warmed up and I'll be right down."

"Now!" she demanded, tugging at his hand, her face twisted into a pouty frown.

Another pair of little boys suddenly appeared in the doorway, both of them brandishing dart guns. "You can't catch us, Omnio!" they taunted, and then unleashed a rapid-fire salvo of foam darts at him.

*"That's it!"* King roared in mock anger, jumping to his feet. "You want to go to war? I'll take you to war!" He beat on his chest like King Kong. "It's time to unleash the whipper-snapper!"

Vonni howled with laughter as chaos ensued. He had no idea what the "whipper-snapper" was, but the mere mention of it evoked terror in every little kid in the room, sending them screaming and running for their lives. It was one of the funniest things he'd ever seen.

"What's the whipper-snapper?" Vonni asked, his stomach hurting from laughter.

King grinned and made a fist, leaving only his middle finger dangling freely. "This is the whipper-snapper, foo!" he said, then snapped his limp middle finger off Vonni's forehead, sounding a loud *thwack.*

"*Minchia…*" Vonni said, rubbing his forehead. "What kind of bullshit was THAT? I ain't scared of no whipper-snapper!" He then fired a stiff jab into King's thigh.

"Arrrrrh, *cornuto!*" King growled, rubbing his leg. "You bastard! Right on the bone."

"Yeah, well, you started it," Vonni said, rubbing the tender red spot on his forehead.

"That's what I like about you, Johnny New York," King said, grinning. "You don't take no shit. Not from no one. Not even from me."

"Yeah, well, why would I? Where I come from, if you take shit from people they'll walk right over you."

"I understand completely," King nodded. "It's the same here." He glanced around the empty room. "Although, nobody gives me no shit these days. They know better. Now come on, let's go terrorize my little cousins."

The basement included a media center, theater room, and a gaming room complete with arcade games, pinball, air hockey, darts, foosball, and a competition-size billiards table. Scattered around the sprawling basement were most of King's younger cousins. Several little boys were hurling small square beanbags at each other, all while blurting obscenities in Italian. A group of little girls were playing with a massive Barbie dollhouse. Over in the theater room, the teenage girls were watching their brothers play Madden Football on a huge projection-screen television.

Dance music was blaring from recessed surround sound, and several little girls immediately charged up to King, demanding he dance with them, which he was more than happy to oblige. Gathering up a few more of his little cousins, he dove

272

right into a personalized rendition of the "Hustle." Since Vonni wasn't much of a dancer, he stepped over to the basement's bar and took a seat on a stool, intrigued by this carefree side of King, which he'd never seen before. Surrounded by his fawning young cousins, King now seemed completely at ease. He obviously adored his family.

But there was one thing Vonni found peculiar. The *Quattro Duchi*. They ignored King like he wasn't even there. Yet King didn't seem to notice their lack of interest. He was having too much fun entertaining his younger cousins, all of them giggling and mimicking his every move. In fact, they were having so much fun that even the little boys decided to join in, all of them giggling and dancing and having the time of their lives. Indeed, King looked like the Pied Piper.

Vonni was so captivated by what he was watching that he flinched when someone tapped him on the shoulder from behind. Startled, he turned around and found himself face-to-face with King's cousin Pamela. He'd noticed her over dinner and thought she was quite cute. Even beautiful. She had a heart-shaped face, short dark hair, and hazel eyes. Her black dress displayed just enough curves to indicate she was physically a full-grown woman, but he knew she couldn't be more than fifteen or sixteen. Too young for the impure thoughts she evoked in his mind, yet from the way she had her chest thrust out at him he wasn't the only one having impure thoughts.

"Who are you?" she asked, studying him with curiosity.

"Vonni," he answered, fighting the urge to look down her dress. "I'm a friend of King's."

"Oh, you're the one from New York," she said, picking up on his accent. "I heard about you."

"You heard about me?" he asked, surprised. "From who?"

"My brothers," she answered, casting a barely perceptible glance toward the media room, where her brothers were sitting.

"And who are your brothers?" he asked, suspecting he already knew the answer.

273

"Anthony and Dino," she said matter-of-factly, confirming his suspicions.

He knew Anthony and Dino had some kind of ongoing feud with King. He hadn't forgotten the morning in the warehouse, when King had asked Dean at gunpoint if Anthony had been the one who sent the assassins. It was no wonder they barely acknowledged each other.

"So what did your brothers say about me?" he asked, still making sure his eyes never dropped below her chin.

She took a seat on the stool next to him and propped herself up on the bar. "They said you saved Omnio's life. Something about you walked in a store when some black kids were trying to rob him. Is that true? Did you save Omnio?"

King suddenly broke away from his dance troupe and stepped over to the bar, sweating and out of breath. "Pamela!" he said, kissing her on the cheek. "You're not bothering my guest, are you?"

"No," she said, blushing. "I was just wondering who he was."

King grabbed a bottle of water from the refrigerator and took a long drink. "I know she's beautiful, paisan," he said, narrowing his eyes on Vonni. "But she's only fourteen so you can put your eyes back in your head."

"I'm fifteen!" she blurted before Vonni could answer.

"Oh, forgive me, Pamela," King chuckled. "I didn't realize you're a woman now. You're growing up so fast. It seems like yesterday you over there playing in the Barbie playhouse. Now look at you, a beautiful young woman." His eyes suddenly became hard and slightly threatening. "But don't let me find out you're talking to any boys. I'd hate to have to pay them a visit." He grinned and set a hand on Vonni's shoulder. "But hey, maybe in a few years when I let you start dating, Vonni here can take you out to dinner? He's a standup guy, as good as they come."

"When you let me start dating?" she scoffed, looking amused, ignoring his remark about Vonni. "Get in line, cousin.

274

You forget about my dad and brothers? If they have it their way, I'll join a convent and be a nun."

"A nun, eh?" King said, scratching his chin. "That's actually not a bad idea."

She punched him playfully on the arm. "Real funny, jerkoff," she said, then jumped off her stool and smiled at Vonni coquettishly. "But I'd go to dinner with your friend here anytime. He's a cutie." With that, she turned and strode from the room. But knowing she had Vonni's attention, she flashed him one last smile and purposely swayed her hips teasingly as she climbed the basement stairs.

"What?" Vonni asked, feeling King's eyes on him. "I would never..."

King shook his head, clearly amused. "Look at you, paisan! You're turning red! Relax, I can't fault you for looking. She's beautiful. But she wasn't joking about her dad and brothers. She's the only girl in her family and they protect her virtue like it's the Crown Jewels. I feel bad for any guy she brings home. Believe me, that kid is gonna have it rough."

"Well it won't be me," Vonni assured him. "I got enough problems."

"Don't we all, paisan," King said, the countenance of his face suddenly pensive and serious, as if something was weighing heavily on his mind. "Oh, that reminds me, my grandpa wants to talk to you. In private."

"Me?" Vonni asked, both surprised and confused. "About what?"

"Oh, I'll let him tell you," King answered, nodding toward the stairs. "Come on."

"Now?"

"Yes, now. And we have to sneak out of here without my little cousins seeing us."

But their attempt to sneak out of the basement was futile. The instant they made a move for the stairs, a gaggle of boisterous young dancers charged up to King and pleaded for

275

him to stay and dance more. They were only slightly appeased when he promised he would be right back.

Upstairs, as Vonni followed King through the sprawling mansion, he suddenly found himself sweating under his suit. What could the don want with him? Was he in some sort of trouble? Had he done something wrong? Had he accidently offended someone? These questions were flashing through his mind when they came to the main living room, where they found Don Falcone and the rest of the men smoking cigars and sipping wine while waiting for the Rose Bowl to kickoff.

"Grandpa, can I have a word with you?" King asked from the doorway.

Don Falcone stood and handed Leoni a ledger and a cellular phone that was attached to a binary scrambler. "Leo, take the book. Any more than five dimes on either side of the spread, call Vegas. Deadline is kickoff."

The don then led King and Vonni to his private den, which King referred to as "The Oval Office." Inside, the don quickly locked the door behind him and motioned to a polished leather sofa. "Take a seat, boys," he said, removing a crystal tumbler and decanter from a small dry bar against the wall. "I need a drink."

As the don poured himself a glass of grappa, Vonni sat on the couch and took in the impressive room. Surely by design, there were no windows. This was probably where the don hosted his most private meetings; no windows rendered FBI laser listening devices completely useless. The mahogany walls were lined with shelves that were packed with hundreds of books. The matching hardwood floor was covered with an intricately woven Persian rug. A full-body mount of a huge grizzly bear stood menacingly in one corner. There were several framed pieces of art, including a beautiful oil portrait of the Virgin Marry cuddling Baby Jesus. On the mantle above a stone fireplace were several framed photos of the don posing with various politicians, celebrities and social luminaries, including

276

Jimmy Hoffa, Joe DiMaggio, Frank Sinatra, Tommy Hearns, Sparky Anderson, Al Kaline, Mike Illitch, and even Lee Iacocca. There were even pictures of him with several local judges. In one picture he was deep-sea fishing with a senator from Florida. But the room's centerpiece was an ornate oak desk that resembled William Evenden's famed Resolute Desk in the White House. It was no wonder King had referred to the room as "The Oval Office."

"Did you have enough to eat, Giovanni?" Don Falcone asked, taking a sip of his beloved Italian brandy, dropping into the plush leather chair behind the massive desk.

"Probably too much," Vonni said, rubbing his belly. "The food was delicious. Almost as good as my own grandmother's."

Don Falcone emitted a soft rumbling chuckle. "I won't tell Momma you said that. She'd never feed you again."

"Well, to be honest, her cooking was really better than my grandma's," Vonni admitted. "I just feel disloyal saying it. But that meal was probably the best I've ever eaten. You can tell her I said that."

"Tell her yourself, my friend," Don Falcone said with another rumbling chortle. "She'd love to hear it. But if you do, be prepared to have dinner with us often. She'll insist you come over every Sunday with Omnio for dinner. Cooking is one of her gifts. Hell, it's one of the reasons I married her. She's a smart woman. She knows the way to a man's heart is through his stomach." He held up his forearm and made a fist to represent an erect phallus. "A man can't perform unless he's well fed. Trust me, I know. I've had five children."

"I'll keep that in mind when I start looking for a wife," Vonni said, glancing at King, who didn't try to mask his amusement with this whole exchange.

Don Falcone turned to King and his eyes became serious. "Omnio, I think it's time we get to business. There's four more games this afternoon and I have to balance the books for Vegas before each one..."

He drained his drink and turned his eyes on Vonni. "Giovanni, I want to ask you a serious question. And I need you to really think about it before you answer..." He paused for effect. "...If you were the leader of, oh, let's say a big company, a corporation, for example, do you think it would be better to be loved by your employees or feared by them? Take your time. Think about your answer."

Vonni knew he was being tested. He glanced at King, who was studying him with the same focused intent as his grandfather. Loved or feared? Which was better? It was a tough choice but it only took him a moment to choose.

"Loved."

"Why not feared?" Don Falcone asked, his earnest expression unwavering.

Vonni shrugged. "Because if people love you, they'll work hard to please you. They'll trust you. And they'll be loyal to you. But if they fear you, they might eventually turn on you."

"Very good," said Don Falcone, relaxing back into his chair. "That's what I hoped you'd say. Indeed it is better to be loved than feared. Fear breeds resentment, but love breeds loyalty. And loyalty is a rare thing these days. Which brings me to why you're here, Giovanni." He cleared his throat and leaned up onto his desk, his ebony eyes boring into him. "Are you familiar with the word *Omerta*?"

"Isn't it a vow of silence?" Vonni answered, almost sheepishly.

"It is," the don answered, nodding pensively. "But it's much more than just that, paisan. *Omerta* is a word that dates back over two thousand years. Its origins are ancient Latin, and it was first used in reference to an oath taken by Greek Sicyons who first colonized Sicily, nearly eight-hundred years before the birth of Christ. Back then, the island was governed by a feudal system of powerful landlords known as *sovrano de omnio*. Which means sovereign lord and is where Omnio derives his name from. Each *omnio* controlled their own territory. Some territories were bigger than others, but each territory was divided into dukedoms, which were overseen by the *omnio's titolare duchi*, his appointed dukes. The *omniosi* leased their lands to the people—their *abitante locatori,* who farmed it, raised livestock on it, hunted it, fished, whatever. But all adult men were sworn to their *omnio*, who could call them to arms at any time. They were sort of like his personal army. His muscle. They were bound to him by the blood oath of *Omerta*. You see, Giovanni, the *omniosi* worked for the betterment of all who lived on their lands. They protected the weak, the old, the infirm. They fed the poor and settled disputes between neighbors. They portioned out food, crops, and livestock during lean times. The *omnio* was a form of local king, sure, but he treated his *locatari* with love and respect. In return, they were loyal and loved him. It was very symbiotic. If a husband died, the *omnio* would take care of the widowed wife and children until she remarried, even if it meant taking care of them the rest of their lives. The *duchi* and *locatari* who were loyal to their *omnio* received protection from invaders, from thieves, from bandits, even neighboring *omniosi* who might try to sell them into slavery or annex their villages into their own territories. Omniosi treated all of their *locatari* like they were members of his own family, but they were also notoriously ruthless when betrayed. If a *duca* or *locatario* ever broke his vow of *Omerta*, him and every male in his family would be dragged into the village square and murdered in cold blood, in front of everyone. Fathers, sons, grandfathers, uncles, cousins, they'd all be killed to ensure against a blood vendetta. Even young children. And the women that were left over were sold into slavery to neighboring *omniosi*. But with loyalty, a *locatario* could eventually earn the right to own the land he lived on. And on rare occasions, the most faithful *locatario* could eventually be made a *titolare duchi* and given his own dukedom."

The don paused and lit a cigar. "But these were tough times for Sicily," he continued, as if narrating an epic saga. "Because of its location in the middle of the Mediterranean, everyone wanted to make it their own personal trading post. First came the Romans, then the Byzantines, the Arabs, the Normans. They pillaged the land with their armies, raping women, taxing the poor, slaughtering anyone who defied them. Eventually, the *omniosi* banned together and formed militias, small guerilla units that would attack outposts and patrols belonging to the invaders. They would ambush their supply trains, sabotage their ships, steal their trade goods. As I'm sure you can imagine, this infuriated the invaders. They would put bounties on the *omniosi* and try to hunt them down. *Omniosi* often had to flee into the mountains with their most trusted *duchi,* hiding for months, even years. Their only ties to their families were through their faithful *locatori*, the men and women who lived on their lands. But sometimes when the invaders suspected certain *locatori* were helping their omnio and his *duchi*, they'd torture and even threaten to kill them if they didn't give up the whereabouts of the *omnio*. But do you know what those *locatori* would do, Giovanni?"

"No, Don Falcone," Vonni said, fascinated by all of this. "What did they do?"

"They'd tell their captors to go ahead and kill them," the don answered, leaning back in his chair, slowly taking a long pull from his cigar. "They would rather die than break *Omerta*. This, Giovanni, is the power of *Omerta*. This is how *Cosa Nostra* began over two-thousand years ago. Today the rest of the world knows it as the Mafia, but it started as nothing more than a few Sicilian peasants fighting to free themselves from persecution by foreign invaders. And do you know where the word Mafia comes from?"

"I don't," Vonni admitted.

Don Falcone stubbed out his cigar in an ashtray. "I want you to know something, Giovanni," he said, a glint of warning in his eyes. "The word Mafia is forbidden in my home. I hate it because Hollywood has made it synonymous with thugs and buffoons who talk with New England accents. People have no idea what the word really means or represents." His face flushed with anger, and he decided to pour himself one more shot of grappa. "In ancient Latin, the word Mafia means boldness. La Mafia was a term used to describe the native Sicilians who defied foreign invaders by choosing death over betraying their *omnio*. It was the oath of *Omerta* that made these Sicilians so bold. So it was actually *Omerta* that made them *La Mafia*. Today this is where we get the term 'Made Man.' When a *locatorio* took the oath, it 'made' him part of *La Mafia*, the bold ones who defied the powerful foreign invaders. And it was—"

The voice of Leoni suddenly crackled from the intercom on the desk. "Peter, the game's about to start. Is everything okay in there?"

Don Falcone furled his brows and frowned. "Everything's fine, Leo," he answered, masking his annoyance. "I'm just having a little chat with Omnio and his paisan. Tell everyone I'll be in back in a few minutes." He then unplugged the intercom and began jotting something down on a notepad, clearly in deep thought.

Meanwhile, Vonni sat rigidly on the sofa, spellbound, playing over the don's words. He had so many questions, starting with why was he even there? Why was he being told the entire history of the Mafia? He had always felt a certain connection to the Mafia, its shadowy existence and larger-than-life figures, yet he now realized that he knew almost nothing about it. Most of what he thought he knew had come from watching embellished Hollywood movies or from neighborhood gossip back in Brooklyn, which was usually just exaggerated hearsay. But he now knew there was so much more. The Mafia had a history dating back thousands of years, a history the rest of the world knew nothing about.

Then there was the don himself, a human quasar emitting a brilliant aura of power and authority. Even now, dressed in a casual outfit of black slacks and split-back suspenders over a simple white button-up, he still possessed an air of nobility. Even though his broken English was spoken with a peasant Sicilian accent, by no means was he illiterate. He may not have attended high school, but from the way he spoke it was obvious he was extremely intelligent. The hundreds of books on the shelves were a testament to his thirst for knowledge. The don was a Mafioso savant, with the smooth cadence and voice of a born orator. His skin was sallow and aged like any man his age, yet he was still very handsome and physically intimidating. His hair, which was more silver than gray, was slicked straight back with pomade. Vonni decided that Hollywood could never cast a better actor to play a Mafioso than God had cast Don Falcone to play a real one.

"Are you alright, Giovanni?" Don Falcone asked, noticing the pensive look on his face.

"Yes, I'm fine," Vonni answered, snapping from his moment of reverie. "Why?"

"You just look distracted, that's all," the don answered. "But I suppose you're wondering what this all has to do with you?"

"Actually, I am," Vonni admitted. "But I want to hear more. I had no idea there was so much history behind the Maf... I mean, *Cosa Nostra*."

Don Falcone relaxed into his chair and took a sip of grappa. "Giovanni, there is much you don't know about Our Thing. And of course this isn't your fault. You weren't born into it." He glanced at King. "But Omnio thinks you were born for it, and I trust his judgment. He believes you're cut from the right stone. After meeting you, I have to agree. It doesn't matter that you're a *difetto*. Look at Omnio. He's also a *difetto,* but I know he was born to lead my Family. He means the world to me. Not just because he's my eldest grandson, but because he's brilliant, cunning, ambitious, and fearless... just like his father was before the Good Lord took him away. Just like I was when I first came to this country. But because his blood is not pure Sicilian, the rest of the *capiregime* look down on him. They treat him like an outcast and I fear they will never accept him. But he's my choice to someday take over this Family. He is a born leader. And as the last Falcone, it's his birthright. But, as it stands, the others will not allow it. There is a rule that was made up by Luciano instilled. To be a full Made Member of Our Thing, a man must be of pure Sicilian blood. Otherwise, he can ever be Made. And if a guy can never be Made, he can never rise above the rank of soldier. But I believe in my heart of hearts that Omnio can and will someday win over the others. He has the brains and integrity to lead the whole Syndicate. I've been preparing him for this his whole life. He knows the old codes of conduct that have governed Our Thing for hundreds of years—codes that most of the younger generations no longer honor or respect."

"But what about Leoni?" Vonni asked, picturing King's menacing uncle.

Don Falcone steeled himself as thoughts of his son-in-law popped in his head. "Unfortunately, right now, Leoni is in line to take over the Family. His father, Vito Gianolla, is my goombadi. We've been allies for many, many years. His crew is very powerful and enforces most of the Syndicate's street rackets. His other two sons, Tony and Little Vito, control the city's demolition and sanitation contracts, two of the Syndicate's most lucrative rackets. An alliance between our Families was the smart thing to do. It keeps the others from trying to muscle us out. Especially me, since I have no heir-apparent, and a lot of my government allies will be retiring over the next few years. This is why I arranged for my daughter Patricia to marry Leoni. Not only did this strengthen both our Families, but it also ensured that all of my other grandsons will grow up to have rank within the Syndicate. Problem is, it also means that my *Famiglia* will die with me. Once I die, or the Commission orders me to step down, Leoni will take over and there will be no more Falcones in the Family. Leoni is not my first choice, but with him in charge at least my men will retain their ranks and positions within the *borgata*. Unfortunately, Leoni will never allow Omnio

283

to be a major part of the Family. Not without the expressed consent of the other *capiregime*. This is why you are here today, Giovanni. I don't trust Leoni. He knows I have hopes of seeing Omnio someday take over the Family, and he feels threatened by this. That is why I believe he was behind this business with Diangelo..."

He paused, the muscles in his jaw twitching with obvious irritation. But before he could continue, King picked up where he left off.

"Vonni, you'll have to forgive my grandfather. He's still very upset over what happened. We can't prove it, but we believe my uncle Leoni had the Scrois put the contract on me. He wants to see my cousin Anthony take over our Family someday. Maybe even become *Capo di tutti Cappi*."

"They're all scared of Omnio," Don Falcone added, his face still flushed with anger. "They see what he's already accomplished at such a young age. It makes them nervous. He's not even eighteen and he's already building a name for himself. He has money pouring in and he commands a crew of faithful *soldati* who follow his orders without question. And do you know why they follow him without question? Because they love him. And as long as I'm still the Boss of this Family they will receive my full protection..."

His eyes glazed over and it suddenly seemed as if he was thinking out loud. "I'm the goddamn Boss! Who the fuck are they to tell me I can't protect my own grandson? As long as I control the judges, the politicians, the police chiefs, I run this fuckin' town. The Commission made me the Boss. I'm the goddamn *Capo di tutti Capi*! This should be enough to make the other *capi* respect Omnio. But this incident with Dean has opened my eyes. Leoni and his power-hungry brothers want him out of the picture. They fear him for three reasons. The first is that he is already finding ways to clean his money by expanding into legitimate operations. The second is that he may begin earning enough money to fatten the pockets of the other *capi*. And the third is

284

that he has already formed soft alliances with some of the *capi* who are not supporters of Leoni. They also know that if he can gain the approval of the others, the Commission may very well overlook his mixed blood and Make him. It's extremely rare, but there have been instances of *difetti* being Made. And if Omnio gets Made, I believe the others will back him. So you can see why Leoni and his brothers would want to get rid of him. They figure if they kill him now they won't have to bow to him later."

Vonni sat there silent, overwhelmed, not knowing what to say or even think. He hadn't expected such an outpouring of Family secrets and Syndicate politics. He had no idea there was such a power struggle taking place. Nor did he realize there was such a fine line between friend and foe within the Syndicate. But it all made sense now. The Syndicate was supposed to be a convivial partnership between several crews, or "Families," each of them led by a *caporegime* who answered to one Boss, the *Capo di tutti Cappi*—Boss of all Bosses. But it was never that easy. Crews were constantly vying for position, always trying to undermine each other in an attempt to gain an edge over the other, all of it driven by money and power. But Vonni wondered what any of it had to do with him.

"Don Falcone," he said, glancing at King, "I haven't known Omnio very long, but I have a lot of respect for him. I can see why his uncles would fear him. I have no doubt that he can do anything he puts his mind to. But I mean no disrespect when I ask: Why are you telling me all this? I'm just some kid from New York who runs a little crew of nobodies. What I did in the store that day... Well, I was just in the right place at the right time. King and I were friends from the gym. I'm sure he would've done the same for me."

Don Falcone leaned forward with his elbows on the desk. "Giovanni, you're no kid," he said, his voice stern and forceful. "You're a young man, and I know more about you than you think. Omnio has kept an eye on you since you arrived in our city, and he likes what he's seen. He believes you're a man of honor and integrity. But more importantly to me, he trusts you. Other than making a little money, and maybe a name for yourself, you have no agenda. You have no ties to any of the other *capi* here in Detroit. You owed Omnio nothing, but you risked your life to save his. This tells me a lot about your character. You and I have a lot more in common than you realize, Giovanni. I also came to Detroit when I was just a teenager. And like you, I quickly made a name for myself. You're a bold and fearless young *soldato*, just like those Sicilians who started this thing of ours two-thousand years ago. Men like you don't come along every day. At least not anymore. Which is why Omnio and I both agree that you should be part of our Family."

"Part of your Family?" Vonni asked, confused. "What do you mean?"

Don Falcone glanced at King before answering. "Omnio wants you to be his *protettore titolare.*"

"His *protettore titolare*?" Vonni asked, even more confused, not recognizing the term.

Don Falcone's eyes seemed to glaze over, as if recalling a distant memory. "It is an ancient title that dates back to the beginning of Our Thing. Each Omnio had one *protettore titolare picchiotti*, a bodyguard he appointed for life. His *protettore* was his most trusted and loyal friend. But he was also his chief enforcer and the overseer of his lands. It was a great honor to be a *protettore titolare*. But it will be our honor if you agree to be part of our Family as Omnio's *protettore*. I know the two of you are relatively new friends, so I'm sure all this must come as a surprise. But something in my gut tells me that you are truly loyal and worthy of this position, and my gut has never failed me. Not once. You're a smart young man, Giovanni. I know this because I checked your school records. You're a good student. You're a born hustler. You're ambitious and hungry to make a name for yourself. And the way you handled those thugs who robbed you? It proved you are both loyal and fearless. Yes, I know about that too. I also know what you've been doing for Joey.

What you don't know, Giovanni, is that it was Omnio all along. He was the one who arranged for you to work for Joey. The pot, the steroids, the stolen goods? All Omnio. He's been testing you all along, and you've passed his every test. You're street savvy and quick to take advantage of an opportunity. You're loyal and know how to take orders. You have honor and integrity. And, as a bonus, you're not from around here. That means you have no ties to the other *capiregime*. Therefore, you are perfectly qualified to be Omnio's *protettore*."

Vonni's mind raced as he tried to process all of this. His mouth was suddenly dry and his hands felt clammy. Never in a million years could he have anticipated the don would ask him to swear his life to King and become part of their *Famiglia*.

"But I thought he just needed me to be his driver?" he asked, still not sure if he fully understood the responsibilities of a *protettore,* a word that translated to "protector."

"On the surface, you will be," answered the don, his onyx eyes glinting conspiratorially. "But you'll be much more. You'll be his business partner, his chief enforcer and full-time bodyguard. The men he has now are loyal, but I fear they could become corrupted by promises of power and position the same way Diangelo was. Some of them may aspire to be more than street soldiers working the ghettos and petty street rackets. If they get approached by one of the other skippers with the right offer... well, they know they can only go so far with Omnio. After what happened with Dean, I refuse to trust just anyone with Omnio's life. Until he's Made—and I believe they will someday let him take the oath—he will need a truly loyal *protettore*. One he can trust completely with his life."

"But I'm still in school, Don Falcone," Vonni said, unsure if he wanted to make such a commitment. "I promised my mom I'd stay until I graduated."

"No worries, paisan," said the don, nodding his understanding. "I have many friends in this town, including some who work for the Detroit public school system. One such friend happens to be the superintendent of your school district. I had him check your records and he told me that you already have more than enough credits to graduate. As favor to me, he even said he'd allow you to graduate early. With honors." He smiled and held his hands apart. "So, my friend, you can tell your mother that not only are you going to graduate early, but you'll also be graduating with honors."

Vonni was silent for a moment while he considered this. "Don Falcone, this is..." he began, still ambivalent. "Well, I don't know what to say."

"Say yes. Because Omnio needs you."

"So what exactly would I be doing?"

"Your most important duty will be to protect Omnio. The continuance of my bloodline will depend on it. But you'll also be his driver and go-between for him and some of his associates. The two of you will be a team. Rarely apart. There will be many responsibilities. You'll be his right hand. His voice. And sometimes even his brains. But he believes you can handle this. And after meeting you myself, I do too. You have that combination of brains, honor, and fearlessness that is so rare these days. It is men like you who made Our Thing strong throughout the centuries. Unfortunately, you are part of a dying breed."

Vonni suddenly felt swollen with pride. "I'm honored that you would even consider me for such a position, Don Falcone, but I'm sure you have men more qualified for this position than me. Wouldn't they be upset that you passed them over for someone like me?"

"It's true," Don Falcone said, nodding thoughtfully. "I do have plenty of men who would jump at the opportunity to take this position. Just like that fuckin' Diangelo did when I offered it to him. And we saw how that ended. He was seduced by false promises of power and position. He thought he could earn Leoni's favor by helping the Scrois get rid of Omnio. That story about the Scrois threatening to kill his little brother was bullshit.

288

They're definitely ruthless *diavoli* but they would never kill an innocent kid. That was Dean just trying to seek mercy from Omnio. But he broke his vow to Omnio, and for that there is no mercy."

"So you have no one you can trust?" Vonni asked, confused. "What about your own men? Don't you have your own *protettore*?"

"I do. His name is Alanso Profaci and he's waiting for me in the living room. Been my *protetttore* for almost thirty years, and I trust him with my life. But, like me, he's getting old. So are the rest of my *capidecina* and *tenente*. They've been with me most of their lives, and I trust them all, but they're slowly dying off, retiring, or getting locked up. *Manchia*, half my guys got indicted last year with that whole Game Tax business. The next generation is positioning to take over. I trust the few captains I have left, but some of their men, their sons and grandsons... well, there's going to be a major shift in power once I step down. Naturally, they want to align themselves with whoever they think will be the next Boss, which they think is going to be Leoni. And Leoni hates Omnio, if only because Omnio poses a threat to his position within the Family. This, Giovanni, is why I can trust no one. Not even my own men. So who do I trust to protect my only living heir? It can't be anyone with ties to any of the other *capi*. It has to be someone with integrity, someone who can't be manipulated by money or the promise of power and position. It has to be someone who has no other loyalties. Someone Omnio feels he can trust with his life. This describes you, Giovanni. You already saved his life once. Now do you understand why he has chosen you?"

"Yes, sir," Vonni nodded. "I think I do. Leoni wants to make sure King is out of the picture by the time you step down."

"Exactly. He thinks he has me fooled, but I'm two steps ahead of him. He has no idea that I've already dealt with the Scroi brothers."

"Are they dead?" Vonni asked, surprised by his indifference.

"No," Don Falcone answered, a frustrated look in his eyes. "I wish they were, but it's not that easy. They're Made men. And since Omnio isn't, the Commission ruled that I couldn't take any action against them—which is goddamn bullshit. They tried to kill my grandson! But as a consolation to me, the Commission shelved the fuckers. Banished them from Detroit. They can no longer operate here and all of their Detroit affiliations have been terminated. They're being relocated to Toronto, where they'll now work for our Canadian affiliates." His dark eyes suddenly became cold as ice. "If it were up to me, I'd cut their fuckin' hearts out. But the Commission wouldn't allow it. They said it could incite a war."

"What exactly is the Commission?" Vonni asked, having heard it referenced to several times now.

Don Falcone seemed to gather his thoughts for a moment. "Giovanni, I have broken many rules today by telling you what I've already told you. You're not even supposed to know there is a Commission. It's a subject that should never be discussed outside the Family. Only amongst Made members of the Family. But because I want you to know how much I trust you, I'm going to break another rule. I have to warn you, though, if you ever repeat to anyone what I am about to say..." He splayed his hands wide. "Well, I'm sure you can guess the consequences."

"You don't have to worry about me, Don Falcone," Vonni said, nodding his understanding. "Oath or no oath, I would never repeat anything you tell me."

Don Falcone grinned slightly. "No, of course you wouldn't. Which is why you're here." Again he paused and seemed to gather his thoughts. "So... the Commission. Consider it a sort of board of directors for Our Thing. The board is made up of ten *Caporegime* from the ten biggest Families in the country, elected by the Commission itself. I am one of them. The Commission used to be led by the heads of the five New York Families, but that was before New York went to shit with its rats and interfamily wars. Now the Commission answers to a *Sovrano Capo Supremo* in Trapani, Sicily."

He paused and rubbed his temples for a moment, the look on his face one for frustration. "There are strict rules, Giovanni. No Made man can be touched without a sit-down and unanimous consent from the Commission. That's why Omnio and I were in Miami. For a sit-down. I brought this whole Scroi business to the table, and I was forbidden from retaliating against the *putani*. Since the Scrois have always been faithful captains and good earners for Don Vito Gianolla, the Commission voted to give them a pass for what they did. Vito also attended the sit-down and swore he had no knowledge of what the Scroi brothers were up to. And I believe him. He would never sanction such a thing. We've been goombadi for too long. He was outraged by such a blatant act of aggression and disrespect. He said he would agree to whatever repercussions I felt necessary. But I know it was his boy, Leoni, behind it all. Vito and I go back to the Old Country. Our fathers were from the same village outside Trapani. But he's also getting old. He's been positioning Leoni to take over his operations for several years now. And on the surface, Leoni seems to be doing a decent job. But he over-values himself. He likes to think he is smarter than everyone else. But he's not. He's a goddamn fool if he thinks..." He suddenly closed his eyes and seemed to drift into deep thought.

"My uncle has become drunk with power," King interjected. "He's already muscling some of the other crews out of their operations. Even whole territories. He hates what I've been doing in the city. He says there is no money left on the other side of 8 Mile, yet here I am making thousands each week from the scraps nobody wants."

"*Diavolo!*" Don Falcone spat vehemently, using the Italian idiom for devil. "He's an arrogant *canooda* and he's going to someday destroy this Family. I only arranged for him to marry Patty because I figured it was smarter to keep him close than have him as our enemy. But I fear I may have made a mistake by doing so. He's been letting his new position go to his head. He masquerades around like he's already the new Boss, using my name and his father's influence to bully the other *capi* out of operations that have been theirs for decades. Now that he's married into my Family, he assumes he's my choice to succeed me. I'm sure he's expecting my full endorsement when it comes time for me to step down. But only the Commission can decide who succeeds me."

He grabbed the bottle of grappa and poured himself another shot. "But none of this concerns you, Giovanni," he said, looking him in the eye. "All that you need to know is that the Scrois no longer pose a threat to Omnio. They're gone. And their operations are mine now, so I'm dividing them up between my captains and lieutenants. Omnio is getting their five nightclubs." He offered Vonni a grin. "One of those clubs will be yours, a gift from me, if you pledge your loyalty to Omnio and agree to become his *giurato protettore.* I'm getting old, paisan. When the Good Lord takes me home, Omnio will need someone close to him he can trust. Someone who can't be bought. Someone who will never betray him for promises of power and position. Because I can assure you, my friend, Leoni will never stop trying to get rid of him. At the very least, he'll squeeze him out of the Family and won't allow him to make a living."

Vonni looked at King. "So is this what you want? You really trust me that much?"

"I do," King nodded. "I know you'll always have my back."

Don Falcone leaned forward and pierced Vonni with the eyes of a hungry raptor. "So, my young friend, what's it going to be? Are you are ready to swear an oath of loyalty and servitude to my grandson? He is more precious to me than all my other grandsons put together. He's the last Falcone, the only one who can carry on my name. If he dies, so does my bloodline. And if my bloodline dies, I will dishonor my ancestors. This is why I need you, Giovanni."

Vonni had a thousand questions running through his head, but he decided none of them mattered. This was his destiny. Becoming King's sworn bodyguard was an intimidating prospect, and it sounded like it would be a dangerous one. But it was his chance to finally be a real someone. He had always dreamed of being part of a real Family. A *Famiglia*. And now he had his chance.

"Don Falcone," he said, weighing his words carefully, "I would be honored to pledge myself to King and be his *giurato protettore*. Whatever you need me to do, I will do it. For *La Famiglia*."

Grinning triumphantly, Don Falcone stood and sauntered over to a bookshelf. From an old humidor he removed a small wood effigy of St. Albert, the patron saint of Trapani, Sicily. It was hand-carved and incredibly detailed, yet no larger than a deck of cards. He studied it for a moment with a reverent look on his face, and then returned to his desk and set the small carving in front of him. After rolling up his sleeve, he removed an old switchblade knife from a leather sheath strapped to his forearm.

"Giovanni..." he began, his voice saturnine and deliberate, his eyes examining the knife almost affectionately. "What we are about to do dates back many hundreds of years. Here in this room we will consecrate a covenant that has bound Our Thing together since those first Sicilians banded together to resist foreign oppressors. The covenant is what makes us who we are. It's what has made us stand the test of time. The Roman Empire fell. The Persian Empire Fell. The Ottoman Empire Fell. All the world's great empires have fallen. But this thing of ours will never fall, because we are bound by honor to the oath, and the oath bounds us by honor. When we are finished here today, you will no longer be a civilian. You will be one of us, forever bound to Our Thing by *Omerta*."

He motioned Vonni to stand. "As I'm sure you probably already know, being a *difetto* means you're not even supposed to know about the oath. But I am making an exception, just as how I hope the Commission will make someday for Omnio. Traditionally, this ceremony is strictly reserved for loyal Sicilian and Italian *gabelloti* who have proven themselves to their *capo* through many years of loyal service. But I believe you have proven yourself enough, and in more ways than one. The most important is that you risked your life to save Omnio's. Such an act of loyalty and bravery deserves great reward. There is nothing I can say or give you that will ever truly express my gratitude. If you hadn't intervened when you did, my name would die with me. And I cannot dishonor my ancestors by allowing my name to die, which is why I need you to make sure Omnio lives. He chose you himself, and he believes in his heart you can be trusted with his life. I also believe he can trust you. Most *capi* would think I'm crazy for inducting you into my Family at such a young age, and only after working for Omnio for such a short time, but I say to hell with them. I see your potential and I believe in my heart you are ready for this. You're going to have a great responsibility, Giovanni. There are perilous times ahead for Omnio and our Family. But my name must live. The oath you are about to take may not make you a Made man in anyone else's eyes, but you will be a Made man in my eyes. I will hold you to all the standards that entails: Death before dishonor. Unquestioning obedience. Loyalty till death. A willingness to lay down your life in an instant for Omnio. And, of course, silence. Today you will swear an oath of secrecy. Which means you can never, ever, repeat what is about to take place in this room. Do you understand this, Giovanni?"

"I understand," Vonni said, never having felt such an overwhelming sense of pride and honor.

"Then I will only ask you this once," said the don, switching to Italian, his tone suggesting the gravity of his next words. "Are you prepared to take the oath or *Omerta* and commit your life to Omnio as his sworn protector? Because if you are not, now is the time to walk away. There will be no hard feelings, and you can go back to your daily business as if today never happened."

Vonni glanced at King, who gave him a barely perceptible nod. "I'm ready," he said confidently. "Even if King never gets Made, I will always protect him with my life."

Don Falcone nodded. "Then it is time you officially become part of our Family."

"I'm honored, Don Falcone," Vonni said, his chest swelled with pride.

Don Falcone walked over and stood in front of both him and King. With a trancelike look in his eyes, he asked each of them to give him their right palm. He then used the knife to make a small incision in each palm. When blood oozed from the cuts, he put the knife to his own palm and pressed it until blood appeared. After making the sign of the cross, he held up the effigy of St. Albert and began the ceremony by quoting a benediction from the Book of Solomon.

"Father God, only You know our hearts. Only You shall judge the righteous and wicked... we now ask that You, Father God, stand as our witness as we consecrate Giovanni's oath of fealty. We ask that You protect him in all things and forgive him for the sins that he may commit in the name of the Family. Bless him with strength, honor and integrity. Protect him from his enemies and guide him on his journey. Watch over him as he protects Omnio throughout all of his days. And if he ever breaks this oath, may he burn in hell like this effigy."

He rolled the St. Albert effigy in his bloody palm before handing it to King and then Vonni so they could do the same. When it was thoroughly covered with their blood, he held it over a burning candle. For several seconds the bloody effigy smoked and smoldered as the blood dried and baked to the wood. When a small flame finally appeared, and a sooty black smoke began rising from it, he turned it over so the flame could spread and consume their blood as one.

"Giovanni," he said, setting the smoldering idol on the desk, "the flame from our blood burning together represents that we are now one Family, bound together through blood and honor.

To break this bond means you will be condemned to death. Do you understand this?"

"I do," Vonni nodded, feeling as if he were in a dream, as if time itself had slowed to a standstill.

The trancelike look on the don's face turned into one of genuine happiness. "Then welcome to our Family, Giovanni!" he said, pulling him into a fatherly embrace. "You are now no less than one of my own sons."

When the don released him, King also embraced him in a powerful hug. "You are now no less than my own brother. Thank you. You have no idea what it means to have you as my *protettore*. I know I'll always be able to count on you. But I want you to know that the oath goes both ways. It is now my job to also protect you, to see that you are successful in all that you do, and be there whenever you need me. We're a team now. And together, someday, you and I are going to run this town. You'll see. My grandfather worked his whole life to build this Family, and I'm not going to just lie down and let my uncle take it from me. I'm the last Falcone. It's rightfully mine. Leoni and the other *capiregime* will someday bow to me. And when they do, you, paisan, will be by my side. Like my grandfather said, my fate is now in your hands. I'm sure you must have many questions, but save them for another day. Today we celebrate. My grandfather taught me that life shouldn't always be about business. There has to be time for family, for friends. We're young men, paisan, so who could blame us for acting like it?"

Don Falcone handed Vonni the scorched remains of the effigy. "Take this. It's yours to keep as a reminder of your oath. Put it somewhere safe. It is your most prized possession. It represents your commitment to Omnio. To our Family. To this thing of ours."

Vonni studied it for a moment. "Thank you, Don Falcone," he said, holding the burnt carving like it was the most precious gem. "I will never forget my oath or what it means."

"I know you won't," said the don, setting a hand on his shoulder. "But for now, we're finished. Like Omnio said, there's more to life than business. We must take advantage of days like this. It's time to relax, eat, and watch some football. You have to get to know our Family, and they have to get to know you. So come on, that's enough business for one day. Let's go enjoy the rest of the afternoon."

Without adding another word, Don Falcone turned and led them from the den. As they went, Vonni tucked the charred effigy of St. Albert into the inside pocket of his suit jacket. The feel of it against his chest was a tangible reminder that life as he knew it had just ceased to exist. He was now officially part of La Cosa Nostra, and would be until he breathed his last breath. There would be no turning back.

# CHAPTER 16

The following day, Vonni quit his job and dropped out of school to begin his tenure as King's new *protettore giurato,* his "sworn protector." But his mother became livid when she learned of this from his aunt. Even when he explained how he was still going to graduate with honors, she was furious and demanded to know why he was ruining his life. She knew from his aunt the type of people he had been hanging around, and feared he would end up like his brother. She tried ordering him to stay in school, but of course this did nothing. He simply told her he had been offered a well-paying job as a nightclub manager and he planned to take it. It broke her heart, for she dreamed of seeing him attend a university and someday go on to become some type of professional. She knew he was exceptionally smart and could do anything he put his mind to. But no matter how much she begged and pleaded with him to reconsider what he was getting himself into, he wouldn't listen. Even when she got his father involved, he refused to listen. He definitely wasn't going to take advice from a two-timing father he no longer had respect for.

As Vonni began his new life as King's *protettore*, he was immediately surprised by several things. Starting with King himself. He had always seen King as a sort of larger-than-life, all-business young Mafioso. But he soon learned King was, in many ways, no different than any other teenage guy. At least at heart. He had a playful nature and an exceptional sense of humor. He loved to laugh and joke with the people he was close to. And, surprisingly, he had many friends who were "civilians," people with no ties to his Family or any criminal activity. When he was alone with Vonni, he was a completely different person than he was in the presence of his crew, most of whom were several years older than him and strictly business associates. It was almost as if he had a split personality. Whenever in the presence of his grandfather or business associates, he was austere and humorless, professional and pragmatic, articulate and well-spoken, as if he were much older. Vonni sometimes thought he talked more like a college-educated businessman than a young street tough. Yet when they were alone, or in the presence of his various girlfriends, King acted his age—silly and jocular, always using himself as the butt of his jokes. He even had two separate wardrobes to go with his two personalities. When out on business, he wore tailored suits and pressed shirts, which made him look the quintessential young Mafioso. But when he was out for a day of leisure, he preferred jeans, sweatshirts, jerseys, sneakers and baseball caps. Vonni quickly learned that when King dressed down like this, he was far more comfortable, always laughing and joking and completely relaxed.

As Vonni got to know King on a more personal level, another thing that surprised him was King's interest in reading. King loved to read. It was one of his favorite pastimes. He spent several hours a day reading books about war, philosophy, history, culture, and business. He studied famous military leaders like Octavian, Alexander The Great, Napoleon, Hannibal, Genghis Khan, and Sun Tzu. He read the works of famous philosophers and political figures like Niccolo Machiavelli, Karl Marx, Lenin, Aristotle, Plato, and Socrates. He read the biographies of famous captains of industry, such as John D. Rockefeller, Andrew Carnegie, and Pierre Du Pont. Another of his favorite pastimes was playing chess. He was constantly studying books on chess strategy. He once told Vonni, "Life is really just one big chess game. In order to win, you always have to think three moves ahead of your opponent."

He prided himself as a chess master, and was always challenging Vonni to games. He would even remove his queen just to give Vonni a fighting chance. Even then, Vonni, who was a decent chess player, never came close to beating him.

Vonni found King to be very easy going and fun to be around. The two of them were constantly laughing and joking with one another. Vonni entertained King with his stories about growing up back in Brooklyn. King entertained Vonni with his animated impressions of celebrities or people from the neighborhood, which Vonni found hilarious. The two of them got along great, and it wasn't long before they were the best of friends.

Vonni would pick King up each morning and together they would set off on their daily rounds, handling business, delving out orders, picking up money, meeting with King's lieutenants and other associates. They would spend hours in Club Vanzetti's devising new schemes and working on ways to strengthen their current operations. But they also spent a lot of time at the homes of their various female "friends." And the mall. King loved the mall. Or rather, he loved shopping. They made several excursions a week to Eastland Mall, on Detroit's 8 Mile Road, where there they would shop and eat and flirt with every cute young girl they encountered. It seemed the mall offered an infinite supply of new girls for them to flirt with. It was the perfect place to hone their pickup skills, and they approached it like a sport, betting on who could get the most numbers. They ate together. They played together. They worked together. They womanized together. When King had to satisfy his sexual needs with one of his girlfriends, Vonni was always there in the next room. And when Vonni needed to do the same, King was always in the next room. Indeed their friendship was symbiotic. They were nearly inseparable.

The more time they spent together, the more Vonni learned about King's various business endeavors. He even sat in on King's meetings with his lieutenants. He learned their order of rank was as follows: Tony "Taps" Tappio was King's second-in-command and unofficial underboss. Next in rank was Paulie "Pal" Palazzolo, who was the oldest member of the crew at 29, and acted as King's unofficial "consigliore," or advisor. Joey "Hollywood" Lombardo, who was a drug dealer and King's liaison to some of the Family's other crews, was next in rank. From there the rest of the crew was essentially equal but each of them had their own specialty. Billy "One Eyed" Profaci, King's second cousin, ran a chop shop out of his uncle's junkyard on 8 Mile. "The Machete" Mianchetti was King's sports bookmaker and chief loan shark enforcer. Georgio "Fats" Corado ran a small escort service but his main racket was selling cocaine. Lastly, there was Victor "Fists" Aquiano, who was a bit of a Renaissance man who handled whatever King needed handled.

The size and scale of their overall operation were much, much larger than Vonni realized. But King made it very clear to them that Vonni was now part of it all. At first Vonni detected some animosity, even resentment for his quick jump in rank. But when King expressed how Don Falcone himself had decided to make Vonni his *protettore*, they accepted him without question, albeit surely with a grain of salt. After all, they had known King all their lives. A few of them, like Georgio, were secretly bitter that they hadn't been considered for the position. Especially over a relative stranger. But they knew Vonni had saved King's life, and that the don had selected him for a reason. They would never question the don's decisions. If they did, they knew it could very well be their last question.

Vonni also became well acquainted with the various Syndicate intricacies, including its politics and how a strict chain-of-command was designed to protect the Boss of each crew. He learned that there were, in fact, five major crews, sometimes referred to as "Families," that made up the Syndicate: the Falcone crew, led by the Boss of Bosses, Don Falcone; the Malacci crew, led by Don Vincenzo Malacci; the Toccio crew, led by Alfonse Toccio; the Zirello crew, led by Tony Zirello; and the

Rubino crew, led by Giuseppe Rubino. Vonni learned who was ranked where in the Syndicate hierarchy, who the *capi* were, who was friend or foe, and who could or couldn't be trusted. He learned which crews controlled which rackets, and which *capi* possessed the most power and influence. And he learned how the Syndicate itself worked together as one unit, under the direction of the Commission, to control or sometimes even monopolize certain rackets, both licit and illicit.

Every day seemed to be a new learning experience for Vonni. One of the things he learned was how King somehow managed to operate just under the fringes of the Syndicate's umbrella. The five Families had their hands in everything from municipal contracts and union corruption, to extortion and gambling, to prostitution and loan sharking, to drugs and robbery. There were literally dozens, even hundreds of scams and hustles taking place at any given time. But King was not allowed to partake in any of them if they were outside of Detroit's city limits. His operations were strictly confined to the inner city ghettos, areas nobody else wanted. Yet with his grandfather's tutelage, he was still managing to squeeze considerable profits from the discarded city rackets. After learning the details of King's entire operation, Vonni not only considered his new boss to be a genius, but he decided that the guy could, if he put his mind to it, squeeze water from a rock.

Vonni also learned why Don Falcone had been forced into semi-retirement. Over the last several years, the FBI had been scrutinizing his every move. They knew he was the Syndicate's top boss, and suspected that he had hidden interests in several Canadian and Indian casinos, which indeed he did. So when he got word from his lawyers that the Feds were working on a grand jury indictment targeting him for RICO—Racketeering Influenced Corrupt Organization—the Commission became nervous and ordered him to relinquish his interests in the casinos. They also forced him to hand over most of his illicit operations to Leoni and his other sons-in-law, all of who were *capi* in the other Families. This was the reason King was not invited to partake in any of the Syndicate's larger, more lucrative rackets. The don was being muscled out and forced into retirement, and there was nothing he could do about it. As it stood, because there was so much federal scrutiny on him, the only thing the don was allowed to retain was his beloved sports book.

Don Falcone had amassed the vast majority of his wealth via gambling, but he wasn't a gambler. He was the house, known in Las Vegas as a "layover bookie," A.K.A. a master bookie. At any given time he had up to two dozen bookies working for his various *capi*, and his job was to balance their books before each game or sporting event. Compulsive gamblers bet on just about anything, and bookies collected from each winning bet a 10% gratuity known as "vig," short for vigorish. A portion of this 10% was kicked up to the master bookie. But in order to make a profit, a bookie had to always make sure his book was perfectly balanced before a particular sporting event, which meant that he had to take an equal amount of bets on both sides of the point-spread. Their goal was to have the book perfectly balanced before the start of each game. This way, no matter who won, the losers would pay the winners, and the bookie would collect his 10% vig. Oftentimes, however, when a bookie was unable to balance his book, meaning he either took in too many bets with or against a spread, he would try to push his excess bets onto another bookie who needed that particular off-balance swing in the spread. Before each game or sporting event, this process was repeated over and over until everyone's books were balanced. But it wasn't always possible to perfectly balance every book. This is where Don Falcone came in. As the master layover bookie, he would take all excess bets and push them onto his associates in Las Vegas. If done right, it was foolproof. Everyone made money, and there was virtually no risk. The profits on certain games, such as the Super Bowl, could extend into the millions. It was a scam that dated back thousands of years to ancient Rome, when elite Roman citizens placed bets on gladiatorial games in Flavian's Great Coliseum.

But with the ever-present FBI having the don under the proverbial microscope, the Commission had instructed him to even downsize his sports book, and instead focus on managing his various legitimate businesses. Which meant that King was, for the most part, left to fend for himself when it came to finding ways to make money. But he was a born hustler and incredibly business savvy for someone his age. He saw potential for profits where nobody else saw them. So rather than beg Leoni and the other *capi* for their scraps, he simply worked around them and managed to eke out a comfortable living for himself and his crew. But he was far from satisfied.

Since Detroit itself had become inhabited by mostly impoverished blacks and Latinos, Leoni and the other *capi* felt that there was little money left to be made within the city limits. So they focused their time and energy outside the city, where opportunities were abundant. The suburbs and adjoining exurbia were inhabited mostly by middle-class, blue-collar, white denizens who had plenty of disposable income. There were countless new businesses popping up to cater to them— everything from grocery stores and restaurants, to tanning salons and movie theaters. And they all presented opportunities for the Syndicate to make money via extortion, robbery, gambling, union corruption, and forced partnerships.

The old-time Syndicate Bosses may have considered Detroit a wasteland, but King found that there was still plenty of money to be made there by establishing business relationships with the city's black and Latino gangs, most of whom knew who exactly who he was. Some treated him like he was already a Syndicate boss, for his reputation as a ruthless young Mafioso well preceded him. He was young, yes, but the streets knew that he was someone to fear, someone who should not be crossed. And street gangs were cheap labor. He used them to do his dirty work, but they reported to his various lieutenants, never him directly. They maintained everything from strings of drug houses and underground gambling establishments, to after-hours clubs and escort services. They even had a very successful chop shop that was overseen by King's cousin Billy. But it was the extortion racket that provided them with their most stable source of income. They shook down dozens of local businesses for protection money, requiring a small largesse each week to keep these businesses from having an "accidental" fire or sudden rash of armed robberies. And of course, the proprietors of these businesses paid without fail, for they knew the local police could do nothing to protect them.

Vonni was impressed by how King was received by these inner city associates, the majority of which were seasoned street hustlers—drug dealers, gang members, pimps, and surely a few killers. But they seemed to have a natural affinity for him. They enjoyed being in the presence of a real-life Mafioso. They would invite him to parties and backyard barbecues. They introduced him to beautiful young women from their neighborhoods. They fraternized with him like they were old friends, and they all accepted Vonni without question, for anyone King brought around had to be someone of importance.

As Vonni became more and more involved in King's day-to-day operations, he became privy to the enormous amounts of money King and his crew were making. In fact, one of his new duties was to help King collect, count, and track his money. There was so much of it coming in that the numbers were nearly overwhelming. In a good week, King would clear over a hundred thousand dollars! But he was very generous with his money. He paid his men well and was constantly surprising them with lavish gifts, new cars, jewelry, and all-inclusive trips to places like Atlantic City and Las Vegas, where Don Falcone had associates who worked in the hotel and gaming industry. And of course, his generosity extended to Vonni. At the end of each week, after they tallied up their take, King would hand him no less than ten percent, which was on top of what Vonni was still making from his pot, steroid, and stolen-goods operations. He began taking in so much money that he didn't know where to put it all, so he began stashing it in safety deposit boxes at banks all over the city.

King was constantly looking for new ways to expand his various rackets into legitimate arenas, and one of those arenas was the nightclub industry. He already owned Club Vanzetti's, which was bringing in considerable profits, but he was about to open a string of new clubs. Or rather, re-open the Scroi brothers' clubs with new names and new management. All he was waiting for was Don Falcone to finish transferring the deeds and liquor licenses. He knew these clubs were going to provide him and his crew a fresh source of legitimate income, as well as a way to clean much of their illicit income. Vonni was especially excited about this, because Don Falcone had promised that one of the clubs would be his to manage and oversee.

Every Sunday afternoon, Vonni would drive King to Don Falcone's home for dinner. Leoni was always there with his family, and after dinner he would join King and Don Falcone in the den for their weekly sit-down, leaving Vonni to entertain himself with King's cousins Anthony, Dino, and Pamela. It was always a little awkward, since Anthony and Dino made no attempts to mask their contempt for him. The fact that their little sister seemed to have a romantic interest in him only made matters worse. She would openly flirt and make eyes at him with little regard for her watching brothers. But he knew better than to reciprocate. There was no denying he was attracted to her. In fact, he found her to be quite beautiful. His heart would race every time he saw her. But to overtly show any interest in her would not only be taken as an insult to her father and brothers, but it would also be disrespectful to King. She was the baby of her family, and like all Sicilian women, she was closely guarded by the men around her who considered her virtue to be the family's most sacred commodity. To encroach on this virtue would not be tolerated. Especially from a half-breed *difetto*.

During King's Sunday afternoon palavers with his grandfather and Uncle Leoni, he would present them with exactly half the weekly take from all of his various operations, a percentage set by the don himself. This money was called "operational expenses." Some was used to always keep a team of high-powered lawyers on retainer. Some was used to bribe the local police and other law enforcement agencies to allow the Syndicate to operate without interference. Some was used to line the pockets of various judges and politicians for certain favors. And some was used to bribe certain city officials in charge of allocating enormous municipal contracts. But most importantly, a portion of this weekly offering was added to the Syndicate's monthly tithe to the Commission, who added it to The Corporate Fund for the Family Bosses. "The Fund," which was rumored to be in the tens of millions, was used to invest in various legitimate corporations, particularly corporations involved in the casino and gaming industry. And of course, Don Falcone always made sure the Commission always knew exactly how much King was bringing to the table. It was his way of planting a seed that he hoped would someday take root.

Vonni was learning the ropes and making more money than he ever dreamed of. Life was good and only getting better by the day. But he did have one thorn in his side. His aunt and uncle. They were always pestering him with questions about what he was doing every day, who he was hanging out with, and where he was going. But he'd never answer them. Or rather, he couldn't answer them. He knew *Omerta* extended to even his own family. When his mother called from New York and demanded to know what he was up to, all he could do was tell her not to worry, that he was a man now and he knew what he was doing. He knew this broke her heart, but he had chosen his path. Or rather, it had chosen him. Like it or not, she would just have to deal with it.

Eventually he grew tired of his aunt and uncle's constant badgering, so he decided to get his own place. After all, he had plenty of money. So he began shopping for apartments, condos, and even houses. But it ended up being Don Falcone who found him the perfect place—an apartment in the prestigious 9 Mile Tower, the only true luxury apartment high-rise on the Eastside. Situated right on the shores of Lake St. Clair, just a five-minute drive from Don Falcone's own home, it was the tallest building for miles, which offered each luxury apartment a panoramic view of Lake St. Clair and the surrounding landscape. Vonni's new apartment included a terrace balcony, underground parking garage, dockage at the adjacent marina, access to a 20,000 square foot clubhouse, a private gym, and even a 24-hour concierge.

This exclusive apartment building usually had an extensive waiting list that was several years long, but its manager was an old friend of Don Falcone's. And this friend happened to owe the don a favor. So when the don asked him if there was an apartment available for a valued member of his family, the manager immediately evicted one of his top-floor tenants for a fabricated contractual infraction. Vonni almost felt sorry for the previous tenant when he moved in and took in the spectacular view from his terrace balcony. Almost. Never in his wildest dreams had he thought he would ever live in such an opulent apartment. Even though rent was costing him a whopping $3,000 a month, it was well worth every penny of it.

After moving into his new apartment, Vonni couldn't help wondering why King still lived in a dilapidated old house back in the city. After all, he knew King could afford to live wherever he wanted. All of his top lieutenants lived in beautiful homes or apartments out in the suburbs. Yet King still lived with his mother in the old neighborhood, in a house that looked like it should be condemned. So, one day while they were in Vonni's apartment counting stacks of cash from their weekly take, Vonni decided to ask him why.

"Not that it's any of my business," he said, flattening a stack of cash onto the coffee table, "but I'm curious as to why you didn't take this place for yourself? I mean, I figured you would've had first dibs on it."

King stopped counting and looked up with regret in his eyes. "Well, paisan," he said, his tone sullen and lined with frustration, "I would love to get out of that shitty fuckin' house of ours. But… it's my mom. She won't leave. Believe me, I've tried getting her to let me buy us a new house. Maybe somewhere out here. But she won't leave. My dad bought that house before I was born, and I guess she has some kind of emotional attachment to it. Don't ask me why. It's a pile of shit. She won't even let me fix it up. She says she wants to remember it just as it was when my dad bought it for her."

And just like that, Vonni understood. King's mother had experienced a series of mental breakdowns after the murder of her husband, King's father, and her mind never fully recovered. In fact, she had only grown progressively worse, particularly over the last several years. She had pictures of King's father all over their house. They were on the fireplace mantle, on shelves, on tables, hung on walls—faded old photos from the seventies and eighties. King looked just like his father. Their physical resemblance was uncanny. They had the same thick dark hair, broad shoulders, and Mediterranean good looks. And, of course, they both had the trademark Falcone eyes. It was no wonder that his mother's mental health had been deteriorating over the past several years. Now that King had grown into a man, he was a constant reminder of her dead husband.

Vonni often tried engaging King's mother in conversation, but she always seemed distant, as if she was mentally somewhere else. She was nice enough, and accepted him as King's new friend, but there was obviously something very wrong with her mind. She usually just sat in the living room, staring out the window while mumbling to herself. When she did speak, her words were monotone and emotionless. Her eyes were always glazed over and she slept nearly 20 hours a day. When she walked, she dragged her feet like a lifeless zombie. She almost never left the house, and always wore an ill-fitting housedress that was stained and faded. Vonni couldn't help but feel sorry for her. She was just a shell of a woman, with a broken heart that had clearly broken her mind. But King still loved her dearly. Even when Don Falcone suggested putting her in a special mental home for people in her condition, King refused to do so. She was still his mother. He did everything in his power to make her happy and comfortable. He did almost all of the household chores. He paid all the bills. He even cooked her dinner every night. He would sometimes insist Vonni join them for dinner, but Vonni always felt awkward eating with them, for she rarely spoke and often sat there mumbling without even touching her plate. He figured King just wanted her to have some company other than himself once in a while.

Yet she wasn't always torpid and incoherent. Occasionally she'd become lucid and even have fairly rational conversations with Vonni while King worked around the house or made dinner. But she was very suspicious of people and didn't seem to trust anyone, which was the reason King couldn't hire a home nurse or maid. She seemed to warm to Vonni on the rare occasion she was coherent. She was intrigued by his New York accent, and enjoyed listening to him talk.

The one thing Vonni found most odd about her was her apathy towards King himself. She rarely thanked him for making dinner or doing all the work around the house. In fact, she barely even spoke to him. But Vonni suspected he knew why. King reminded her of her long-lost husband. Just the sight of him was a cruel reminder of her loss, the only man she ever loved, a man who had died in her arms mere days after King's birth. Though she was broken of heart and spirit, she wasn't completely witless. She knew exactly what King had become. She knew he was following in the footsteps of his father, and that he could very well meet the same fate at any moment. It was almost as if she was afraid to love him in fear of someday losing him like she had lost his father. Although King did his best to hide his emotions, it was obvious her listless apathy towards him bothered him. But some things were better left unsaid, so Vonni never pursued the subject.

Each day became a new learning experience for Vonni, and he was learning so much. He studied King's chess moves and various business strategies. He learned how King's mind worked, how King looked upon the world as both a giant chessboard and playground of opportunity. Before beginning his tenure as King's *protettore*, Vonni had always seen him as some sort of larger-than-life wiseguy, an almost mythical being of great power and stature. But now that he really knew him, he realized King was just a regular guy. Well, a regular guy with an exceptionally brilliant mind and a mob boss for a grandfather. Yet he was surprisingly humble and independent. He was his own man and didn't need to flaunt the fact that his grandfather was the Boss of Bosses. He knew exactly where he wanted to be, and had a well-thought plan on how to get there. It was almost as if he had his whole life mapped out.

Another thing that surprised Vonni was King's insatiable appetite for women. It seemed King had girlfriends spread throughout the entire metropolitan area. He made a point of spending several hours a week with each of them, treating every one of them as if they were the love of his life, showering them with gifts and affection. There was no denying he was a ladies man, but it was Mary, the petite little Italian girl from Vonni's school, that he seemed to have a special place in his heart for. She was from a poor family and her mother was an invalid confined to a wheelchair. Maybe it was that they both had sick mothers, but King clearly had a special thing for her. He treated her differently than his other girlfriends. He showed her genuine emotion. When he tried buying her gifts, she refused them claiming they made her feel cheap, as if he was trying to buy her. She did, however, allow him to pay some of her mother's medical expenses, which were extensive. Sometimes he would even spend the night with her, which he never, ever, did with his other girlfriends, though he was indeed sleeping with them all.

Another thing Vonni found interesting about King was his need to spend time away from the city. King liked to frequent places where nobody knew him, where he could blend in and be a normal eighteen-year-old. He often had Vonni drive him far out into the suburbs to shop at the big malls, or catch an afternoon matinee, or shoot some pool. At night, using expertly-crafted counterfeit ID cards, they would hang out at small pubs and bars that had no ties to any of the Families. It was in these places that he really seemed to relax and enjoy life, laughing and horseplaying, even doing a bit of casual drinking. They were places where he could let his guard down and escape the responsibility of being the last Falcone.

Unfortunately for Vonni, he wasn't afforded the same luxury of relaxing and letting his guard down. He had no illusions as to what his responsibilities were when they were together. Sure they laughed and joked and had a good time, but he was always on high alert and never without his pistol. No matter where they were, he was constantly scanning the room for anyone who might be paying King a little too much attention. That day in Don Falcone's den, when he swore his oath of fealty to King, the don made it perfectly clear that his first priority was to always protect King. If he failed at this, he knew he would never live to explain why. Yet there was now more than just an oath that bonded them. There was genuine love. They were brothers, and he would gladly take a bullet for him. It was this love and devotion, he finally understood, that was the very essence of *Omerta*. It wasn't fear that kept those ancient Sicilians from breaking their oath of *Omerta*. It was love.

# CHAPTER 17

Because of certain municipal statutes and legal minutiae, it took Don Falcone longer than expected to take legal possession of the five nightclubs that had belonged to the deposed Scroi brothers. It wasn't until early spring that the process was finally complete. But just as he'd promised, the don gave one of the clubs to Vonni, which he aptly named "Johnny New York's." Located in an east side suburb several miles north of Detroit, the club was fairly new and modern, but Vonni still spent several weeks remodeling it, upgrading its sound system, adding laser lighting, installing new bars and a massive parquet dancefloor. But all of this still wasn't enough. He wanted it to be more than just another local nightclub. He wanted it to be unique. And after giving it some thought, he came up with a perfect way to do so. A theme. One that perfectly fit his personality. He had the interior made to resemble a 1920s New York speakeasy, with the décor matching the popular decor of that era. The walls were covered with framed black-and-white prints of people dressed in 1920s regalia, all of them drinking and swing-dancing merrily in underground speakeasies. There were pictures of famous celebrities from the 1920s, such as flapper Louise Brooks, actress Gloria Swanson, and actor Rudolph Valentino. On the dining room walls hung blown-up mug shots of infamous outlaws, such as bootlegger Billy McCoy, bank robber Clyde Barrow, and of course gangsters like Lucky Luciano, Bugs Moran, and Al Capone. All of it gave the club an authentic New York speakeasy feel, which Vonni hoped would transport his patrons back to the roaring twenties and offer them a whole new nightclub experience.

Since his eighteenth birthday was in May, Vonni decided to open his club for business on his birthday, as a sort of birthday party for himself. During the weeks preceding his birthday party grand opening, he promoted Johnny New York's aggressively, handing out hundreds of flyers and VIP passes, even paying for a few radio plugs. As a result, his grand opening was a smash success. With the onset of spring, people were eager to get out and celebrate the coming of summer. They arrived in droves to drink, dance, and party away their cabin fever. By midnight, the place was packed to capacity with a long line out the door. Though the club wasn't nearly as large as King's Club Vanzetti's, everyone really seemed to enjoy the 1920's speakeasy theme.

Over the last several months, King's lieutenants had slowly begun to accept Vonni as a legitimate part of their crew. And as a show of respect, they arrived at his grand opening in style, stepping out of tinted limousines wearing tailored suits, with beautiful young ladies under their arms, bodyguards by their sides. Even though he was much younger than they were and had no real rank within the crew other than as King's bodyguard, they paid him homage like he was a real someone, offering him respectful hugs and kisses on the cheek, wishing him great success with his new club. Having them publicly acknowledge him like this was a big deal, because it told people who were watching that he was "with them," the infamous King Falcone crew.

As Vonni mingled with his guests, King was never far from his side. Playing the part to the fullest, both of them were clad in 1920's style—black pinstriped zoot suits and fedoras. Together they walked around the club shaking hands, personally greeting people of importance, delving out complimentary vintage cocktails to friends and valued associates. Hordes of beautiful young women flitted around them, vying for their attention.

Young wiseguys from all over the city dropped by to pay their respects to "Johnny New York," King Falcone's new right-hand-man. At the end of the night, not only did he declare it the greatest birthday of his life, but the greatest night of his life.


Unfortunately, now that Vonni was King's full-time *protettore*, he was left with little time to manage his new nightclub, which meant he had no choice but to assign this responsibility to someone else. But it had to be someone he trusted. Naturally, he chose the one person he trusted most, his own right-hand-man, Tommy Guns Moceri, who was thrilled to take the job. Ever since Vonni became King's *protettore*, they had been seeing less and less of each other. Tommy had missed his goombadi. But now that he was managing Johnny New York's, he got to see Vonni almost every day. Although managing a popular nightclub was a lot of work, it was worth it. Not only did it allow him to see Vonni every day, but it let everyone in town know that he, too, was "with" the King Falcone crew.

But Vonni did feel a little guilty about dumping all the responsibility of managing Johnny New York's on Tommy. Sure his name was on the marquee out front, and people assumed he was the owner, but in truth, the club still belonged to Don Falcone. Other than show up a few times a week to collect money, Vonni had very little to do with its day-to-day operations. Tommy was the one actually doing all the work. He hired and managed the entire staff, from waitresses and bartenders, to disc jockeys and bouncers. He ordered and inventoried all the food and liquor. He did all the books and payroll. He kept track of the banking. Sometimes it was overwhelming, but he was compensated well for his efforts. Vonni paid him 10% of the club's weekly take, while Vonni himself was allowed to keep 25%. The rest went to King, who in turn kicked half of his cut up to Don Falcone. The club was earning Vonni a couple of thousand dollars extra a week, but Johnny New York's was more of a status symbol than anything. It was Don Falcone's way of telling the other crews that Vonni, who was already known around town as "Johnny New York," was now part of the Falcone Family.

The Scrois' other four clubs met similar fates. Don Falcone handed all of them over to King, who divided them up amongst his top lieutenants. His second-in-command, Tony Tappio, always the enterprising young entrepreneur, decided to turn his club into a high-end gentlemen's club. Joey Lombardo did the same. But obtaining licenses and permits for such clubs was not easy. Certain conservative city officials resisted the idea of having a strip clubs in their districts. Some even banded together to take a stand, citing various zoning laws and city ordinances that made it illegal to operate such establishments in their districts. In the end, however, Don Falcone did what he did best—he used his influence to change their minds, calling in several favors, making a few subtle threats. Several city ordinances and zoning laws were reworked, permits and licenses were issued, and the clubs were eventually allowed to open as high-end gentlemen's clubs.

As each club quickly grew in popularity, it wasn't long before King and his crew had much of the local nightclub market monopolized. Some of their clubs were bringing in enormous amounts of legitimate revenue. More importantly, though, they acted as giant laundry machines to clean much of the crew's illicit proceeds. Even more importantly, the clubs put them on the map. No longer were they considered just a ragtag crew of street hustlers and low-level wiseguys. They were now a well-oiled crew of legitimate businessmen, a growing force the other crews had no choice but to recognize as an extension of Don Falcone's Family. But inwardly the Syndicate *capi* were not happy that King had muscled his way into the suburbs and its extremely lucrative nightclub racket. Some of them were downright furious. But as long as Don Falcone was backing him, there was nothing they could do but bite their tongues and bide their time.


Word of King's crew as up-and-comers was spreading throughout the Syndicate ranks, and Vonni's name soon became synonymous with King's name. That raised a lot of questions amongst some of the other crews. Mafiosi were intrinsically cautious and skeptical about newcomers. Naturally, they wondered who Vonni was, where he had come from, and how he had worked his way into King's favor so quickly. Yet most were eager to shake his hand and make themselves known to him. Young hustlers from their side of town were constantly approaching him with business opportunities— various scams and hustles. Though most of these opportunities posed more trouble than their worth, he did incorporate several of them into his existing operations.

With his time split between King, Johnny New York's, and his various business ventures, it wasn't long before Vonni had more on his plate than he could handle, which meant it was time he began expanding his crew. He started by promoting his stolen goods mavens, Jimmy and Carlo, who he charged with recruiting new soldiers for their crew, soldiers who would be used to manage certain aspects of their street rackets. And of course, he made sure to implement a strict chain-of-command. All the new recruits reported to Jimmy and Carlo, who then reported to the Campisi brothers, Vitor and Luigi, who reported to Tommy, who finally reported to Vonni. He made sure this chain-of-command was strictly adhered to. Because, after all, he and his crew were really just an extension of King's crew, which was essentially an extension Don Falcone's Family.

As was the modus operandi for all Mafia factions, Vonni's crew was structured with a strict operational hierarchy that allowed for a buffer between himself and members of his crew who were involved in regular illicit activities. It was this buffer that kept him protected if one of them were to get busted by authorities. The local police posed little threat. They were on the Syndicate payroll and paid well to "look the other way." But it was the FBI all Mafiosi had to worry about. The Federal Bureau of Investigations had an Organized Crime Unit, whose sole purpose was to monitor the activities of the local Mafia *borgata*. They kept their ears to the street and were constantly looking for new informants to infiltrate the *borgata* and provide them with information. Don Falcone did have some "friends" in the FBI, even one or two who worked with the local Organized Crime Unit, but one could never be too careful. The FBI had limitless resources, and most of its agents could not be bought or coerced by intimidation. This is why Vonni and his young crew operated under a well-defined chain-of-command that kept King, and ultimately Don Falcone, from being implemented in anything illegal if one of their subordinates were to turn FBI informant.

As well as learning how to structure and manage his crew, Vonni learned the many codes and decrees that governed the Mafia as a whole, some of which had been in place for hundreds, even thousands of years. King lived by these codes and decrees, and expected nothing less from every member of his crew. If anyone failed to honor these codes and decrees, he'd immediately implement sanctions. Or worse. Every member of his crew knew the consequences of betrayal. His one-time driver, Diangelo "Big Dean" D'Anatto, was a reminder of those consequences. Even though Dean had been reported as a missing person, rumor on the street was that his disappearance was related to him somehow betraying the Family.

One of Cosa Nostra's most powerful indoctrination practices was to explain in great detail the consequences of betrayal. That was why each new recruit, no matter who they were or what role they would play within the crew, was required to provide the addresses of all close relatives. It was made very clear to everyone who worked with the crew that if they were to betray the crew in any way, shape, or form, revenge would not only be sought on them, but also on their family. No one was exempt. Mothers, fathers, siblings, even children were potential targets for retribution. It was a ruthless practice, but it wasn't until the second time Vonni witnessed King's vengeance on a betrayer that he realized just how ruthless his new boss could be.

Victor "Fists" Aquiano, one of King's top enforcers, had met a Mexican cocaine dealer while serving several months in the Wayne County jail for beating the son of a local judge half-to-death in a bar fight. After getting to know this Mexican, he learned that the guy was a mid-level distributor for a large drug cartel in Tijuana, Mexico. Upon his release, the guy began supplying him with large consignments of high-grade cocaine. Victor would then advance the coke to a network of mid-level dealers throughout the city. These dealers, most of who belonged to one of the black or Latino gangs that worked with King's crew, had their own small networks of street-level dealers who sold crack from street corners or abandoned houses. For many months this arrangement worked smoothly, bringing in tens of thousands of dollars for Victor and, ultimately, King.

But the drug business was not a racket that King particularly cared for. Not only did his grandfather disapprove of it, but he didn't like the caliber of people involved in it. He was also aware of how hard drugs could devastate entire neighborhoods and destroy the lives of the addicts who used them. But it was a racket he couldn't pass up. At least not now. There was just too much money to be made. He knew addicts would get their fix no matter who sold it to them, so he decided it might as well be his crew who sold it to them. But it was a dangerous racket. Not only because federal drug charges carried draconian prison sentences, but because the Syndicate already had a major hand in it. Giuseppe Rubino, a powerful *capo* who commanded a ruthless crew of street soldiers, was the Syndicate's primary drug czar. He imported everything from cocaine and heroin, to

319

marijuana and methamphetamine–literally tons of it. His crew had wholesalers spread throughout the city, but by no means did they monopolize the market. It was impossible to completely control a drug market the size of Detroit's. There were just too many freelance dealers and importers, everything from mid-level wholesalers to teenage crack dealers who sold nickel rocks on the corner. But Rubino and his crew did control a significant portion of the city's drug market, taking in millions annually for the Syndicate coffers. Which was what made it such a dangerous racket for King. He knew Rubino and the other *capi* would not be happy if they learned he was siphoning from their cash cow.

One early summer evening, while Vonni and King were making their rounds to their respective clubs, King received an unsettling call from his lieutenant, Victor Aquiano. It seemed one of Victor's dealers had run off with a fairly large consignment of cocaine. Four kilos to be exact, with a wholesale value of nearly a $100,000. This was the first time since the morning of the Big Dean incident that Vonni saw King truly furious. For starters, someone was going to have to pay for the dope. The Mexicans were an integral part of his operation, helping him and his crew earn tens of thousands of dollars each month. And they were a particularly ruthless bunch. They had no idea who his grandfather was, and even if they did it wouldn't matter. They had their own organization that was vast, powerful, and well-funded. He had no intentions of going to war with them over such a paltry sum of money. If it came down to it, he would pay them out of his own pocket. But it wasn't the money that had him vexed. It was the infraction itself, the blatant disrespect to him and his crew. He knew he could never allow anyone to steal from them. If he did, it would be taken as a sign of weakness. In their world, the weak were eaten alive by the strong.

The dealer who had disappeared with the dope was a black gang member by the name of Terrance "T-Bone" Jones. King had never met him before, but Victor had vouched for him several months previously when he began advancing him kilos of cocaine. Terrance had been a good earner, moving considerable amounts of product and always paying on time. But it seemed he hadn't taken Victor's warning about betrayal seriously, which was not acceptable. So the first thing King did was order surveillance on the dealer's house, his girlfriend's house, and his mother's house. But when Terrance failed to turn up after two days, King decided it was time to take a more aggressive approach. He knew if he wanted to save face with his crew as well as send a message to anyone else who thought they could get away with disrespecting them, he would have to handle it personally—and quickly.

On the third morning, Vonni drove King to meet Victor and Billy, who were parked in a stolen Suburban several houses down the block from the home of Terrance's mother, a rundown old colonial on the city's upper east side. It was just after 8:30 in the morning, and after Victor relayed that there had still been no sign of Terrance, King had Vonni drive down the street and pull up in the mother's driveway. After taking a quick glance around the quiet street, King walked up to the front door and knocked. A moment later, a heavy-set black woman opened the door.

"Sorry to bother you, ma'am," he said, flashing her a disarming smile, "but I'm looking for Terrance. He hasn't been at his house the last few days, and he's not answering his phone. I'm starting to worry about him."

"Oh, him and that damn phone," she said, a look of understanding on her matronly old face. "He don't answer when I call either. What's the point of having a cell phone if you don't answer it?"

King flashed her another smile. "I was thinking he might've broke or lost it."

"Maybe," she nodded. "Have you tried his girlfriend's house?"

"Cheyanne?" he asked, knowing there had been no sign of Terrance at the girlfriend's house either.

321

"No, not her fast ass. She just his baby momma. He got a new girlfriend on the west side. Name's Keysha. I only met her once, but she seem alright."

"Oh, yes, Keysha," he said, never having heard of her. "He told me about her. You wouldn't happen to have her address, would you?"

"No, I don't. I just know she live over there off Joy Road somewhere."

"Well, I guess I'll just wait for him to call me then. But if you see him, could you do me a favor and have him to call Vic?"

"Sure," she said. "But there's no tellin' when I might see him. You know how he is."

"Yes, ma'am, I sure do. Again, sorry to bother you. Have a great day."

"You, too," she said, and then cast a quick look up and down the street before shutting the door.

Since he had no address to the new girlfriend's house, he decided to pay a visit to some of Terrance's dope houses in a seedy old ghetto near Mt. Elliot and Gratiot. At the first house, he played dumb and asked the "trap" workers if they had seen Terrance over the last few days. They said they hadn't. Nor did they claim to know where his girlfriend lived. But the fact that they had bags of crack to sell was proof that they were lying. The second house yielded him the same result. Nobody seemed to know anything.

King finally lost his patience at the third house, when one of two teenage dealers there called him a "crackhead cracker." Deciding it was time to make a statement, he pulled out his pistol and shot the kid in the face. Terrified and in shock, the kid's partner began begging for his life, saying he knew where Terrance was hiding. He even provided King with an address, which indeed belonged to the new girlfriend. King then dispatched the young crack dealer with two head shots. He hated a rat and wasn't going to leave a witness.

322

Now that he had an address, King ordered Victor and Billy to park down the block from the home of Terrance's mother and wait for his call. He then had Vonni drive across town to the girlfriend's house, which was located in a run-down neighborhood on the city's west side. When they pulled up out front, there were two cars in the driveway but neither belonged to Terrance. King then ordered Vonni to wait in the car while he stepped up to the front door and knocked. When nobody answered, he knocked harder. Finally, a disheveled-looking black girl in her twenties yanked the door open and glared at him.

"Who the fuck are you?" she demanded, eyeing him up and down with contempt. "And why the hell are you pounding on my door? You a cop or somethin'?"

He examined her briefly. She was wearing jean shorts and a T-shirt. Her hair was a mess like she had just woken up, but she was wearing fresh makeup. She was actually quite pretty, but clearly had a bad attitude. He wondered if she even knew her boyfriend was on the lam for stealing somebody's dope.

"No, I'm definitely not a cop," he assured her, feigning amusement. "I'm looking for Terrance. I've been trying to get ahold of him but he hasn't been answering his phone."

She examined him suspiciously but avoided eye contact. "So what makes you think I know where the hell he is? I ain't his mother."

He immediately suspected she was hiding something. "Well, it's funny you say that because it was actually his mother who told me he's staying here with you."

"His momma?" she said, an incredulous look on her face. "How you know his momma?"

He shrugged indifferently. "Me and T-Bone go way back."

Again she eyed him suspiciously. "That's funny, 'cause I know all his friends and I ain't never seen you before. He don't hang with no white boys. Which means you're either a cop or a crackhead. Either way, you can take your cracker ass off my porch so I can go back to sleep."

A hot wave of anger washed over him, but he remained calm and pragmatic. "Well, I apologize for waking you. But again, I'm not a cop and definitely not a crackhead. Me and Terrance are old friends. So if you see him, do me a favor and have him call Vic. It's important. I really need to talk to him."

"*Whatever*," she said, and then slammed the door in his face.

Back in the car, he told Vonni to drive around the block and park down the street so they could watch the house. He then placed a call to Victor. "Bring her here," he said, then hung up and looked at Vonni. "Now we wait."

"Wait for what?" Vonni asked, confused.

King stared at the girlfriend's house. "She was definitely hiding something. I'm pretty sure the fucker is in there. But if he isn't, she's on the phone with him right now, telling him we were there. If he's smart, he'll grab his shit and try to run. But then again, we already know the fucker ain't too smart. He stole from us."

Vonni looked at the house. "How do you know she was hiding something?"

"Because she was nervous. She wouldn't look me in the eye, and she was very defensive. That's what people do when they're hiding something. They get defensive to cover up their nervousness. It's basic Freudian behavior. Plus, she tried to make it look like she just woke up. Her hair was all fucked up, but she was wearing fresh makeup and dressed like she was going out."

Vonni nodded. "So who's Vic and Billy bringing here?"

"His mother," King said matter-of-factly. He then removed a silencer from his pocket and screwed it into the barrel of his .45 semi-automatic.

Thirty minutes later, Billy pulled up next to them in the stolen Suburban. Bound and gagged in the back seat was

324

Terrance's mother, a distraught and confused look on her face. King simply motioned Billy to follow them to the girlfriend's house, where Vonni came to a stop along the curb out front. Billy parked the Suburban directly behind them. This time King had Vonni accompany him to the front door. After knocking several times, the same girl yanked the door open with the same annoyed look.

"*What the fuck do you want*?" she boomed, glaring at King. "I already told you Terrance ain't here!"

"Tell him to look out the window," King drawled menacingly, gesturing towards the parked Suburban.

When she looked towards the Suburban, Billy powered down the tinted back window to expose Victor holding a sawed-off shotgun to the head of Terrance's terrified mother, duct tape around her mouth, tears streaming down her face.

"Wha..." she mumbled, her impudent attitude suddenly vanishing. "What the hell is going on? Is that—"

"Yeah, it's his mother," King interrupted, amused by the mortified look on her face. "And I suggest you invite us in, because my paisan over there has a very heavy trigger finger. I'd hate for him to blow Momma T-Bone's head all over your front lawn."

When she just stared at the Suburban, paralyzed with consternation, he simply drew his silenced pistol from his waist and forced her back into the house. Vonni immediately drew his own pistol and shut the door behind them.

"Who else is here?" King asked calmly, aiming the pistol at her face. When she hesitated, he cocked the hammer. "You should seriously consider your next words, sweetheart, because I don't want to kill any unexpected family or heroes. Now, who else is in the house?"

"Just...," she stammered, staring down the barrel of the pistol. "It's just... just me and Terrance. Please don't shoot me. I don't know what he did, but I had nothing to do with it. *Please!*"

"Where is he?" he demanded, his tone making it very clear that he meant business.

"Upstairs," she whispered, motioning a trembling finger towards the ceiling. "He told me to get rid of you."

King turned and aimed his pistol at the staircase leading upstairs. "Terrance!" he yelled. "Look out the window and wave good-bye to your mother, because this may be the last time you ever see her alive."

Terrance was locked in an upstairs bedroom, clutching an AK-47 assault rifle against his side. Since running off with Victor's dope, he'd been confident that no one would ever find him there at his new girlfriend's home on the opposite side of the city. He figured Victor would eventually give up looking for him after a few weeks, and then he would use the four kilos of coke as a foundation to build his drug empire. But as he now looked out the window and saw his mother gagged and bound with a sawed-off shotgun pointed at her head, his grandiose dreams of being a cocaine kingpin instantly turned into a nightmare. Even the most hardened gangsters had a weak spot, and he was looking at his.

Knowing he had no choice, Terrance now unlocked the bedroom door and slowly made his way downstairs, still clutching the assault rifle. When he stepped into the living room, he saw his girlfriend seated on the couch, a look of pure terror on her face. There were two young white guys in the room, neither of whom he recognized. One was posted by the door with a semi-automatic pistol aimed at him. The other was casually seated on the recliner in the corner of the room, a silenced pistol propped across his lap. It wasn't hard to tell which one was in charge.

"Hello, Terrance," King said, offering him a grin. "Nice of you to join the party."

"Who the fuck are you?" Terrance demanded defiantly, aiming the AK-47 at him. "And what do you want?"

326

"Put the chopper down, paisan," King said, his words calm but threatening. "If my partner outside hears gunshots in here..." He tapped the barrel of his silencer against his head. "Well, your mother will end up with a serious headache."

Terrance looked into those dark eyes, and a sense of pure dread washed over him. He'd grown up on the streets, associating with nothing but gang members, hardened street toughs and drug dealers. But none had ever unnerved him like this. This young guy had the eyes of a cold-blooded killer. For the first time in his life Terrance felt true fear, because he suddenly realized that his mother's life was now in the hands of this young killer.

"Alright," Terrance said, lowering the rifle to his side. "Who are you and what do you want?"

"First of all, I'll be asking the questions," King said, and then motioned to Vonni. "Second, hand my partner the chopper. Nice and slow."

Vonni, who had learned to trust King and followed his orders without fail, immediately stepped over and took possession of the AK-47, while keeping his pistol trained on him the whole time.

"As to who I am..." King continued, leaning forward in the recliner. "Well, I'm the Boogie Man. You know, the bad man parents tell their kids about to scare them into being good kids."

"Yeah?" Terrance said, casting a glance out the front window. "Well good for you, dude. But what the fuck you want with me? And why the fuck you got my mom out there?"

"Paisan, you know why we're here," King growled, almost maniacally. "And it's your fault your mother's involved. You obviously didn't take Victor seriously when he explained the consequences of betraying us. Did you really think you could just run off with our dope and get away with it?"

Terrance felt a wave of trepidation wash over him as he suddenly realized who he was dealing with. "I didn't steal your dope!" he blurted. "It was stolen from me. Some fuckin' stickup kids busted in my spot and jacked me!"

King considered this for a moment. "Oh, we didn't know that, T-Bone. You could have just told us this. I mean, these things happen. It's part of the business we're in. You didn't have to go into hiding. We would have worked with you. Maybe fronted you some more weight so you could work off the loss."

The wave of trepidation that had just washed over Terrance was suddenly replaced with a wave of relief. Maybe if he stuck to his story he could talk his way out of this and still keep the dope. He wondered why he hadn't come up with this story in the first place. "I didn't tell Vic because I thought he'd freak out," he said, doing his best to sound sincere. "I knew he'd think I was lying and probably do some crazy ass shit like this. So I figured I'd just hunt down them fools who jacked me and get the dope back. I mean. I have a pretty good idea who they were."

King suddenly jumped to his feet. "Enough bullshit!" he roared, pointing a finger at the girlfriend. "Your loud-mouth hood-rat here likes to think all white guys are crackheads or cops. Well guess what? I ain't no crackhead. And I definitely ain't a cop. I'm your worst motherfuckin' nightmare, Terrance. I'm the guy who has your mother tied up in the back of a truck with a twelve-gauge pinned to her head. And if I give the order, my guy will blow her brains across the front lawn. It's that simple. I don't want that to happen, but I won't lose any sleep if it does. She means nothing to me. Neither do you. I just want my dope back. You got greedy. It happens. You figured you could just run and hide for a few weeks until things settled down. You figured Victor was just some punk ass white boy you could get down on. And part of me can't blame you. I mean, shit, that's a hundred grand worth of dope. Break it down and you could triple that. That's a nice start, but you failed to consider one thing. When you began working for us, Vic made it clear what would happen if you ever betrayed us. And yet here we are. Clearly you have no idea who you're dealing with. This ain't no fuckin' rap video, my man. And

I ain't Puff Daddy. We run this town! You, your little gang, you're a joke to us. Nothing but ants. And we step on ants for fun."

He paused and visibly seemed to calm himself. "But that being said, it's not too late to redeem yourself, Terrance. You can start by giving our dope back. And to make up for your infraction, you'll pay us a penalty of..." He looked up, as if picking a number from the air. "Oh, say fifty grand... Yes, fifty should do it. I'll even give you a few months to pay it."

The girl, deciding her life was no longer in danger, jumped to her feet. "Fifty grand?" she blurted insolently. "That's bullshit! Why would he pay you anything? He just told you he got robbed. He doesn't have your dope! Who the fuck do you think you are?"

King raised his pistol and aimed it at her forehead. "Why, I'm King Falcone," he said, and calmly squeezed the trigger.

The silenced Colt .45 coughed softly, and the back of her head exploded, sending a geyser of crimson gore splattering onto the wall, her body crumpling to the floor. Vonni didn't even flinch. He calmly kept his pistol trained on Terrance, not even seeming to notice the girl lying on the floor, the exit wound in the back of her head gushing blood to the fading rhythm of her dying heart.

"*Fuck, man!*" Terrance yelled, staring at his girl twitching on the floor in death throes. "Why...? "

King leveled the smoking pistol on him. "Because she had a big mouth," he said, his face twisted into the mask of a hardened killer. "And you're next. Then your mother, your brothers, sisters, kids, everyone you love. This is how it works. This is how we operate. Victor told you this you before he began fronting you dope. But you obviously didn't take him seriously. You thought he was just some dumb white boy you could get down on." He lowered his pistol and seemed to soften. "But I believe you've learned your lesson, Terrance. Yeah, your girl's dead. These things happen. Collateral damage. But you're still alive. Girls come and go, but you only get one life. So let's stop playing games. Let's move forward and get back to business. All I want is my dope back. Plus the fifty grand. Or would you like to do it the other way?"

Terrance looked up at him, his eyes filled with confusion. "What other way?"

King shrugged indifferently. "I just kill you and cut my losses."

Terrance began begging for his life and quickly led King down to the basement, where he opened an old Brinks safe concealed under a massive pile of dirty laundry. Inside it were three of the four missing kilos, over $20,000 in cash, two pistols, and several pieces of expensive jewelry. King had him load it all into an empty pillowcase and then shot him in the head. Twice. He and Vonni then casually strode from the house and walked up to the Suburban.

"Take this back to the stash house," he said, tossing the stuffed pillow case in the back seat next to the mother. "But first blindfold her and dump her in an alley somewhere. Alive. She's served her purpose."

With that, he had Vonni drive him to Vanzetti's so they could get back to their usual business. He felt no remorse for what he did. Terrance had sealed his fate when he decided he could get away with disrespecting the crew. He had to be made an example of. A message had to be sent to anyone who thought they could get away with disrespecting the crew. Terrance was just an expendable gambit in King's chess game of life, a sacrificial pawn.

It was this day that Vonni saw the stark contrast in King's two personalities. Usually, King was very easygoing, relaxed and fun to be around—a loving and compassionate leader to his crew. But he was still a Mafioso, a Falcone, and to cross him could be fatal. He'd been trained by Don Falcone himself to show no mercy to those who betrayed him. For to show mercy was to show weakness. And after word got out how he handled Terrance, nobody could ever claim King Falcone was weak.

# CHAPTER 18

Just as Don Falcone had promised, Vonni was allowed to graduate with the rest of his senior class. Wanting his parents and sister to be there to watch him receive his diploma, he paid for them to be flown in for his commencement ceremony. He even sent a limousine to pick them up at the airport and drive them straight to his club, where he and King were eagerly awaiting their arrival. The instant they stepped through the door, he jumped up greeted them with enthusiastic hugs. After formally introducing them to King, he took them on a quick tour of his club, excited for them see what a success he had become there in Detroit.

As his father took in the room, he discreetly studied Vonni, barely able to believe he was looking at his son. It seemed Detroit had turned his boy into a man, and he had to admit, he was impressed. "So you actually run this place?" he asked, finding it hard to believe that an eighteen-year-old kid was managing his own nightclub.

"Yeah, Dad, this is all me," Vonni answered, taking in the club with pride. "What do you think? Like the theme?"

"I do," his father admitted, looking at a picture of Coco Chanel on the wall. "Very classy. But who actually owns it?"

"My grandfather," King answered, gesturing towards a table that was already set with dinnerware. "And you are my guests, so please sit down. I know you've had a long trip, so I imagine you're hungry. I brought my chef over from my club to prepare us a special meal. He was trained in Florence and he's best in town. So please, sit down and relax. I've heard so much about you all, and I've been looking forward to meeting each of you."

After seating themselves at the table, King began asking about their flight and how long they planned to stay in town. He was gracious and articulate, full of jokes and witticisms, but Vonni's mother was not impressed. She knew from her sister that he was the grandson of a local mob boss, but she was not expecting what she was looking at. She expected him to be a gangly young thug dressed in a tacky jogging suit and gold chains. This "King," however, was a tall, handsome young Adonis in a three-piece suit. He was mature, articulate, and looked like a college quarterback, an all-American boy next door. But there was something unnerving about him. He possessed a self-assurance that was far beyond his years. Growing up in Brooklyn, she had gone to school with several young Mafiosi. She even made the mistake of dating one for a short time. But they all had one thing in common: the same cocky self-assurance that this one possessed, as if rules didn't apply to them. But this one's cocky self-assurance trumped them all. This one carried himself like he came from some kind of royal lineage. Then there were his eyes. They were unnervingly dark and penetrating, as if he was constantly trying to read her every thought. But there was more to his eyes than that. They screamed danger. Though he was smiling and doing his best to come across as just a harmless teenager, she knew exactly what he was—a young Mafioso. And as she now watched him interact with her son, she felt a sinking sense of dread, for she knew how the Mafia worked. Once you were in, you were in for life.

As they dined on fine Italian cuisine, Vonni made small talk with his parents and sister, who brought him up to speed on all the neighborhood gossip from back in Brooklyn. King, for the most part, just sat back and listened. When he did speak, he tried to impress them with his charm and wit. But Vonni's mother wasn't fooled. She knew he was simply putting on an act, that men like him, no matter what age, were accomplished actors. And as she now watched his act, it was easy to see how her son had become so enchanted with him. The exact same thing had happened to her eldest son, who consequently ended up with a bullet in his head, floating in the East River. That was why she had come there with hopes of convincing her only remaining son to give up the path he was on. But as she now saw how he looked upon his charismatic new friend, she feared it was too late.

After dinner, Vonni brought them to see his new apartment in the prestigious 9 Mile Tower. His parents had never seen anything like it, and found it hard to believe that their son, a mere eighteen-year-old, was living in the lap of such a luxury. But it was his sister who was most impressed. Her little brother was living like a superstar. Over the last several months, her mother had told her several times that he was associating with some sort of Mafia sect there in Detroit, but she refused to believe that he was a dangerous criminal. To her, he would always be the sweet little brother who had defended her honor so vehemently when they were kids. Yet there was no denying he was a man now. Handsome and fit, he was quite a sight to behold in his shiny new suit. But it was his manner that had changed the most. He had obviously matured since moving to Detroit, and whatever he was doing for money, he was clearly good at it. So regardless of who he was associating with, she couldn't help being impressed. After all, he had come from nothing and grown up an outsider, with no money and even less social status. But there in Detroit he clearly had both, and even though her parents disapproved of his new lifestyle, deep down she was proud of him.

After showing them his apartment, Vonni paid to put them up in a pair of luxury suites at the Renaissance Marriott. Located in the city's largest and most iconic downtown skyscraper, each suite of rooms offered a spectacular view of the Detroit River,

Canada and beyond. At first, his parents, especially his mother, tried to refuse his generosity.

"Giovanni," his mother said, taking in the first room. "This is too much. A pair of economy rooms would do just fine."

But of course, he wouldn't listen. "Take the rooms, Mom," he insisted. "They're presidential suites. They're already paid for so enjoy them. Order room service. Take a swim in the pool. There's a salon downstairs. Go get your hair and nails done. Whatever. Get a workout in the gym. Checkout the spa. They got a four-star restaurant here. There's even a masseuse."

It didn't take much more convincing. None of them had ever stayed in a luxury hotel before, and by the end of the weekend they would take full advantage of the hotel's amenities. Even his mother would end up getting her hair and nails done at the hotel's salon, all of it charged to his account.

The following morning, a limousine delivered Vonni's parents and sister to his commencement ceremony. After greeting them excitedly in his cap and gown, he escorted them to their seats and then took a seat at the front of the auditorium with the rest of his graduating class. When he was finally called up on stage to collect his diploma, even he was surprised by the applause he received. Hundreds of kids began clapping and calling out his name, for it was well known that he was now King Falcone's right-hand-man. But the acceptance of his peers was not what made the ceremony so special. Nor was it that his family was there to watch him collect his diploma. It was the fact that Don Falcone himself was in attendance. Seated next to King in the back of the auditorium, the don was flanked by his own *protettore* and another of his bodyguards. Although he was trying his best to blend into the crowd, most of the people there knew exactly who he was—the alleged head of the local Mafia.

When the ceremony was finally over, Vonni excitedly introduced his family to Don Falcone. And, as always, the don was his usual charming self, looking dapper in his three-piece suit, his hair slicked and glistening with pomade. But Vonni's parents were noticeably unnerved by the two suit-clad men posted behind him like a pair of Secret Servicemen protecting the president. He was gracious and friendly enough, but he gave the impression that he was a man who took what he wanted, even if it was by force. Even though he and his grandson were separated in age by several decades, they both had the same self-assured cockiness that seemed universal to all Mafiosi. It was easy for Vonni's parents to see why their son would want to emulate them.

After introductions were made, Don Falcone invited everyone to dinner at the Roma Café, one of the city's oldest and most renowned Italian restaurants. Located downtown only a few blocks from the don's Eastern Market headquarters, the famous Italian eatery was owned by one of the don's personal friends. So of course, he received the VIP treatment. The instant they stepped through the door, a beautiful young hostess greeted them excitedly and led them straight to a reserved table at the back of the dining room. A moment later, an eager young waiter delivered baskets of freshly baked Italian bread and complimentary bottles of house wine.

Always the gracious host, Don Falcone took the liberty of ordering for everyone. He went with one of his favorites—*osso bucco*, a classic Italian dish made of braised veal shanks cooked in a white wine sauce, served over angel hair pasta. While they waited for their meals, he engaged Vonni's parents in light conversation, generally interested in learning more about them. He asked about New York, their family origins, and what they did for a living. But he sensed their apprehension toward him, so he tried to put them at ease by sharing stories from his own life and humble Sicilian roots. He told a few jokes and tried to come across as nothing more than a benign old grandfather.

Vonni's father and sister were enchanted by Don Falcone, prattling away with him like they were old friends. But Vonni's mother was not so easily duped. She knew the game the old mobster was playing, and could see right through his amiable masquerade. But of course, she didn't dare voice this. As much as she despised the man for who he was and what he represented, she would never say it to his face. So all she could do was sit there and hope that her son was not fully under his corrupted spell.

When they finished feasting on their plates of *osso bucco*, Don Falcone ordered tiramisu for dessert, with glasses of anisette to wash it down. And while they enjoyed this rich Italian dessert, he surprised everyone at the table with an announcement.

"Giovanni..." he began, casually lighting a cigar. "It's no small feat to graduate high school. Especially with honors. Such an occasion only comes along once in a lifetime. I'm sure your parents are very proud of you. I know I am. So to commemorate your graduation, I've arranged for a little party in your honor at the Gourmet House. Real swanky place up on Jefferson. A friend of mine owns it, and he took care of everything. I even had Omnio invite your entire senior class. So enjoy. I myself never finished high school. I wish I had, but, unfortunately, back when I first came to America, I could barely speak English. The teachers didn't know what to do with me. And, to be honest, a lot of us immigrants weren't very welcome in the public schools. The other kids treated us like lepers. So I ended up dropping out and taking a job loading trucks in the Eastern Market. Only a few blocks from here, actually. Fortunately, when I turned eighteen, I was able to enlist in the Marines, even without a high school diploma."

"Did you ever see combat?" Vonni's father asked, having spent four years in the Army.

"Oh, yes," Don Falcone said, a nostalgic look in his eyes. "Several times. I was with the 26th Marines, part of the 1st Marines, 5th Regiment. My company was a recon unit attached to the Marine Expeditionary Force. We were one of the first units to hit the beaches in Pusan, South Korea. That donkey's ass MacArthur picked the rainy season for the landing. It was a terrible mess. We were ambushed the second we hit the beach. Everything was mud and our mechanized units just sunk in. It took us six weeks to finally secure Pusan. I lost a lot of friends during those six weeks."

Vonni had no idea the don was a war hero. "Were you ever wounded?" he asked, fascinated and wanting to hear more.

Don Falcone held up two fingers. "Twice," he admitted. "But only once in actual combat. I was hit with a grenade fragment." He pointed at an ancient scar on his forearm. "It's still in there. The doctor said it would do more damage to take out, so there it still sits after all these years. Sometimes it aches when it gets cold, but I usually forget it's even there."

"What about the second time you were wounded?" King prompted, grinning mischievously. He had heard the story many times and knew it was one Vonni would appreciate.

Don Falcone shot him a look, knowing quite well what his grandson was doing. "Omnio, that's a story better left unsaid. At least here at the dinner table. But you could say it was my own fault I got wounded."

"Come on!" Vonni urged, sensing this was a story he didn't want to miss. "You can't just leave it at that. Tell us what happened."

Don Falcone thought for a moment and finally acquiesced. "Giovanni, if you insist, I will tell you. But only because I think there is a lesson to be learned from it, and I want you to know this is something I am not proud of. I was injured in a bar fight. Stabbed, actually. Like I said, it was my own fault. I was a stupid, loud-mouth kid who got drunk and let my guard down. I was lucky to walk out of there alive. But I learned a valuable lesson that night: It's okay to do a little social drinking, but there's no greater fool than a drunkard. When a man is drunk, he is compromised both physically and mentally. You boys should always consider that before you drink."

As Vonni's mother listened to the don's dogmatic narrative, she noticed the awe and wonderment in her son's eyes. He was

337

obviously enamored with the enigmatic old mob boss. It caused her to feel a terrible sense of loss and frustration, for she suddenly realized her son would never escape this man's grip. As a mother, her job was to protect her son from men like this. But she had clearly failed at the job. Her son had grown up to be a gangster, a Mafioso, seduced into a dangerous and shadowy world that she could never understand. As she now watched him hang on the old mobster's every word, her heart was heavy with sadness, for she suddenly felt as if she had lost a second son.

After bantering back and forth with Vonni's father for a few more minutes about his time in the Marines, Don Falcone produced an envelope from his inside pocket. "Oh, I almost forgot," he said, sliding the envelope over to Vonni. "This is for you. A little gift to show my appreciation for doing such a great job managing the club."

Vonni opened the envelope and peered inside. "Vegas?" he said, removing two first-class plane tickets to Las Vegas.

"Yes," Don Falcone said, grinning at King. "You boys have been working so hard I figured you could use a little vacation. So I reserved a suite for you at the Flamingo. Relax by the pool. Look at the pretty girls. Take in some shows. Maybe learn to golf."

"Golf?" Vonni's sister asked, confused. "In Las Vegas? Isn't it just desert out there?"

"Oh, no, honey," Don Falcone answered, chuckling at her naiveté. "Las Vegas has some of the most beautiful golf courses in the world. Compliments of the Colorado River." He turned to her parents as if a sudden thought occurred to him. "You know, I was going to suggest the boys take their girlfriends, but I just had a better idea. Why don't you join them? My treat. I'm sure the boys would love to have you."

Vonni's mother narrowed her eyes at him. "With all due respect, Mr. Falcone," she said, her tone that of a concerned mother. "May I ask why you're doing all this for my son?"

Don Falcone's eyes glazed over, as if recounting a distant memory. "Well, Mrs. Battaglia, I must admit I have a special place in my heart for your son." He smiled at Vonni affectionately. "I've never told him this, but I also moved to Detroit as a very young man—and under similar circumstances. Back in Sicily my family had been involved in a feud with another family. Many men died, including my father and two older brothers. So, before I could become another casualty in this feud, my mother put me on a boat and shipped me to America to live with an aunt I'd never even met before. It was tough. I was only fifteen and I struggled to find my identity... I suppose this is the reason I feel so inclined to help your son. I know how hard it is to be a young man in a foreign place. I'm only trying to give him a head start in life. I hope this doesn't make you uncomfortable."

This slightly appeased her, but only slightly. "Well, Mr. Falcone," she said, trying not to sound too abrasive, "I appreciate your concern for our son, and I thank you for being so generous with him, but I don't see what he's done to deserve it. After all, you barely even know him."

"Oh, I think I know him quite well," he said, again smiling fondly at Vonni. "I've gotten to know him over the last several months. He's a good boy. Very bright. Respectful. Ambitious. Reminds me of myself at his age."

"Regardless," she said, standing her ground. "I think he's too young to be vacationing in a place like Las Vegas."

"Too young?" he repeated, as if he had no idea what she was implying. "He's eighteen now. He and Omnio will love it down there. Vegas is more than just a bunch of nightclubs and casinos. It's a wonderful place to relax and vacation. There are plenty of fun things for them to do, and I have friends there who will treat them like royalty. I thought it would be a great opportunity for them to get out and see the world a little."

She glanced at her estranged husband, hoping to get his support. But when he simply shrugged, she became even more frustrated. "Frankly, Mr. Falcone, I don't approve," she said, her anger audible. "I still think these boys are too young to be running around Las Vegas by themselves. As far as I'm concerned, there's nothing but trouble for them down there."

"Nonsense," he said, dismissing this with a wave of his hand. "They'll be fine. I even made arrangements with some friends to look after them, and again, if you're that concerned, you and your husband are welcome to join them. Make it a family affair. Do some shopping. Take in some shows. Relax by the pool. I'll see to all the arrangements. You'll want for nothing. My friends down there will roll out the red carpet for you."

She looked him in the eye and could tell he was not used to being questioned. He was clearly trying to win her over with generosity, but she saw right through his altruistic facade. He was masterfully trying to tighten his grip around her son. It was just more of his sophistry and manipulation, but she knew it would be a frivolous waste of time to call him on it. Her son was going to do whatever he wanted no matter she said.

"That's very generous of you, Mr. Falcone," she said, offering him a forced smile. "Unfortunately, I have a job and I can't afford to take any more time off. But thank you for the offer."

Vonni's father also had a job to get back to, but he was tempted to take the don up on his offer. He had never been to Las Vegas and could use a vacation. But he knew if he went, his wife would be furious. He also knew his son would not be happy about it. They had grown distant over the last few years, and rarely even talked. So he also respectfully declined.

Vonni's sister, however, had no such reservations. School was out for the summer, and she had no immediate plans. She had never been to Las Vegas and she missed her little brother. This was the perfect opportunity for her to spend some time with him away from their parents, where she could ask him all the questions she wanted to ask without putting him on the spot.

"I'll go!" she blurted, casting an excited look at Vonni. "Can I go?"

"Of course, sis," Vonni said, offering her a smile. "I'd love to have you down there with us."

His mother shot her a dirty look but did not say anything to discourage her. As much as she detested the idea of her eighteen-year-old son and twenty-year-old daughter vacationing in Las Vegas—paid for by some Detroit mob boss—she did not want to keep them from spending time together. After all, they had barely seen each other over the last four years.


Vonni's graduation party turned out to be an extravagant affair, complete with a five-course dinner, disc jockey, open bar, ice luge, even a burlesque show. Don Falcone had spared no expense, but he did not attend the party. Vonni's parents, however, did stay until midnight. For the first time, they were able to see a glimpse of who their son had become there in Detroit. Throughout the night, they watched as dozens of young Italian men, most of them several years older, offered him congratulatory hugs and handshakes. They wore expensive suits, alligator-skin shoes, and diamond pinky rings. Obviously they were young Mafiosi, and they treated him like he was a celebrity, which made his mother wonder what he had done to earn such reverence. Especially from men who barely even knew him. Whatever it was, by the end of the night she had a terrible feeling that her son was now a very bad person who had done some very bad things there in Detroit. And it only compounded her sense of loss and failure.

The following morning, before heading to the airport, Vonni's mother tried one last time to convince him that he was making a mistake by getting involved with the mob. She even suggested he move back home with her. But her words fell on deaf ears. It was too late. He had been seduced into the Mafia's dangerous abyss, which broke her heart, for she had lost one

341

son to this abyss. And as she kissed him good-bye with tears in her eyes, she knew deep down that she had already lost her second son to it.

# CHAPTER 19

Neither King nor Vonni had ever been to Las Vegas, the infamous "Sin City." King was very intrigued by the business of legitimate gaming, and Vonni was looking forward to spending some quality time with his sister, who would be arriving there just one day after them.

Their plane touched down just before noon, and like nearly every day in Las Vegas the sun was blazing down from a cloudless azurite sky, the temperature outside already approaching 100°. Inside the airport, however, it was cool and comfortable, like a metaphor for the city itself—a bustling oasis in the middle of the Sierra Nevada dessert.

The instant they stepped into the baggage claim area, they were met by a pair of large men who introduced themselves simply as Stan and Milo. In their dark suits, dark sunglasses, and radio earpieces, they looked exactly like what they were—professional bodyguards. Milo, a 6'5" giant with the body of an NFL lineman, curtly explained that he and his partner would be their security detail for the next four days. Then, without adding another word, he collected their luggage from the conveyor and led them out to a waiting limousine, which promptly delivered them to the legendary Flamingo Hotel and Casino Resort.

When their limousine pulled up out front, an enthusiastic bellhop quickly loaded their luggage onto a brass cart and directed them inside to the reception counter. But when they stepped inside, they were instantly taken aback by what they saw. Chaos! Loud, organized chaos—an incongruous theatrical stage where the actors were mostly blue-collar vacationers gambling away their hard-earned dollars on dreams of hitting it big. Never in their young lives had King or Vonni seen anything like it. It reminded them of a scene from a movie. So much pomp and glitz it almost caused sensory overload. The flashing lights. The noise. The beautiful women! The two of them were impressed to the point of awe, for they could only imagine how much the casino was raking in by the second.

Built in the 1940's by infamous gangster Bugsy Siegel, the Flamingo was one of the first true casino "resorts" in Las Vegas. Wanting it to be more than just a casino, Siegel designed it to be a first-class vacation destination, where people went to enjoy the beautiful weather, relax by the pool, dine on the finest food, take in the live shows, pamper themselves and indulge their every whim. And though the building itself had been rebuilt several times since its inception, its appeal to hedonists and gamblers alike still remained the same. The hotel's current owner, wanting to give people a taste of old the Vegas charm and mystique, had purposely tried to keep the theme and décor as original as possible. Though it was the oldest casino on the strip, it was still a major draw that attracted tens of thousands of people from around the world each year.

Even now, in the middle of the afternoon, the Flamingo's casino floor was loud, crowded, and alive with activity. Dozens of people were playing blackjack, roulette, poker, baccarat, craps, and of course, slot machines. What seemed like hundreds of slot machines were trilling their melodic tunes all at once, the metallic clang of coins dropping into payout trays mingling with the joyous cries of lucky winners. Throughout the casino, gamblers displayed their luck on their faces—winners grinning merrily, losers frowning with frustration. Scantily clad cocktail waitresses scurried across the floor, serving complimentary drinks to winners and losers alike. A small army of bellhops shuffled about the lobby, pushing brass carts stacked with luggage.

When King gave his name to a woman at the reception counter, she glanced at him curiously before placing a call on the house phone. After a brief and hushed conversation with someone unknown, she offered him a smile and informed him that someone would be with him shortly. A moment later, a handsome older man with a British accent sidled up behind him and introduced himself.

"Mr. Falcone!" the man said excitedly, shaking his hand. "Welcome to the Flamingo. My name is Rubin Gold, and I'm the hotel manager. I know your grandfather. He and I are old friends. It's a pleasure to have you here with us at the Flamingo. If there is anything you require during your stay, anything at all, please feel free to ask for me personally. You and your friend are Platinum VIP Guests, which entitles you to all of the hotel's complimentary amenities. Your grandfather also arranged for your markers. Would you like to sign for them now?"

"Markers?" Vonni asked, confused. "What's a marker?"

King flashed him a grin. "Gambling money," he said, and then looked at the manager. "I'll sign for them later, thanks. Right now we want to get changed and have something to eat."

"Not a problem, Mr. Falcone," said the manager, nodding his understanding. "Your luggage is already being delivered to your suite. As for satisfying your hunger, you can order up room service or, if you wish, I can reserve you a table at one of our restaurants."

"You have a buffet, don't you?" King asked. "I've heard Vegas has some of the best buffets in the world."

"Indeed it does," the manager confirmed proudly. "And ours is the best in town. I will have a table reserved for you immediately. Just give the hostess your name."

"Great," King said, offering Vonni a wink. "I think we're going to like this Platinum VIP status."

The manager then waved a concierge from behind the reception counter. "These two gentlemen are Platinum Guests," he said, gesturing towards them. "See that they are made aware of all the perks and amenities that entails."

Looking eager to please, the concierge shook their hands excitedly and then led them up to a penthouse suite on the top floor, where he proceeded to give them a quick tour of what would be their accommodations for the next four days. Each of the suite's five rooms had parquet floors, Persian rugs, suede furniture and expensive artwork. There was a fully-stocked bar and hot tub in the main parlor, which included an impressive media center that was complete with projection screen television and surround sound. The two bedrooms came equipped with canopied king-sized beds, cheval glass mirrors, and walk-in closets. Every room offered a spectacular view of the entire Las Vegas strip. Taking it all in, King and Vonni could hardly believe it was all theirs for the next four days.

After showing them around the suite, the concierge explained the many perks that came with being a Platinum VIP Guest, including complimentary room service, a personal barber, dry-cleaning, a fitness center, laundry service, massage therapists, limousine service, and reserved VIP seating at all of the hotel's restaurants and shows. He also explained that, if they were interested, he had access to the finest prostitutes in all of Las Vegas.

Excited to see what else Vegas had to offer a couple of testosterone-fueled teenagers from Detroit, they quickly tipped the concierge and began preparing for a night on the town. After showering and donning clean suits, they headed downstairs to the hotel's legendary "Paradise Garden" buffet. But even in Las Vegas two teenagers flanked by a pair of huge bodyguards was not a common sight. As they made their way across the casino floor, people stared at them, surely wondering if they were celebrities. It was exactly what they felt like.

Vonni's sister, Ann Marie, arrived the following morning. A suite had been reserved for her, and King made sure that all of the hotel's complimentary courtesies were extended to her as well. Except, or course, for the $20,000 markers Don Falcone had arranged for him and Vonni. But not wanting his sister to feel left out, Vonni gave her a $10,000 gambling largesse out of his own pocket. It wasn't until he handed her this money that it actually sunk in who he had become. She had no idea how it happened or when he had made the transition, but he was a real Mafioso—and apparently quite a successful one. The $10,000 he gave her was more money than she had ever seen, yet he acted like it was mere pocket change. And from the way the hotel's staff was treating him and his friend, they were obviously more than just low-level wiseguys trying to play the role of big shot Mafiosi. They were the real thing. She hadn't the faintest clue as to what they did for money, but they clearly had a lot of it. Even though she knew her little brother was probably making his money illegally, it didn't matter. She was still proud of him. If he was going to be a mobster, she figured he might as well be a successful one.

For the next two days, King, Vonni, and Ann Marie took full advantage of their Platinum VIP status. They ordered decadent breakfasts every morning, delivered by room service. They lounged by the pool by day and hit the city's club circuit by night. They shopped the designer fashion boutiques. They dined at the finest restaurants in town. They took in a couple of sold-out shows. They even did some light drinking at the nightclubs. In one afternoon alone they went skydiving over the desert and rented jet skis on Lake Mead, and of course, they gambled away most of their money. Las Vegas was a fantasyland, and they took full advantage of every moment they were there.

On the third morning, Vonni decided to spend some private time with his sister. She was scheduled to fly home that afternoon, and he could tell she wanted some alone time with him. So, while King stayed in the casino and played blackjack,

Vonni took her on a little shopping excursion. For several hours they bounced from casino to casino, mall to mall, hitting all the high-end retail outlets—Prada, Gucci, Chanel, Coach, Louis Vuitton, and Tiffany's. He bought her shoes, dresses, handbags, and jewelry. He even bought a few gifts for their mother.

As they shopped, the two of them laughed, joked, and seemed to rekindle their sibling relationship. He expressed how much he had enjoyed having her down there with him, and she stated how genuinely proud she was of him. He shared his goals of someday being a successful businessman, and she confessed her desire to pursue a career as a pop singer. He advised her to never give up on her dreams, and she told him not to worry about what their parents thought of his new lifestyle. When she voiced her love for him and thanked him profusely for all the gifts, he responded by telling her how much he loved her, and thanked her for not judging him. By the time they returned to the hotel, they seemed closer than they'd ever been, each of them vowing to always be there for the other no matter what happened in life.

Back at the hotel, Vonni ordered up one of the hotel's complimentary limousines to take his sister to the airport. After helping a bellhop load her luggage into the trunk, he removed several thousand dollars from his pocket and handed it to her.

"What's this for?" she asked, confused, staring down at the money.

"For studio time," he said, offering her a brotherly smile. "If you're serious about this singing shit, you're gonna need a demo. That means you'll need studio time and a producer. But studio time and producers cost money. There's plenty of good ones in New York, so do your homework and find one who believes in your talent." He pointed at the wad of cash. "Let me know if you need more. I got you covered."

She looked at him with tears in her eyes. "Thank you, little brother," she said, hugging him lovingly. "You've always been my protector. It's been so nice getting to spend these last few days with you."

"Tell mom I'm sorry I didn't turn out the way she hoped," he said, then stepped back and looked her in the eye. "But I want you to know something, Ann Marie. I'm not ashamed of who I am. This is who I was meant to be. I hope mom can someday accept this."

"She will, brother," she said, a tear escaping from her eye. "Just give her some time. You know how she is. She sees everything in black and white. But I don't. I know you're not a bad person. I'm proud of you. You've come a long ways from Brooklyn. Just be careful and don't go getting yourself in any trouble. I don't want you to end up like..." She let her words trail off, unable to say the name of their dead brother.

King, who had been standing off to the side quietly listening, stepped over and smiled down at her. "Don't worry," he said, setting a reassuring hand on her shoulder. "I'll take good care of him." He gestured toward the hotel. "Someday your brother and I are going to own a place like this. More than one. Legitimate places. So don't worry, *bella mia*. I won't let anything happen to him."

"Thank you, King," she said, giving him a hug and peck on the cheek. "I'm going to hold you to that. I've already lost one brother. Don't let me lose another."

"I won't," King promised. "You have my word."

With that, Vonni gave her one last hug and watched the limousine take her away. He would miss her dearly in the years to come, for he would not see her often. But he was at peace knowing that their childhood bond was still intact.


Later that evening, King and Vonni experienced a strange series of events that would forever alter the course of their lives, starting with the fact that they were both winning at the tables. Over the last three days, the two of them had consistently lost nearly every time they gambled. In fact, they had quickly burned through their $20,000 markers and eventually requested an additional $50,000 credit line. Which, of course, was immediately approved after the hotel manager placed a call to Don Falcone, who was not happy about it but said he would personally cover the marker if needed.

Now on their last night in town, however, they were actually winning. King was up nearly $50,000, while Vonni was up over $20,000. Splitting pairs, doubling down, upping their bets, it seemed they couldn't lose. Along with their ever-present bodyguards, a small crowd of onlookers had gathered behind them to watch them play, surely wondering who they were. After all, it wasn't a common sight to see a pair of teenagers gambling for such high stakes, let alone teenagers clad in designer suits and shadowed by a pair of professional bodyguards. Every time they won a hand, the crowd of onlookers would ooh and ahh, even clap. Not even they could believe their string of good luck.


Hector Arpionis, longtime owner of the legendary Flamingo Hotel and Casino Resort, was making a final walk-through of his casino before heading home to meet some business associates he was having over for dinner and poker. But while talking to one of his pit bosses, he heard cheering coming from a small crowd gathered around one of his blackjack tables. Someone was obviously winning his money. He was tempted to go see who it was but decided against it since he was already running late. And the men waiting for him at his home were not the type of men who liked to be kept waiting.

For a number of years, business at the Flamingo had been slowly declining. In fact, it had lost money several years in a row. Such an antiquated old casino simply could no longer compete with the new mega resorts that had been steadily popping up all over town. Hector, one of only a few non-corporate casino owners in Vegas, knew his hotel was the last of a dying breed.

His "whales," an elite group of super gamblers who accounted for nearly half his annual profits, were being lured away by the over-the-top glitz and opulence of these new theme resorts. So, never one to remain static in business, he decided it was time to embark on a new business venture. Since gaming was his passion, naturally another casino was what he had in mind. Unfortunately, real estate, licensing, and construction costs in Las Vegas had become astronomical in recent years, making the prospect of opening another casino there beyond even his reach. He did try to acquire funding from traditional lenders, such as banks and venture groups, but the amount needed to build a modern casino resort, one that could compete with the corporately-funded mega resorts, was far more than even they were willing to lend. Atlantic City was the answer. Real estate was much more affordable there, and the city's gaming industry was booming. It also had far fewer competitors.

But Hector knew it was going to require some serious startup capital to build a modern casino resort on Atlantic City's boardwalk strip. Even if he leveraged all of his assets, including his stake in the Flamingo, he was still going to fall several hundred million short, which is why he'd decided to seek funding from private investors. Lucky for him, he knew some extremely wealthy private investors.

Hector's first successful business venture had been a very lucrative shipping company based in Athens, Greece. Using a small flotilla of mid-sized cargo ships, he moved merchant goods all over the world. One of those goods had been Turkish opium, which he smuggled by the ton all over the world for some associates in Sicily. Associates in the Mafia. Their partnership had lasted many years, netting both parties tens of millions. Eventually, he became such a trusted confidant to the Sicilians that their American counterparts came to him with a business proposition. They wanted him to buy a casino. Or rather, they wanted him to be their front man at a casino they wanted to buy—so they could skim pre-taxed cash from the casino's count room. Since he was a squeaky clean, legitimate businessman with a naturalized American citizenship, he made the perfect front man.

Ever since Howard Hughes had pressured the FBI to expose the Mafia's influence in Las Vegas, known organized crime figures had been under intense scrutiny in Sin City. Though Hughes had managed to force the Mafia out of many casinos by simply buying them out, the FBI knew the mob still managed to maintain a tentative foothold in Las Vegas. The bosses back in Chicago, Detroit, and New York were not just going to give up their skims without a fight. Not when the skims accounted for a huge percentage of their annual profits. The mob's answer was to just buy or build more casinos, and to avoid FBI scrutiny, they did it by using legitimate businessmen as "bag men," or front men. That was how Hector had come to own the Flamingo—a secret partnership that had earned him and his Sicilian associates tens of millions.

But then came the indictment. When an FBI wiretap recorded a low-level wiseguy from Kansas City talking about "the Flamingo skim," the Feds began investigating Hector, suspecting he was backed by a Detroit Mafia faction who allegedly extorted Jimmy Hoffa out of nearly twenty million dollars of Teamster pension funds to purchase the casino. Using these wiretaps to record conversations between Mafia bosses in Detroit and Jimmy Hoffa, the FBI intended to pressure Hoffa into testifying against the mob bosses. But before this ever happened, Hoffa disappeared, never to be seen again.

Nevertheless, the FBI still ended up indicting Hector for connivance, racketeering, and conspiracy to commit tax evasion by allowing the Mafia to skim from his count room. But the charges were eventually dropped. There was no irrefutable evidence that he had purchased the casino using anything other than legitimate means, or that he had knowledge of a "skim." Unfortunately, because of the wiretaps, a number of high-level Mafiosi back in Detroit were indicted on federal charges, including extortion, conspiracy to defraud the federal government, and tax evasion. Some were even sent to prison for several years.

But that had all been in the mid-1970's, over twenty-five years ago. Since then, Hector had been forced to distance himself from his Sicilian associates. Because of FBI scrutiny, he had even been forced to stop importing heroin for them. He paid them back, with interest, for their initial investment in the Flamingo, and he maintained a cordial, if somewhat discreet, relationship with them, always making sure to send them an occasional perquisite, usually in the form of a duffel bag full of cash—a million dollars or more. He'd kept his mouth shut when indicted, and made sure to stay in good standing with his one-time partners. As a result, they had a deep respect for him.

Unfortunately, because of the FBI's constant scrutiny, he knew he couldn't just ask his old mob partners for backing in his new Atlantic City project. This was why he was hosting tonight's poker game.

Now, as Hector now did a final check-in with his pit bosses to see if there had been any big winners in the casino, again he heard clapping and cheering coming from the same blackjack table. Wondering who was winning his money, he let his curiosity get the best of him. Even though he was running late, he had to see who was taking money out of his pockets. But when he stepped over to the table, he was surprised to find that it was none other than Omnio Falcone, the handsome young grandson of his old friend, Peter Paul Falcone, one of his old Sicilian partners who had collected the Flamingo skim before being federally indicted with several other Detroit mob bosses. Since then, he had become a don, Boss of the entire Detroit Syndicate.

As Hector stood there watching Falcone's grandson, a thought suddenly occurred to him. Was it mere coincidence that this young Mafioso was in town on this particularly important weekend? Had the old Detroit mobster sent his grandson down there for a reason? Don Falcone had called him the previous week to make arrangements for his grandson to stay at the Flamingo for an extended weekend holiday. At the time, Hector had thought nothing of it and assured the old Mafioso that his grandson would receive the best the hotel had to offer. And over the last several days, Hector had heard from his staff that the young Mafia prodigy and his friend had been taking full advantage of their Platinum VIP status. At the time, he found that amusing. But as he now considered what was about to take place at his home, he couldn't help wondering if there was a connection, if the old mob boss had a reason for sending his grandson down on this weekend of all weekends. It seemed almost too coincidental.

King doubled down a $5,000 bet on split tens and caused the dealer to push. The crowd of onlookers clapped yet again as he added his winnings to the pile of chips in front of him.

"I see Lady Luck is smiling on you boys tonight," a deep voice with an accent said from behind him.

King glanced over his shoulder and saw a tall, handsome man smiling down at him. Right away something told him that the man was someone of importance. He was wearing a perfectly tailored tropical wool suit, and had an air of gentility about him. He looked Italian, though he could be anything from Spanish to Middle Eastern. But what really denoted that he was someone of importance was the four-man security detail standing behind him, all of them clad in black suits and wearing radio ear-pieces.

"Good evening, Mr. Arpionis," said the pit boss, snapping to attention like a private might in the presence of a general.

"Good evening, Gordon," Hector replied to the pit boss, and offered everyone at the table an affable smile. "Ladies and gentlemen, I hope you are enjoying your stay with us here at the Flamingo. We appreciate having you as our guests, and as a house courtesy I'd like to comp each of you a one-thousand-dollar marker if you would allow me to relocate you to another table."

Along with King and Vonni, there were two Asian women and a fat older black man at the table. All of them were more than happy to relocate to another table for a free thousand bucks. After all, there were over two dozen blackjack tables in the casino, none any luckier than the next. But King wondered who the man was and what was going on, which his eyes expressed as he and Vonni began gathering up their chips. But as they were about to follow the others over to a new table, the older man in the silk suit set a hand on his shoulder.

"I was hoping I might have a word with you, Mr. Falcone," said the man, extending a hand to him. "My name is Hector Arpionis. I own the Flamingo."

"Pleasure to meet you, sir," King said respectfully, shaking his hand, not failing to notice the power in the man's grip. "But how do you know my name?"

Hector was impressed. Young people were rarely so polite and respectful these days. One of the things he admired about the Mafia was they taught their young the value of respect and honor, which he thought was so rare in today's youth.

"The pleasure is all mine, Omnio," Hector said, offering him a smile. "I know your grandfather. He's told me a lot about you."

"Really?" King said, both surprised and impressed. "He said he had friends in Vegas but never mentioned that he knew the owner of this place."

Hector cast a pensive look around his bustling casino. "My friend, it was your grandfather and his associates who helped me get started in this business nearly thirty years ago."

"Interesting," King replied, wondering why his grandfather had never talked about this man before. "I didn't know that."

Hector looked from King to Vonni. "So tell me, boys, how has my staff been treating you?"

"Your staff has been exemplary," King answered. "They made us feel like royalty."

"Exemplary?" Hector chuckled. "I see you've already learned how it works down here. A bit of sycophancy goes a long way."

"I'll remember that, Mr. Arpionis..." King said, and then slowly took in the bustling casino. "...when I open my own casino."

"Your own casino?" Hector echoed, grinning, not even trying to mask his amusement. "Wow. Big dreams. I like that. Your grandfather said you were a smart young man, but he never mentioned you had plans to open your own casino. That's very ambitious. But I would never call it lofty. Look at me. I'm living proof it can be done. I must warn you, though, my friend, running a casino is hard work. Like a newborn child, it requires your constant attention. You can't trust anyone, because everyone is out to get you. Your staff. Your patrons. The IRS. The Gaming Board. They are all out to steal your money."

King grinned cryptically at Vonni. "Sounds like the story of my life, Mr. Arpionis."

Hector studied him for a moment, impressed by his poise and equanimity. "So are you really interested in the gaming industry?"

King looked him in the eye. "Alexander The Great said, 'Fortune favors the ambitious.'"

Hector cocked his head. "Actually, I believe he said, 'Fortune favors the bold.'"

King shrugged. "Semantics."

"Yes, I suppose so," Hector chuckled, amused but impressed at the same time.

"As far as me opening a casino?" King continued, again taking in the crowded room. "Yes, I'm serious. Until a few days ago I knew nothing about the casino business. But now that I see how it works, Vegas is more than just somewhere to go gamble. It's a vacation destination where gambling happens to

356

be legal. But of course, that's just marketing, isn't it Mr. Arpionis? We both know everything here is designed to encourage gambling. It must feel like stealing. I mean, look these people. They save up all year just so they can come down here for a few days on vacation, and they gamble it all away."

"Not everyone loses," Hector said, pointing at the stack of chips in King's hand. "If they did, I'd be out of business in no time."

"Beginner's luck," King said, looking at the chips. "But let's face it, Mr. Arpionis, more lose than win. It's a numbers game. Simple math. The house has the odds stacked in its favor. Sure, people come down here with dreams of hitting it big. And sure, every once in a while someone does. But nobody consistently beats the house. My grandfather taught me that a long time ago. Knowing they have a chance to win free money every time they place a bet is what keeps them betting. And we both know they'll keep betting, don't we? The rush of occasionally winning becomes addictive. Personally, I can't think of a better racket. At least not a legal one."

"Your grandfather was right," Hector said, expelling another rumbling chortle. "You are indeed a very smart young man. But I have to tell you, Omnio, these new corporate mega resorts are becoming harder and harder to compete with. The Flamingo's main attraction is that it's the last original casino on the strip. They come here to experience a taste of the old Vegas."

"You could always eliminate your competition," King suggested half-jokingly, looking him in the eye.

But Hector knew that the young Mafioso was, en passant, really implying that he could take out his competitors. He found such a remark to be a little unnerving. Yet it made him think of something: He may very well need this young Mafioso someday. In fact, he could use him tonight.

"Omnio," he said, glancing at Vonni, "do you and your friend here know how to play poker?"

357

"You're joking, right?" King answered, looking almost offended. "My grandfather taught me how to play penny poker when I was five. I started housing games when I was fourteen. Why?"

"Well…" Hector said, glancing towards his poker pit. "I'm hosting a little poker tournament tonight at my home. Just me and a few associates. How would you like to join us?"

"We'd be honored, Mr. Arpionis," King said with unfettered excitement. "But how high is the buy-in? We only have so much cash on us."

"No worries, my friend," Hector said, shooting a quick look at his platinum Breitling timepiece, suddenly looking pressed for time. "I will personally cover all your bets. But my associates should be arriving any minute. So, unless you boys have other plans, our chariot awaits."

With that, Hector Arpionis, esteemed owner of the legendary Flamingo Hotel and Casino Resort, beckoned King and Vonni, a pair of teenage wiseguys from Detroit, to follow him over to the private elevator at the back of the casino. As they went, their retinue of six total bodyguards formed a protective circle around them, causing dozens of people in the casino to stop and stare with curiosity.

The elevator took them straight to the roof, where a pilot was already warming Hector's "chariot," a Sikorsky S-76 luxury helicopter. Neither King nor Vonni had even seen the inside of a helicopter, let alone flown in one. Naturally, they were apprehensive. But Hector assured them it was perfectly safe and that the flight to his Henderson home would take less than ten minutes. Still a bit reluctant, the two of them glanced at each other, shrugged, and climbed into the impressive helicopter, which had an interior that rivaled even the most luxurious limousine.

During the short flight, King began asking Hector a series of questions, starting with how the old gaming mogul had gotten started in the casino business. He also asked how much it had cost him to buy his casino. He figured he might as get as much information from the man while he could. After all, it wasn't every day he had a multi-millionaire gaming tycoon at his disposal.

Hector enjoyed talking to King. Though the young Falcone still had the hardened edges of a teenage street tough, he also possessed the poise and maturity of someone who was much older. He also had a glowing intelligence in his eyes, which Hector rarely encountered—and never in the eyes of such a young man. He had an inquisitive nature and asked question after question about Hector's various business ventures. By the end of the flight, Hector felt like he had just been interviewed for a job.

Hector's palatial estate was located on a remote expanse of private land some 10 miles outside Henderson, Nevada, and he had spared no expense when building it. Situated on the eastern shores of Lake Las Vegas, it boasted a private golf course, horse stable, a pair of guesthouses, and rooftop helipad. But the home itself was most impressive. Constructed to resemble a Rococo French chateau, it was more of a castle than a mansion.

As the helicopter approached the rooftop helipad, Vonni and King were struck silent by the sheer size and magnitude of the home. Back in Michigan, they had been exposed to the ostentatious homes of Grosse Pointe, but never had they seen anything like this. Built on an outcropping of land that jutted several acres out into the lake, it was surrounded by beautifully manicured lawns, flower gardens, and groves of perfectly pruned ornamental trees. It was such a stark contrast to the arid landscape just beyond the property—miles of rolling desert hills blanketed with sage and saguaro cactus. Though there a few other beautiful homes built on the lake, his was by far the largest and most extravagant, making it stand out like a lone quasar on a dark night.

But Hector's home was even more impressive on the inside. As he led King and Vonni to his private gaming pavilion, the two of them took it all in with both awe and wonderment. Intricately patterned Corinthian marble flowed from room to room. There were beautiful works of art everywhere, including paintings by Rembrandt and Picasso, and sculptures by Remington and even Michelangelo. In a Grecian-themed dining hall, the walls were covered with intricate frescos and a plafond cathedral ceiling that was supported by towering marble columns. In the center of this expansive dining hall was a hand-carved oak table that stretched nearly the entire length of the room. At the head of this table was a massive, jewel-encrusted replica of the legendary throne of Zeus. But the room's most impressive feature was a colossal granite sculpture of Dionysus, the Greek god of wine and ecstasy. Towering twenty feet high, it stood like a giant sentry at the back of the room, clearly there to evoke awe from Hector's dinner guests, which is exactly what it did to King and Vonni.

After Hector led them through only a small portion of his home, they came to a large vestibule, where a number of bodyguards were lounging about. His majordomo, a stately old black man in a tuxedo, was posted in front of a pair of massive oak doors.

"Good evening, sir," said the butler with a British accent, gesturing towards the doors. "Your guests are waiting inside."

"All of them?" Hector asked.

"Yes, sir," the butler confirmed.

Relieved that all of his guests had arrived, Hector pushed open the double doors and beckoned King and Vonni into his private gaming pavilion. They were instantly taken aback by what they saw. It seemed Hector had an entire casino in his home! There were craps tables, blackjack tables, roulette tables, poker tables, and a variety of slot machines. A bartender was pouring drinks from behind a full wet bar, which was stocked with the finest spirits the world had to offer. A pair of cocktail waitresses hurried about the room, serving drinks and trays of hors d'oeuvres to the guests. In the center of the room was a plush lounge area, where several beautiful women were casually sipping drinks and chatting amongst themselves. At a baize-topped poker table, a tuxedo-clad croupier was dealing cards to a group of older men, all of whom were smoking cigars and sipping drinks.

King didn't overtly register recognition on his face, but he had seen several of the men at the Flamingo over the last three days. They hadn't been hard to miss. Crowds had gathered around to watch them wager huge sums of money at the tables. They always had at least two bodyguards lingering close by, and the casino's staff catered to them like they were heads of state. He had watched some of them toss around hundreds of thousands of dollars like it was mere pocket change.

But one man stood out from the rest, and King now locked eyes with him. The previous afternoon, while Vonni had been out shopping with his sister, the man had sat down next to him at a blackjack table and introduced himself as Russell Loduca. After playing side-by-side for nearly an hour, out of the blue the man invited him to play craps at a nearby craps table. At the time, King had found it odd that a perfect stranger, one who was probably twice his age and obviously very wealthy, would extend such an invitation to him. But he was on a losing streak and the man seemed friendly enough, so he agreed to join him. As the two of them began making their way over to the craps table, however, the man divulged the real reason he had wanted to talk to him privately. It turned out, he knew Don Falcone. King had no idea how the man had recognized him, or even knew who he was, but any friend of his grandfather's was a friend of his. After winning a few thousand dollars playing craps, they ended up having lunch together. Over lunch, the man explained that he was a real estate developer who had previously partnered with some of Don Falcone's associates on a large development project in Florida. He even said the don was currently helping him with a problem up in Michigan, though he did not specify what the problem was. After lunch, he handed King a business card.

"Call me if you're ever in the market for some commercial properties," he said, offering him a cryptic wink. "Nobody will beat my price."

When they parted ways, King was left with a strange feeling that his grandfather, the master of strategy and manipulation, had sent him and Vonni there for the sole purpose of meeting this millionaire real estate developer. He just didn't know why his grandfather just hadn't arranged a formal meeting between them.

"Gentlemen!" Hector exclaimed, greeting his associates excitedly. "Please forgive my tardiness, but I have good reason for being late." He gestured toward King and Vonni. "I'd like you to meet some young friends of mine." He put a hand on King's shoulder. "This handsome young stallion is Omnio Falcone. He's the grandson of one of my longtime associates in Detroit. His business partner is Giovanni Battaglia. I ran into them back at the casino. They're some very, oh, industrious young men. Much like yourselves at their age, no doubt. I thought you might enjoy meeting them, so I invited them to sit in on tonight's game. Both say they know how to play poker."

"Is their money green?" drawled a powerfully-built older man in a cowboy hat and ill-fitting suit.

Hector gestured towards the man. "Boys, allow me to introduce my good friend, Lawrence Delance, President of Delance Petroleum. His company operates a number of very lucrative offshore oil rigs." He grinned at Delance. "And yes, Larry, their money is green. I'll be covering their bets. In fact, I've decided to abdicate my seat at the table and let them play for me. Though I must warn you, they were on a bit of a winning streak before we left the casino. It's one of the reasons I invited them to join us. I had to get them out of there before they broke the house."

This evoked a round of laughter from the men at the table, and eased some of King and Vonni's nervous apprehension. After all, they had no idea who these men were or why Hector had invited them to his private poker game. But whoever they were, and whatever Hector's reasons were, King and Vonni had a feeling it was going to be an interesting night.

"Five thousand ante?" one of the men suggested.

Everyone at the table voiced their agreement.

"Well then, let's get started, shall we?" Hector said to the croupier, gesturing to King and Vonni. "Start my young friends off with one hundred thousand each."

"Yes, sir, Mr. Arpionis," said the croupier, who immediately began counting out stacks of thousand-dollar chips.

As King and Vonni seated themselves at the table and collected their chips, Hector sauntered over to the bar and ordered a scotch on the rocks. He was pleased with himself, for his plan was coming together quite nicely. He knew his associates had world-class egos, and that those egos would transform them into self-inflated braggarts just to impress his young guests. They would bet big and toss their money around like it grew on trees. But it wasn't their poker money he was after. Later tonight, after they loosened up with some alcohol and friendly wagering, he would ask them to invest over half a billion dollars into his Atlantic City project.

At first, King and Vonni felt out of place and out of their league. They were young enough to be the sons, if not grandsons, of most of these men. And they had never played poker for such high stakes. Nor had they ever played against such seasoned players. But this pantheon of high-rollers turned out to be surprisingly friendly and surprisingly easy to play against. They told jokes and laughed and made sure to include King and Vonni in all of their conversations. Just as Hector had expected, they began putting on a show for them, trying to one-up each other with witty quips and inflated machismo. They hurled vulgarities and jestful verbal jabs at each other like they were a bunch of frat boys. They talked of their world travels, extravagant vacation homes, toys, money, and various business exploits—all while tossing around literally tens of thousands of dollars at the table like it was mere play money. Which to them it was. But the more boastful and self-inflated they became, the easier it was for King and Vonni to pick up on their "tells," the cracks in their "poker faces." King especially had a knack for picking up on tells.

Soon King was playing like a seasoned poker pro, betting big and calling bluffs. As he became more comfortable, he began laughing and joking right along with this eclectic fraternity of mega millionaires. As he played and studied their poker faces, he began asking each of them what they did for a living, where they were from, and how they knew Hector. He even shared some of his own business goals. He figured the more he could get them talking, the easier it would be for him to read their tells. His plan worked. Before long, he was winning consistently against them.

Hector had assembled quite an interesting cast of characters, most of whom were of questionable moral integrity and operated their various enterprises on the outer fringes of legality. But owning a reputedly Mafia-backed casino seemed to attract this type of men to him. They were men who had an excess of money and a shortage of morals, and they loved Las Vegas for this very reason. It was a city where they could indulge their every whim, which was exactly how Hector had gotten to know them. Whenever they came to town, he made sure to put them up in his finest penthouse suites and catered to their every desire. He comped their rooms, their meals, their drinks, and anything else they wanted. He provided them with limousines, bodyguards, tickets to the best shows in town, and all the high-end prostitutes they could handle. All he asked in return was that they gamble at his casino. And they did. Sometimes they won, but more often than not they lost. And usually lost big.

Lawrence Delance, the Texas oil tycoon in the ten-gallon hat, had made his fortune drilling for oil in the Gulf of Mexico. He was highly connected to certain high-level politicians in

Washington, which was how he had bribed his way into a government contract that made his company one of only a handful of oil companies that provided oil for the country's strategic oil reserves.

Then there was Vlado Ivanoff, a huge 400-pound Russian with a ruddy face and a rumbling laugh that seemed to shake the windows. He could barely speak English but enjoyed citing corny American jokes from a tattered old joke book he carried everywhere. His benign, jocular nature, however, was just a facade. He was a notoriously ruthless and unscrupulous businessman who was rumored to have ties to the Russian Mafia. He'd made his fortune, said to be in the billions, by liquidating stockpiles of Russian Cold War munitions after the fall of the Soviet Union.

Next there was Armando Valderez, a Mexican telecommunications mogul. A short, handsome little man with slicked black hair and a pencil mustachio, he had become one of the wealthiest men in the world by monopolizing nearly all of Mexico's mobile telecommunications market. Rumor had it that he was backed by both Colombian and Mexican drug cartels, which was how he had muscled all of his competitors out of business. Forbes Magazine estimated his net worth to be upward of twenty billion. A practical and conservative businessman, he was anything but practical and conservative in his personal life. A hedonist through and through, he enjoyed not just the finer things in life, but the *finest* things in life. Along with homes all over the globe, he owned nearly one hundred cars, several private jets, and five yachts, one of which was amongst the largest in the world. He loved beautiful toys, beautiful places, and beautiful women. But what he loved most was gambling. Considered to be one of the world's largest "whales," he almost never failed to lose several million dollars whenever he visited Las Vegas. He once lost fifteen million dollars in one night at the Flamingo. But ever since the corporate mega resorts began

365

luring him away with their palatial rooftop suites and glamorous villas, he had been staying at the Flamingo less and less.

Another handsome billionaire at the table was Dimitry Popadomis, son of Hector's old partner in the shipping business. After Hector sold his half of the company to his partner in order to pay off his silent Sicilian partners in the Flamingo, his old partner had gone on to build their company into one of the largest and most successful shipping companies in the world, comprised of nearly one hundred freighters moving goods around the world every day. Unfortunately, his old partner hadn't lived to enjoy the fruits of his labors. Nearly twenty years ago, at only age forty-five, he died of a heart attack while in bed with his mistress. His son Dimitry, however, was very much alive and enjoying the fruits of his father's labors. And there was a lot to enjoy. The Popadomis International Shipping Corporation was worth over fifteen billion dollars. Like the rest of the men at the table, Dimitry Popadomis was a man who loved to jet-set, travel and spoil himself with the finest things life had to offer, including fast cars. For a short time in his twenties, he had even been a professional Formula One driver. Nowadays, he owned not one but two F-1 teams. He loved all things fast, from cars to women. But his favorite vice was gambling. High-stakes gambling. It was the one thing that still gave him a rush, and rumor had it that he once won a twenty-million-dollar Tuscan villa in a single hand of poker with the Prince of Monaco. On any given day, Dimitry could be found gambling in casinos from Monte Carlo to Las Vegas, often wagering millions of his inherited fortune on a single hand of baccarat or poker. And out of respect for his father's old friend and one-time partner, he always made sure to stay at the Flamingo whenever he visited Las Vegas.

Next was Zoron Petrovonich, a tall, burly Serbian who was built like a bear and looked more Grecian than Slavic. With his deep, baritone voice and massive bulk, he had a commanding presence and was the one man at the table everyone had an intrinsic fear of—and for good reason. Petrovonich had once been a general in the Serbian Army during the country's civil war between the Serbs and Croats. He was said to be partly responsible for the Serb's attempted genocide of the Croatians during the war. It was rumored that he was responsible for killing tens of thousands of innocent Croatians. After the war, with the backing of his friends in the new Serbian government, he launched the "Global Arm & Security Corporation," an international arms brokerage and private security firm based in Titograd, Montenegro. He made his fortune supplying arms and military training to paramilitary organizations such as the Palestine Liberation Organization in Jordan, the Taliban in Syria, the Northern Alliance in Afghanistan, the FARC in Columbia, and the IRA in Ireland. The CIA had a dossier on him that was six thousand pages long, and the American government had him listed as "persona non grata." That was one of the reasons he loved visiting America, particularly Las Vegas. He enjoyed the rush of sneaking into the country using one of his private jets. He was a chronic gambler, drinker, and womanizer who found no better place than Las Vegas to indulge such vices. Even though he wasn't welcome in the country, Hector always made sure to roll out the red carpet for him, which was how they had become such good friends.

Lastly, there was Russ Loduca, the stocky Italian who had introduced himself to King the previous afternoon. At age thirty-five, he was the youngest man at the table. He also looked nothing like the others. While they wore designer silk suits, he wore a tight V-neck polo shirt and khaki slacks. Whereas the others were mostly corpulent and out of shape, he was fit, muscular and powerfully built. The most reserved man at the table, he spent more time listening than talking. With a net worth of barely fifty million, he was by far the poorest of them. While they bragged and boasted about their wealth and various exploits, he mostly observed and listened, because even he felt out of place amongst men of such wealth and power. At one point, he showed mild offense when they referred to him as "nouveau riche," since his wealth was still in its infancy. But Loduca was well on his way to becoming a man of their wealth and stature. Straight out of high school he began buying and selling real estate. Small residential properties at first, but as his capital reserves grew so did the size of his investment properties. By age twenty-five, he was already a multi-millionaire. Then he stumbled upon the opportunity of a lifetime, a chance to get into commercial development, where there was real money to be made. An old widow had died and her estate had gone up for auction. Part of that estate was a huge tract of undeveloped land between the coastal metropolis of Tampa, Florida, and the much smaller community of Clearwater. He bought the property with intentions of building a massive shopping mall on it, where his plan was to lease space to retail outlets. Unfortunately, at the time, he lacked the capital and credit to see the project through. Conventional lenders wouldn't back him, citing that his project was "over ambitious and too high-risk." But he hadn't been ready to give up. He knew there were millions to be made, so he forewent conventional financiers and sought financing from some less conventional lenders. A friend from his hometown of Miami introduced him to a discreet group of Italian businessmen who had plenty of money and were always looking for "high return" investments. One of those businessmen was a mysterious, dangerous-looking man from Detroit named Peter Falcone. Now, nearly ten years later, the mall was one of the busiest malls in America.

As the night wore on, Russ Loduca found himself drawn to his old business partner's grandson, Omnio. He knew it was no coincidence that the young Mafioso was in town. Less than a month ago, Loduca had called Don Falcone in need of a favor. He was in the process of developing a large tract of land in Rochester Hills, an affluent suburb some thirty miles north of Detroit. His intentions were to build a gated community consisting of several dozen multi-million dollar homes, but a particularly unreasonable zoning official was giving him trouble, stalling the project and costing him thousands of dollars each day as his construction crews waited to resume work. Since he knew the don had influence in the area, he'd asked him if there was anything he could do to help. Of course, Don Falcone promised to see what he could do, but during their conversation Loduca happened to mention that he'd been invited to attend tonight's poker game, which was being hosted by their mutual associate, Hector Arpionis. This was when the old Mafioso had brought up his grandson, the handsome young man now seated across from him at the poker table. Don Falcone said he was planning to send his grandson down to Las Vegas this same weekend. He suggested they meet, stating that his grandson was a very "ambitious young entrepreneur" who might need him someday. And Loduca was always looking to make friends with ambitious young entrepreneurs. Especially ones connected to men like Don Falcone. So, yesterday in the casino, he had asked the hotel manager to point out the young Falcone. After introducing himself, they did a little gambling and even had lunch together. But he certainly hadn't expected to see him here at tonight's poker game. Nor did he expect to find himself so impressed with him. He had no children of his own, and rarely interacted with young people, but he knew it was rare to see such a young man carry himself so poised and confident, especially amongst the caliber of men seated at the table. It was impressive. But he was most impressed by the kid's ambition. The young Mafioso already owned several businesses and even expressed an interest in someday opening a casino. By the end of the night, Loduca would make a personal note to keep in touch with him. Because like the don implied on the phone, they may very well need each other someday.

Sometime around 1:00 AM, Hector hinted to King that it was getting late. But of course, King knew this was just Hector's way of politely dismissing them so he could be alone with his associates. Which was fine. After three days of nearly no sleep and nonstop running around Vegas, he and Vonni were in desperate need of sleep. They also had to be up early for their return flight home in the morning. So, not wanting to overstay their welcome, they stood and prepared to leave. Each man at the table got to their feet and shook their hands good-bye, voicing how much they had enjoyed their company. It was rare that they fraternized with young people—most of them barely even saw their own children—and spending a few hours with such charismatic young men had been a welcome break from the norm.

After King and Vonni had expressed what a pleasure it had been to meet each of them, Hector began walking them toward his majordomo, who was waiting by the room's huge oak doors to take them back to the helipad. But before they got there, Russell Loduca got up from the table and rushed over.

"Omnio," Loduca said, "before you go, I want to remind you again to stay in touch. Make sure you hold onto my card. When you're ready to build that casino, give me a call. We'll find you a nice piece or property to build it on. And if you're ever in South Florida, give me a call. I own a number of timeshare rentals in the Miami area. You're welcome to stay at any of them as long as you like, and do me a favor... when you get home, give my regards to your grandfather. Tell him I said you lived up to everything he told me about you."

Hector, who was standing next to them, gave Loduca a puzzled look. "Wait, you know Peter Falcone?" he asked, confused, wondering how Russ Loduca, a young real estate developer from southern Florida, could possibly know an old mob boss from Detroit.

Loduca cast an oblique glance at the poker table, making sure the other men were out of earshot. "Yes..." he said, grinning at Hector's surprise. "Mr. Falcone and I have done some business together in the past. Some of his associates were partners of mine on my first major development project."

And just like that, a light bulb went off in Hector's head. Now it all made sense. It had been Russ Loduca who tipped Don

Falcone to tonight's poker game, and the old mob boss had no doubt sent his grandson down for the weekend with hopes of him getting acquainted with Loduca. It seemed as if his plan had worked out perfectly. Not only had his grandson gotten acquainted with Loduca, but he'd also become acquainted with the rest of Hector's VIP players. Because of tonight, they would forever remember him as the charismatic young man from Detroit who had charmed them with his youthful wit and big dreams.

*That slick old devil,* Hector thought to himself, picturing Don Falcone. He had arranged tonight's game to solicit investment capital from these extremely wealthy and powerful men. Yet right under his nose, without him even realizing it, the Detroit mob boss had made allies out of every single one of them by using his enigmatic young grandson. *Well played, old friend.* He knew a day may very well come when Don Falcone, or even young Omnio here, might seek out these men for investment capital in one of their own ventures. It pleased Hector to know that it was he who had brought them together, even unintentionally, to serve this purpose.

Hector extended a hand to King. "It's been a pleasure, Omnio," he said, gripping his hand firmly. "I really enjoyed having you with us tonight. You're a fine young man. I hope you enjoyed your time in Las Vegas. I want you to know you're always welcome in my home and my hotel." He glanced at Loduca with a knowing look. "And please, Omnio, also give my regards to your grandfather. In fact, have him call me when you get home. I have something I would like to discuss with him."

"I will, Mr. Arpionis," King promised. "And thank you for your hospitality. My partner and I have had a great time down here. It's been a pleasure meeting you and an honor being a guest in your home. I'm sure my grandfather will be grateful."

"Anything for an old friend," Hector said with a wink, knowing the don's masterful plan had unfolded perfectly.

King extended a hand to Loduca. "Mr. Loduca, I will definitely keep in touch. Don't be surprised when I take you up on that offer to stay at one of your time shares."

"You're welcome to them anytime, my friend," said Russ, giving him a firm handshake. "You'll love it down there. I have several properties right on the beach. Beautiful women everywhere, and they're always looking to sink their teeth in a couple of young bucks like you and your friend. Just give me a few days notice to make the arrangements. If I'm in town, we'll get together for dinner. Or maybe some deep-sea fishing on my boat... but you might see me up in your neck of the woods first. I have a large project in the works up there Michigan. Rochester Hills, actually. Not far from you. So next time I'm in town, maybe you can show me around? I hear you got a couple of pretty hoppin' clubs up there."

King was about to tell him about Club Vanzetti's, but noticed the impatient look on Hector's face. The handsome old casino owner obviously had some pressing business he wanted to discuss with his associates. King was smart enough to know that Hector hadn't assembled this group of powerful men just for a casual night of drinks and poker. The game was surely just an ice-breaker, a way of getting them half drunk and softened up before they talked business.

"I'd love to show you around Detroit," King said to Loduca, offering him a parting smile. "Make sure you look me up next time you're in town." He then turned to the butler, who was still waiting patiently by the pavilion doors. "After you, Benson," he said with a grin, making reference to the 1980's sitcom character.

But before he could take a step, Hector gestured towards the poker table. "Aren't you forgetting something?" he asked, an amused smile on his face.

King glanced at the poker table. "Um... not that I know of. Why, have I forgotten something?"

"Your winnings?" Hector said matter-of-factly.

"Not my winnings," King said, shaking his head. "Your winnings. I was playing with your money."

Hector considered this for a moment and then nodded. "But the money you won wasn't mine. It belonged to my associates. Trust me, they won't miss it. Take it. You earned it. I know a lot of poker players, and believe me when I tell you, those men are some of the best there are. So whatever you won over there, you deserve to keep."

King glanced at Vonni. "But my paisan lost a hundred grand of your money tonight. I was up just over two hundred grand..." He shrugged. "So the way I see it, it's a wash. We're even."

Hector shook his head with disbelief, unable to believe that this young man, barely nineteen years old, would turn down a free hundred thousand dollars. "Omnio," he said, extending a hand to him, "I admire your integrity. I look forward to seeing you again. Have a safe trip home. And don't forget to have your grandfather call me. We have a lot to talk about."

King gave him a firm handshake. "I won't forget, Mr. Arpionis," he assured him. Then, without adding another word, he motioned for the butler to lead him and Vonni out to Hector's warming helicopter.

The following morning, as they were checking out of the Flamingo, the hotel manager came over and handed King a Gucci valise. Inside it was $105,000 in cash and a note that read:

*You earned it. If only for reminding me that there are things in life more valuable than money, such as honor and integrity. Thank you for making my associates and me feel young again. We enjoyed your company. Come back soon.*

*Sincerely, Hector Arpionis,*
*President, Flamingo Hotel and Casino Resort*

# CHAPTER 20

Hector had been right. Don Falcone did indeed have a plan, and it worked out even better than he could have ever imagined. Knowing that it was likely the other Syndicate bosses would never fully accept Omnio as a ranking member of his Family, he had to take preemptive measures. He refused to stand by and watch his beloved grandson settle into a life of mediocrity as a simple street soldier, forever bullied by the other Families. Not when he knew Omnio had the potential to be something special. Not just for the Family, but for Cosa Nostra as a whole. The key would be for Omnio to make himself invaluable, which he could only do by positioning himself in a way that the other bosses, and ultimately the Commission, needed him more than he needed them. It would come down to money and power. It *always* came down to money and power. The only way the Commission would overlook his *difetto* blood and still allow him to take the Oath was if he became so powerful that they had no choice.

Also as Hector presumed, Don Falcone had learned of Hector's private poker game from Russell Loduca. This was the reason he sent King down to Las Vegas. He wanted him to begin meeting men like Loduca, men who were extremely successful but not part of Cosa Nostra. He wanted him to see that there was an entire world outside of Detroit, a world where the most successful men were not Mafioso, but in fact legitimate businessmen. His pride, of course, hadn't allowed him to come right out and explain this. After all, he was the *Capo Crimini* of a

Cosa Nostra Family, a Boss of Bosses, a Mafioso through and through. He'd been a career criminal nearly his entire life. How could he tell his grandson, who looked up to him with such admiration, to begin considering a life outside of Cosa Nostra? How could he openly discredit who he was and what he had stood for his entire life? He couldn't. His pride wouldn't allow it, and it was this pride that had kept him from coming right out and asking Hector to introduce Omnio to his powerful associates. His pride had not, however, kept him from asking Russ Loduca to introduce himself to Omnio. He knew his grandson's natural charm and magnetic personality would leave a mark on Loduca.

But he was not expecting the news he received when Hector called. Not only had Omnio become acquainted with Loduca, but it seemed he had become acquainted with all of Hector's billionaire associates. And from what Hector had to say, he had made quite an impression on them.


King returned from Las Vegas with a whole new perspective on life and business. Particularly the world of big business. His time in Vegas made him realize that it was possible to build a legitimate empire without breaking the law. Or at the very least, only bending a few laws from time to time. He now saw a much bigger picture, one that revealed exactly why his grandfather had sent him to Las Vegas. Not just for a bit of relaxation and fun in the sun, but to be exposed to a realm of business and success far beyond anything he could have ever imagined in Detroit. It motivated him to start setting his goals much higher.

Las Vegas changed something in him. A seed had been planted in his mind, a seed that quickly took root and began to grow. He now knew that he could be more than just a low-level Detroit wiseguy. Or even a *capo*. After being exposed to Hector and his wealthy associates, he realized that he was only limited by his own imagination. If he set his goals high, applied himself, and used what his grandfather taught him, he could be anything he set his mind to. Someday he could even be like the men he had played poker with. He'd been selling himself short. But now, memories of his time in Vegas would be a constant reminder of what could be accomplished, even through legitimate means.

One of the first changes he made was removing the crew from its involvement in the drug business. Particularly hard drugs, such as cocaine and heroin. Though drugs were an incredibly lucrative racket, federal judges tended to hand out draconian prison sentences for large drug convictions. As a result, busted dealers were quick to turn informant in exchange for leniency. King's network of dealers were not bound to silence by *Omerta,* which made him fear they could turn state's evidence if one of them were to get pinched by the feds. The money was good, but the risk just wasn't worth it. So, acting on his grandfather's advice, he relinquished all of his interests in both the cocaine and heroin business to Don Giuseppe Rubino, who had several long-standing relationships with high-level federal judges, whom he kept on his payroll in case one of his dealers were to ever get pinched. King did, however, allow his crew to retain their marijuana operations, a drug the federal authorities had little interest in, yet that still produced considerable profits.

With the subsequent loss of income from hard drugs, King knew he had to start finding new ways to replace this income, especially if he wanted to maintain his regular largesse to the other Syndicate bosses, who only allowed him to operate under their protective umbrella because of his regular financial contributions. So one of the first things he did upon returning from Las Vegas was have a sit-down with his lieutenants. During this sit-down he told them about Hector and his associates, how the powerful businessmen had inspired him to think differently.

"If we make the right business decisions..." he said, pacing the room. "...we can build an empire that will someday trump all the Syndicate Families combined! Once we have enough capital... once the time is right... we'll leave the street shit behind. That's what the bosses do. They invest in legitimate companies, then their friends in the government help them land the big municipal contracts. Friends they helped get elected using the unions. Now they don't have to worry about being sent to prison for the type of petty street shit we do."

He also explained the obstacles they would have to overcome in order to achieve this—starting with aligning themselves with the Syndicate bosses, who were always watching, always demanding a piece of their weekly take. Unless he could make them genuine allies, they would continue doing whatever they could to keep the crew from growing into a recognized extension of Don Falcone's *Famiglia*.


If there was one thing that young wiseguys loved to do, it was spend money and have a good time. They hustled by day and spent their money by night, usually drinking and philandering at local bars and strip clubs. Most of King's crew blew through their money as fast as they made it. Sometimes faster. Clothes, cars, jewelry, women, whatever. They ate at the finest restaurants in town. They took their girlfriends on extravagant shopping sprees. They gambled. They bought whatever shiny thing met their fancy. This was "the life," the reason they did what they did. Money was like a hot potato—if they held onto it for too long, it'd burn their hands. There was a simple explanation for this. They knew, at least on a subconscious level, that they could very well end up in prison, or worse, on any given day. So they lived each day to the fullest, spending nearly every dollar they made having fun. The notion of saving for the future was as foreign as getting a regular 9-to-5 job. It was almost beyond their comprehension.

But now that King realized the richest men in the world were not criminals, but in fact brilliant-minded businessmen, he began stressing to the crew the importance of putting aside money for future investments. He also stressed the importance of opening legitimate businesses that would supply them with a source of "clean" income. So the first thing he did was ramp up promoting their various nightclubs, which were providing them with a considerable source of legitimate revenue. Next thing he did was have them open a number of small businesses—a chain of pizzerias, a pair of laundromats, half a dozen car washes, and a landscaping company. In the months that followed, more businesses were added—a bakery, a used car lot, an arcade, a hair salon, even a tattoo parlor. All of these fledgling businesses were slow to start, and many of them lost money in the beginning, but they eventually began trickling in clean, legitimate profits. But they did more than just provide the crew with a little extra cash. They acted as laundry machines to clean their illicit proceeds.

Unfortunately, with what King had planned for the future, he needed to start making more money. A lot more. And he knew these new businesses were not going to provide it. The streets were where he knew how to make money, so he also began branching into some new illicit rackets, such as loansharking, sports books, and chop shops. But his most profitable source of new income came from a unique type of protection racket Vonni had suggested during one of their regular late-night conversations. It was a brilliant idea, and after giving it some thought he presented it to his grandfather for authorization. Don Falcone not only thought it was genius, but wondered why he had never thought of it himself.

The traditional protection racket was simple and straightforward. Each Family, or "crew," had a well-defined territory, where its street soldiers shook down businesses for protection money. Local liquor stores, grocery stores, garages, nightclubs, gas stations, restaurants, car lots, retail stores, etcetera paid a monthly "tribute" to whichever Family controlled that particular territory. These cash payments were a sort of insurance policy. If a business owner refused to pay this minor indemnity, their business would be vandalized, robbed, or in some cases even burned to the ground. Sometimes when an example needed to be made, an owner would be beaten. In some extreme cases, such as if an owner refused to pay or threatened to go to the cops, he or someone close to him was killed. This racket was primarily plied in the suburbs, because most of the Syndicate bosses believed there wasn't enough money in the city to bother with it, which of course worked in King's favor. The suburbs were certainly more profitable and offered many more opportunities, but he and his crew still generated considerable revenue from the protection racket in the city.

Vonni's idea, however, put a whole new spin on the protection racket. His idea made it mutually beneficial for both parties. It was bold, and required some panache, but it eventually paid big dividends. Together they began researching large, privately owned businesses with major competitors in the area. Once they marked a business, they would approach its owner with what they referred to as "The Service." Rather than threaten them into paying a protection fee, they offered them a service that would boost their sales and, consequently, their profits. For example, if there were two major construction companies competing in one area for the same market share, King would, for a small fee, arrange for one of those companies to be decommissioned for several weeks, or even several months. This would allow the remaining company to monopolize the local market, thus significantly increasing its sales and profits. Arson was the preferred method for decommissioning a business. Burn it to the ground and it would usually be out of commission for at least 6-8 weeks, which would result in a huge spike in business for the company receiving "The Service." There were hundreds of businesses competing with each other for market share in the metropolitan Detroit area. Car dealerships, construction companies, retail chains, grocery stores, gas stations, gyms, restaurants, garages, trucking companies, even manufacturing factories. There was a limitless supply of businesses competing for the same customers, and all of them could profit greatly by taking advantage of The Service.

King and Vonni made a perfect sales team. After targeting a particular business for The Service, they would thoroughly research it—find out who owned it, who the target demographic was, and how much business it lost to local competitors. They even used one of Don Falcone's connections in the IRS to obtain tax records that listed exactly how much money a business made monthly, quarterly, and annually. Once all of this data was compiled and analyzed, King would then contact the owner and request a private meeting to discuss providing them with a service that would significantly boost their business' profitability. Clad in tailored suits, he and Vonni would pitch The Service like a pair of seasoned sales professionals. Upon hearing their proposal, some business owners had a hard time taking them seriously, but one piercing look from King told them all they needed to know—the offer was indeed serious and the two young men offering it were part of the local Mafia. Some of them declined The Service, not wanting to climb into bed with the Mafia. Others told them they would consider it and get back to them. But more often than not they would leap at the opportunity to eliminate their competitors and significantly increase their sales.

Best of all, the companies weren't even required to pay in advance for The Service. Since King already knew exactly how much money they were making monthly, quarterly, and yearly, all he required from them was a nominal 35% gratuity from the subsequent spike in sales. Which, depending on the type of business, could be upwards of several hundred thousand dollars.

The Service proved to be an incredibly lucrative new racket, and King quickly compiled an extensive list of clients interested in receiving it. All he had to do was send a couple of capable arsonists to burn down the headquarters of a client's largest competitor. And since there seemed to be no rhyme or reason to the types of businesses being burned, investigators were unable to find any correlation between them. Nothing was sacred. No business was off-limits. But The Service was a tricky and dangerous racket. Not because King was worried about the police, but because some of the businesses he torched in the suburbs were in fact under the protective aegis of various Syndicate Families. That was why he took extra care to always keep the recipients of The Service confined within his innermost circle. Because if the other Families were to ever learn he was torching businesses under their protection, not even his grandfather would be able to protect him.

While King expanded his operations, Don Falcone continued mentoring him, emphasizing the importance of making new friends. Particularly friends in legitimate business arenas. He also made sure King always tithed to the other bosses who allowed him to work his rackets in their territories. As the months wore on, they were astonished by how much money he was tithing. Even Leoni, who inwardly detested him, was impressed. Though almost all the other bosses still saw him as a maverick *difetto*, they couldn't help but respect his hustle.

Of all the other Bosses, Don Giuseppe Rubino was King's only true Syndicate ally, which was no surprise. Ever since King had plugged him into his Mexican cocaine pipeline, Rubino's cocaine profits had skyrocketed. Though their relationship was tentative at best, Rubino's crew had no problem with King or the fact that he was a *difetto*. Don Rubino was a thoroughbred hustler. He strictly adhered to the rules of his oath, but what mattered most to him was money. A guy's bloodline wasn't as important as how much he earned for the crew, and he knew the young King was a serious "earner." Not just for himself, or even his crew, but for Don Falcone and even some of the other Bosses.

As King began stockpiling money, Don Falcone reminded him to always  invest in the local "community," a euphemism for greasing the palms of certain government officials. So King began giving hefty cash payoffs to various police chiefs, city officials, judges and prosecutors—monies above and beyond what the Syndicate bosses were already paying them. He contributed to the campaign funds of high-ranking politicians, congressmen, even a Michigan Senator. He put huge sums of money in escrow for various circuit court judges—advance insurance policies taken out in the event that one of his crew were pinched by local police. He paid for their lavish vacations and deposited money into their children's college funds. There was always someone to bribe or "grease." But Don Falcone had taught him long ago that these operational expenses were necessary if the Syndicate wanted to exist without major government interference.

But King took investing in the community one step further by actually investing in the community. He donated money to local churches and other charities. He had truckloads of food—usually stolen by his crew from local warehouses—to be delivered to local homeless shelters and soup kitchens. He even provided financial support for several old widows in the neighborhood, making sure someone always drove them to their doctor appointments and Sunday church services. He bought food and diapers for more than a dozen single young mothers in the neighborhood, and if they fell behind on bills, he always stepped in to provide them with financial support, daycare, school tuition, and job training. He even put a few of them to work at his new businesses.

People in the neighborhood began to liken him to a sort of modern day Robin Hood. Young and old people alike got to know him on a personal level. A few even grew to love him like a son or brother. Wherever he went, he was greeted with smiles and friendly handshakes. If some thugs moved into the neighborhood and were causing trouble, neighbors didn't call the police. They called King Falcone, for they knew he would handle them quickly and efficiently. Though the surrounding area was mostly black ghettos, he did not tolerate hoodlums and thugs trying to muscle their way into the neighborhood.

One day while faced with such a problem, King was struck with an epiphany, an idea for another sort of protection racket, one that could provide him and the crew with a huge infusion of new income. The idea stemmed from an incident that happened in front of Vonni's aunt and uncle's house. Vonni often stopped by their house for dinner out of love for his aunt, and on this day King joined him. After a wholesome meal of pork chops and mashed potatoes, the two of them joined Vonni's cousin Jack in the backyard to digest their dinner and shoot a little basketball. It was a hot summer evening and Jack's sister, Erika, who had recently turned seventeen, was in the driveway out front, washing her parents' car. She was playing music and quietly enjoying herself when she suddenly started yelling and cursing at someone. Wondering what was happening, Vonni dropped the basketball and dashed down the driveway.

"One of those jerks grabbed my ass!" she yelled, pointing a group of thugs standing on the sidewalk in front of the neighbor's house.

Vonni looked at her and almost couldn't blame them. She was a beautiful girl, and wearing only a skimpy bikini. But such a disrespectful act was intolerable, and he instantly felt his blood pressure boil with outrage. There were four thugs, two blacks, two Latinos, all of them appearing to be in their twenties. None of them looked familiar, but all of them looked ready for a fight. Being that he was in front of his aunt and uncle's house, he really didn't want to get into it with them, but when they began taunting him and laughing at him, he snapped. Enraged, he began reaching for the pistol he had tucked under his shirt at the small of his back.

"Don't!" King whispered, grabbing his wrist in a vice-like grip.

Vonni spun around with furry in his eyes. "Why the fuck not?" he growled. "You hear these motherfuckers?"

383

King ignored him and turned to the thugs, who were postured on the sidewalk as if readying for a fight. "We don't want no trouble, fellas," he said, forcefully shoving Vonni back up the driveway. "It's just a misunderstanding."

The thugs relaxed and began backing down the sidewalk, laughing and taunting them with crude expletives until they disappeared around the corner.

"Go inside," King ordered Erika, pointing at the house.

Up until this moment, she had always seen King as the type of guy who would never back down from anyone, especially not some ghetto punks. She was about to call him on it when she noticed the look in his eyes—a look that told her he was not done with the punks, that he would make them pay for their disrespect. She smiled in this knowledge as she did what she was told and went inside.

"What?" Vonni asked, wondering why King was glaring at him. "I'm supposed to just stand here and let these punk motherfuckers disrespect me and my family?"

Still glaring at him, King motioned him into the garage. "And what were you going to do?" he asked when they were alone. "Shoot them in broad daylight? In front of your aunt and uncle's house? With your little cousin standing there? What are you, some kind of homicidal maniac? Come on, Giovanni, you're smarter than that. So what if some punk grabbed your cousin's ass? I'm not saying something shouldn't be done about it, but there are ways to handle these things. You of all people should know this. I'm telling you, Vonni, if you don't learn to control that temper of yours, it's going to get you in trouble someday. Only a fool reacts on impulse. You know better."

Those words cut like a knife, and Vonni suddenly felt ashamed for acting so foolishly. He knew King was right. He needed to learn how to control his temper. Even if it had only been for a brief moment, he'd allowed his emotions to cloud his judgment. If King hadn't been there to intervene, he might very well have shot one of those punks.

384

"Sorry, I wasn't thinking," he apologized, pained by the disappointment on his boss' face. "You're right, I need to control my temper better."

King saw the shame and regret in his *protettore's* eyes, so he set a hand on his shoulder. "No worries, *prottetore mia*," he said, offering him a brotherly smile. "We'll find those punks and make them pay for their disrespect."

"Yeah?" Vonni asked, the shame in his eyes turning into excitement.

King waved Jack into the garage. "You recognize any of those punks?"

"Actually, yeah..." Jack answered. "They've been hanging out at the park a lot. One of them moved in a house over on Ashland. My boy, Jim Antonelli, lives down the block. Says they sell dope from the house. I guess they got crackheads coming and going all night. They're a bunch of fuckin' assholes, too. Always loud and fuckin' with people, starting fights with the neighbors, hitting on people's girlfriends. Real dicks!"

King gave Vonni a barely perceptible grin. "Jack, do me a favor and have your buddy Jim get me the address to this house. And see what else you can learn about them."

"Why?" Jack asked.

"Because we're going to pay them a visit."

Jack nodded, knowing exactly what that meant.


It only took Jack's friend two days to get the address and the name of the guy living there. Located on Ashland Road, the unofficial border between King's neighborhood and the adjacent ghetto, and less than five blocks from his own home, it was a street that always seemed to attract undesirables. Particularly drug dealers. And as of late, more and more of these opportunistic drug dealers had been renting houses on the fringes of his neighborhood. To some degree, King had been tolerating them, if only because he knew there was only so much

385

he could do to stop them. As families with money moved out to the suburbs, the impoverished lower class inevitably moved in and transformed entire neighborhoods into ghettos. Same story all over America.

But these newest punks were harassing and bullying people, disrespecting their neighbors, inviting junkies into the neighborhood to score dope and steal anything that wasn't bolted down. And this King would not stand for. He'd known for some time that he would eventually have to make an example out of one of these ghetto transplants, but they had no idea who he was and knew nothing about his Family. As a result, he feared the only way to rid them from the neighborhood would be to use violence, which he'd been hoping to avoid. After all, he didn't want to turn his neighborhood into a war zone. But when this new batch of punks blatantly disrespected him and Vonni, he decided it was time to make an example.

Any other time, he would have simply assigned one of his soldiers to handle the problem, but he wanted to personally send a message to any more thugs who thought they could muscle their way into his neighborhood, sell drugs, and terrorize people. He wanted them to know exactly who he was and what they were up against.

The thug running this new dope house was a guy named Jose "Joker" Torres, a 22-year-old Puerto Rican implant who knew nothing about the Mafia or its presence in Detroit. But that was about to change. Two days after the incident with Vonni's cousin, King and Vonni paid Joker a visit. It was late morning, just before noon, and Vonni parked in the driveway. When they stepped from the car, all appeared quiet in the house, which was normal for dope houses at this time of day. King knocked on the door, but nobody answered. When he knocked harder, almost pounding, someone peeked through the front blinds. A moment later, Jose yanked the door open, wearing nothing but underwear. His hair was disheveled, his eyes were bloodshot, and he did not look happy. For a moment he stood there looking at them, his mind trying to recall why they looked familiar. Then he remembered.

"What the fuck do you two clowns want?" he said, surprised they had the nerve to come to his house.

King offered him a forced smile. "Jose, my name is Omnio Falcone. People call me King. I didn't mean to wake you, but we need to talk."

"Talk about what?" Jose asked, scratching his crotch.

"I have a deal I'd like to offer you."

"A deal?" Jose scoffed with contempt. "What the fuck you talkin' about?"

King glanced up and down the street. "Maybe we should step inside."

Annoyed but curious, Jose stepped aside and let them in. The house was a disaster. The living room carpet was matted and stained. A coffee table was littered with carryout containers, overflowing ashtrays, and empty 40-ounce beer bottles. The room reeked of marijuana, body odor, cigarettes, and filth. Two of the guys from the other day were asleep on a pair of tattered couches, both of them snoring. One had what appeared to be a hooker tucked under his arm. A dilapidated old entertainment center had a TV and Nintendo gaming system in it. A creaky ceiling fan was stirring the musty hot air.

"Alright, what the fuck you want, kid?" Jose asked, folding his arms over his chest, his face a mask of contempt and annoyance.

King quickly surveyed the room. He immediately noted a sawed-off shotgun leaning against one of the couches, and amongst the clutter on the coffee table was a chrome revolver. He and Vonni were both armed with semi-automatic pistols, but he had given Vonni a direct order to hold both his pistol and tongue in check unless things went bad.

"This is my neighborhood," King said matter-of-factly, an icy look in his ebon eyes. "I've lived here my whole life. Everyone knows me. The people who live here don't have much money, but they like their peace and quiet, which is why I can no longer allow you to sell drugs from this house. But like I said, I came to make you an offer. I can help you relocate your operation and we can be friends…" He splayed his hands wide. "Or you can choose to stay and we can be enemies. The choice is yours. It makes no difference to me. Either way, you're done selling dope from this house. And if you ever disrespect me or any of my people again, you—"

Jose cut him off with a roaring fit of laughter. "Holy shit, kid, you've got fuckin' balls!" he exclaimed, and then gave him an icy look of his own. "Who the fuck do you think you are, coming in here givin' orders like you runnin' shit? Fool, do you know who you're talking to?"

King looked him deadpan in the eye. "I know exactly who I'm talking to. Your name is Jose Torres. They call you Joker. You recently moved here from Miami. And you obviously have no idea who *you* are talking to. If you did, you would think twice before talking to me with such disrespect. You see that's the difference between you and me. I know exactly who I am talking to, but you have no idea who you're talking to. I came here to offer you a business opportunity, not to disrespect you. I will only offer you this opportunity once."

Jose suddenly didn't feel so cocky. There was something in this kid's eyes that made him nervous. "Okay, let's suppose I give a fuck who you are," he said, now more curious than amused. "What kind of business opportunity you talking about?"

"One that benefits us both," King said, his tone pragmatic and professional. "You can continue living in this house, but you can no longer sell drugs from it. No more junkies coming and going all night. No more harassing the neighbors." He gestured a hand around the room. "You'll clean this place up and take care of the outside. But as far as your business goes, I will help you open another dope house in another neighborhood. And to ensure that house is successful, my associates and I will personally eliminate all competitors within a one-mile radius. I'll also see that the local cops allow you to operate without interference. And for this service, I will only require a ten percent cut from your profits."

Jose actually took a moment to consider this. It was true, he did compete with dozens of nearby dope houses. The ghettos just to the south and west had dope houses on almost every block. It was the main reason he had rented this house in the first place. He knew the closer he got to the suburbs, the closer he was to the throngs of junkies who made a daily pilgrimage into the city to score dope. Being closer to the suburbs gave him a geographical and tactical advantage. But what this kid was offering could very well give him an even greater advantage. It would allow him to monopolize the market for an entire mile. He might even have to open another house just to keep up with sales. But it sounded too good to be true, and after a moment he decided there was no way this kid could possibly hold up his end of the bargain.

"How's this for a deal?" he said, more annoyed than ever. "Fuck you and fuck your neighborhood. I'll do whatever I want from this house, and you ain't gonna do shit about it." He pointed at the door. "Now get fuck out my crib before you really piss me off. And do me a favor, have that cute little bitch in the bikini from the other day drop by. I'll show her who's runnin' shit around here."

Vonni's face flushed with rage as he fought the urge to draw his pistol and shoot the punk in the face. But he remained calm, remembering his orders.

King's jaw muscles flexed as he also bit back his anger. "Ask around," he said, knowing this was neither the time nor place to put the punk in check. "Like I said, everyone knows me. You have one day to shut down your operation. After that, if you continue selling from this house... well, don't say I didn't warn you."

With that, he turned and led Vonni from the house.

389

Jose followed them out onto the porch. "Sure, boss," he laughed. "I'll get right on it. You just don't forget to have that little bikini bitch drop by. I'm gonna put her to work for me. She can be my new bottom bitch." He was still laughing when he stepped inside and slammed the door shut.

Three nights later, at 3:00 AM in the morning, four of King's soldiers surrounded the house and tossed gasoline bombs through the windows. The house instantly exploded into an inferno. When Jose and his crew came charging out the front door, they were gunned down before they ever made it off the porch. Several neighbors who had heard the initial explosions looked out their windows and actually witnessed the carnage, but told the police nothing of what they saw. They knew who was behind it and figured the drug-dealing thugs got what they had coming.

Not only did this rid the neighborhood of a growing cancer, but it also inspired an idea in King's mind: He could begin providing "The Service" to drug dealers in the ghetto. When he proposed his idea to Don Rubino, who controlled a network of mid-level drug dealers throughout the city, each of who ran a series of dope houses that competed with dozens of freelance dope houses, the tenured drug czar thought it was genius. So, for a small fee, King began eliminating these freelance dealers who competed with Don Rubino's dealers, an arrangement that worked out so well that the don's drug sales nearly quadrupled in certain areas. Not only did King receive a significant percentage of this new spike in business, it helped him forge an alliance with Don Rubino, an alliance the other Families were not happy about. For Don Rubino led one of the most powerful crews in the Syndicate.

# CHAPTER 21

Over the next two years, King continued expanding his operations, both legitimate and illicit, into new arenas. And with this expansion came serious profits, which of course he shared with the Syndicate bosses, including Leoni—proxy boss of the Falcone Family. Though he knew some of them still looked down at him for his impure blood, at least they were finally beginning to accept him as an extension of his grandfather's *Famiglia*. Even Leoni seemed to outwardly accept him, although King knew it was only as a show of respect for Don Falcone. Some of the Syndicate bosses even allowed him to expand his operations into their territories, including the surrounding suburbs of East Detroit, Roseville, Warren, Fraser, St. Clair Shores, and Mt. Clemens. Of course, they required a significant portion of his profits from these operations, but at least he was finally getting the respect and acceptance he deserved. After all, he was a Falcone. The last Falcone. Grandson of Peter Paul Falcone, *Capo di tutti Capi,* Syndicate Boss of Bosses.

Leoni and the other Syndicate bosses, however, were not the only ones watching King and his crew grow into a recognized extension of Don Falcone's Family. The FBI had also taken notice and they now had King on their organized crime watch list. Ever since Don Falcone had been released from federal prison for his involvement in skimming from several Las Vegas hotels, the FBI had maintained a vigilant eye on him. Which was the primary reason that the Commission had nudged him into retirement by tentatively "suggesting" he hand over the reins of his Family to his son-in-law, Leoni. The FBI knew he had amassed most of his wealth via criminal means, but they'd never been able to prove it. For nearly thirty years they had been investigating him, and during that time not a single informant would agree to testify against him, even if it meant being sent to prison for the rest of their lives. They knew testifying against the infamous Butcher might very well result in a death sentence for their entire family.

Though certain low-level informants claimed that Don Falcone was retired from any criminal activities, the FBI believed he was still heavily involved in the criminal rackets. They knew the Syndicate Boss of Bosses would never fully step down from his throne, and suspected that he was simply using corrupted bankers, front men, and various legitimate businesses to launder monies earned from illicit rackets that were now managed by his son-in-law, Leoni Gianolla. He was just maintaining a facade of retirement. But the FBI was in no hurry. Time was on their side. They were always there. Watching. Waiting. Lurking in the shadows. Probing. Investigating. Tapping phones. Recruiting informants. Listening to the streets.

Ever since the highly-publicized escapades of the New York Families—particularly the conflict between John "The Teflon Don" Gotti and his underboss-turned-informant Salvatore "Sammy The Bull" Gravano—the Commission had ordered all Cosa Nostra factions to tighten their circles and maintain a low profile. And none were better at maintaining a low profile than the Detroit faction, which they did by paying exorbitant bribes to city officials, local media outlets, and police chiefs. They also made sure to avoid violence and conflicts between Families, as well as refrained from flaunting their influence. Under Don Falcone's leadership, the Syndicate bosses maintained a veneer of legitimacy and did everything in their power to stay off the FBI's omnipresent radar.

But this didn't deter FBI efforts. Their network of street informants supplied them with fragments of information that helped piece together a vague picture of the Syndicate's hierarchy. It was common knowledge that Don Falcone now played only a small part in running the *borgata*. Rumor had it that his only illicit activity was managing a small sports book, and only as a hobby in his spare time. The OCT (Organized Crime Taskforce) knew he earned more than enough money from his legitimate businesses—several nightclubs, restaurants, and a wholesale produce business in the Eastern Market—to maintain a comfortable lifestyle for the rest of his life. Because of this, the Federal Bureau of Investigations had come to the realization that if they wanted to see him back behind bars, it wasn't going to result from something new, but rather from something in his past.

The FBI did, however, begin looking closer at the don's handsome young grandson, Omnio. Rumor had it he was quickly becoming a serious Syndicate player, even as a mere street soldier operating semi-autonomously from his grandfather's Family. They were certain he was involved in the criminal rackets, but were unsure as to what extent. They knew he was the leader of a small crew of notorious young street hustlers, but none of them had ties to any particular Family. That made it next to impossible for FBI informants to penetrate their circle. Like his grandfather, it seemed young Omnio was also very feared on the streets, because nobody would even talk about him. Or rather, FBI informants claimed to know nothing of "King" Falcone's activities, which was obviously a lie. They were just scared to talk. But in the grand scheme, the FBI saw Omnio Falcone as nothing more than a blip on their radar. The Organized Crime Taskforce considered him and his crew to be nothing more than a disorganized band of petty street hustlers. They had no idea how wrong they were.


Don Falcone couldn't have been more pleased with the progress of his favorite grandson. So pleased, in fact, that he threw him a surprise twenty-first birthday party. It was a Saturday evening, mid-July, and the party was at Leoni's headquarters, "Leo's On The Lake," an exclusive restaurant and nightclub adjoined to a large marina along the shores of Lake St. Clair. Don Falcone had made sure to invite the entire family, as well as the Syndicate's ranking *capiregime*. But he did not expect such a large turnout. Nearly two hundred people came to celebrate the event.

The evening was beautiful, warm and cloudless. A live band was playing top-forty dance music from a small bandstand. Inside, the dining room was packed with people eating and drinking. Outside on the deck, several dozen people were seated around canopied terrace tables. Everyone was in high spirits, drinking and socializing. King, the guest of honor, was in the dining room, seated at his own table, completely surrounded by his crew. And as he enjoyed the festive ambiance, a steady stream of uncles, cousins, and family associates stopped by his table to wish him a happy birthday, each of them kissing his cheek before handing him an envelope of cash—a standard show of respect. Even his cousins Anthony and Dino, who resented the special relationship he had with their grandfather, paid him homage with an envelope stuffed with hundred dollar bills.

But of course, King wasn't fooled by the generosity of his cousins. He knew they despised him and would stop at nothing to usurp him as their grandfather's favorite. They were jealous of his success and knew he was slowly beginning to win over the Syndicate *capi*. Even their father had grown to accept him. Or at least tolerate him. They feared it would only be a matter of time before other *capi* overlooked his *difetto* blood and approved of him taking the oath, which meant he could someday become their boss. And this he knew they could never accept. They were just biding their time, waiting for the right opportunity. An opportunity to kill him and be rid of him once and for all. But he would never give it to them. He was too smart. No matter where he went or what he did, he always made sure he was well-protected. Ever since Vonni saved him from the assassins in Gus' store, he knew his treacherous young cousins would stop at nothing to get rid of him. But soon, very soon, his grandfather would contact Don Vincenzo Valacci, current Boss of New York's Genovese Family and unofficial chairman of the Commission, to request a sit-down where they would discuss the possibility of him being Made. And if he were Made, he would be untouchable. Not even his insidious cousins or Uncle Leoni would dare make an attempt on his life. Not unless the Commission and all of the Syndicate bosses collectively sanctioned it. He knew as long as he continued to put serious money in their pockets, this would never happen. Not unless he broke the cardinal rule of killing a Made man without their unanimous consent.

As guest of honor, King eventually stood and began making his rounds, personally thanking everyone for coming. He stopped and played with all his young cousins, who swarmed around him and begged for his attention. He socialized with all of his aunts, complimenting each of them on how beautiful they looked. He shook the hands of cousins and uncles he hadn't seen in years, most of who were not part of Cosa Nostra.

He was very much enjoying mingling with everyone, but when he came to the table where his cousins Anthony, Dino, and Pamela were sitting, he froze in his tracks. Seated next to Pamela was the most beautiful girl he'd ever seen. So beautiful, in fact, that he just stood there staring at her, paralyzed, his heart pounding in his chest. Petite and no more than 5'3" in height, her white summer sundress displayed curves in all the right places. Her long dark hair, olive skin, and soft features were indicative Mediterranean origins. But her eyes were her most striking feature. They were the brightest, most beautiful cerulean blue eyes he'd ever seen. And as she now turned them on him, he felt like a deer in headlights, for he could not look away. In fact, he was so enraptured by her beauty that he failed to notice his cousin Anthony sneering up at him with contempt.

"What's up, cousin?" Anthony said, his sneer twisting into a crooked smirk. "Cat got your tongue?"

King snapped out of his trance and leaned down to kiss Pamela on the cheek. "Hello, Pamela," he said, ignoring Anthony's remark. "How's my favorite baby cousin?"

"I'm nineteen, Omnio," she said, feigning anger. "When are you going to stop calling me a baby?"

"Never," he teased, and then turned his attention to the beautiful blue-eyed angel sitting next to her. "So who's your friend? I don't think we've met."

Pamela instantly noticed the lascivious look in his eyes. It was a look she'd never seen in them before. She knew he loved girls. All kinds of girls. And they loved him. Growing up, all of her friends had swooned over her "beautiful" cousin Omnio. Yet he always acted like he had no idea why girls were so captivated by his looks, which she found amusing. She was perfectly aware of his philandering ways, that he rotated a small harem of girlfriends. But never had she seen him look at a girl the way he was looking at this one—a look of unabated lust.

She turned to the girl seated next to her. "Contessa, allow me to introduce my cousin Omnio. This is his party."

The girl smiled up at him coyly. "Hello, Omnio," she said, her Italian accent making her words hard to understand. "Happy birthday."

"Thank you," he said in Italian, figuring she would be more comfortable speaking her native tongue. "So you're a countess?"

"No," she said in English, giggling melodically. "It is just a name. Like yours. Unless you really are a king?"

He flashed her his most charming smile. "I am the king of my own domain."

Anthony rolled his eyes. "Well ain't that some shit," he scoffed, his sneer returning. "What do you know, guys? We're in the presence of royalty."

396

King ignored him and continued staring at Pamela's friend with overt intrigue. "So where are you from, Contessa?" he asked, again speaking in Italian, if only because he knew Anthony wasn't fluent. "Are you Siciliano?"

"Yes," she said, also in Italian, a distant look in her eyes. "I was born in Palermo but moved to Pozzuoli when I was very young."

He thought for a moment, scanning his knowledge of Italian geography. "Pozzuoli? That's just south of Naples, yes?"

"Yes!" she said, her face lighting up. "That's exactly where it is. How do you know this?"

"Oh…" he said, tapping the side of his head. "I have all kinds of useless knowledge swimming around up here."

"But today it wasn't useless," she said, smiling coquettishly.

"I have my moments," he said, flashing her a smile of his own. "So… I have to say, Contessa, I think you may very well be the most beautiful girl I've ever seen. Are you spoken for?"

She instantly began to blush. "Thank you, Omnio," she said, suddenly aware that everyone was staring at her. "That's very sweet. But if you are asking if I have a boyfriend, the answer is no. I had one back home, but he has moved on. We haven't spoken in months."

"You writing a book, cousin?" Anthony asked smugly, his tone dripping with sarcasm.

Again, King ignored him and continued addressing Contessa. "So judging by your accent, you haven't been in the States very long. Are you on vacation or here to stay?"

"I'm here attending university," she said, casting a quick look at Pamela.

"She goes to school with me," Pamela said in English, understanding some of their discussion and not liking where it was going. "We shared a dorm last semester. Her father and grandpa are friends, so she's staying at my house for the summer. But when we go back to school this fall we're going to get an apartment together."

King nodded, even more intrigued. Pamela had just finished her freshman year at the University of Michigan, where she was earning her degree and setting her sights on med school. He was very proud of her. Unlike her two brothers, he knew she had a deep love for him. Growing up, they'd always had a special relationship, one unlike any they had with their other cousins. He really had no idea how it came about, but she was the closest thing he ever had to a sibling. He found that ironic, considering her two brothers were his mortal enemies. But she was no longer just his baby cousin. Indeed she was a grown woman. A beautiful and exceptionally intelligent woman who was hoping to one day become a pediatrician. Over the last year, while she was away at school, he missed her dearly. Before heading off to college, she'd always joined the family at their grandparent's house for Sunday dinners. After dinner they always found a quiet place to talk in private, usually just to catch up on gossip or joke about their odd family dynamic. He missed their Sunday afternoon time together, the two of them laughing and joking as they tried to outwit each other with random trivia and famous quotes. She always brought out the best in him, and he loved her like a sister. He'd barely seen her over the last year, but when she did come home for the holidays or occasional weekend, they would pick right up where they left off, sometimes talking alone in their grandparents' basement for hours. He enjoyed hearing about her studies and goals for the future, and she seemed generally interested in his own goals for the future. Their relationship had always been separate from the complexities and politics of their family structure. She shared her innermost thoughts and secrets with him, and for the most part he did the same with her. But now he couldn't help but wonder why she had never mentioned her beautiful college roommate.

Then the answer hit him. Anthony. The malevolent sneer on his cousin's face told him all he needed to know. Pamela had never mentioned Contessa because her brother had a crush on her. No matter what kind of special relationship he had with

Pamela, her brother would always come first. For all he knew, Anthony and this Contessa were already dating, which would explain Anthony's attitude. So, not wanting to further aggravate his nefarious cousin, he decided it was time to back off. At least until he learned more about her. But it took all his strength to not grab her by the hand and run from the room.

"Well, it was a pleasure meeting you, Contessa," he said formally, gesturing a hand around the table. "Maybe we can all get together sometime for dinner at my club? I've been so busy lately I barely get to see my cousins anymore."

"You're not the only one who's been busy, cousin," Anthony said, casting a cryptic glance at his brother, Dino.

Before King could reply, Vonni sidled up behind him and whispered in his ear that Don Falcone wanted to speak to him out on the deck.

"Well, thank you for coming, you guys," King said to his cousins, his eyes stopping on Contessa. "And again, it was a pleasure meeting you. Enjoy your evening and hopefully I'll see you again soon." He offered her one last smile, and then followed Vonni out onto the deck.

Behind the club was an expansive wooden deck that was famous for supposedly being the largest deck in Michigan. Built along the edges of a large lagoon that connected the marina, it had two levels, one several feet higher than the other. The lower deck was for regular patrons, but the upper deck was a VIP terrace that offered a bird's-eye view of the entire marina, where hundreds of sailboats, cabin cruisers, and speedboats were moored to a series of docks and piers. On the VIP terrace were a number of umbrella covered tables that were illuminated by paraffin candles. Seated at one of these tables was Don Falcone, Leoni, and three other men, all of them sipping drinks, smoking cigars, and casually talking amongst each other.

"Nonno?" King said to Don Falcone. "You looking for me?"

"There you are, bambino!" Don Falcone boomed, mildly inebriated from several glasses of wine. "Yes, I wanted to know... are enjoying your party?"

"I'm having a great time, Nonno," King replied, glancing back toward the dining room. "I can't believe so many people showed up. I haven't seen half of them in years. I forgot how big our family is."

Don Falcone chuckled and reached for a bottle of cognac on the table. "Well, everyone wanted to see how you've grown," he said, pouring shots into a pair of glasses. "Now sit and have a drink with us. After all, you're finally of age." He handed each King and Vonni a glass, then raised his own glass. "Salute!"

Everyone at the table hoisted their glasses in the air and saluted the guest of honor, but King and Vonni only took small sips, for they had never forgotten the don's pithy maxim about alcohol: Only a fool gets drunk, and they definitely did not want to look like fools tonight. Not with so many people watching them. But it would be disrespectful for King not to have at least one drink with his grandfather and this assemblage of Syndicate royalty. So, as a show of respect, he drank his celebratory drink and displayed none of the abhorrence he felt for some of the men at the table. Though they had grown to accept him as an extension of his grandfather's Family, he knew most of them still considered him to be nothing more than a maverick *difetto*. They only tolerated him because he was lining their pockets with cash, and because they still feared his grandfather. He could see the contempt in their eyes when they looked at him, hear it in their voices when they spoke to him. But he knew it was more than contempt. In their eyes was also a twinge of fear. Barely perceptible, but there nonetheless. It only fueled him, for the slightest show of fear was the slightest show of weakness. They'd seen what he was capable of over the last two years, even with little support from his grandfather. King was barely twenty-one, and his crew was already growing into a powerhouse. It made them nervous. And knowing he made them nervous was the best birthday gift he could ever get, which of course was exactly why Don Falcone had invited them to the party.

Along with Don Falcone and Leoni, seated at the table were Giuseppe Rubino, Alfonse Toccio, Vincenzo Malacci and Tony Zirello. All dons. All distinguished Syndicate *capi*, and all very dangerous Mafiosi in their own right. They represented the five Families of the Syndicate "Partnership." Out of respect for Don Falcone, they'd brought their sons and grandsons with them tonight, several of whom were captains and lieutenants for their respective Families. They had honored King with praise and accolades, congratulating him on all of his recent successes, kissing him on the cheek like he was an extension of their own Families. But they were treacherous men, masters of deception and Machiavellian tactics. Though the Partnership was supposed to work together as one syndicated collective, they all had their own goals and agendas. Subterfuge was a common practice. They never stopped bickering over who should control which rackets and which territories. They were constantly trying to undermine and outflank each other, always vying for the favor of Don Falcone and the other Commission bosses. Dissension was the norm, and one of the things they worked hardest at was hiding their money from each other. Because the more money they earned, the larger the cut the Bosses and Commission required, which created a bit of a paradox. They were constantly appealing to the Commission for larger territories and more opportunities outside of Detroit, yet when they were given these larger territories and opportunities, they complained they weren't making enough money to pay the Commission its due share. That was why the Commission had backed Don Falcone for so long. They trusted him and knew he was a man of honor. Most of all, they knew the others feared him. And fear was what kept them in line.

Though the men at the table were smiling in King's face, he knew some of them were already plotting to muscle him out of his various operations. If it weren't for his grandfather, they would have no doubt already muscled him out, even if it meant killing him. But there was one of them he trusted. Don Rubino. Not just because they had forged a sort of symbiotic relationship in the drug business, but because Don Rubino was the only one who openly expressed his distaste for Leoni, who he knew was in line to become the next Syndicate Boss of Bosses.

But as King now sat there sipping his drink, laughing at their jokes, pretending to be listening to their bad quips and self-inflated tidbits of wisdom, his mind was somewhere else—on the beautiful Contessa. She was just inside, sitting with his cousins. Never had he felt so drawn to another human being. It was almost as if he could feel her presence, a magnetic pull drawing him to her. He wanted to look into those magnificent blue eyes and learn her most intimate thoughts. He wanted to run away with her and meld her soul to his.

"Omnio, I almost forgot," Don Falcone said, snapping him from his reverie. "I got you a little something for your birthday. Just arrived from Canada yesterday. I think you'll like it."

"Well, what is it?" Don Rubino asked. "Don't leave the poor boy in limbo."

Don Falcone turned towards the lagoon. "That one there," he said, pointing at a boat moored to the first dock.

King couldn't believe his eyes. It was a beautiful offshore race boat, which was something he'd already been shopping for. He loved boats and knew the Zirello crew was involved in a very lucrative stolen boat racket, which was surprisingly simple. Boats from the Canadian side of Lake St. Clair were stolen from their docks and brought over to the American side, where they were then re-tagged and given new paperwork. And vice versa—boats from the American side were stolen and delivered to the Canadian side to be re-tagged and sold at standard Blue Book rates. A quarter-million dollar boat could be stolen and re-tagged for under $10,000, and then sold to buyers all over the country at standard retail prices. Some were even shipped overseas to be sold.

Since King had an interest in boats, he even tried to get in on the racket. But Tony Zirello's son, Pauly, who oversaw the operation, claimed he was too young and inexperienced to be involved. Of course, King knew the real reason was simply because Pauly didn't want him, or anyone else for that matter, getting a piece of his action. Especially not some young *difetto*, even if the *difetto* was the Boss' favorite grandson.

"Grandpa, I know you didn't get me that for my birthday?" King said, wondering if this might be some kind of joke.

"Yes I did," Don Falcone replied, winking at Don Zirello. "You mentioned you were thinking about buying one, so I thought I'd surprise you. Tony and his boy gave me a deal on it. Go take a look. It's a beautiful piece of work. Pauly says it can top ninety miles per hour. It's all fueled up and ready to go. Maybe you can take some of your cousins out for a ride?"

King gave him a look. "Grandpa, don't you don't think such a boat is a little excessive for a birthday gift? Not to mention flashy?"

Don Falcone dismissed this with a wave of his hand. "Nonsense. I told you, Tony gave me a deal. As for flashy? Well, we all deserve a few nice things in life. It's your twenty-first birthday, Omnio. And you've been working so hard. I just wanted to reward you with something special. Now go take it for a spin. Enjoy it. I know you don't want to sit around with us boring old men all night. Just be careful. Driving a boat is not as easy. They have no brakes."

This evoked a good laugh from everyone at the table, but it was not entirely a joke. Driving a boat, especially such a large and powerful boat, took skill. Leoni especially knew this to be true, since he owned a 42-foot cabin cruiser named "Patty," after his wife, and a 32-foot offshore racer named "Triton," after the Greek god of the sea.

"Have Anthony show you how to drive it," Leoni suggested, motioning to the seawall at the edge of the deck, where his two boats were moored. "He takes mine out all the time. Your grandfather is right. Driving a boat is dangerous if you don't know what you're doing. It takes practice. Let Anthony show you the ropes."

"That's a good idea, Uncle Leo," King said, shooting Vonni a grin. "You up for taking a spin on my new boat?"

Vonni looked at the impressive black race boat. "You think you can keep from killing us?" he asked, only half-jokingly, drawing a round of laughter from the table of old Mafiosi.

"Don't worry, you'll be fine," Leoni assured him. "It's like riding a bike. Once you figure it out, it's second nature."

"Yeah, it's not rocket science," King said, and then glanced inside, where the party was still going strong. "Come on, let's go get Anthony to show us how to drive the thing."

Inside, everyone was still casually drinking and socializing. Several young children were dancing on the dance floor, half of them with cake smeared on their faces, all of them having the time of their lives. As King made his way through the crowded room, people began cheering and raising their drinks to him. Little girls darted up to him and demanded he dance with them. Happy to see everyone feeling so festive, he decided to make a quick cameo on the dance floor, where he performed his trademark hustle. Which, of course, caused his guests to roar with applause.

After a few minutes of dancing with his young cousins, King found Anthony still seated at the same table with Dino, Pamela, and the beautiful Contessa. He knew Anthony had a deeply rooted hatred for him, one that dated back to their childhood. He did not want to compound this hatred by intentionally asserting himself in front of Pamela's beautiful friend, whom he sensed Anthony had a crush on. He was aware that Anthony had always resented him for being bigger, stronger, and better looking. Anthony, at only 5'6", 145 pounds, looked like a runt standing next to him. But by no means was Anthony ugly. On the contrary, he was extremely handsome, with brooding good looks that easily rivaled King's. Though he had a slightly hawkish nose and lacked King's powerful build, he possessed a certain swagger that most women found irresistible. Sometimes he came off as cocky, but his self-assuredness was well warranted. After all, he was the eldest son of the Syndicate's current underboss and future Boss of Bosses. Someday he would become a Made man and likely take over his father's entire operation.

But King didn't hate Anthony. In fact, he regretted how they had grown apart over the years. Though Anthony was abrasive and arrogant, King knew he was simply a product of his father, which Leoni had turned him against him. King only wished that they could set aside their differences and become allies, maybe even join forces to strengthen their Family, rather than divide it with petty jealousies.

Unfortunately, like King, Anthony was a thoroughbred alpha male. Thanks to his father's brainwashing, he considered King to be nothing but a half-breed *difetto* who should never be allowed to rise above the rank of street soldier. Therefore, he would never see him as an equal. This saddened King. They had been such good friends as kids, back when together they had ruled the world as leaders of the *Quattro Duchi,* the Four Dukes. But now that they were grown, King made a conscious effort to avoid him. And when they did come in contact, he did his best not to offend him, which was not easy with Anthony's inferiority complex. It seemed no matter what King said or did, Anthony responded with an attitude and snide remarks. But, until the time was right, he had no choice but to keep his cocky young cousin pacified. That was why he now took extra care not to even look at Contessa as he stepped up to their table.

"Anthony, you know how to drive a boat, right?" he asked, already knowing the answer.

"Yeah, why?" Anthony replied with a touch of pugnacity.

King gestured towards the marina. "Grandpa got me a boat for my birthday, but I have no idea how to drive the freakin' thing. I was hoping you could teach me how to drive it."

For a moment, Anthony sat there staring up at him, annoyed. It seemed once again their biased grandfather had shown his precious Omnio favor. But Anthony was consoled by the fact that Omnio was now coming to him for help. Especially in front of Contessa, who Omnio was obviously smitten with.

"Where is it?" Anthony asked, taking a casual sip from his Molson, his chest suddenly swelled with self-worth.

"First dock," King said, and then looked around the table. "Pam, Dino, Contessa, would you like to join us?"

"I would love to take a ride on your new boat," Contessa said excitedly. "I grew up by the water, and I love boating."

"Great," King said, and then looked at Anthony. "I'm ready when you are, cousin."

Anthony, looking mildly annoyed, stood and led their procession out to the dock, where King took a moment to appreciate his grandfather's flamboyant birthday gift—a custom 38-foot Fountain offshore racer with twin 750-horsepower engines! Its hull had been freshly painted jet black, and stenciled down its side in bold red letters were the words "OMNIOUS MAXIMUS." Inside, the upholstery was a plush gray leather with red piping. Down below, the cabin had a small teak bar, bathroom, leather benches and an alcove bed covered with silk throw pillows. As he took it all in, he considered what such a boat would cost brand-new. He figured upward of $250,000.

Anthony fired up both engines in quick succession, expertly backing the boat from the dock before piloting it from the marina. Once he reached the open waters of Lake St. Clair, he jammed the throttles forward and the twin engines thundered to life with a deafening roar, their 1,500 collective horsepower causing the boat to practically leap from the water, thrusting everyone into their seats. Within seconds he finessed the trim settings and the boat settled into an even plane, skipping across the waves at speeds exceeding 70 mph.

When they were several miles offshore where there was little danger of boat traffic, Anthony began familiarizing King with the throttles, the trim settings, and the boat's brute horsepower. King instantly fell in love with it. Just as he'd expected, driving it came naturally. The boat became an extension of himself, and soon he felt completely in control. Racing it across the open water was one of the most exhilarating experiences of his life. The thunder of its mighty engines. The rush of the wind in his face. Skipping across the waves at high speeds. It was euphoric. Primal. Invigorating. Almost spiritual. But what made it even more thrilling was that she was watching. The beautiful Contessa. He pretended not to notice, but he felt her eyes on him. Several times he glanced back and they locked eyes. Even at night, her magnificent azure eyes stood out like lucent blue beacons calling out to his soul. But there was more to her than just beauty. Something far more intriguing. There seemed to be a certain power radiating from her, an aura of nobility, as if she were indeed a real countess. It stirred something in him he had never felt before.

He wondered what she thought of him. For some reason, she was very reticent and only spoke when spoken to. He knew she probably wondered why so many people had been doting over him back at the party. And she was obviously surprised that his grandfather had given him such an extravagant gift for his birthday. Had Pamela told her about their Family? Could she be intimidated by him? Or was she just shy? Maybe she was just being respectful, knowing Anthony had a crush on her. Whatever the case, when he finally returned to the marina and pulled up to the dock, he yearned to take her back out on the lake, just the two of them, so he could anchor somewhere under the stars, stare into those eyes, and make her fall in love with him. Unfortunately, he was certain Anthony had already laid claim to her. And, at least for now, he was not ready to go to war with his cousin. Especially not over a girl.

Back at the party, King resumed mingling with his many guests. But as the night wore on, he found his eyes drawn to Contessa. Especially her fit yet curvaceous body. Never had he seen such an exquisite example of physical perfection. It took all of his strength to keep from staring at her. But he caught her looking at him several times. Maybe it was just his imagination running wild, but he felt there was something special happening between them.

Around midnight, the party finally began to disperse. And as a show of respect, King stood by the exit, respectfully thanking each of his guests for coming, delving out hugs and kisses to friends and family alike. But when Pamela and her friend stepped over to say good-bye, his heart began to race.

"Drive carefully," he said, kissing Pamela on the cheek before locking eyes with Contessa. "And thank *you* for coming, Contessa. It was a pleasure meeting you."

"It was also a pleasure meeting you, Omnio," she replied, her eyes reading his. "I had a great time. Thank you for taking me for a ride in your new boat. That was fun."

He could almost feel his heart pounding in his chest. "Well, if you and Pam ever want to get together for some inner-tubing or water skiing, give me a call. I'd love to take you out." When she smiled at his choice of words, he added, "On the boat, I mean..."

As they continued bantering back and forth, flirting with their eyes, Pamela glanced nervously at Anthony, who was across the room with several of their other cousins. She hoped he wouldn't look over and see Omnio talking to Contessa. She knew exactly what Omnio was doing. He was only inviting her and Contessa back out on his boat because he wanted to see Contessa again. But from the way they were now looking at each other, Pamela knew that would be a bad idea. Not when she knew how Anthony felt about her. He had voiced his interest in her on many occasions, but Contessa had expressed no interest in him, claiming he just wasn't her type. Pamela knew he lacked the intellect, charm, and wit required to impress a girl of Contessa's caliber. Omnio, on the other hand, was her perfect match.

This scared Pamela. She loved her brother dearly, but knew he could never compete with Omnio. Not on any level. Especially not when it came to girls, which was why Anthony had always been jealous of him. But Omnio was very dear to her. In many ways, she was closer to him than her own brother, and she did not want to see them fighting over a girl. Even though she knew Contessa would probably never develop an interest in Anthony, she did not want to see her fall under Omnio's spell, because she knew Contessa was exactly his type. Petite, voluptuous, and drop-dead gorgeous. On top of that, she was extremely intelligent. That was why Pamela had purposely tried to keep them from ever meeting. Unfortunately, she had accidently slipped up and mentioned tonight's party to her. And since they now lived together, it would have been rude not to invite her along. But what she feared would happen, was exactly what happened. From the instant they set eyes on each other, the chemistry between them was almost tangible. And as Pamela now looked over and saw Anthony watching them from across the room, she realized she had made a terrible mistake by bringing her along.

# CHAPTER 22

In the days following his birthday party, King was consumed by thoughts of the gorgeous Contessa. He had a number of beautiful young women that he used to satisfy his sexual needs, but he had almost no true amorous feelings for any of them. Over the years, he'd been in several fairly serious relationships, but he had never been in love. Until now, he hadn't even been sure if he was capable of truly loving a woman. But he now knew with complete certainty he was. No woman had ever stirred in him the feelings that he felt when he looked into those beautiful blue eyes. Her exquisite beauty, her regal poise, it awoke feelings in him he never knew existed. Yet he tried to tell himself that what he was feeling couldn't possibly be love. Or could it? Was it even possible to love someone he didn't know? Or was he just infatuated with her striking beauty? Was it just a boyish crush? Had he only imagined the silent connection they'd made that night? Whatever the case, he had to learn more about her.

Several days after his birthday party, he began discreetly inquiring about Contessa. First, he asked some of Pamela's friends if they knew anything about her. None of them seemed to know anything more than that she had been Pamela's college roommate. So he decided to take a more direct approach by having his cousin Billy ask Pamela about her. What Billy learned was quite interesting. It seemed Contessa could very well be, in a sense, a real countess. Her last name was Ferraro, a name King had heard his grandfather use on several occasions. Don Toriano Ferraro was a legendary Mafioso serving a life sentence in an Italian prison. But before being sent to prison, he had been *La Capo Supremo,* the single most powerful Mafioso on the planet, listed as number two on Interpol's most wanted list, second only to an Islamic terrorist. When Rome had declared war on the Mafia, Don Ferraro responded by declaring war on Rome. It had taken a special Italian military task force to finally capture him. But not before he had killed hundreds of federal officials—police inspectors, military leaders, judges, magistrates, politicians, and anyone else who dared cross him.

King wondered if Contessa was somehow related to the infamous Don Ferraro. When he asked his grandfather if this was possible, he was shocked to learn that not only was she related to Don Ferraro, but she was his actual granddaughter! It seemed her father, Ettore Ferraro, was now the interim *Capo Supremo*, advisor to every La Cosa Nostra faction on the planet. He was the only man the Commission bosses answered to. But since Contessa was his only daughter, he had purposely sheltered her from his world, not wanting her exposed to the violence and dangers of Sicily. Wanting her to live a normal life, to grow up in a normal home, far removed from his dangerous world, he had sent her as a young girl to live with distant relatives Central Italy. But even though she did not live with him, he still made sure she was well cared for. He sent her to the best schools money could buy, and made sure she never wanted for anything. After high school, when she told him she was interested in pursuing a career in medicine, he encouraged her to attend university in the United States, which was known for having the best medical schools in the world. After applying at several colleges of her choice, she was accepted into the University of Michigan, only a few short miles from Detroit, where her father had "friends."

This was how Contessa had come to be roommates with Pamela. When Ettore Ferraro learned that his daughter would be attending college at the University of Michigan, he contacted Don Falcone, Detroit's *Capo di Tutti Cappi.* He knew Don

Falcone was a respected and loyal *caporegime* who could be trusted to take good care of her. Don Falcone was honored to be charged with her care, and assured him that he would look after her as if she was his own daughter. He immediately arranged for her to be Pamela's roommate at college. Since they were both hoping to become doctors, their friendship quickly blossomed.

But King's inquiry about Contessa immediately raised a red flag with Don Falcone, who was well-aware of his grandson's philandering ways. Under any other circumstances he was fine with it, as long as those philandering ways didn't involve the young daughters or granddaughters of Syndicate *capi*. It was one thing if he planned to marry them, but to play with their hearts could be very, very dangerous. Because if there was one thing all fathers were quick to defend, it was the hearts of their daughters. But this was worse. Far worse. This girl was the only daughter of Ettore Ferraro, the highest-ranking Cosa Nostra Boss on the planet.

Worried that King might get himself into trouble with this girl, Don Falcone more than just warned him about toying with her emotions. He gave him a direct order to stay away from her, and not just because of who her father was, or even because he knew of Anthony's obsession with her. But because he knew of King's regular indiscretions with women. He refused to let Ettore Ferarro's daughter become another of King's conquests. Because if he did, and her father were to ever learn of it, Ettore Ferarro would take it as the ultimate act of disrespect. Don Ettore Ferraro was from the old country and strictly adhered to the old codes of conduct and honor. And if King were to offend Contessa, or tarnish her chastity in any way, there would be nothing even Don Falcone could do to save him.

But Don Falcone was not biased when it came to his reproaches about Contessa. He issued the same warning to Anthony. Unfortunately, he doubted Anthony would heed his warning. Anthony, that treacherous son of his daughter, always did what he pleased and only listened to his equally treacherous

412

father. Fortunately, thus far, Contessa had shown little interest in him, which was no surprise. He was a repugnant, arrogant little marauder who was short on brains but high on self-worth. Omnio, however, was a different story. He had a way with women, and Don Falcone knew it was very possible that Contessa could fall under his spell, which was why he ordered him not to even consider pursuing her. Too many empires had fallen at the hands of a beautiful woman. Particularly when two men of power fought over the same one. Omnio and Anthony already had enough animosity towards each other. Don Falcone did not want this young woman, beautiful as she was, be the cause of an open vendetta between them. Such a scenario could very well tear their Family apart.

In the end, King followed his grandfather's orders and stopped inquiring about Contessa. But this didn't stop him from thinking about her. He was constantly haunted by the memory of her. No matter where he was, or what he was doing, she was always there, looming at the back of his thoughts. Where was she? What was she doing? Might she be thinking of him? He found the only way to distract himself from thoughts of her was to stay busy, which he did by focusing on business. But he also took Don Falcone's advice and did a little splurging. Like his grandfather so often decreed, life was too short to not at least occasionally taste the fruits of his labors, and King's favorite taste was travel. He loved traveling with Vonni to places where they were free to act their age and not be burdened by the weight of their responsibilities back home. They spent weekends in Miami, where they stayed at beachfront condominiums owned by Russell Loduca. They flew to New York to shop and visited with Vonni's family. They visited Family associates in Philadelphia, Chicago, Los Angeles, and Atlantic City. Wherever they went, they ate at the finest restaurants, shopped at high-end fashion outlets, and frequented the hottest nightclubs. They would drink and party and throw away money like it grew on trees, because they didn't have to worry about the FBI watching their every move.

When out of town, they were free to act like what they were—rich young men with more money than they knew what to do with. But back in Detroit, King always made sure to maintain a low profile, for he did not want to attract the attention of the Feds. He even sold his Corvette. The only flashy thing he still owned was his boat, which he loved. On weekends, he would take some of the crew and as many girls as the boat would fit out for a day on the water. They'd drop by all the popular hotspots along the lake, like Metropolitan Beach, where tens of thousands of people gathered each weekend. There was Gull Island, a tiny island oasis in the middle of the lake, where hundreds of people would gather to drink and barbecue and party without reservation. And of course, there were the nightclubs: Beach Grill, Jack's, Lagos, Mac & Ray's, Gino's Surf Lounge, Terry's Terrace, and many more. OMNIOUS MAXIMUS became a regular fixture at them all. The boat itself was an attention-getter, but so was King. People wondered who he was, for it was not common to see such a young man pull up in a quarter-million-dollar race boat. But there were whispers. Rumors. Some people recognized him and his crew, and before long everyone knew that he was, in fact, an up-and-coming young Mafioso.

Yet King wasn't the only up-and-coming young Mafioso often seen at these lakefront hotspots. Anthony used his father's boats like they were his own, especially his father's offshore racer, TRITON, which was even more impressive than King's OMNIOUS MAXIMUS. In fact, it was touted as one of the fastest boats on the lake. With its four engines and nearly 3,000 horsepower, it could be heard thundering across the lake from miles away. And wherever Anthony went in it, he was treated like a superstar. Because, unlike King, he made it no secret who he was. Or rather, who his father was. He liked to brag and boast that he was in the Mafia, that his father was the city's new Boss of Bosses.

Anthony may have used his father's boat like it was his own, but by no means did he live off his daddy. Instead, he was quite independent. He ran his own crew of very capable young wiseguys, most of whom were childhood friends or cousins on his father's side. Together they handled some of Leoni's street level operations, including gambling, loansharking, collections, and extortion. They also operated half a dozen legitimate businesses. But like his father, Anthony was drunk with power. Because his father was a notoriously ruthless *capo*, he often felt inclined to throw his weight around. He even muscled some of the other Families out of several minor territories and street rackets, which thoroughly irritated Don Falcone and the other Bosses. Yet Anthony didn't care. He operated under his own set of rules. Rules that his father enforced if anyone dared question them. Not even Don Falcone, with his infinite wisdom and pragmatism, could talk any sense into him. Anthony knew the Commission had already selected his father to be the next *Capo di tutti Capi,* because they knew the other *capi* feared him and would stay in line under his regime. His father had also promised to make him Syndicate street boss, and even someday his *Sotto Capo*—underboss. Until then, he took pride in his pure Sicilian blood and the knowledge that father had spoken to the other bosses, who had unanimously approved his "button," if only because they feared what his father would do if they voted against it. Now it was up to the Commission to "open the books" and allow him to take the Oath. And once he took the Oath, he would transition his crew from the petty street rackets into the far more lucrative racket of municipal contracts, which generated millions of dollars annually for the Syndicate.

Even now, as he waited to be Made, Anthony and his crew were well-known street enforcers for the Gianolla Family. Leoni used them to collect back payments from bookies, loan sharks, union leaders, business owners, drug dealers, and anyone else who owed him money. There were many parallels between Anthony's crew and King's, but there was one major difference: Anthony was allowed to operate in the far more profitable suburban territories, and was given the full support of all the Syndicate Families. King, for the most part, was only allowed to operate within the inner city, and received almost no support from the other Families.

King kept his boat docked in the boathouse behind his grandparents' home, and used it almost daily. But as much as he enjoyed entertaining on it, he also enjoyed taking it out alone, sometimes even without Vonni. He loved being by himself on the lake, racing across the water with the wind in his face. He rarely got to be alone, and he found it to be very liberating. His favorite maritime jaunt was cruising along the shores of Grosse Pointe to look at the beautiful waterfront homes, where he would fantasize about someday owning one himself. He found these lone cruises to be almost therapeutic, a time when he could meditate on his future and formulate his thoughts.

But Vonni never liked it when King went out alone on the boat. He took his duties as *protettore* very seriously, and rarely let him out of his sight. Even though he knew King was safe by himself on the boat, he always felt uneasy while waiting for him to return. But he also understood that there were times when a man needed to be alone with his thoughts. So he would patiently wait inside the house with King's grandparents, which was always entertaining. He enjoyed Don Falcone's company, but enjoyed Signora Falcone's cooking even more. Every time he was there, she'd insist he sit down and let her feed him.

On one such occasion, Vonni was enjoying a meatball sandwich Signora Falcone had prepared for him, when in walked King's cousin Billy. He had stopped by to drop off some paperwork for Don Falcone, but Signora Falcone insisted he sit and join Vonni for a meatball sandwich. As they sat at the kitchen table enjoying their sandwiches, Billy began catching him up to speed on the latest Syndicate gossip. Vonni was only half-listening until Billy mentioned something that King would definitely want to hear.

Billy was more than just one of King's lieutenants. He was also an unofficial, if somewhat low-level liaison, between Don Falcone and the other Families. His father worked for a Made guy who happened to be married to Leoni's sister, Gina. This made Billy's father an extension of the Gianolla Family. He owned a demolition company called "Detroit Wrecking," and with Leoni's help, he had landed a huge city contract that entailed tearing down several hundred of Detroit's abandoned buildings. It was a contract worth millions. Of course, Leoni demanded a significant portion of the profits, but Billy didn't care. He was just happy his father was in tight with the Gianolla Family, which was now through marriage an extension of Don Falcone's Family. Unfortunately, because Billy was a *difetto* like King, he could never be Made. And since he really had no blood ties to anyone, King had assimilated him into his motley crew of independents. He was one of King's longest standing lieutenants, but because his father worked for one of Leoni's captains, he was occasionally charged with minor errands, which sometimes put him in direct contact with constituents from the other Families. It was during one such errand that he ran into Anthony's lieutenant, Frankie Bommarito.

Billy still ran a chop-shop operation out of a local junkyard on the city's east side, and one day he received a strange order from his father. He was to deliver a re-tagged Mercedes-Benz to a used car lot owned by one of Leoni's brothers. But when he drove to the lot with the luxury sedan, he found Frankie waiting to pick it up. It seemed the car was actually for Leoni, who ordered it up as a back-to-school gift for his daughter Pamela. Of course, when Billy learned the car was for Leoni, he knew better than to ask Frankie for the $10,000 he was expecting for it. But during their conversation, Frankie happened to mention that their cousin Anthony was planning a small back-to-school party for Pamela this weekend at his father's club, Leo's On The Lake. It was this news that Vonni knew King would be interested in hearing. When he later relayed it to him, King had grinned excitedly.

"Well, we can't miss sending my cousin off to school, can we?" King said with a wink.

But Vonni knew he was only excited because Contessa would be there.

Since the night of the party was hot and muggy, they forewent their standard evening attire of suits, instead opting for a more comfortable ensemble of dress shorts, silk shirts, and loafers. Yet dressed down as they were, they still commanded attention as King piloted OMNIOUS MAXIMUS into the lagoon, which was already crowded with a line of boats waiting to be valeted. Uniformed marine valet attendants stood posted along the deck like sentries, parking each newly arrived boat based on its size and grandiosity. Already moored to the seawall were several yachts and cabin cruisers, the most impressive of which had purposely been secured along the deck so they could be appreciated up close by those who could only dream of owning such ostentatious toys.

Summer was near its end, and there was a certain festive ambiance in the air. In only a few short days the temperatures would begin dropping and the nautical nightclubs along Lake St. Clair would close their decks for the summer. As a result, everyone on the deck was in high spirits. Caribbean dance music was playing from a series of unseen speakers. Tiki torches cast a shimmering golden luminescence onto the calm black waters of the lagoon. But even with all of this noise and activity, nearly everyone on the deck turned and looked when a low resonant rumble signaled the arrival of another thunderboat easing its way up to the deck for dockage.

On the main deck, groups of people were standing around, casually drinking and socializing. On the upper deck, VIPs lounged around candlelit terrace tables. Sitting at one such table were King's cousins Pamela, Anthony, Dino, Frankie, Billy, and several of their friends. Enjoying the view from their elevated position above the lagoon, they lounged in cushioned deck chairs, casually sipping umbrella drinks while enjoying the warm evening. All of them were just quietly talking and taking in the scene when one of Pamela's friends looked down toward the lagoon.

"Pam, isn't that your cousin, Omnio?" she asked, pointing to a sleek black offshore race boat being moored to the edge of the deck.

When Pamela peered over the railing, she saw King handing money to a pair of valet attendants. "Yeah, that's Omnio," she said, feeling a ping of trepidation, not expecting to see him there tonight.

As everyone else peered over the railing, Pamela glanced cautiously at her two brothers. Neither looked happy to see Omnio and his sidekick, Vonni, stepping from the boat. Omnio looked as if he hadn't a care in the world, but as always Vonni looked tense, his eyes scanning the crowd for potential enemies. Seeing them gave her a bad feeling in the pit of her stomach. They weren't supposed to know about tonight. She had purposely avoided bringing Contessa around Omnio all summer. And as she now noticed Contessa, who was usually unimpressed by boys, stiffen uncomfortably at the mere mention of Omnio, she remembered why. Immediately upon leaving his birthday party over two months ago, Contessa had asked about him, voicing how handsome he was. Fortunately, Pamela had been able to deflate her interest in him by telling her what a libertine womanizer he was, which Contessa had found to be disgusting. Yet she looked anything but disgusted as she now watched him make his way across the crowded deck. Her eyes were suddenly wide and alert, and she made a discreet examination of herself, adjusting her dress, pushing back a lock of hair, straightening her posture.

King's rigorous weight training regime had his muscles bulging from under his shirt as he made his way across the deck, drawing stares from every female in his vicinity. Including an attractive young waitress who flirtatiously called him a teetotaler when he asked her for a glass of ice water. But he wasn't there to drink. He was there for one reason, and that reason was up on the VIP deck. He purposely hadn't looked in that direction, but he could feel her presence, that same magnetic pull he'd felt the first time he saw her.

"Aren't you going to invite him up?" asked Pamela's friend.

For a moment Pamela didn't answer. But she knew he would inevitably see them, and she already felt bad enough for not personally inviting him to tonight's little get-together. Acting like she didn't see him would only make her feel worse.

"I'm going down to say hi," she said, intentionally avoiding eye contact with Contessa. "I probably won't get to see him again until Thanksgiving."

Anthony felt the hair on the back of his neck stand up. The last thing he wanted was for King to join them, but if he didn't at least suggest they invite him up, he would appear callous and insecure in front of Contessa. And this he could not have. He wasn't used to being rejected by girls. Yet this one had rejected his advances all summer, and that made him want her even more. But he was now faced with a quandary. If he invited Omnio up to join them, he knew he would be eclipsed by his cousin's commanding presence. But if he didn't, he would appear invidious and begrudging, which was even worse. After all, he had no reason to be invidious and begrudging of his cousin. Omnio was a lowly *difetto*, a nobody. And Contessa was Mafia royalty. She would never be interested in a nobody *difetto*.

No, Anthony decided, he refused to be usurped by him in front of her. Not here, not tonight. Not at his father's club, where he was tonight's host. This was his last chance to impress Contessa. His sole purpose for arranging this little soiree was to make one final attempt at impressing her before she went back to school with his sister. He would not allow his cousin to ruin it by simply showing up. He did, however, find it ironic that Omnio would show up there tonight of all nights. Over the summer, they'd run into each other on several occasions at other popular nightspots along the lake, but never once had he seen him there at his father's club. That told him Omnio's unexpected appearance tonight was no coincidence.

"No," Anthony said, standing and motioning for Pamela to sit. "I'll go bring him up myself."

Mildly inebriated on alcohol, but fully drunk with self-worth, Anthony quickly made his way down onto the main deck, intent on showing Contessa he was not threatened by anyone, especially not his *difetto* cousin.

"Cousin!" he shouted, extending a hand as King approached him through the crowd. "I'm glad you're here. Pam goes back to school tomorrow, and we're having a little sendoff party for her. I meant to invite you but... shit, you know how it is. I got busy and totally fuckin' forgot. But I'm sure she'll be happy to see you. Come on up. Join us. Dino, Billy, Frankie, they're already up there. Paulie and Joe and some of my other guys should be here any minute."

King shook Anthony's outstretched hand and gave him a hug, wondering why his normally emulous cousin was being so amiable. "A sendoff for Pam?" he asked, feigning ignorance. "I had no idea you guys were all here. We were heading to Beach Grill but decided to pop in here first. We almost didn't stop." He looked him in the eye, trying to read him. "So how are things, cousin? Everything good with you?"

Anthony offered him a forced smile. "Everything's great. How's things with you guys?"

As they exchanged pleasantries and began bantering back and forth, Vonni stood off to the side and listened. Even from a few feet away he could smell alcohol on Anthony's breath, and he could see right through his act. He was fully aware of how Anthony felt about King, and vice versa. In fact, he was privy to every idiosyncrasy of King's life, including the strange Machiavellian relationship King had with Anthony. He knew Anthony hated him with a passion. And as Vonni now saw the guileful look in Anthony's eyes, he wondered if he had made a mistake by telling King about tonight's party.

"Come on," Anthony said, gesturing towards the VIP terrace. "We're all up there. Can I get you guys a drink? Something to eat? The kitchen is still open. I can have our chef make you anything you want. On the house, of course. How about I order us some steak and lobster? Yeah, that sounds good. A little surf and turf. I could use something to eat."

"Thanks," King said, "but grandma made us dinner before we left. I'll take a beer, though."

"A beer it is," Anthony said, pleased with his own act. "Now come on up, it's too fuckin' crowded down here."

Up on the VIP terrace, as King was greeted by his cousins with hugs and kisses on the cheek, Contessa remained seated, silently observing, her brilliant azurite eyes fixated on him. Like the first time they met, she found herself utterly captivated. Back home in Italy, she had known many handsome young men, some of whom had vied for her attention. But none had ever evoked the feeling she now felt—pure carnal desire. He was more than handsome. He was beautiful. A perfect male specimen. Tall, lean, and built like a professional athlete. His dark hair accentuated his dark features. But there was more to him than just his outward appearance. He had a certain presence. He exuded an air of confidence and poise that she had never encountered in such a young man. In fact, in all her life she had only encountered one man who possessed the same level of tacit certitude. And that man was her father. All the boys back home, or even at college, had been just that—boys. They were immature, precocious, and lacked any form of chivalry or intellect. Even her boyfriend back home, who was handsome and athletic, had been an immature dolt she only dated because he showered her with gifts and treated her like a queen. Unfortunately for him, his benevolence had earned him nothing more than an occasional kiss.

But this Omnio was different. His dark eyes were aglow with intelligence. He was articulate, charming, and seemed far more mature than his twenty-one years. Even Anthony, who also had a commanding presence, seemed to shrink into obscurity in his presence. She knew Anthony was infatuated with her, but she was turned off by his immaturity, arrogance, and foul mouth. Yet she had to admit there were times when she found him somewhat attractive. He could be very sweet, persistent, and he made her feel wanted. He was handsome, confident, and even occasionally showed glimpses of wit. Everyone wanted to be his friend. Although, she knew this was mostly because of who he was. Or rather, who his father was. Back home, people treated her father the same way, and it wasn't because they liked him. It was because they feared him. Even though she had grown up far away from her family in Sicily, she wasn't naive. She knew exactly what her father was. Just as she knew exactly what Anthony and Omnio were. Mafiosi. She also knew that much of their confidence came from being feared. But it was Omnio who looked fearsome, and she sensed that Anthony resented him for it.

After being greeted by his cousins, King said hello to all of Pamela's friends, who smiled at him like love-struck school girls. He knew what they thought of him. Growing up, Pamela had told him many times that all of her friends had crushes on him. So he made sure his chivalry was on full display, addressing each one of them by name, for he never forgot a name. But when his eyes came to Contessa, he acted as if he hadn't noticed her sitting there. Which of course, she knew he had.

"Contessa!" he said, feigning surprise. "Long time no see. How have you been?"

"I'm doing great, Omnio," she replied, her eyes locked on his. "How have *you* been?"

He shot a loving smile at Pamela. "I'm great now that I'm here with my favorite baby cousin. I can't believe I almost missed her little sendoff party here. I'm glad I stopped by."

Pamela felt a pang of guilt, knowing he was sending her a message. It was no coincidence he was there. She should have called and invited him herself, but she had her reasons for not doing so. Or rather, one reason: Contessa. She had purposely avoided him all summer while Contessa was around, which was pretty much all the time. From the way Contessa was now looking at him, she had done the right thing. She and Contessa had become like sisters. Over the last year, they had done everything together and shared their most intimate thoughts. What she learned was that there was much more to Contessa than her beautiful exterior. She was exceptionally intelligent and cultured, having attended the best private schools in all of Italy. Growing up, she had wanted for nothing. Her father had spoiled her beyond imagination, giving her anything she wanted. But there was one thing that Pamela found odd. Contessa expressed very little interest in boys. Anthony had pursued her all summer, yet she had been completely unresponsive, claiming he just wasn't her type. But of course, Pamela understood this. She knew her brother could never satisfy a woman like Contessa. He lacked the intellectual capacity to keep her engaged. Omnio, on the other hand, was a different story. He had a brilliant mind and had a way of bewitching every woman he set eyes on, which was exactly what it seemed he had done to Contessa. Even after Pamela had warned her of his philandering ways, she still expressed an interest in him. And from the way she was now looking at him, her interest had only grown.

But Pamela's thoughts of King and Contessa were fleeting, for she had a secret attraction of her own. Vonni. Whenever she was around him, she found it impossible to take her eyes off him. Ever since she was fourteen, she had fantasized about Omnio's mysterious friend from New York. She considered him to be the most handsome and interesting boy she had ever met. She liked his tough exterior and his New York swagger. He was funny and witty and had that bad boy image she found irresistible. The strange thing was, she knew almost nothing about him, only that he had saved King's life when they were seventeen, and that he was now his *protettore*—sworn bodyguard for life. She was impressed by how serious he took his job as her cousin's protector. No matter where they were, or what they were doing, he was always hyper-vigilant, his eyes wide and alert like that of a cat preparing to pounce. He never drank and was almost never more than a few feet from Omnio. It was this loyalty to her cousin that had caused her to fall in love with him. But of course, she kept these feelings closely guarded. Not only would her father and brothers disapprove, but so would Omnio, for it would be considered a violation of trust. So, just as she had done for years, tonight she hid her secret feelings for Vonni from the world. If only for his own sake.

King stayed only long enough to finish his one beer. He could tell his presence made some of the people at the table uncomfortable. Particularly Anthony, who was going all out with his pretentious act in an attempt to impress Contessa. But he had accomplished what he had set out to do. He needed to look into Contessa's magnificent blue eyes one last time to be sure his feelings for her were mutual. And now he knew for certain that they were. The way she looked at him told all he needed to know—she was feeling the same thing he was feeling. It made him vow to someday, when he no longer had to worry about offending Anthony, make her his wife. Until then, he would bide his time and pacify his cousin by showing no overt interest in her. Unfortunately, his next encounter with her would spark into motion a chain of events that would ultimately result in his downfall.

# CHAPTER 23

Contrary to popular belief, the Mafia was more than just an underworld criminal organization made of thugs, street hustlers, and violent sociopaths. The reality was that La Cosa Nostra was a very proficient network of intelligent and ambitious businessmen. Though some were unscrupulous in their business practices, their goal was always the same: to maximize profits. Most upper echelon Mafiosi owned legitimate businesses that accounted for a significant portion of their wealth. Some barely engaged in illicit activities at all, only occasionally bending laws or manipulating labor unions to their advantage.

The Detroit faction of La Cosa Nostra owned dozens of legitimate businesses, many of them very successful in their own right. Every *capodecina*, or crew boss, owned "front businesses" that generated considerable clean, legitimate revenue. This made it next to impossible for the FBI to prove that any significant percentage of their income derived from illegal rackets. Nevertheless, the FBI still closely monitored all of the Syndicate's top bosses, as well as some well-known lieutenants and street soldiers. The local Organized Crime Taskforce had a rough idea of who was doing what, but like always when dealing with the Mafia, they found it impossible to penetrate even the Syndicate's outermost circle, let alone its inner circle. Federal agents knew the Families were involved in everything from illegal gambling and loansharking, to extortion and murder. But proving it was another story. It was a game of cat and mouse the FBI had been playing with the Mafia since the 1920's, when Mafiosi like Al Capone made millions selling liquor during Prohibition. But when all else failed, they focused on the one thing the Mafia had trouble with—hiding their money, which often resulted in tax fraud. Hiding large sums of illicit proceeds was not nearly as easy as one might think. Banks were required to keep meticulous records for the Internal Revenue Service. Federal law also required banks to report all deposits and/or transactions over $10,000. If a bank failed to do so, it could face felony charges for conspiring to defraud the federal government.

Of course, there were always corrupted bankers who, for the right price, were more than willing to help such large transactions go unreported. For decades this was how Don Falcone had managed to hide much of his wealth, but the IRS loosely monitored his financial transactions. Unbeknownst to him, when he made a large, suspicious transaction between himself and a boat brokerage owned by Paul Zirello, another local Mafioso on the OTC watch list, a red flag went up. It seemed the infamous Don Falcone, who had always been so meticulous and crafty at hiding his money, had slipped up. When he purchased a used race boat from Zirello's boat brokerage, he made the mistake of putting the boat in the name of a company he owned, using his personal bank to facilitate the transaction. When the IRS learned of this, they looked into the boat's background. The bill of sale said it had been purchased from a Canadian seller, with Zirello's company acting as a consignment broker. But there was no record of it in the Canadian Ministry of Transportation. It seemed as if the boat had just popped up out of thin air. Though its lack of registration history was more than a little suspicious, the only legal infraction Don Falcone had committed was failing to pay the required sales and import tax on the purchase. It was a fairly minor offense, but it gave the IRS legal grounds to further investigate his tax records. During their inquest into his recent financial history, they found he had made a number of questionable purchases over the last several years, including the purchase of five very successful nightclubs for prices significantly below market value. When these findings were relayed to the FBI, a federal magistrate assigned a special tax fraud unit to further investigate his financial records, as well as the financial records of his known associates. Their goal was to indict them all on the dreaded RICO Act.

Meanwhile, King and his crew continued expanding their operations, especially their legitimate operations. He was even working on opening a large construction company that would build commercial office buildings, industrial complexes, and large residential homes. And he already had a number of contracts lined up with land developers, including his grandfather's old friend, Russell Loduca. Money was pouring in, and by the time he turned twenty-two, he was already a multi-millionaire. Yet even with things going so well, there was one thing that had him frustrated and downtrodden. The Commission. Once again they had denied Don Falcone's request to have him Made.

The Commission, made up of Bosses of the ten largest Cosa Nostra Families in the country, was extremely well-connected with many powerful friends. Some of these friends employed "associates" who worked in the inner sanctum of certain FBI offices. Once such associate had learned that the Detroit Organized Crime Taskforce was digging deep into Don Falcone's financial records. Particularly his tax records. It seemed the FBI and IRS were going back decades to see if he had defrauded the government out of its due share. Because of this, the Commission needed to distance themselves from him, which included distancing themselves from his ambitious young grandson, Omnio. Who, rumor had it, was becoming a bit of a problem for some of the other Detroit Bosses.

With Don Falcone aging and under such intense government scrutiny, the Commission had decided it was time for him to finally step down and name a new Boss as his successor. In an attempt to retain some control of the *borgata* and keep his enemies close, he named his son-in-law, Leoni Gianolla, the new Boss. It was no surprise to anyone. Everyone had known for years that Leoni would inherit the crown. And of course, Leoni quickly restructured the Family's administration to make sure he was surrounded by people he could fully trust. His brother-in-law, Piero Antonelli, was named *Sotto Capo*— Underboss. His Father, Vito Gianolla, was named *Consigliore*. And of course, he wanted a street boss he could trust implicitly. Naturally, he wanted it to be his eldest son, Anthony. Which was why he had, unbeknownst to Don Falcone or any of the other Syndicate Bosses, recently flown to New York to discuss this very prospect with the Commission delegates. But while he was there, he had purposely mentioned how his maverick nephew had become flamboyant and reckless, claiming King was buying up new cars and boats, flashing money in public, acting like he was a young John Gotti in his heyday.

Leoni was only exaggerating the truth in an attempt to make King look bad, but it worked. The Commission bought it. They respected Don Falcone, and knew King had become a significant earner for the Family, but they could not afford any unwanted federal attention in Detroit. Not now. Not when the city was on the precipice of legalizing gambling. Because once gambling was legalized, the Commission Bosses had plans to pool their money together and erect a casino there, which was why they issued Don Falcone a stern warning to rein in his reckless young grandson. Though Don Falcone had received this warning gracefully, assuring them he would reprimand his grandson, he was livid. Obviously one of the Syndicate *capi* had gone behind his back and lied about Omnio, and he had little doubt that it was his treacherous son-in-law, Leoni. He was so enraged by this blatant act of disrespect that he was tempted to have Leoni killed. Unfortunately, he couldn't. The Commission had made it perfectly clear that there was to be no trouble in Detroit. Not with so much at stake. So, with a grain of salt, he did what he was told and reproached Omnio, ordering him to quell his spending and tone down his crew's public persona.

After his grandfather's reprimand, King was angry with himself. He had broken one of Cosa Nostra's cardinal rules by drawing unwanted attention to himself. He had always been conservative with his money and public persona, but in his quest to impress the other Families he had allowed his crew to become flamboyant. Although, a small part of him couldn't help but to blame his grandfather. After all, it had been Don Falcone who had decreed that life was too short to not at least occasionally taste the fruits of his labors. But then he also knew his grandfather had only wanted the other Families to see his success and know he was worthy of being Made. Unfortunately, it seemed to have backfired. The Commission now saw him as a liability, and he knew it was Leoni who planted this malignant seed in their head. Because, after all, they had mentioned nothing of Anthony's flamboyant ways, which were far more excessive than King's or any of his crew's.

The Commission needed Leoni. With gaming soon to be legalized in Detroit, they needed a young, strong, and fearsome *capo* to run the Syndicate. Mostly because they knew that once their casino was opened, all the Syndicate's crews would try to muscle in on the skim, as well as many other rackets surrounding a casino—union manipulation, food service, security, sanitation, valet, escorts, drugs, corrupted dealers, prostitution, limousine services, and many more. Infighting was liable to erupt. And this the Commission could not have. Not when they intended to invest tens of millions into at least one Detroit casino. Of course, they knew Don Falcone had always been a strong and fearsome Boss, able to keep the whole *borgata* in line. But his leadership qualities had nothing to do with him having to step down as Boss. It was the fact that he was being investigated for tax evasion, coupled with the fact that he had a history of skimming from casinos. The FBI would be scrutinizing his every move. That was why the Commission unanimously agreed that someone else had to lead the Syndicate and manage their interests in the city's gaming industry. Someone they could trust while keeping on a short leash. They decided that someone was Leoni—a strong bull with a small brain.

It was family tradition that Don Falcone host all holiday dinners at his Grosse Pointe home, and he required all immediate family members to attend. He even insisted that Pamela come home from college to be with the family for the holidays. But King was always disappointed when she would arrive for dinner without Contessa. Thanksgiving, Christmas, Easter, they all came and went with no sign of Contessa. After dinner he would ask Pamela about her in casual conversation, but she would become curt and standoffish, telling him only that Contessa was fine and busy with her studies. He did his best to seem indifferent, but of course, Pamela saw right through him. She knew him as well as anyone, and his interest in Contessa was more than obvious. That was why she always made sure to leave her back at school whenever she came home for the holidays.


Over the winter, several trips to Miami had spoiled King and Vonni with southern Florida's beautiful weather. But now that it was June, the weather in Detroit was finally warming. Finally, it was time to wax up their cars, break out their motorcycles, and open the decks at their nightclubs. Things were going well and they planned to fully enjoy the summer—even if Leoni thought they were being flamboyant with their public persona. After all, they were still considered to be nothing more than a small independent crew operating on the outer fringes of Don Falcone's protective umbrella. Which meant technically, they didn't have to answer to anyone but the don himself.

One hot Sunday afternoon while working out at the gym with Vonni, King was paged to the front desk for an urgent phone call. He usually never took calls while he was working out, but when the front desk girl told him the person on the phone said it was an emergency, he put the phone to his ear and heard his cousin Billy relay a very straightforward message from Don Falcone himself.

"Your grandpa says he doesn't give a shit what you're doing, get your ass to this party and show your cousin some respect."

The previous week, Don Falcone had asked King to make an appearance at his cousin Nina's high school graduation party. But he had blown it off to go workout with Vonni. Mostly because he knew his grandfather only wanted to show him off, which he did at all the family functions. But he now felt guilty for not showing up. High school graduation was a big deal for the Family. It signified adulthood and represented great achievement. Even though Nina was only his second cousin, it would be disrespectful of him not to at least show up and give her a gift.

So, after he hung up the phone, he and Vonni quickly showered and changed. Since it was a hot, sunny afternoon, they decided to take their motorcycles straight from the gym to the party. Together they raced across town, weaving in and out of traffic at breakneck speeds, acting like traffic laws didn't apply to them. They were having so much fun that King was tempted to forego the party and just head downtown to Belle Isle, where they were sure to find an abundance of bikini-clad girls wanting rides on their bikes. But of course, he continued on to the party. He didn't want to upset or disappoint his grandfather, who had given him a direct order through Billy. Yet he was dreading yet another Family function, where he was likely to run into his Uncle Leoni and some of the other *capi* who regarded him with such disdain.

Nina was the daughter of King's "Aunt" Fiorella, who was Don Falcone's sister's daughter. Fiorella was married to Alfonzo Miseraca, a *capo* who ran an underground casino for the Zirello

432

crew at a local country club. They lived in a posh neighborhood of Grosse Pointe Park, in a beautiful old colonial. When King came racing down the street on his bike, he was surprised to find nearly the entire block lined with parked cars. It seemed he had seriously underestimated the size of the party. When he and Vonni pulled up out front, a group of little girls were on the lawn, chasing each other around in a heated game of tag, while several young boys darted across the grass playing a game of touch football. The instant King parked on the sidewalk and removed his helmet, he was mobbed by this boisterous throng of children. Some were his cousins, others belonged to friends of the family. But as he knelt and gave several of them hugs and kisses, they all began chanting his name and demanding he stay and play with them. After tossing the football with them for a few minutes, he promised he'd play more later and then headed for the party.

The sounds of music and chatter emanating from behind the house made it clear where the party was. But when King led Vonni into the backyard, he was surprised by what he saw. In an open-walled circus style tent, there were at least a hundred people seated at a couple dozen round tables. In the back of tent was a long, rectangular table covered with steaming pots, pans, and trays of food. Standing behind this buffet of deliciousness were several of King's aunts, all of them studiously preparing plates of homemade Italian cuisine for anyone who was hungry. Everyone was feasting, drinking, and chattering away, many of them speaking in Italian. More little kids darted around, chasing each other, yelling and giggling gleefully while their parents pretended not to notice.

There were several tables of teenagers, but King didn't recognize any of them. He figured they were Nina's high school friends. There were, however, plenty of familiar faces in the crowd, including a number of Syndicate soldiers and lieutenants. There were even a couple of *capi* in attendance. Cousins, aunts, uncles, family and friends were all there to celebrate Nina's graduation. But they were also there to make a social statement, to be seen and to engage in a bit of intra-*Famiglia* fraternization.

As King made his way into the backyard, people began shouting salutations to him in Italian. He waved and responded in kind, but made a beeline straight for a large table at the center of the tent, where his grandparents were seated with several of his aunts and uncles, including Nina's parents.

"Omnio!" Don Falcone shouted over the din of the crowd. "There you are. Get over here. Come say hello to your Aunt Fiorella and Uncle Alfonzo. They were just asking about you."

Like any good *protettore*, Vonni stood off to the side, posted like a sentry as King kissed his aunt and uncle on the cheek. Strangely, nobody seemed to acknowledge him. They knew who was, and they had become so used to him silently shadowing King that they barely even noticed him anymore.

"I was beginning to worry about you," said Don Falcone, looking mildly annoyed. "You boys and those damn motorcycles..." He shot Vonni a look, conveying he didn't approve. "Yes, we heard you pull up. I really wish you would get rid of that thing before you kill yourself on it."

"Grandpa, you're starting to sound like Grandma," King said, bending down to kiss him on the cheek.

"That's because she worries about you," Don Falcone replied, smiling wryly. "Every time she sees you on that thing, she thinks the next time she sees you will be in a casket."

"No worries, Poppa," King said affectionately, casting a barely perceivable glance at Leoni. "I'm like a cat. I have nine lives. It's going to take more than a motorcycle accident to get rid of me."

"The young," Don Falcone chuckled, looking around the table. "They all think they're invincible. If only they knew how precious life is, they wouldn't be so eager to test fate." He paused and admired King affectionately for a moment. "And you, my dear grandson, are the last Falcone. Testing fate on that God-forsaken motorcycle could very well result in the extinction of our bloodline. You should consider that next time you go racing around town like a madman."

King took a quick account of the party. "Nonno, you've become such a party pooper in your old age," he said, goading him with a playful smile. "But point taken. I'll definitely be more careful next time I race around town like a madman."

"Smart aleck," Don Falcone laughed.

King's Aunt Fiorella smiled up at him. "Honey, we're so glad you made it. Nina was hoping you would come. Have you seen her yet?"

He shot another look around the backyard. "No, not yet. Where is she?"

"Inside," his Uncle Alfonzo answered, gesturing towards the house. "She and her friends just went in to eat. You should grab a plate and join them."

"That's a good idea," King said, his mouth already salivating from the aroma emanating from the buffet table. "We just came from the gym and we're starving "

His Uncle Alfonzo studied him for a moment. "*Mannaggia gaguzzalonga*, Omnio, you sure have grown up. You look just like your father. I'm not sure if you know this, but he and I went to school together. He was also built like a brick shit house too. The girls used to fight over him."

King's eyes glazed over with regret. "Yes, I've seen pictures," he said, having no real memories of his father.

His uncle quickly changed the subject. "Anyway, I know Nina will be happy to see you. Grab yourself a plate and go join her and her friends inside."

"Yes, I think I'll do that," King said, glancing at the house

He then led Vonni over to the buffet table, where several of his aunts piled their plates with pasta aioli, sausage, meatballs and artichoke hearts. When their plates could take no more, they thanked his aunts and headed for the house.

King was not close to Fiorella and Alfonzo, whom he referred to respectfully as "aunt and uncle." And the truth was that he barely even knew his cousin Nina. In fact, he had only met her a few times at various family functions, the last of which was over four years ago. At the time she had only been fourteen. He vaguely remembered her as a cute but timid girl with wispy dark hair and big brown eyes. But as he now stepped through the back slider, he wondered if he would even recognize her. But he did. The instant he stepped inside, he saw her standing in the kitchen, pouring wine into several glasses on a large silver tray. She looked the same, only now a young woman. The surprise on her face was obvious.

"Hello, Nina—" he began, but stopped mid-sentence when he thought he heard the familiar voice of his cousin Pamela coming from the next room.

"Omnio!" Nina shrieked excitedly. "How are you? It seems like forever since I last saw you."

He heard her, but wasn't listening. He was too focused on the voices coming from the adjacent dining room. If Pamela was in there, it was very possible Contessa was with her, and such a thought instantly caused his heart to begin racing. But he quickly regained himself and removed an envelope from his back pocket. Inside it was one thousand dollars in cash.

"I'm great," he said, handing her the envelope. "And yes, it does seem like forever. Last time I saw you, you still looked like a little girl. But now you're all grown up." He pointed at the envelope. "Congratulations on your graduation. I heard you graduated with honors. I'm impressed. You should be very proud of yourself." He paused, and there was an awkward silence between them. "So... have you picked a college yet?"

Nina gestured towards the dining room. "Actually, it's funny you ask. I was just in there talking about schools with Pamela. She's trying to sell me on Michigan."

"Pamela?" he asked, feigning surprise, forcing back another wave of excitement. "Our cousin Pamela?"

"Yeah," Nina said, wondering why he looked so surprised. "She's in there with my friends. We were just sitting down to eat

436

but I wanted to get us some wine. My parents don't want us drinking but, hey, what they don't know won't hurt them, right?" She pointed at his plate of food. "Come sit down and join us."

When King followed her into the adjoining dining room, he found both Pamela and Contessa seated at a large dining room table, both of them engaged in conversation with several teenage girls. Both stopped mid-sentence the instant they saw him and Vonni step into the room.

Nina looked at her friends and gestured to King. "You guys, I'd like you to meet my cousin Omnio."

"Hello, ladies," he said, offering up one of his bewitching smiles. "Would you mind if my paisan and I join you?"

"Of course not," Nina said, pointing at the table. "Sit down. Eat. Pamela and her friend were just telling us about U of M. I was leaning towards State, but they're trying to change my mind."

King grinned mischievously at Pamela. "Go Blue!" he said, snatching a glass of wine off the tray and tipping it to her. "May your Wolverines finally beat those pesky Buckeyes this year."

Pamela narrowed her eyes on him. "Hello, Omnio," she said, rolling her eyes at his chivalrous act. "I wasn't expecting to see you here."

He pulled a chair out and sat directly across the table from Contessa. "Surprised?" he said, pretending to be confused. "Why would you be surprised?" He smiled up at Nina. "You should have known I'd come to congratulate Nina on her graduation. But I'm actually surprised to see *you* here, cousin. Aren't you supposed to be at school getting your pre-med on?

Pamela inwardly groaned. He was obviously enjoying his little performance. And with a table full of teenage girls already practically drooling over him, he had quite the captive audience. But she knew his performance wasn't for them. It was for Contessa, whose eyes looked almost feral as she stared at him from across the table, studying his every mannerism.

437

"The semester ended three days ago," Pamela said, glancing at Contessa. "We just got home this morning. When Grandma said Nina was having trouble picking a school, we decided to come here and see if we could steer her in the right direction."

He took a sip of wine and smiled at Contessa. "Contessa, I almost didn't see you there. How are you? It seems like forever..." He took another sip of wine and stared directly into her eyes.

"Hello, Omnio," she replied, grinning, meeting his gaze. "I'm great. How have *you* been?"

He shrugged and glanced at Pamela affectionately. "Well, I'm glad to see my baby cousin. I've missed her." He gestured towards Nina. "But don't let me interrupt. Please, Pam, tell us more about life at Michigan. Grandma tells me you've joined a sorority. Is this true?"

Pamela knew he was really pouring it on. He didn't care about her sorority. Nor did he care to hear about her life at college. He was simply playing for the crowd, trying to impress Contessa. But since Pamela didn't want to seem rude in front of Nina and her friends, she had no choice but to play along. So, as everyone at the table dove into their plates of food, she dove into a description about the many wonders of college life. But she could tell Omnio was barely listening. As he devoured his plate of food, his focus was clearly on Contessa, who hadn't taken her eyes off him since he stepped into the room. Once again, they looked like two little kids with grade school crushes, making eyes at each other, smiling back and forth as they ate. Pamela was just thankful her brother wasn't there to witness it.

Indeed King was barely listening. The rest of the world seemed to have melted away, leaving only him and Contessa. Even in shorts and a V-neck T-shirt, she looked regal and noble. He could feel his heart beating in his chest, a lump in his throat. All he could think about was kissing her, touching her, what her body might feel like against his. He studied every contour of her

438

beautiful face, her neck, the swell of her breasts under her shirt. He could smell her musky perfume, the same one she had been wearing the last time he saw her. He *needed* to know what her naked body felt like against his, her lips on his.

Little did he know, she was nearly paralyzed with her own amorous need for him. Her body felt hot and flush all over, especially between her legs. She ached for him. She was mesmerized by him, unable to look away. As she watched him eat, she began fantasizing about what it would be like to make love to him.

While Pamela told Nina and her friends about pledging for her new sorority, she happened to glance over and notice a look in Contessa's eyes, a look she had never seen before. Though Contessa wasn't saying a word, she didn't have to. Her eyes said it all. They were drunk with lust. As were Omnio's. This was exactly what she had feared, the reason she had purposefully kept them apart. The look they were giving each other made Pamela realize she had to get Contessa out of there before Omnio made his move. Unfortunately, fate was about to intervene.

King may have been focused on Contessa, but he was not so focused that he failed to notice how Pamela was looking at Vonni. It was the same way she had always looked Vonni. He knew what it meant, and finally admitted to himself that he could no longer deny the truth. She had a secret crush on his *protettore*. Deep down, he'd known about it for many years. She'd had a crush on Vonni since the day she first saw him in their grandparents' basement. Back then she had been his baby cousin, but she had grown into a beautiful young woman. He recognized the look she was now giving Vonni. It was the same look girls often gave him. But before he could decide whether or not he approved or disapproved, his thoughts were interrupted when his two teenage cousins, Rocco and Michael, burst into the dining room.

439

"Omnio!" Rocco shouted. "Are those your motorcycles out front?"

"They are," King said, casually taking a sip of wine. "Why?"

"Can me and Mikey take them for a ride?"

King considered this for a moment. "That depends," he said, knowing they were only sixteen and probably had never driven a motorcycle. "Do you know how to drive them?"

Rocco looked at his twin brother. "No, but we had mini-bikes when we were little. How much different can it be?"

King chuckled. "Oh, there's quite a difference between a mini-bike and a crotch rocket," he said, amused by their confidence. "And I'll show it to you. But not today. Your parents would kill me. And so would my grandparents. But I'll make you a deal: Tomorrow afternoon, stop by my club and I'll have some work for you guys. When you finish, I'll teach you how to drive a real motorcycle. Just don't tell your parents."

"Work?" Rocco asked, an incredulous look on his face. "What kind of work?"

"Oh, I'm sure we'll think of something," King answered, glancing at Vonni. "Maybe you can pass out some promotional flyers for us. Or maybe you can wax my boat. Maybe both. Whatever it is, when you're done Vonni and I will teach you how to ride. If you're any good, maybe we'll let you guys take the bikes next weekend. But you can't tell your parents. They'd want my head on a platter. *Capisce*?"

"*Capisce!*" Rocco exclaimed excitedly, glancing at his brother. "We'll be there."

Contessa glanced towards the front of the house. "You have a motorcycle here?" she asked in Italian, her eyes alight with excitement.

"Yes," he grinned, hoping he was correctly reading into the question. "Why, would you like to take a ride?"

"You won't kill me?" she asked, half-jokingly.

440

"Kill the beautiful Countess Ferraro?" he countered, feigning offense. "And what kind of Omnio would I be if I let harm befall a countess?"

"So..." she said, with a playful smile. "Are you telling me you really *are* a king?"

"I like to think so," he shrugged, flashing her a grin. Then he beckoned her toward the door. "Come on, let's go for a ride."

Pamela suddenly looked panicked. "Omnio, I don't think that's a good idea. It's dangerous and you know Grandma and Grandpa will freak out."

"They won't know," King said, pointing at Vonni. "Because you're riding with him."

For a moment, Pamela sat there looking flustered and uncomfortable, but then happened to notice how Vonni was eyeing her. "Okay, a quick ride," she acquiesced, feeling mixed emotions. "But you better not drive crazy, Johnny New York."

Vonni was surprised King would suggest he take Pamela for a ride, but he understood the motive. If King wanted to get anywhere near Contessa, he would have to win over Pamela. Of course, Vonni had known for years that Pamela had a secret crush on him, but he never thought King was aware of it. Not until now. It was definitely going to be awkward having Pamela wrapped around him on the back of his motorcycle, but he would never deny his boss.

Outside, as the girls slipped on the spare helmets that King and Vonni always kept strapped to their bikes for just such occasions, both of them felt their respective hearts racing with anticipation. But it wasn't fear that had their hearts racing. It was excitement, the fact that they were about to have their arms wrapped around the men they had fantasized about for so long.

After Contessa climbed onto the back of King's bike, she wrapped her arms around him and felt a jolt of electricity surge through her, ending between her legs, which were straddling his hips. His body was so firm and powerful. For over a year now she had been dreaming about what it would be like to touch him,

441

to feel her body pressed against his. But never could she have anticipated it would evoke such a primal response. She literally ached for him and quickly found herself imagining what his naked body would feel like pressed against hers. But just as she began to let her mind drift into this fantasy, she was suddenly jolted back to reality when he twisted the throttle and they went rocketing down the street at breakneck speeds.

With her small hands clutched to his chest, King was having similar thoughts. Except he wished the tables were turned, that she was driving and he had his hands clutched to *her* chest. He was picturing this in his mind when he noticed something that instantly made this amusing thought vanish. Parked down the block, in a black Crown Victoria, were two men wearing suits and dark sunglasses. As he approached them, he could clearly see they were FBI agents. They stared directly at him as he sped past. He was used to seeing FBI agents. They sometimes hung around his clubs or other businesses, always taking pictures and acting like nobody could see them. Fitting the common stereotype perfectly, they always drove burgundy or black Crown Victorias, always wore dark sunglasses, and were always clad in cheap suits. He often wondered if they actually thought they blended in like this. He sometimes found their failed attempts to be inconspicuous comical. But not today. For some reason, he had a bad feeling about these two Feds staking out his cousin's graduation party. And his intuition would prove correct. The FBI were about to make a statement.

But with Contessa clung tightly to his back, thoughts of the FBI quickly vanished. He had more pressing matters to attend to. Like ditching Vonni. He'd been dreaming of having Contessa all to himself since the moment he first saw her, but losing Vonni wasn't going to be easy. His *protettore* took his protective duties very seriously, and would never agree to just leave him alone with Contessa. Nor would Pamela. But Vonni would never endanger Pamela's life by driving recklessly. So as they cruised down Alter Road, King suddenly twisted his throttle and raced ahead of him several blocks. When he came to Jefferson Avenue, he made a quick left and again twisted his throttle full bore, sending them rocketing to nearly a 100 mph within seconds. And before Vonni even got to Jefferson, he made a quick right and then turned left into an alleyway behind St. Ambrose Church, where he parked and listened. A moment later, he heard Vonni's bike race by.

"Omnio, what are you doing?" Contessa asked, listening to the sound of Vonni's motorcycle vanish in the distance.

King lifted his visor and smiled at her. "Pamela has had a crush on Vonni for years. I figured she'd appreciate her ride better without me around."

"You know?" Contessa asked, her eyes wide with surprise.

"I know everything."

"Everything?" she asked, smiling up at him coyly.

"I know he knows why I ditched him."

"So he could be alone with her?"

"There's another reason," he said, peering into her mesmeric blue eyes.

"And what would that be?" she asked, still smiling up at him coyly.

He studied the countenance of her angelic face. "I think you know the answer to that."

"Let me guess," she giggled. "So I'll better appreciate my ride without Pamela around?"

"Exactly!" he said, then slammed his visor shut and twisted the throttle.

After ditching Vonni and Pamela, King took Contessa on a guided tour of the city. First, they cruised down Lakeshore Drive to look at all the beautiful waterfront mansions. From there they headed down to Detroit's famous Greek Town, where they stopped for a slice of pizza at Niki's, Detroit's most famous pizzeria. Next it was to Belle Isle Park, where they took a few trips down the park's giant slide. From there he took her to see Club Vanzetti's, where they had a glass of wine. And finally, they

443

ended up at Metropolitan Beach, a beautiful waterfront park on the shores of Lake St. Clair.

He'd been enjoying acting as her cicerone so much that he completely lost track of time, and by the time they arrived at the beach the sun was already beginning to set, its rays casting a magnificent kaleidoscope of brilliant oranges, ambers and yellows over the water. After turning off the main thoroughfare, he followed a small dirt trail that meandered through a grove of weeping willows, ending at a secluded little picnic area along the lake.

When they finally came to the end of the trail, he shut the bike off and took in his surroundings. Fifty yards away a pair of young lovers were cuddled on a blanket under a large willow. Further down the beach another young couple was walking barefoot in the surf. The evening was still and quiet, and the lake was almost dead calm. The last of the sun's rays were reflecting off the lake's surface, which was dotted with several distant sailboats. A flock of gulls were foraging along the beach, their haunting cries echoing into the quiet evening.

After removing his helmet, he breathed deeply and filled his lungs with the fresh marine air. He couldn't have asked for a more romantic setting. It was perfect, which was exactly why he had taken her there. And as he now helped her off his bike, he felt like he was on top of the world. It had been a perfect day. It was about to get even better.

For several minutes they walked hand-in-hand down the beach, saying nothing, taking in their surroundings. Strangely, they both felt shy and at a loss for words, which was rare for both of them. Eventually they settled onto a bench under a majestic old willow. As they sat there soaking in the romantic ambiance, he found himself discreetly studying her. Again he decided that was the most beautiful woman he had ever seen. Even in a casual summer outfit of jean shorts and a V-neck top, she looked almost royal. Her body was so petite and perfectly proportioned, with just the right combination of muscle and curves. She was exquisite, the perfect combination of strength, beauty, and intelligence. He was completely mesmerized.

"Omnio..." she said, finally breaking the silence. "Why are we here?"

The melodic sound of her accented voice made his heart race, and as he looked into her eyes he suddenly felt a strange sense of weakness, which was something he had never experienced before. He was supposed to be a tough Detroit wiseguy, but as he gazed into those incredible blue eyes he felt as vulnerable as a newborn baby. At that moment, he knew he would forever be at her mercy.

"I thought you might like it here," he said, unable to look away. "Why, do you want to leave?"

She turned and looked at the placid lake. "No," she said, snuggling into him. "You were right... I love it here. It reminds me of home. There was a bay on the Tyrrhanian near where I grew up. It looked much like this. I used to go for walks there with my uncle when I was little. It was always so peaceful and beautiful... like this."

"Do you miss home?" he asked, hearing the sadness in her voice.

"Sometimes," she admitted, still looking straight ahead. "But I like it here. There is so much opportunity."

"Will you stay after you finish school?

"Why?" she asked, finally turning to look at him. "Do you think I should?"

"Yes," he said without hesitation.

"Why?" she asked, staring up at him longingly.

"Because I don't want to lose you."

"Does that mean—" she began, but he leaned down and kissed her.

For a moment, she was taken aback by his boldness, but instinct kicked in and she suddenly found herself kissing him passionately. She moaned softly and melted into his powerful arms as he probed her mouth with his tongue. Her body became flush with a wanton need for him, and she suddenly felt like she was floating through one of the many amorous fantasies she'd had about him over the last year. But this was real, and she never wanted it to end.

For the next hour, as the sky darkened and became alive with thousands of twinkling stars, they sat on there on the bench, snuggling and kissing and finally getting to express the feelings they felt for one another. Each admitted how they had been secretly thinking about the other since the night of his birthday party. Finally, they were able to relax and get to know each other. She shared with him what it was like growing up in rural Italy, and he shared with her what it was like growing up on the mean streets of Detroit. She told him what it was like being the only daughter of Ettore Ferarro, and he told her what it was like being the *difetto* grandson of Don Falcone. She voiced to him her dream of someday becoming a neurosurgeon, and he voiced his dream of someday owning a casino. But there was one thing they did not talk about. Anthony. They knew he would be enraged if he were to learn of their little romantic interlude. For now, it was just the two of them, young lovers, alone in their own little world, appreciating each other and the beautiful setting.

They were not, however, the only ones making a love connection. Vonni had driven around for nearly an hour in search of King. At one point, he considered going back to the party to just wait for him there, but decided against it. Don Falcone would ask where King was, and Vonni was not prepared to face the don without an answer. So, left with no other choice, he went to the one place he figured King would eventually show up. His apartment.

But as he keyed open the door and let Pamela in, he wondered if he had made a mistake by taking her there. It wasn't that he was worried what King might think. Nor was he worried about Pamela getting the wrong impression. He was worried about himself. She had grown into such a beautiful woman—tall, thin, with pert breasts and long legs. That in itself was enough to drive him wild. But he was even more impressed by her brain. He often found himself fantasizing about her. But of course, he never voiced any interest in her. Not to anyone. Especially not to King, who would never approve. But now that he found himself alone with her, it took all his strength to show no overt interest in her.

Alone in his apartment, they sat on the couch to watch television and wait for King to show up. But halfway through an old episode of *21 Jump Street*, she attacked him. Instantly his self-control went out the window. He was powerless to resist her sexual aggression. All the pent up sexual tension between them exploded into an inferno of passion, and within seconds they were making love right there on his living room couch. Then on the floor. Then in his bedroom. But it was more than casual sex. It was ardent, passionate lovemaking. Never had either of them experienced such ecstasy. Back and forth they went, indulging their bodies. An hour turned into two hours. Then three. The very fabric of time seemed to stop as they made love over and over until their bodies were completely spent.

Yet as much as Vonni was enjoying himself, he eventually began to seriously worry about King, who had made no attempt to contact him. Not even a phone call. Then a sudden thought occurred to him. Perhaps his boss was having the same luck with Contessa. But then he remembered who Contessa was. Getting a girl like her into bed would require a lot more work than what it had just taken him to get Pamela in bed, a thought that now made him now laugh aloud.

By 10:00 PM and still no word from King, Vonni decided it would be inappropriate if he kept Pamela any longer. So he put her in his Cadillac and drove her home. But when he began walking her up to the front door, Anthony came charging outside with rage in his eyes.

"Where the fuck is Omnio?" Anthony barked, ignoring his disheveled sister.

"I have no idea," Vonni admitted. "We took Pam and Contessa for a ride on the bikes but got separated. I haven't seen him since."

Anthony glared at Pamela. "So Contessa is still with Omnio?"

"I don't know," Pamela said, suddenly looking timid and submissive. "Like he said, we got separated."

Anthony turned back to Vonni. "And how long ago was that?" he asked, his face flushed with anger.

At first Vonni assumed Anthony was only mad because King had slipped off with Contessa, but now he sensed there was something else. "A few hours ago. Why?"

Anthony looked at Pamela. "Go inside," he ordered, pointing at the house.

"No," she protested. "Not until you calm down. Why are you so upset? The party was boring, so Omnio and Giovanni took us for a ride on their motorcycles. What's the big deal?"

Anthony continued glaring at her. "Pam, I won't tell you again. Go the fuck in the house!"

She glanced at the driveway and noticed both her parents' cars were gone. "Where's Mom and Dad?" she asked, knowing he would never talk to her like this if they were home.

Anthony suddenly turned his scowl on Vonni. "While you assholes were out joyriding with my sister and Contessa, the Feds raided Nina's graduation party. My grandfather was arrested, and my father was brought in for questioning. They're being held downtown in a Federal bullpen." He turned to his sister with a softer look. "Mom and grandma are already down there with the lawyers trying to get them out."

Vonni's head began to spin and his mouth instantly went dry. This could be catastrophic for their crew. With Don Falcone in jail, they would be at the mercy of Leoni. Even worse, the Feds could be looking for King. It was even possible King had already been picked up, which would explain his sudden disappearance.

448

"I need to go," Vonni said, already moving towards his car. "I have to find King. If he shows up, have him call me on my cell."

"If you find him first, make sure he fuckin' calls me," Anthony said, his inflection making it clear it was an order.

"I will," Vonni assured him, and then turned to Pamela when he saw the distraught look on her face. "Don't worry, I'm sure your grandfather has the best lawyers money can buy." He then got into his car and prepared to pull off. But just as he put the car in gear, Anthony stepped over and leaned in the driver's window so their faces were only inches apart.

"Let me tell you something, Giovanni," Anthony growled. "You risked my sister's life on that fuckin' bike today. Don't let it happen again. Stay the fuck away from her. And you can tell Omnio to do the same with Contessa. *Capisce*?"

Vonni stared up at him and bit back what he wanted to say, which was to fuck off. "Yeah, I got it, Tony," he said instead, not wanting to dig himself any deeper. "Settle down. It was just a ride."

Anthony shot a look at his sister and sensed they had done more than just take a ride, which made him think of King and Contessa. "You can also tell my cousin I don't think Contessa's father would appreciate her driving around town on the back of some fuckin' *difetto's* motorcycle."

This enraged Vonni, but before he said something he would regret, he stepped on the gas and tore off in search of his boss.

After a harried search of the neighborhood, Vonni found King at Mr. Q's Billiards Hall, shooting a casual game of pool with Contessa. The two of them looked like a pair of love-struck teenagers, smiling and flirting and fawning over each other with no regard for the people around them. But when King saw the look on Vonni's face, he immediately knew something was wrong.

"What is it?" King asked, setting down his cue stick.

449

Vonni took a quick account of the billiards hall. The place was packed, and there were many people discreetly watching them. King was rarely seen at Mr. Q's anymore, but nearly everyone there knew exactly who he was. They were also all surely wondering who his beautiful companion was.

"Maybe we should step outside," Vonni suggested, motioning towards the door.

A wave of trepidation suddenly washed over King. "Giovanni, tell me Pamela is home safe."

"She's fine," Vonni assured him, again taking in the room nervously. "I dropped her off at home a half-hour ago. But I ran into Anthony and..." He let his words trail off and looked at Contessa.

"And what?" King prompted. "He's pissed we took the girls for a ride?"

Vonni looked him in the eye. "Nina's party got raided by the Feds. Your grandfather was arrested and they brought Leoni in for questioning."

For a moment, King just stood there and said nothing, the neurotransmitters of his brain clicking into high gear. "Did Anthony say why my grandfather was arrested?" he finally asked.

"No. He just said he was taken to a Federal bullpen downtown. I guess your grandma is already down there with the lawyers."

As Contessa stood there listening, she witnessed King transform from the playful romantic he had been all day, to the dangerous young Mafiso she had forgotten he was. His dark eyes suddenly became cold and menacing, and she recognized the look in them. Anger. Dread. Frustration. She'd seen the look in her father's eyes when her own grandfather had been arrested after years of being on the lam. And as she now watched him formulate his thoughts, she realized the old adage was true—girls often fall in love with men who emulate their own father.

450

Finally, King turned to Vonni and said, "Take her home and meet me downtown."

"I'll come with you," Contessa said, her eyes pleading.

He knew Anthony was probably at home fuming, surely plotting his revenge. It made King realize what a mistake he had made today by running off with her. He had no idea how much trouble his grandfather was in, but without his grandfather's protection, Anthony and Leoni would quickly begin muscling him out of everything he had worked so hard for. Or worse. And to keep Contessa with him any longer would only make things worse.

"No," he said firmly. "I have to get you home. Pam is going to need you right now."

"But I don't want to go home," she pleaded. "I want to stay with you!"

He didn't want her around as a distraction, and he no longer had time to entertain her with his chivalry. So even though he knew it would surely hurt her feelings, he became cold and ignored her pleas. "Take her home," he ordered Vonni. "Then meet me downtown. I'm heading there now on my bike."

"Why don't we just drop her off together?" Vonni asked, knowing this was no time to leave him unprotected.

King's eyes suddenly turned hard as diamonds. "Do what I said, Giovanni." And without another word, or even a second glance at Contessa, he turned and walked out the door.

# CHAPTER 24

After the FBI and IRS dug deeper into Don Falcone's tax records, dozens of tax violations were revealed, most of them facilitated by local banks. Several bank branch managers were promptly arrested and charged with conspiracy to defraud the government. Federal prosecutors then threatened them with long prison terms if they refused to testify against the don. Of course, they knew how dangerous it could be for them to testify against a reputed Mafia Boss, but agents from the Organized Crime Taskforce were able to convince one of them that his family was in danger whether he did or didn't testify. Concerned for the welfare of his family, he agreed to testify in exchange for immunity from prosecution and acceptance into WITSEC, the Federal Witness Protection Program. This was how Don Falcone's indictment came about.

Don Falcone was charged with sixty-one counts of tax evasion, conspiracy to commit tax fraud, and the RICO Act—maintaining a "Racketeering Influenced Corrupt Organization." He was also questioned about everything from being the leader of the Detroit Mafia, to several cold case murders suspected of being mob related. They even asked about Jimmy Hoffa, who FBI sources believed had been killed by the don's cousin at a home in Bloomfield, Michigan, a home that had once belonged to him. But of course, he adhered to *Omerta* and said nothing. They knew he was a dangerous and ruthless Mafioso who had built his vast empire through criminal means, but knowing and proving were two different things.

Two days after his arrest, Don Falcone was released on a one-million-dollar bail. But facing a long trial and potential prison term, the Commission immediately sent word that he was to completely remove himself from all Syndicate activities. Even his crew, who had been working with him for nearly thirty years, had to break ties with him. With the FBI still monitoring his every move, all he could do was sit back and await the outcome of his grand jury indictment.

Leoni felt like he had hit the lottery. With his father-in-law awaiting trial, he wasted no time in officially restructuring the Family hierarchy. Because he didn't trust any of the don's top men, he promptly promoted several of his captains and lieutenants to take over the don's operations, while redistributing the majority of the don's men amongst the other four Families, giving them his blessing to work for the other *capiregime*.

Unfortunately, because King had been working under the don's flag, Leoni also took it upon himself to dismantle King's crew and take over their most profitable operations. Naturally, this infuriated King. But he knew there was nothing he could do about it. Leoni tried to pacify him with assurances that his operations would be returned once things cooled down, but King knew better. His treacherous uncle had always planned to muscle him out. Don Falcon's arrest only expedited the process. And if Don Falcone was sent to prison for any length of time, King knew his uncle would try to muscle him out of the Family permanently. Or worse.


As Don Falcone awaited trial, it wasn't long before King and his crew began feeling Leoni's oppressive hand weighing heavily on them. Under Leoni's despotic rule, they were relegated to once again working the low-level street rackets, grunt work they hadn't done in years. But they had no choice. Leoni was the new Boss. Even though they couldn't stand him, if they wanted to continue working under the protective umbrella of the Syndicate, they had no choice but to follow his orders. The Boss was the Boss. Not everyone liked him, but everyone had to follow his orders. Leoni had a large crew of faithful followers who would carry out his orders without question. Even if that order was to kill Don Falcone's favorite grandson. King knew to defy his uncle could very well mean a contract on his head.

King was devastated by the dismantling of his crew and operations, but this was the least depressing consequence of his grandfather's arrest. Over the last several years, he had entrusted nearly two million dollars of his crew's money to his grandfather, who had used various corrupted bankers to deposit it in a number of offshore accounts. Unfortunately, one of those bankers had turned state's evidence and provided the FBI with the locations of these numbered accounts. As a result, the accounts were frozen pending the don's trial, leaving King and his crew with next to nothing. All the money they had worked so hard for over the last five years would likely be seized by the federal government. Even though it would be nearly impossible to prove the money was obtained through illicit means, Don Falcone had no documentation proving it wasn't. Thus, the IRS would claim it was untaxed and declare it property of the Federal government.

From a financial standpoint, Don Falcone was in an even worse situation than King. Pending his trial, all of his bank accounts were frozen, including two that had several million dollars in each of them. Nearly all of his assets were also frozen, including his four restaurants, his wholesale produce business, a grocery store, and the five nightclubs that King and his crew had been making considerable profits from. The IRS and FBI were claiming that the don owed upward of several million dollars in back taxes. And if he were convicted of tax fraud, he would owe millions more in fines. The IRS was even threatening to seize his waterfront home.

Though King and his crew were relegated to minor street rackets, Leoni did allow them to retain their legitimate businesses, if only because these businesses could be used to help the Family launder money that had been earned illicitly. But Leoni demanded a significant cut of all profits from these legitimate businesses, and that significant cut was half of everything earned. It was just one more way that Leoni was able to lord himself over King. To add insult to injury, Anthony was the one who personally picked up that cut each week.

King hated being having to answer to Leoni and Anthony while his grandfather awaited trial, but knew it was the smart play. At least for now, until the FBI eased off the Syndicate's back. He figured once things cooled down, he would just cut his losses and start over. After all, he had started from the bottom once. And if he did it once, he could do it again. In the meantime, he focused on doing whatever he could do to help his grandfather.

Though Don Falcone had no friends in the federal court system, he did have friends in the state courts, including a number of judges and prosecutors, some of whom did indeed have friends in the federal court system. And for a sizable donation, one of these friends was able to obtain a list of witnesses the prosecution intended to subpoena for testimony in Don Falcone indictment. There were five total, all branch managers of various local banks. When Don Falcone finally got this list, he passed it on to the one person he trusted most—his faithful grandson, Omnio.

King immediately gathered a hit squad made of his crew's most trusted street soldiers, and together they began systematically hunting down these witnesses. Four of them were easy to convince that it would be in their family's best interest to refuse to testify, even if it meant being charged with perjury and contempt of court. They were smart enough to know what might happen if they worked with the prosecution. Unfortunately, the prosecution's primary witness, who had smartly opted to enter the Federal Witness Protection Program, was nowhere to be found.

Due to a number of postponements by both prosecution and defense, Don Falcone's hearing was delayed until nearly twelve months after his initial arrest. And like so often was the case with notorious Mafiosi, the media made a spectacle out of the proceedings, especially when it was rumored that several of the prosecution's key witnesses had mysteriously disappeared or suddenly refused to testify. New crews documented everything as the prosecution presented their case to a federal grand jury. Each day as the proceedings began, the courtroom would become crowded with camera crews and reporters, as well as the don's many friends and associates. But of course none of the Syndicate's top echelons dared show their face, for to do so would make them look guilty by association.

The trial dragged on for weeks, and King found himself in a perpetual state of gloom. It seemed his whole world was crashing down around him. He tried to be optimistic, hoping the lawyers might get all the charges dismissed, but deep down he knew his grandfather was about to be sent to prison for a considerable stretch. All of his money was now property of the federal government, and the vast majority of his operations had been appropriated by his Uncle Leoni. Even his crew had been dismantled and divided up amongst Leoni and Anthony.

But worse than all this, he was haunted by thoughts of Contessa. He hadn't seen her since the afternoon of Nina's graduation party, and memories of their short time together tormented him. He could still feel her lips on his, her firm body pressed against his. The ambrosia of her subtle perfume lingered in his memory. Several times he had considered calling her, but knew Anthony would become enraged if he found out. And this was no time to poke a lion with a stick. Not when the lion had an inferiority complex and was still trying to prove his mettle to father and the other Syndicate *capi*.

So all King had were the bittersweet memories of his one afternoon with Contessa. He was certain she felt the same for him, but also knew she was smart enough to know why he hadn't reached out to her. With his grandfather facing prison, and Anthony's father taking over the Syndicate, she had to know how vulnerable he was. All Leoni had to do was give the word, and he would be a dead man.

Thanks to King's strategic witness tampering, the prosecution was left with mostly circumstantial evidence. Unfortunately, the one remaining witness was willing to testify that he had personally laundered millions of dollars for the don. Yet the prosecution did not want to put the fate of their case into the hands of a jury they believed may have already been corrupted by bribery and collusion. So, thirteen months after the don's arrest, the defense and prosecution reached an agreement. Don Falcone would plea guilty to six counts of Federal tax evasion, and the prosecution would dismiss all other charges. Much to King's chagrin, however, the agreement stipulated that his grandfather had to forfeit all of the money in his offshore accounts, as well as nearly all of his assets, which would be auctioned off to pay the astronomical fines levied on him by the IRS. The only thing he was allowed to retain was his Grosse Pointe home.

One week before King's twenty-third birthday, in a courtroom packed with news camera and reporters, a judge sentenced the infamous Peter "The Butcher" Falcone to eleven years in Federal prison. With good behavior, he could be out in as little as eight. It was better than the original twenty years he had been facing.

As U.S. marshals led him away in shackles, his wife and daughters began sobbing uncontrollably. Even King's eyes watered as he watched his beloved grandfather being led away. But his tears were more of anger than sadness. His fury erupted when he saw several news cameras filming his bereaved family. Enraged by this act of disrespect, he charged over and began barking expletives at them, even shoving a camera off the shoulder of one particularly bold cameraman who ignored him. When he shot the rest of them murderous looks, they scurried off to interview the gloating prosecutors.

During the sentencing proceedings, Pamela, Contessa, and King's Aunt Patricia had been seated in the back of the courtroom with Anthony, Dino, and Leoni. King had caught Contessa looking at him several times from the corner of her eye, and they even exchanged a couple of fleeting smiles. But Anthony was very observant and did not look happy to see their little exchanges. Even though he had never even kissed her, he considered Contessa his property. In his mind, he still thought it would only be a matter of time before she succumbed to his irresistible charm.

The afternoon of Don Falcone's sentencing, his family gathered at his home for a somber dinner to console Signora Falcone. Leoni and her other sons-in-law assured her she would be well taken care of in Don Falcone's absence, but this did little to diminish the fact that should be without her life-long companion for the next eight years.

After dinner, while King's aunts and uncles retreated to the outdoor pavilion for coffee, his cousins headed down to the basement media room. But he was in no mood for socializing. He especially wanted to avoid Pamela and Contessa, at least while Anthony was around. So while his cousins gathered in the basement to shoot pool and play video games, he and Vonni discreetly made their exit. But just as they slipped out the side door, Pamela and Contessa came running out after them.

"Where are you guys going?" Pamela asked, avoiding eye contact with Vonni. "Home," King said curtly, casting a painful glance at Contessa.

"Why?" Pamela asked.

"Pam, you know I'm not wanted in there. They've never considered me part of this family. I'm just a fuckin' half-breed *difetto* to them."

458

"You weren't just a *difetto* to Nonno," Pamela said. "And Grandma wants you here. She doesn't care about your mixed blood. She loves you, Omnio. You really shouldn't leave without at least saying good-bye."

He glanced at the house, feeling a pang of guilt. "Tell her I'll be back later when everyone leaves."

He turned to walk away, but she grabbed his arm. "I know what Anthony and my dad are doing to you," she said, looking him in the eye. "And for the record, I think it's bullshit."

He offered her a small smile. "Yeah, well, it's good to know I'm not the only one."

She reached her arms around him and hugged him. "Call me sometime, eh, cousin?" she said, casting a quick glance at Vonni. "I miss you. Maybe we can all meet up and go out sometime. Just the four of us."

He looked at Vonni, knowing something had happened between them. He sensed they had real feelings for each other, but hoped his *protettore* knew better than to even think of pursuing her. After making a mental note to warn Vonni about her, he turned and locked eyes with Contessa. She seemed to be peering into his soul, those mesmerizing azurite eyes, so wide and innocent, reflecting his own need for her. But she was dangerous. He knew if he were to follow his heart and disregard Anthony's unspoken claim to her, the consequences could be catastrophic. Even fatal. And if he intended to carry on his grandfather's blood legacy, he had to live, which meant he needed to get her out of his head and focus on surviving the next eight years without his grandfather's protection. So, as much it pained him, he knew he had to walk away. And he did.

"No, Pam," he said, breaking eye contact with Contessa, "The four of us hanging out is a bad idea."

He then turned and walked away, not wanting Contessa to see the pain and shame in his eyes.

# CHAPTER 25

With Don Falcone out of the picture for the next eight years, Leoni quickly began lording himself over King. At first, he only took his fifty percent cut from King's legitimate businesses, but when he realized how much money King and his crew were still making off the streets, he began demanding a cut from that too. It was his way of keeping King on a short leash.

Nevertheless, King scraped by. He still had Club Vanzetti's, which had been purchased legally from the Scroi Brothers, albeit far under market value. And even though most of his crew's major operations had been absorbed by Leoni and his *capidecina*, King and his crew still maintained their street rackets within the city limits—loan sharking, sports books, poker games, numbers lottery, escort services, extortion, and shaking down drug dealers and pimps. But for every dollar they made, Leoni wanted half. Paying this "tribute" made them feel like they were the ones actually being shaken down, but they understood that it was a necessary operational expense if they wanted Leoni's protection from the local police as well as the other Syndicate crews.

Adding insult to injury, Anthony was the one who collected these regular tributes to Leoni. He and his equally loathsome brother, Dino, would show up at Vanzetti's unannounced, always escorted by their bodyguards, and offer King nothing more than contemptuous looks and snide remarks. There was nothing King could do about it. Leoni was The Boss. Anthony was had recently taken the oath and was now trying to step out from under his father's shadow. To prove his moxie, he even began muscling his way into territories the other Families had been working for decades. His crew was quickly growing, expanding, and asserting itself as a new Syndicate force. And of course, with Leoni backing him, nobody dared challenge him. He and his crew began taking in serious revenue, and Leoni always made sure a significant cut of it went to the Commission's Corporate Fund, a strategic play to make sure they were aware of Anthony's progress.

The Commission bosses may have been impressed by Anthony's progress, but some of the Syndicate bosses were not so impressed. They didn't appreciate how he was throwing his weight around, muscling in on their rackets and territories. Don Guiseppi Rubino was especially bothered by Anthony's megalomania, and soon found himself wishing Don Falcone was still around to put him in his place.

To make matters even worse, Leoni had convinced most of the Syndicate crews to distance themselves from King, calling him a "loose cannon with no loyalties to anyone." He convinced them to ostracize him and restrict him from any involvement in their operations. Even King's lieutenants, though still loyal and committed to him, were ordered to distance themselves from him. Before long, King found himself alone on an island, his crew having been reduced to just Vonni, Billy, Tommy, Carlo, Jimmy, and the Campisi twins.

But this tiny crew of outcasts was enough. Together they slowly began putting the pieces of their dismantled operation back together. Things were slow in the beginning, but King was determined to rise up from the ashes like a phoenix. He promoted Carlo and Tommy to lieutenants, and then had them begin putting together small crews of their own, each with their own territories and specific rackets. They returned to their old cash cows—fencing stolen goods, commercial larceny, auto theft, and robbery. They shook down drug dealers and pimps. They extorted small businesses for protection money. They ran

461

dice and poker games. Once again, they began offering their reverse protection insurance to drug dealers and local businesses, taking out their competitors for a cut of their increased profits. Slowly but surely, they began taking in revenue that Anthony and Leoni knew nothing about.

The money King and his crew were making was considerable, but it was nothing compared to what they had been making before Don Falcone's incarceration. And of course, the more they made, the more Leoni wanted. Yet King was still able to put away several hundred thousand dollars in cash. He planned to use it as seed money to branch into some new business arenas once the FBI stopped scrutinizing his every move.


Several months after Don Falcone's imprisonment, King received a message from one of his grandfather's associates who worked for the local sheriff. It seemed the FBI's Organized Crime Taskforce had determined King to be nothing more than minor Syndicate player who dabbled in the street rackets, and thus they had terminated surveillance on him. This was the news he had been waiting for. Finally, he could start making some moves. His first order of business was recruiting some manpower, but his recruits had to meet a very specific set of criteria. First and foremost, they had to understand the consequences of betrayal. None of them could have blood ties to any of the Syndicate bosses, and they had to fully accept him as their leader.

His new recruits were far from the cream of the crop, but with Leoni always watching and listening, he took what he could get. Blacks, Latinos, gangbangers, it didn't matter. As long as they were loyal and steady earners, he found a way to use them to his advantage. Drug dealers, stickup kids, larcenists, car thieves, safecrackers—all facets of underworld characters were recruited and assigned specific territories to ply their respective skill-sets. With their help, King almost immediately saw a huge spike in his crew's earnings. It was nothing like the good old days, but within a year he was once again stockpiling considerable money. This time he forewent storing it in banks, and instead stashed the money in a series of storage lockers and safehouses.

Leoni's crew, the Gianolla Family, was vast, with *capidecina* and crews spread throughout all of Metropolitan Detroit. They were constantly trying to earn his favor by reporting on the doings of the other crews. This was how Leoni learned that King was once again milking the ghettos by using outsourced street soldiers. And to keep him from gaining too much traction, he began demanding an even a larger percentage of King's weekly take, which of course irritated King to no end. Yet he had no choice but to pay it. He knew the only reason his uncle hadn't cut him off or had him killed was because he was putting so much money in his greedy pockets.

Even though Leoni had turned most of the other Families against him, King still had several Syndicate allies. One of them was his old friend, Don Giuseppe Rubino, who had always been a close friend to Don Falcone. Over the last several years he had grown fond of King and considered him to be a thoroughbred Mafioso, even if his blood was not pure Sicilian. Unbeknownst to Leoni, Don Rubino decided to help King by advancing him large consignments of cocaine, heroin, and marijuana. The drug business was not something King particularly wanted to get into, but he needed the money. Because if he wanted to reestablish his power base and earn the alliance of the other bosses, he would have to start paying more than Leoni a cut of his weekly take. He would once again have to start paying all of them a cut.

Without Leoni's knowledge, King still maintained discreet working relationships with all of his old lieutenants, some of whom still managed aspects of his remaining operations. They constantly expressed how much they hated working for Leoni and Anthony, who treated them like bottom-rung grunts. But because they had once been part of King's infamous crew, many of the Syndicate's street-level *capi* and lieutenants still showed them a lot of respect. They rubbed elbows with associates from other crews almost daily. They'd see them in clubs, or pop in at each other's headquarters to catch up on Syndicate gossip. They played poker and dice together. They corroborated on various hustles and scams. Everyone in the community talked, and because of it there was very little that everyone didn't know about. And the hot topic of late was legalized gambling.

For decades, the Syndicate had adamantly opposed legalized gambling—and for good reason. A huge portion of the Syndicate's wealth derived from illegal gambling. Some of the Families, including Don Falcone's, made over half their income from illegal gambling. But the Commission saw the legalization of gaming in Detroit as an immense opportunity. If the city were to legalize gambling, they could pool their resources and open legitimate casinos. With this objective in mind, they had Leoni and the other Syndicate *capi* begin bribing certain city officials who had previously opposed legalized gambling.

After years of legislative red tape and bickering amongst city, county, and state officials, the City of Detroit finally decided to offer its people a chance to vote on legalizing gambling. When the ballots were collected, legalization was approved nearly 2-to-1. The people had big hopes that a few casinos would encourage tourism and inject an infusion of new jobs and money into the local economy.

The ten Commission *Capi* managed a secret cache of money known as The Corporate Fund, or simply, "The Fund." There were tens of millions stashed in The Fund, almost all of it in offshore accounts, protected by layers of fictitious shell companies, including several obscure investments groups who specialized in the hotel and gaming industry. Just as they'd once done in places like Las Vegas, Atlantic City, and even Cuba at one time, the Commission intended to use these obscure corporate investment groups to build casinos in Detroit.

Unfortunately, there was a problem. A big one. The state's fledgling Gaming Board refused to issue a gaming license to a foreign investment group, especially one that would not disclose the identities of its investors. Apparently, the City Council had stipulated that the licenses had to be issued to someone local, preferably a resident of the Detroit area. That meant that the Syndicate was going to need a front man. It would be inconvenient, but their friends in the City Council assured them that they would approve, even endorse, whomever they selected as long as he was a legitimate businessman with impeccable credentials and no criminal record.

Leoni spearheaded the search for a perfect front man, and after several weeks he came up with one: Gregory Tammer, a local businessman who owned a string of very successful car dealerships. He had no criminal history, no overt ties to the Syndicate, and was well known locally. He also had plenty of friends in high places. Over the years, he had used several Syndicate associates for various favors, including a number of large cash loans, as well as help obtaining building permits. That meant he owed them a favor, and it was time they called it in.

Unfortunately, Leoni soon ran into another problem. Gregory Tammer was white. Since the vast majority of the city's residents were African American, they demanded that the new casino owners to be African Americans. After all, it was their vote that had gotten gambling legalized in the first place. The City Council agreed. So, left with no choice, Leoni scrapped Tammer and set out to find an African American front man. It took a while, but eventually he found one.

Insert Henry Davis, known to his closest friends and confidants as "Hank." Raised on the mean streets of South Chicago, Davis was a born hustler. Blessed with a slick tongue, uncanny drive, and a mind for business, he'd been destined to be rich. Filthy rich. His first foray into the capitalist arena was selling cocaine nearly twenty years earlier, at the height of the 1980's crack epidemic. He started as a small-time dealer working local parks and street corners, but quickly worked his way up. Within a year he had over a dozen street dealers working under him. But his southside neighborhood was run by a crew of Italian wiseguys who belonged to the Cicero crew, a powerful faction of the "Outfit," Chicago's resident Mafia *borgata*. And they did not fail to notice Hank's new enterprise. Yet he was surprised when they offered to help him expand his operation, as long as he cut them in on a percentage of his profits. This was his first encounter with the Mafia. It would not be his last. Over the next several years, he worked with the Cicero crew to establish a very lucrative cocaine pipeline from Miami to Chicago. Their symbiotic partnership made millions as the crack epidemic spread across the country. But when Ronald Reagan declared a war on drugs, Hank wisely decided to relinquish all of his interests in the cocaine business to his Italian partners.

Hank was, however, only getting started in business. Sitting on several million dollars in cash, he began looking for new investment opportunities. He found one in the clothing industry. He had a passion for men's fashion, particularly high-end fashion. He loved wearing suits and designer clothes. His favorite place to shop for them was New York. During one of his many shopping excursions there, he became acquainted with a wholesaler who sold overstock of high-end fashion garments. It was this acquaintance who helped him invest his money into several high-end fashion outlets in the Chicago area. But after saturating metropolitan Chicago with his stores, he knew he had to expand into new markets if he wanted to continue growing his empire. So he spent the next five years opening nearly a hundred more stores in the Midwest and New England. Eleven of those stores were in Metropolitan Detroit. Although he was required to pay a tax to certain Syndicate bosses for operating their territories, he was accustomed to paying such tributes from his many years of operating in Chicago.

By age thirty-three, Hank's legitimate net-worth was close to one hundred million dollars. And at age thirty-four, when Leoni offered him that chance to be the face of the Syndicate's new Detroit casino, he couldn't have been more excited. After all, every street hustler's dream was to own a casino, and he was about to do just that.

After some negotiating, an agreement was reached. Leoni would act as the liaison between Hank and his new silent partners, "The Matador Investment Group," one of the Commission's shell companies based in the Spanish Canary Islands. Hank's stake in the casino was a mere 3%, but he was not required to put up any of the two hundred million dollars needed to actually build it.

Once this arrangement was finalized, Davis submitted a proposal and application for a gaming license to the Detroit City Council, who immediately accepted it and forwarded to the state's new Gaming Board. After a thorough vetting by the FBI, he was issued Detroit's first gaming license. Eleven months later, his temporary "Motown Casino" was opened until riverfront real estate could be secured for a permanent hotel casino resort.

Motown Casino was an immediate success. Thousands of local Michiganders flocked there each day to try their luck at the tables. Of course, it didn't generate the enormous draws of Las Vegas or Atlantic City, but the daily take was still considerable. Using hand-selected managers, Leoni was soon skimming tens of thousands of untaxed dollars from the count room each week, all of it divided up between the bosses who had money invested in The Fund. But they were also splitting the casino's legitimate profits, a dollar amount that was growing exponentially each day.

These were good times for the Syndicate. After the initial success of their first casino, they soon opened a second casino, "The Odyssey," in the city's famous Greek Town district. Both casinos had trickle-down effects on the local economy, especially the downtown area. Restaurants, hotels, cab services, bars, theaters, and nightclubs all saw huge spikes in business. So did prostitution, strip clubs, drugs and loan sharking. Of course, the Syndicate controlled all of these rackets, both legal and illegal.

Leoni and the Commission bosses were becoming fat and rich, but it wasn't long before trouble began brewing for Leoni. Some of the other Syndicate had also invested in the project and believed he wasn't paying them their due share. They also believed he was skimming from the Commission's cut. But this was only the beginning of the problems the casinos would end up causing. In the years to come, dissension over the casinos would fracture the Syndicate's unity and cause it to break into two factions. Those who were with Leoni, and those who were against him.

In the ensuing years, King would use the Syndicate's infighting and bickering to his advantage. While the bosses focused their energy on making sure Leoni was paying them their due share of the casino skims, he quietly continued to strengthen and expand his operations. It had been almost four years since the government seized all his money, and only now was he finally beginning to recoup his losses. Leoni saw him as no threat, and had once again accepted him as an extension of his Family, albeit only because King was consistent and timely with his weekly tributes. But for the most part, as long as King kept his crew confined to the inner city and petty street rackets, Leoni left him alone. That is, provided King handed Anthony a fat envelope of cash each week.

King had purposefully distanced himself from much of his family. Particularly from his uncles, all of who now worked for Leoni. He knew Leoni had turned them against him, so he avoided interaction with them unless he absolutely had to. No longer did he have Sunday dinners with them at his grandparents' house. Rarely did he attend family functions, and he only visited his grandmother when he knew for sure they wouldn't be there.

In many ways, he felt cut off from his family. He missed the camaraderie and kinship he felt as a kid, when he had spent so much time with his aunts, uncles, and cousins. Back then he'd felt truly loved and accepted by his family. But those times were long gone. Now he was on his own, almost completely cut off from them. But he did have Vonni, who had grown to be like his brother. He even accepted Vonni's secret relationship with Pamela. He knew his faithful *protettore* had genuine feelings for her. He didn't need to be Sherlock Holmes to figure it out. The signs were obvious. After Nina's graduation party, Vonni began getting mysterious phone calls from a female he would only identify as "a friend." Also, he suddenly stopped dating, which was the biggest indicator considering he had always been a prolific philanderer. But the most incriminating evidence was how he began disappearing on the weekends for several hours at a time, always when she was home from school.

In the beginning, King was admittedly unsettled by Vonni's interest in Pamela. But he eventually came to terms with it. He knew Vonni was a good man and could be trusted to treat her right. Yet he still issued him a stern warning to always respect her and to never play with her emotions. Because he knew if he mistreated her in any way, there would be nothing he could do to protect him from Leoni. But Vonni assured him that he would always respect her and treat her right. Not just out of respect for him, or even out of fear of Leoni, but because he was genuinely in love with her.

After Vonni had admitted he was in love with Pamela, he and King rarely discussed the subject. Whenever Vonni made his regular trips to see Pamela at college, he would leave Tommy behind to be King's interim *protettore*. During these trips to see Pamela, Vonni often saw Contessa, who would always ask about King. When he got home, King would always ask about her. But King never joined Vonni on these regular trips to see Pamela and Contessa. Not because he didn't want to see Contessa. He did. There was nothing he wanted more than to see her. He didn't go because he knew Anthony was still pursuing her, and he didn't want to get Anthony any more riled up than he already was. Not when he was so vulnerable. But what he didn't know was that Anthony's relentless pursuit of Contessa was about to finally pay off.

As much as King would have loved to charge in on his white horse and sweep Contessa off her feet, doing so would have been far too dangerous. He was already walking a fine line with Anthony, who was only tolerating him because he was paying for that tolerance. Which was why, as much as it pained him, he'd made no attempt to pursue Contessa. Even when she invited him to come visit her, he was cold and curt, acting as if he was no longer interested in her. That couldn't have been further from the truth. He was only doing what he had to do in order to survive. It was all about self-preservation. But even after four years, his feelings for her were just as strong as that day at Nina's party. No, in fact they were stronger. But he was too smart to let his feelings cloud his judgment. Not when Anthony was waiting for any excuse to try and kill him. So whenever Pamela came home from school with Contessa, he made sure to avoid running into them. For he knew if he were to come face-to-face with her, he would not be able to keep his emotions in check.

Eventually, after four years, Contessa finally accepted what happened between her and King to be nothing more than youthful infatuation. She was a woman now, with womanly needs. She yearned for the companionship and intimacy of a man, and Anthony had been patiently waiting to supply it. After years of resisting his constant pursuit and attempts to woo her, she finally relented. Over the last few years, he had surrendered a bit of his childhood egomania to maturity. No longer was he quite so inflated with arrogance and self-worth. He was handsome and romantic, and he treated her like a queen. He would pick her up from college on weekends and whisk her back to the city, where he would spoil her with lavish gifts, spa days, and extravagant dinners at the finest restaurants in town. Though she would never outwardly admit it, she did find herself intrigued by his status. She was well aware of how the Mafia worked, how its highest-ranking members were revered and treated with the utmost respect. Wherever she went with Anthony, this was exactly how people treated him, which she found impressive considering he was barely twenty-five years old.

Intrigued as she was, there was also something she found unnerving about Anthony. He could become very angry and combative when he drank, which was more often than she liked. Several times while he was drunk, she'd overheard him talking about hurting, even killing people as if it was nothing but a daily chore. She suspected that he could be a very dangerous young man, capable of doing very bad things. It was why she knew she could never date anyone else. If she did, he would surely chase them away. Or worse. So, lonely and yearning for male companionship, she submitted to his pursuit and began dating him. And though she didn't love him, he filled the gaping void King had left in her heart.


King was both sickened and hurt when he learned of Contessa's relationship with Anthony. Not just because he couldn't stand Anthony, but because it told him that she had

471

finally given up on waiting for him. That was bad enough in of itself, but what made it feel like a dagger to his heart was the fact that she knew Anthony was the actual reason he'd given up on pursuing her. It felt like a slap in the face and a punch in the gut at the same time. He knew she probably thought he was a coward for bowing to Anthony, but she had no idea how dangerous his cousin was. Nor did she know that Anthony had already tried to kill him twice.

To keep his mind off of Contessa, King did what he always did when he needed a distraction. He focused on business. With his crew constantly growing and expanding their presence on the streets, money was once again pouring in. Aside from his love life, things were looking up. Then, things took a turn for the worst.

In the spring of 2004, both Pamela and Contessa graduated from the University of Michigan. To celebrate the occasion, Leoni threw them a party for them at his headquarters, Leo's On The Lake. King knew if he didn't at least make an appearance, he would seem bitter and jealous of Anthony's conquest over Contessa. So he and Vonni showed up at the party dressed to impress. But they quickly found themselves feeling out of place and uncomfortable, for two different reasons.

Vonni was uncomfortable because Pamela was lingering by him, laughing and flirting and making it obvious that she was romantically interested in him. King was uncomfortable because every time he turned around he saw Anthony kissing Contessa on the cheek, holding her hand and introducing her to everyone as his girlfriend. Though her face was a mask of indifference, King caught her discreetly watching him several times. It seemed she knew better than to show any overt interest in him, but seeing her with Anthony felt like a cold stake in his heart. It stirred in him an anger that he'd never felt before. Eventually, when he tired of Anthony's overt gloating, he made his exit.

But little did he know that his appearance at the party had rekindled feelings in Contessa she'd tried to suppress for years, feelings she knew she could never feel for Anthony. One look at him and memories of their brief time together came flooding back. It made her heart ache for him, and for the next several days he was all she could think about. After nearly two weeks, when Anthony was in Miami for the weekend on business, she decided she had to see him. But knowing he would never agree to see her under his own volition, she tricked him.

Vonni and Pamela met regularly for dinner, after which they usually headed back to his apartment for a few hours of passionate lovemaking. But on this afternoon, Vonni knew something was amiss when Pamela called and asked him to bring King along for dinner. Since he knew Anthony was out of town, he had a pretty good feeling what it was.

When King and Vonni arrived at the restaurant, they found Pamela and Contessa seated at a reserved table for four, both of them looking gorgeous in their summer finery. This was the first time King had seen Contessa without Anthony since the day of Nina's graduation party, over four years ago. The sight of her made his heart race with excitement. At first, he was a bit awkward and nervous. But after a few glasses of wine and some casual conversation, he eventually began to relax. As the four of them enjoyed a romantic candle-lit dinner, it wasn't long before they were laughing and flirting like any other young twentysomethings.

King and Vonni were enjoying themselves immensely, but they were not prepared for what happened next. After some dancing and more wine at a local nightclub, the girls directed them downtown to the Renaissance Marriott, where they had already reserved a pair of luxury suites for the weekend.

When King found himself alone with Contessa for the first time, he was surprisingly nervous. He'd dreamed of this moment since the first night he laid eyes on her. She had matured over the last six years, and now looked more like a beautiful woman than a beautiful girl. Her body had filled out and become even more curvaceous. But there was one thing that hadn't changed. Her eyes. They were still the most magnificent eyes he had ever seen. Pools of indigo, brighter than the summer sky. She was exquisite in every sense of the word. And as he now sat next to her on the couch, he gently ran a finger down the countenance of her face, as if to make sure she was real.

"You're an angel," he whispered, looking into her eyes, and then leaned in to kiss her.

With his kiss, she completely and fully surrendered to him. In one momentous eruption, all of her suppressed feelings for him came exploding forth. She kissed him like she had never kissed a man before. Never had she felt such an overwhelming physical need for a man. Within moments they were in the bedroom with their clothes off, his naked body pressing into hers. He was the most incredible looking man she had ever seen, as if God Himself had personally molded him into perfection. He was magnificent. And when she saw his swollen erection, her body ached to have it inside her.

Looking down at her, he was feeling much the same. He was awed by her beauty. Her compact body was so perfectly proportioned. Her small waist only accentuated the curves of her breasts and hips. Her skin was without blemish and silky smooth. Locks of raven hair curled under her chin and smelled like flowers. All of it all made his heart race and his loins throb with excitement. His instinct was to pin her down and ravage her, but he wanted to… no, he *had* to slow down and make sure he satisfied her. After all, he only had one chance to make a first impression.

Fighting to restrain himself, he gently eased her onto the bed and began kissing every inch of her body, fulfilling a fantasy he had dreamed of for years. She moaned and gasped softly as he stopped to tease her erect nipples with his tongue before working his way down her navel. When he began probing her with two fingers and licking her clitoris, she shuddered and began moaning louder. Then she cried out the words he had been waiting to hear since the moment he first set eyes on her.

"Make love to me, Omnio!"

Suddenly he was inside her, their bodies melding together in body and soul. As he slowly thrust himself into her, deep and hard, she expelled a series of throaty moans. The feel of his heavily muscled body atop hers, his full length deep inside her, was far more erotic than any of her fantasies about him. When he began thrusting faster and harder, grunting with each push, it was more than she could handle. Within seconds she began clawing at his back, crying out his name, thrusting her pelvis into him. Then, with a primal, almost animalistic explosion of ecstasy, they climaxed simultaneously.

Neither of them had ever experienced such a perfect sexual union. Time seemed to stand still. Minutes turned to hours as they made love over and over. But it was more than just sex. It was the physical bonding of their souls.

Late into the night, after she finally drifted into a deep post-coital slumber, he found himself watching her, envisioning them together as a real couple. He pictured traveling the world with her, starting a family with her, giving her everything she could ever dream of. Just the two of them, husband and wife. The way they were meant to be.

"Someday..." he mused softly. "Someday you'll be my queen."


King and Vonni spent the entire weekend enjoying Contessa and Pamela, taking advantage of their short time together while Anthony was out of town. They laughed and flirted and acted like what they were—young couples in love. They hung out mostly in King's neighborhood, where people treated him like a celebrity. They shot pool at Mr. Q's Billiards Hall. They ate at his favorites restaurants, and they took romantic walks along the beach. King even brought Contessa to meet his godparents, Nick and Vicky, when he went to get his hair cut.

As Contessa got to know King better, she was surprised by how fun he was. She was impressed by his self-deprecating sense of humor and quick wit. He was constantly joking and making her laugh, yet he was also exceptionally intelligent and worldly. Especially for someone who had no formal education. It seemed he was a savant, with knowledge on a great many subjects. When she inquired as to how he had gotten so smart, he shrugged and answered, "I like to read."

But the thing that she found most impressive about him wasn't his looks or even his brains. It was how he was received by people in his neighborhood. It was similar to how people received Anthony, except there was one major difference: People showed him respect because they loved him, while people showed Anthony respect only because they feared him. After really getting to know King, she realized there was no comparison between the two. Anthony may consider him an infidel because of his mixed blood, but he wasn't half the man King was. By the end of the weekend, she knew she could never love Anthony, because her heart already belonged to King.

Both couples enjoyed their time together immensely, but the weekend seemed to go far too quickly. Before they knew it, it was Sunday night. King and Vonni were saddened that it was over, but knew it was time they got back to reality. When they parted ways with the girls, there was no talk of the future. Vonni knew he had to continue hiding his relationship from Pamela's father and brothers. And though King had enjoyed every second of his time with Contessa, he knew nothing would come of it. She was still property of Anthony, and if Anthony were to ever learn of what happened over the weekend, he would stop at nothing to kill him. King would be on his own in an open war against the entire Gianolla Family. He knew he would find no asylum with the other Families, for they would never side with a lowly *difetto* over the Boss' prodigy son.

476

Anthony may have been a maniacal, scheming, backstabbing narcissist, but he was no fool. He'd never forgotten how Contessa had looked at King during Pamela's graduation party. For years he'd suspected she had hidden feelings for him. So when he went out of town for the weekend with his father, he'd had her followed. When he learned of who she had been with all weekend, he flew into a fit of rage. But he knew better than to react on impulse. His father had taught him better than that. No, this was no time to be impulsive. This was a time to be cold and calculating. He had a small army of street soldiers at his disposal, and he would use them to do his dirty work. Yes, he knew exactly how to deal with his *difetto* cousin, the infamous king of the ghettos.

# CHAPTER 26

Blackballed from the Syndicate's most lucrative rackets, such as bid-rigging, municipal contracts, and union shakedowns, King was left to eke out a living working the petty street rackets. But with the inception of the casinos, the streets offered plenty of new opportunities. One was loan sharking. As Detroit's new gambling scene grew in popularity, the city soon became awash in gambling addicts. When they needed a quick a cash fix to satisfy their addiction, King's network of street lenders were there to provide it to them—at an exorbitant interest rate, of course.

Another of his rackets that saw a significant spike in productivity was Billy's stolen car operation. Each day, droves of wealthy suburbanites flocked downtown to the new casinos. While they were inside trying their luck at the tables, Billy's team of skilled of car thieves would go to work. The system they used was surprisingly sophisticated, but very efficient. Billy employed a number of valet attendants who, using a computer, could duplicate a car's alarm key fob. They also had a key-making machine on site, which they used to quickly make a duplicate key for the target cars. Jaguars, Mercedes, BMWs, Cadillacs, luxury SUVs, and exotic sports cars were the primary targets. But Billy's team couldn't just steal them from the casino's parking structure or surrounding lots. Not only would this bring too much heat from the cops, but it would also bring too much heat from the other Syndicate bosses, who owned the valet services at the casinos and nearly all of the surrounding the parking lots. So they would simply have a team lying in wait. When the owner of a target car left the casino, the team would follow him home. Once they knew where the car was, they'd later return and steal it using the fabricated alarm fob and key. There was no way to tie the theft back to the casinos. Once the cars were brought to a large warehouse, King would have them re-tagged and shipped to Canada or Europe, where they were sold at retail price. It was an extremely lucrative racket that often made them tens of thousands each week.

But the casinos offered many more financial opportunities, which King's crew took full advantage of. King had a number of "watchers" working inside the casinos—bartenders, valet attendants, waitresses, card dealers, and security guards. He paid them to inform him whenever someone was at the casino flashing large sums of money, or had won a particularly large jackpot. When they called him with a mark, he'd send a pair of his men to follow them from the casino and relieve them of their money or winnings.

However, his biggest infusion of new money resulting from the casinos was from after-hours clubs. Since Michigan law prohibited all drinking establishments, including casinos, from serving alcohol after 2:00 AM in the morning, anyone interested in continuing their night after this hour was, quite literally, left high and dry. Many people were just getting started at 2:00 AM. So, seeing this as a great opportunity, King opened a string of after-hours clubs. And thanks to the casinos, he never had a shortage of patrons. Strippers from dozens of the city's gentlemen's clubs, gamblers from the casinos, nightclub staff, restaurant staff, evening shift workers, and pretty much anyone not ready to call it a night at 2:00 AM flocked to his exclusive after-hours clubs to drink and dance and party the night away.

There was, however, much more than just drinking and dancing going on at King's late night social clubs. He had dozens of soldiers working them, each offering a variety of illicit vices. Every drug was available, from cocaine to nitrous oxide gas. And for those interested in a little more than drugs, booze, and dancing, prostitutes were also available. But the latest craze was MDMA, or better known as "ecstasy." Over the last several years the drug had exploded onto the club scene and established a cult-like following. Also known as "the love drug," users expressed a sense of euphoria and heightened sexuality that was beyond description. There were huge profits to be made from selling this seemingly harmless drug. For a mere $25,000, King's old friend and confidant, Don Giuseppe Rubino, began supplying him with 10,000 ecstasy tablets a week. Each pill was sold for $15 to $25, depending on how many a buyer bought. From the sale of just this one drug alone, King and his crew began pulling in tens of thousands a week in their after-hours clubs. But of course, he was only allowed to operate these clubs because Leoni was letting him. When Leoni learned of King's success in the afterhours business, he demanded half of King's weekly take. Fortunately for King, there was no way for Leoni to know just how much he was actually making, which was more than triple what he was reporting to his uncle.

Between his after-hours clubs and the rest of his operations, King was once again stockpiling money. Serious money. It wasn't uncommon for him to deposit a quarter-million dollars or more every week at his various stash houses. Soon, if things continued going the way they were, he would have enough to implement the first phase of his master stratagem. Which was to present a business proposal to some of his grandfather's old associates, including the Las Vegas casino owner, Hector Arpionis. Unfortunately, before he ever got the chance to do so, things took a turn for the worse.


When Anthony learned of King's secret weekend with Contessa, his initial impulse was to kill him himself. But of course, this was out of the question. His father would never approve. Not when King was earning so much money for the

480

Family. Anthony knew he had to find a way to kill him without implementing himself. After much thought, he decided to once again contract outside help to do his dirty work for him. And this time he would make sure they finished the job. But what he didn't know was that fate would again intervene.

Don Rubino's headquarters was an obscure little delicatessen in Grosse Pointe, right on Mack Avenue. In the back was a small office, from which he directed his operations with the precession of a symphony conductor. King often met him there for impromptu business meetings, as to keep potential FBI surveillance from establishing any routine interactions between them. He always enjoyed spending time with the stately old don. But when he stepped into the office on this day, he immediately knew something was wrong.

"Sit down, Omnio," said Don Rubino, motioning to a chair in front of his desk, his tone both somber and forceful. "We got problems."

"Problems?" King echoed, dropping into the chair. "What kind of problems?"

"The kind we need to discuss alone."

King glanced at Vonni, who was posted by the door with a stoic look on his face. "No disrespect, Joe, but Vonni's my *protettore*. If I can't trust him, who can I trust?"

Don Rubino looked Vonni for a moment. "Fine," he said, deciding King was right. If a guy couldn't trust his own *protettore*, he was already a dead man. "Omnio, I don't know what you did to piss off Anthony, but he has it out for you."

"Yeah?" King chuckled, glancing at Vonni. "Tell us something we don't know."

Don Rubino leaned forward and gave him a stern look. "This is serious, Omnio. He wants you dead."

"He's wanted me dead for years," King shrugged. "He's already tried to kill me twice. But that was before I became his daddy's personal ATM machine. Leoni won't let him kill me. I make his ass too much money."

481

"Yeah?" Don Rubino asked incredulously, looking him in the eye. "Do you know Bruno DiCarlo?"

King indeed knew Bruno "The Hammer" DiCarlo, and he now pictured the man in his mind. Older guy. Mid-forties. Big brute with a pocked face and sunken beady eyes. He was a sort of autonomous auxiliary soldier used by all the Syndicate bosses. He owned a dumpy garage off Detroit's 7 Mile Road, but he was also, among other things, a contract assassin. Since he was technically freelance muscle, he wasn't bound to any one Family or crew. But all the Families used him from time to time. Usually to collect debts, persuade certain unresponsive business owners, or track down individuals who owned large sums of money. Known for his savage brutality, he often tortured his victims to get his point across. His modus operandi: A ball-peen hammer, which was how he had earned his moniker "The Hammer." Usually, he was only used for certain sensitive matters, such as sending someone a message. King had met him several times over the years, and considered him to be a lowlife sociopath who could never be trusted.

"Yeah, I'm familiar with The Hammer," he said, meeting the old boss' stare, no longer looking amused. "Why?"

Don Rubino took a deep breath and gathered his words. "Omnio, you've grown to be like part of my own Family. And I'm not just blowing smoke up your ass. I mean it. You have honor and integrity. You respect the rules, which is more than I can say for most of your generation. Your grandfather and I..." He paused and leaned back in his chair, a nostalgic look in his eyes. "Don Falcone and I have a long history. I don't think I've ever told you this, but back when he first learned of my involvement in the drug business, he didn't order me to stop. He could have, but he didn't. He respected me enough to leave the decision to me. And for that, I have always had a special place in my heart for him. So out of respect for him, I feel it's my duty to tell you that Anthony has contracted Bruno and his brother to kill you."

"And how do you know this?" King asked, shifting uncomfortably in his seat.

Don Rubino leaned back in his chair and took a sip of coffee from the cup on his desk. "Bruno's brother, Mario, runs some porn dens on 8 Mile for Joey Sapio. Joey's one of my guys. Works for my son, Santino. Sometimes Joey Saps sends Mario to collect delinquent markers for Tino's bookies. So the other day Saps sends Mario to collect from some welsh who owes a couple grand. Mario is supposed to tune him up a little. You know, send him a message. Make sure he pays on time next time. But kid's a known thief, so Mario tells him he'll squash his debt with Saps if he can get him a hot ride and silenced pistol he needs for a job. He even asked the kid to help him get rid of the car after the job. Well, the kid agreed because he was scared shitless of Mario. But he got nervous. Ended up mentioning it to Joey. Probably figured he was getting in way over his head. And Joey ain't no dummy. He knew someone was about to get whacked, so he brought it to Tino. And Tino brought it to me. But when I asked around, nobody knew anything about Mario taking on any contract wet work. So I had Tino bring him in to find out what the hell was going on. And that scumbag knew better than to pass off some bullshit to Tino. He said the hot car and piece were for a contract his brother got from the Gianolla crew. So, since the *diavolo* fuck knows nothing of my relationship with you, he had no reason not to tell Tino you were the mark. Contracted by none other than your cousin Anthony. But of course, Tino played it cool. He even said he'd help him with anything he needed to make sure the hit went smoothly."

King looked over at Vonni and they locked eyes. They were thinking the same thing: Anthony must have somehow learned of what happened last weekend while he was in Florida on business.

Don Rubino leaned forward with his elbows on his desk. "The DiCarlo brothers are supposed to visit you sometime this week. They'll come under the guise of business. Something

483

about offering you a piece of Mario's peepshow operation in exchange for a piece of your afterhours operation. But it's all bullshit. Mario told Tino your cousin Anthony Gianolla promised him your afterhours operation if he takes you out. But he won't give that *faccia brutta cetriolo* shit. In fact, I'm sure he plans to whack both those DiCarlo fucks after they finish the job. That way there's nobody who can point the finger at him. Not even his *canooda* father."

"The slimy little fucker..." King said, more to himself, his mind already plotting his next move.

Don Rubino lit a cigar and nodded. "Yeah, he is," he said, chewing on the nub of the cigar. "So be ready. They plan to make it look like a robbery." He pointed the cigar at him. "I like you, Omnio. You're a good kid. Your grandfather would cut my balls off if I let anything happen to you. I'm just thankful I caught wind of this before it was too late."

King sat silent, his face flush with anger. He'd known for years this was coming, that it was only a matter of time before Anthony tried to kill him again. It seemed the time had finally come. But considering the events of last weekend, the timing was obviously not a coincidence.

"I'm forever in your debt, Joe," he said, standing to extend a hand to the old don. "I know what I have to do."

Don Rubino ignored his hand and stepped around the desk to embrace him in a fatherly hug. "Be careful, kiddo. Take precautions. Keep plenty of muscle around. But whatever you do, don't retaliate. If you do, you'll only make matters worse. Anthony's got his button. You don't. And much as I can't stand the little fucker, his father is still the Boss. If you strike against Anthony, Leoni will rally the whole fuckin' *borgata* against you. Sure, you got a nice little crew who will fight for you, but a war against the whole Partnership is one you can't win. They'll hunt you down like a dog. Leoni would kill you, your *protettore* here, and everyone you love. But you do have an ace in the hole— your grandfather. Leoni and the others are still scared shitless of him. As they should be. Don Falcone still has quite a few loyal men on the street. His *protettore*, Alfonse Profaci, has strong ties to the New York Families. They would never openly sanction a hit on you because they know he'll be home in a few years. Trust me, his wrath is something they want no part of. That's why Anthony contracted the DiCarlo brothers. They have no ties or loyalties to any of the Families. But you kill those fuckers, Omnio. You may not be able to touch Anthony right now, but you can send him a message that you ain't going out that easy."


Ever since Anthony first attempt to have him killed, King had always made sure to keep himself well protected. His first line of defense, of course, was Vonni. But sometimes when he'd frequent public places, he would bring Tommy along as backup. He even had his cars bullet-proofed and equipped with sophisticated alarm systems to protect against car bombs. But now that he knew Anthony had once again contracted assassins to kill him, he took even more precautions. Starting with an around-the-clock security detail led by Gino Mianchette, his chief street enforcer.

But a week went by and the DiCarlo brothers made no attempt to contact him. Then two weeks. Eventually, after three weeks, King figured Anthony must have called the hit off. So, with no need to have a small army hanging around him all the time, he reduced his security detail down to just Vonni and Tommy. This was when the DiCarlo brothers decided to finally make their appearance.

Early one Monday morning, King was at Vanzetti's in his upstairs office when Tommy stuck his head in the door to tell him that Bruno and Mario DiCarlo were downstairs asking to see him. It seemed they had picked an opportune moment to pay him a surprise visit. Not only was it just him, Tommy, and Vonni at the club, but he was in the middle of counting thousands of

485

dollars from the weekend take. But he was ready. Vonni and Tommy had already been briefed on what to do next.

Vonni greeted the DiCarlo brothers at the front door like any of the other visitors who dropped by to see King each day. He was friendly, cordial, and asked what their business was. Bruno "The Hammer" explained quite convincingly that he and his brother were there to see King about a business proposal. Vonni simply nodded and sent Tommy to tell King they were there. He then politely escorted them down to club's basement office, where King held his most private meetings. But as he led them through the clutter—stacked cases of liquor, kegs, and piles of discarded promotional materials—he did not fail to notice the slight bulges under their shirts at the small of their backs.

"King's upstairs finishing payroll," he said, opening the door to the office, motioning them inside. "He'll be down as soon as he's finished. Shouldn't be more than a few minutes." He offered them a friendly smile. "Can I get you guys anything? The kitchen's closed but I can get you a drink."

"Nah, we're good, kid," said Bruno, dropping his immense bulk onto a leather sofa. "It's too fuckin' early to be drinkin'."

"I'll take an ice water," Mario said, his face glistening with sweat. "It's hot as balls out there today."

"No problem, paisan," Vonni said, offing him another benign smile. "Make yourselves comfortable and I'll be right back."

The instant he stepped from the room, Tommy burst in wielding a sawed-off shotgun. *"Don't move, motherfuckers!"* he barked, aiming the menacing twelve-gauge at Bruno's head.

"Yo what the fuck is this?" Bruno demanded, his face twisted into a pug-ugly mask of outrage. "You know who the fuck I am, kid?"

"Shut up and don't move," Tommy growled. "If you do, I'll blow your fat fuckin' head off."

Vonni casually strode back into the room carrying a Colt 1911 automatic. "Gentlemen," he said, gesturing towards Tommy, "I would take my paisan here very seriously. He has

486

orders to shoot you even if he thinks you might move. And he's very good with that *lupara* of his."

Mario gave him a confused look. "What the hell is going on, kid?"

"First of all, I ain't no fuckin' kid," Vonni answered coldly, aiming his pistol at him. "Second, my advice is shut the fuck up and don't move. Now... I'll be needing your burners." He then stepped over and relieved both brothers of the pistols they had discreetly tucked under their shirts.

"You're fucking up, kid," Bruno growled, sneered up at him. "Do you even know who we are?"

Vonni smashed the side of his pistol into his head. "I just told you, asshole, I ain't no kid!" he said, aiming his pistol at Bruno's face. "And yeah, we know exactly who you are. We also know why you're here. So this will be the last time I tell you: Sit there and shut the fuck up. If you move, I'll blow that fuckin' pea brain of yours across the floor. *Capisce*?"

Bruno's beady eyes were suddenly burning with rage. "I don't know what the fuck is going on, kid, but you're digging yourself a big hole," he said, rubbing the side of his head, where a lump was already leaking blood.

Vonni examined Bruno's pistol, a Colt .380 with Parker-Hale sound suppressor. "Nice piece," he said, looking genuinely impressed. "But what's with the silencer? You always carry a silenced piece to business meetings?"

"Actually, I do," Bruno replied, looking at the blood on his hand, his cockiness was clearly wavering.

"Yeah, sure you do, pal," Vonni chuckled, then stood by the door and waited.

Five minutes later, King stepped into the room carrying a ball-peen hammer. "Gentlemen!" he said, flashing a smile at the DiCarlo brothers. "So glad you finally made it. We were beginning to wonder if you would ever show up."

Bruno glared up at him, feigning confusion. "Uh, King, I think there's been some kind of misunderstanding. I'm just here

487

to see if you wanted in on a couple of peep show joints I'm opening over on Outer Drive and 7 Mile. You got a couple afterhours joints over there, so I figured you—"

King held up a hand and cut him off. "Did you really think you could just walk in here and take me out that easy? Are you really that stupid? But of course you are. You actually believed Anthony would give you my afterhours operation if you took me out. You're too stupid to even realize he was planning to kill you after you finished the job." He chuckled and shook his head. "Fucking *gavone*. But hey, at least he would have killed you quickly. Me? I'm not such a nice guy."

Both brothers suddenly looked stricken with terror. "Listen, King," Bruno said, glancing at his brother. "We have no idea what the fuck you're talking about. I don't know where you're getting your information, but I'm only here to see if you want to make a little money together. That's all. I heard you're always looking to make an extra buck. Well, me too. I even worked for your grandfather a couple times over the years. He was always good to me. I don't know what you heard, but I would never come here to whack you. That's crazy, man. *Pazzo!*"

King stared at him for a long moment, as if in he might actually believe him, and then motioned to Vonni. "Shoot these fuckers," he ordered coldly. "But not in the head. It makes too much of a mess. Lung shots. Two apiece."

Both brothers began pleading for their lives, but their pleas fell on deaf ears. Vonni raised Bruno's silenced .380 and fired four shots in quick succession. Two into Bruno's chest, two in Mario's chest. Their eyes went wide with shock and they crumpled to the floor, choking on their own blood. It took a while before they finally expired, but after several minutes both of them lay still, eyes wide open, blank stares looking at the ceiling,

"Get Billy on the phone," King said, staring at their lifeless bodies with contempt. "Tell him to get down here with a van. We're gonna send Anthony a little message..."

The following morning, just as the sun was coming up, a fisherman was heading out for a day of angling when he saw two bodies floating face down in the marina behind Leoni's nightclub. When the police arrived, they found both bodies naked and had their own genitalia stuffed in their mouths. Projecting from Bruno's anus was a ball-peen hammer.

Later that day, when the local media caught wind of this gruesome double murder, the Detroit Free Press featured a front-page article about how the bodies were found floating behind the nightclub of an alleged mob boss, citing that such gangland violence harkened back to the city's legendary Purple Gang of the 1930's.

Leoni was livid when he learned that Anthony had contracted the DiCarlo brothers to kill King. But he was even more enraged by King's disrespectful act of dumping the bodies behind his club. And he wasn't the only one pissed off. When the Commission Bosses caught wind of it, they were not happy. With the casinos pouring in millions, they could not afford any extra attention on the Syndicate. Not when the Feds were already monitoring the Families so closely, which was why they decided to intervene before a full-scale war erupted between King and Anthony.

# CHAPTER 27

King heeded Don Rubino's advice and refrained from retaliating against Anthony directly, but dumping the mutilated bodies of the DiCarlo brothers behind his father's club was his way of sending both Anthony and Leoni a message. He figured if they wanted to go to war over it, so be it. He was ready. He refused to stand by and let Anthony keep trying to kill him. He was tired of Leoni exploiting him simply because he wasn't pure Sicilian. He decided it was finally time he took a stand and showed them he would no longer let them bully him around. *Difetto* or not, he was still a Falcone, grandson of Don Falcone. He deserved respect, and he'd fight for it if he had to.

Dumping the bodies of the DiCarlo brothers behind Leoni's club was King's first open act of defiance against Anthony and Leoni. Next, he refused to meet with either of them when they called him in for a sit-down. But the straw that broke the proverbial camel's back was when he sent word that he refused to continue paying Leoni's weekly tribute.

This was when Leoni decided he no longer had a use for his cocky nephew. Unfortunately, he knew he couldn't just kill him. As much as he wanted to, he still had to consider Don Falcone. If he found out he killed King, his father-in-law would declare war on him the instant he stepped out of prison. He knew Don Falcone still had plenty of loyalists in the Syndicate, including most of the bosses and their many *capidecina*, which was why he needed the Commission to sanction the hit themselves. That way, the blame would be on them, not him. So, he met with several of the senior Commission members during one of their regular summits in Fort Lauderdale, Florida, where they gathered several times a year to discuss Cosa Nostra business. During this meeting, he painted King out to be a dangerous rogue who was bringing too much heat on the Syndicate, which could threaten their interests in the casinos. He was certain they would sanction a hit on him. After all, he was a nobody *difetto* who hadn't even taken the oath. But to his surprise, they refused to sanction a hit on him. They were Old World Sicilians, many of whom had known Don Falcone most of their lives. One of them, Don Piatro Cadatto of New York's Gambino Family, even knew the don from their childhood days back in Sicily. They all respected him deeply, and knew King was the last male of his bloodline. So even though they knew something had to be done about King's blatant disregard for Leoni's authority, they refused to sanction a hit on him. Mostly because they knew Don Falcone would come home from prison and declare war on anyone and everyone he even suspected was involved. That would bring far too much attention on the Syndicate—attention they could not afford. Not with the Detroit casinos bringing in so much money.

Yet Leoni was still able to convince them that something had to be done before King stirred up more trouble, trouble that would attract more attention from the Feds. With the casinos pouring in millions, they could not afford to have the Feds investigating a Mafia war in Detroit. So it was agreed that King had to go, but there were other ways to get rid of him than killing him.


A month after the DiCarlo brothers were found floating behind Leoni's club, local police swarmed all over King's crew, raiding their homes and places of business, arresting them on charges that ranged from extortion to murder. But this was only the beginning. Because of the amount of drugs and guns found during these raids, the local police passed jurisdiction over to the FBI's drug unit. Nearly two dozen members of King's crew were charged with, among other things, the dreaded RICO Act. But because he had always taken extreme care to make sure he was far removed from anyone actually committing crimes, he was initially able to avoid arrest during this blitz roundup.

Unfortunately, a number of his street soldiers were black and Latino gang members who had no true loyalties to him. Even though he had warned them of the consequences of betrayal, thoughts of spending decades in prison trumped their thoughts of those consequences. When several of them were offered immunity in exchange for their testimony against him, they agreed. Immune from prosecution, they admitted to committing numerous crimes on his orders, claiming that he was the ringleader of a citywide criminal organization that was involved in everything from drugs to extortion. But they were smart enough to avoid implementing anyone in the Syndicate, swearing in their depositions that they had no knowledge of an Italian Mafia in Detroit.

Of course, it was all facilitated by Leoni and the Commission. The Fed's involvement was by design, and every arrest was also by design. By having the local police pass jurisdiction off to the FBI, the Commission strengthened their relationship with them, securing future favors. In a sense, King was an olive branch, a sacrificial lamb. The Commission got rid of him without having to kill him, Leoni got rid of most of King's faithful followers, and in the process, they strengthened relations with their friends in the FBI. It was a win-win for everyone.

King was arrested and charged with RICO—maintaining a Racketeering Influenced Criminal Organization—as well as a litany of other crimes, including conspiracy to distribute narcotics, felony firearms, and tax evasion. To ensure he couldn't post bail and flee prosecution, a federal magistrate slapped him with a ten-million-dollar cash bond. And because his last name was synonymous with his grandfather, the local media quickly latched onto the story, making him out to be one of the Syndicate's major players. This did not sit well with the Commission. The whole purpose of arranging his arrest was to ensure the Syndicate maintained its usual low profile. But his headline-making arrest ended up having the exact opposite effect. So they quickly called upon their associates in the FBI to deflate these allegations. Two days after King's arrest, the FBI released a public statement, claiming King had been working independently and had no suspected ties to any organized crime organizations, including the Italian Mafia.

The one person surprised to be left out of the federal roundup was Vonni. He didn't know that King had already made a contingency plan to protect him in case of such an event. The day after the incident with the DiCarlo brothers, he called Pamela and insisted that she make her feelings for Vonni known to her father. And Pamela knew why. Her father may not approve of Vonni, but he wouldn't harm him if he knew she was in love with him. Admitting she loved him was her only way to save him, and it worked. When the Feds swarmed in on King and his crew, Leoni made sure Vonni was not implemented in any of the crimes they were charged with.

It wasn't until the day of King's arrest that Vonni learned of Pamela's confession to her father. That night, while King sat in a federal bullpen, she paid Vonni a visit and explained that King had asked that she make her father privy to their relationship. But there was one more thing King had insisted. She had to also tell her father that she and Vonni were engaged to get married. Though Vonni never asked her to marry him, he understood why King insisted on this. It was to protect him. But he didn't mind one bit. The truth was, he had dreamed of proposing to her for years. He just wasn't expecting it to be so soon, or under such mitigating circumstances. But he was very much in love with her. She was everything he could ever want in a woman—beautiful, smart, ambitious, independent, witty and funny. But most of all, she loved and accepted him for who he was. A Mafioso. How could she not? After all, she was a Mafia princess herself.

Though Leoni was not happy to learn of Pamela's relationship with Vonni, he could tell she was genuinely in love with him. Being that she was his only daughter, nothing was more important to him than seeing her happy. So, as much as he disapproved of him, he accepted Vonni and even offered to pay for their wedding.


Vonni was relieved he had somehow avoided arrest, and excited that he would soon be married to Pamela, but he was far from happy. In fact, he was miserable. With King facing several life sentences in prison and their entire operation dismantled, he suddenly found himself lost and alone. For the first time since becoming King's *protettore,* he had no idea what his next move should be. With his life in complete limbo, all he could do was wait out King's trial and hope the charges would somehow get dismissed or reduced. But deep down he knew this was never going to happen. King had some of the best criminal defense attorneys in town, but even they knew the prosecution's case was just too strong. There was too much evidence against him, too many witnesses prepared to testify. And the Syndicate bosses were giving him no help. They could have used their resources and connections to make most of the charges go away, but they stood by and did nothing. That made it obvious to Vonni that they wanted to get rid of King once and for all. And that's exactly what they did.

King's trial was short compared to Don Falcon's lengthy, six-week trial. His trial proceedings only lasted three days, during which the prosecution grilled five black and Latino street gang members who had worked for him. In exchange for immunity, they testified that he was the sole leader of a criminal network that was involved in everything from drugs to extortion, and spanned across the entire city of Detroit. His lawyers tried to discredit these cooperating witnesses by claiming they were simply implementing King as a means to cover up their own criminal exploits. Unfortunately, each of these witnesses recounted in great detail how King led them in every aspect of their various criminal enterprises. The jury believed them. After three days of testimony, and over 200 evidentiary exhibits, it took them less than two hours to find him guilty on nearly all charges.

A month later, he was sentenced to 75 years to life in federal prison. Vonni was devastated. At that moment, his whole world came crashing down. Their entire operation had been compromised. All their legitimate businesses had been seized by the government or annexed into the Gianolla Family by Leoni and Anthony. Their crew was gone. He was now all alone, completely on his own. All he had left was a few hundred-thousand dollars stashed in his apartment. Since he had nothing else to do with it, he figured he might as well use it to open a legitimate business. Or maybe start a crew of his own. But whatever he did, his life changed forever the instant that judge dropped his gavel and sentenced King to 75 years in prison.

When Don Falcone learned of King's fate, he was wracked with heartbreak and despair. He knew if King died in prison, so would his family name. All was lost. He had failed his ancestors. He would die dishonored.

But then, one day while in his prison cell watching TV, he happened across a presidential address and was reminded of a favor he had kept on the books for nearly a half a century. And the man who owned it to him could very well save his bloodline from extinction.

# CHAPTER 28

Not long after King was sent to prison, Vonni married Pamela in a small ceremony at St. Ambros church. But with nothing left for him in Detroit, he moved in with her while she attended medical school at the University of Michigan. Eventually, they rented a modest home in Plymouth, Michigan, a few miles from Pamela's campus. He got a job managing a local nightclub and settled into a life of domestic mediocracy. But he soon found that he hated the domestic life. It was boring and mundane. He missed action. He missed fast money. He missed King.

As the months dragged into years, he often found himself feeling bored and yearning for his old high-octane lifestyle—the lifestyle of a Mafioso. He missed being part of something. He missed being a someone. But what he missed most was the respect people had once given him. It was all gone now. He was just another average Joe, living in a little college town, where nobody knew his name or cared who he once was. And he hated every minute of it.

Pamela was aware of his unhappiness, but there was nothing she could do about it. At least not until she graduated from medical school. But every time she looked at him, she felt a pang of guilt knowing that it was her own father who had destroyed his life. Compounding her guilt was the fact that they barely even saw each other. With her attending classes by day, and him managing the club by night, sometimes entire days would go by without them having a single conversation.

But as disconnected as they were, Vonni was still very much in love with her. He was proud to have her as his wife and honored to be her husband. She wasn't the problem. It was their boring domestic life he couldn't stand. He hated feeling like a nobody. He hated having no money in his pocket. Most of all, he hated how the college kids who frequented his club looked at him like he was nothing. Sometimes he wanted to teach them a lesson. Maybe slap them around a little as a reminder that just because they went to college, it didn't make them better than him. King was the only thing that kept him from dragging one of them into an alley to show them who he really was. He stayed in regular contact with him via letters and phone calls, and King was constantly reminding him to control his temper, stay out of trouble, and keep Leoni appeased until he found a way to get home.


Pamela eventually graduated from medical school at the top of her class, with a doctorate in pediatric medicine. As a graduation gift, her father gave her and Vonni a respectable home in Grosse Pointe, only a few miles from his own Grosse Pointe home. Shortly after they moved in, she landed a position at nearby Bon Secours Hospital. But Leoni couldn't have his only son-in-law doing nothing, so he put Vonni to work managing a seedy little strip club called "Duchess," which was owned by a member of Anthony's crew. Located off 7 Mile Road in one of the city's most notorious eastside ghettos, the place was a dive. The position didn't pay much, but he was allowed to supplement his income by hosting regular poker games in the basement. Of course, Anthony took half the cut from these games. But at least it was work that Vonni enjoyed. It gave him back a little of his dignity. Being an extension of Anthony's crew at least afforded him some status on the street. Working at Duchess also brought him in regular contact with wiseguys from all the Families and their respective crews. Some even remembered him from his days as King's *protettore*, and showed him a little extra respect because of it.

Even though managing Duchess was far better than catering to drunken college kids every night, he still missed the good old days when he and King ran around the city like they owned it. He missed the respect and fast money, but most of all he just missed King, his *capo* and best friend. He couldn't stand Leoni and hated being one of Anthony's lackeys. They only treated him with a modicum of respect out of love for Pamela. He knew they considered him a parasitic *difetto*. But he was a parasitic *difetto* who had married Pamela, and not for one minute did he forget that she was the only reason he wasn't in prison or dead.


As King rotted in prison and Vonni managed one of Anthony's strip clubs, trouble was brewing in the Syndicate. And it all stemmed from the casinos. Some of the Syndicate *capi* had invested millions into the casinos, yet Leoni was keeping the lion's share of the skims and accompanying rackets for himself, claiming that as Boss, he was entitled to it. The other *capi* disagreed, but knew better than to confront him about it. They were fully aware of his delusions of grandeur, that in his mind he somehow saw himself as beyond reproach and would likely kill anyone who dared defy him.

But the Syndicate Bosses weren't the only ones disillusioned with Leoni. The frontmen who owned the casinos were growing tired of Leoni's erratic behavior. Though they knew part of the deal was to let the Syndicate skim untaxed dollars from the count rooms, he was becoming excessive. He wasn't even trying to be discreet. The deal was supposed to entail hand-selected managers collecting the skims, and then delivering them to Leoni's intermediaries off the premises. But he had decided that he wanted to personally collect the skims. Whenever he felt inclined, he'd simply walk into the casinos, order the managers to open the count rooms, and remove several hundred thousand dollars for himself, as if the casinos were his own personal bank vaults.

Yet this was only the beginning of Leoni's unpredictable behavior. Sometimes he would walk around the casinos acting like he actually owned them, handing out gambling markers to friends, welcoming people to "his place," comping tabs, ordering around managers and pit bosses, and berating them in front of guests. His arrogance had no end, and his power-tripping ego seemed to be consuming his mind. He was wracked with paranoia and began suspecting the other *capi* were plotting against him. He even had several of his own guys killed when he thought they were conspiring with the other Bosses to kill him. Though he seemed relatively capable in the Commission's eyes, anyone who had regular interactions with him could see the pressures of being the Boss were affecting his mental stability. But, of course, nobody dared confront him about it. If they did, they knew it might very well be the end of them. Because if there was one thing Leoni still was, it was merciless.

While Vonni settled into his life as one of Anthony's minor minions, he still tried to maintain discreet relationships with some of the guys from the old crew—Joey, Victor, Gino, Billy, Georgio, even Jimmy and Carlo—most of whom now worked for the Anthony and the Gianolla Family in some capacity. Whenever they dropped by Duchess to pay him a quick visit, they always expressed how much they hated working for Anthony and how much they missed working for King. They'd also relay the latest Syndicate gossip, which Vonni would in turn relay to King via letters. But because he knew King's correspondence was being monitored by prison faculty, he had to use a special system that involved mailing letters to King's associates in the prison. These associates would then forward the letters to King, allowing him and Vonni to discuss business without being directly in contact with each other. These cryptic letters were Vonni's only way of keeping King up to speed on all that was happening in the streets, and what was happening would soon play to King's advantage.

After seven years and nine months, Don Falcone was finally paroled from prison. The day he was released, the family gathered at his home to celebrate the occasion. It was an intimate affair, made up of only immediate family. Everyone was thrilled to have him home. His young grandchildren cheered with excitement the instant he stepped through the door. His daughters kissed him with tears in their eyes. Their husbands, all of whom were now Leoni's *capidecina*, welcomed him home with respectful embraces and envelopes of cash.

After everyone had a chance to personally welcome him home, they gathered in the dining room for dinner. But as they devoured Signora Falcone's feast, Vonni found himself thinking back to the first time he'd ever been there, the day he'd saved

King from two would-be assassins. Over twelve years had passed, yet it seemed like yesterday. Since then his life had gone full circle. He'd gone from a nobody, to part of a notorious crew making millions, and back to a nobody. He had seen and done things most people could never dream of. And as he now reflected on the road life had taken him, he found himself missing King more than ever. Without King, there was a huge void in his life, and there was nothing he could do to fill it.

As the evening wore on, Vonni found himself discreetly studying Don Falcone, just as he had done the first time they had met, all those years ago. Though the man was in his mid-seventies, he looked spritely and fit. Prison had obviously been good to him. He still had broad shoulders and the musculature of a much younger man. Though his hair was almost completely silver, he still had a full head of it, every strand neatly slicked with pomade. And of course, there were his eyes. They were just as dark and menacing as ever. But Vonni noticed something else in them whenever the don glanced in his direction. It was barely perceptible but there nonetheless. Pain. Regret. Sadness. And Vonni knew why. His very presence was a reminder that his beloved Omnio was still locked away in prison.

As everyone caught Don Falcone up to speed on the latest family affairs, Vonni also found himself watching Anthony and Contessa. Particularly how they interacted with their young son, Angelo. Shortly after King was sent to prison, Contessa married Anthony. Not long after that, she announced that she was pregnant. Over the years, Vonni saw them from time to time at family functions, and always found himself intrigued by little Angelo. He had watched him grow from an infant into a handsome little boy. But now, watching him interact with his other young cousins, Vonni was reminded of what could have been King's. If King had married Contessa, little Angelo would be his, not Anthony's. Unfortunately, fate had decided otherwise. It made Vonni despise Anthony that much more, though he did not hold it against Angelo. It wasn't the boy's fault that his father was a murderous megalomaniac who had tried to kill his own cousin simply out of jealousy. He was innocent. He was also quite impressive for a boy of four—handsome and well-mannered. Even though he looked more like his mother, it was obvious he was a Falcone, for his hair and eyes were black as onyx. Watching him dart around the room, playing with his cousins, a small part of Vonni was thankful that King wasn't there to see what could have been his.

After his release from prison, Don Falcone had a hard time adjusting to his new life of retirement. He wanted to do what he had always done—run his *Famiglia*. But because the FBI were surely monitoring his every move, the Commission had advised him to stay out of any Syndicate affairs. His *Famiglia* was Leoni's now. There were no more crews to run. No more operations. No *sotto capo*, no *capiregime*, no *capidecina*, nobody. Nothing. He couldn't even run a simple sports book, the one thing from his past that had brought him so much joy. He'd been completely stripped of his identity, and the reality of this was hard to deal with. He was a man who had spent his entire life working, building his Family and the Detroit Partnership into one of the most powerful and lucrative Mafia Syndicates in the country. And yet now he had no choice but to leave it all behind.

Worst of all, Omnio was still locked away in prison, and Don Falcone knew it was Leoni's fault. Every fiber of his being wanted to kill Leoni. But he couldn't. The Commission had spoken. Too many people had money invested in the casinos. If he were to kill Leoni, a war between the other bosses could erupt over who would fill his shoes, which would surely rile up the Feds and draw far too much attention to the *borgata*.

Nevertheless, the dissension amongst the Syndicate bosses was growing. Some even expressed to Don Falcone their disapproval of how Leoni was lording himself over them and not giving them their fair share of the rackets. They were especially displeased with how he'd been cheating them out of their cut of the skims. They knew Don Falcone still had friends in the Commission and hoped he might take their grievances to them. Or even better, help them remove Leoni from power. Unfortunately, their grievances made no difference to the Commission bosses, all of whom were heavily invested in the casinos. They knew Leoni was feared by the Syndicate's other *capiregime,* and that was enough for them. With the casinos raking in millions, a war over who should be Detroit's Boss of Bosses was not an option.

What the Commission didn't realize, however, was just how unstable Leoni had become. Nor did they know he was cheating some of the other local bosses who had also invested in the casinos. They had no idea he'd become so paranoid that he had been strategically killing anyone he thought was conspiring against him. They had no idea that the Partnership Families were already plotting to remove him from power, with or without a green light from the Commission. Nor did they know Don Falcone was more than willing to help them.

The Commission, of which Don Falcone was still a member, acted much like Cosa Nostra's Board of Directors. Having been established in 1931 by Charles "Lucky" Luciano, it was designed to moderate disputes and see that all the country's Mafia families worked together as a whole, not against each other. But when it came to the regional politics and Family structure, the Commission only acted as a sort of advisory board. Although in the case of Detroit, because of the money they had invested in the casinos, they often tried to intercede in an attempt to keep the peace.

The Commission did, however, have connections to most of the Detroit Families through various relatives who had cross-family married, and they soon learned that Don Falcone had been reasserting his influence over the Syndicate. Some of the Commission *capi* began fearing that the one-time Detroit Boss of Bosses might even try having Leoni killed so he could resume

503

his place on the Syndicate throne, which they could not have. Not when the Feds were watching his every move. Plus, an unsanctioned hit on an acting Boss would likely incite a full-scale war between the Families. Some of the *capiregime* would surely rally behind Don Falcone, while others would side with Anthony out of fear. And if known Mafiosi started turning up dead all over town, an army of federal agents would converge on the city like a plague of locusts.

Fearing this scenario, several high-ranking members of the Commission had an informal sit-down to discuss how to handle Don Falcone. All agreed that something had to be done before he incited a war. Though killing him was an option, they all agreed it would be their last resort.

Most of the old Commission bosses had been friends with Don Falcone for years, even decades. They knew he was a man of honor and integrity. In the past, he had always respected their advisory input. So, before things escalated, they summoned him to New York for a face-to-face sit-down, where they intended to "advise" him one last time to stand down and stay out of Syndicate affairs. If he refused, then they would have no other choice but to kill him. There was just too much at stake to have him interfering. It was strictly business, nothing personal.

Fortunately for Commission bosses, before the sit-down could ever happen, they received a stroke of luck. For nearly four decades the FBI had been trying to pin Jimmy Hoffa's disappearance on the Mafia, and they finally caught their break when an old Syndicate associate named Vito Storing was arrested for possession of five kilos of heroin. In exchange for immunity and acceptance into the Federal Witness Protection Program, he did the unthinkable and offered to testify that not only had he helped Don Falcone extort Hoffa out of millions of Teamster dollars, but also that he had helped him dispose of Hoffa's body by grinding it into pig feed at a local slaughterhouse. Once again, Don Falcone was arrested and charged with a litany of crimes, including conspiracy to murder

James Hoffa. The evidence was all circumstantial hearsay, but if convicted he would spend the rest of his life in prison, and the Commission would no longer have to worry about him interfering with their interests in Detroit. It seemed the infamous "Butcher" had finally reached the end of his road.

At this point, King had been in prison nearly five years and had exhausted all his avenues for appeal. And with his grandfather likely headed back to prison for the rest of his life, he had finally come to terms with the fact he was never going home. So rather than rub salt in his wounds by hanging on to any hope, he decided to cut all ties with the outside world. He started by sending Vonni one last letter, in which he told his faithful *protettore* to forget about him, to go on with his life and always make sure to take care of Pamela. Vonni was devastated by this letter, and swore he would never give up on him. He wrote back and promised to do whenever it took to get him out, even if it meant bribing a Supreme Court judge. But King told him to save his money, that trying to bribe a Supreme Court judge was just too risky. In the end, Vonni knew he was right. Attempting to bribe a Supreme Court judge could very well backfire and end up landing him in prison, too. And prison was not at option for Vonni. Not now. Not when Pamela had just given birth to their first child, a beautiful baby boy they named Omnio.

Don Falcone was miserable. The days leading up to his trial were some of the darkest of his life. With the Feds monitoring him so closely, the entire Syndicate treated him like a leper. Of course, he couldn't blame them. He would have done the same in their shoes. But to make matters worse, his lawyers were sucking up all his money. Not even Leoni was helping him financially. And since the IRS had seized most of his money and assets before his last imprisonment, his only legal income was from Social Security and a paltry military pension. But money was the least of his problems. The stress of facing yet another long prison sentence was beginning to take its toll on his health. He was losing weight, and his stomach was giving him problems. He had ulcers and his doctors wanted to run tests, suspecting he had early stage prostate cancer. His old age was not turning out as he imagined. His tyrannical son-in-law was now the boss of his Family, a Family he had spent his entire life building on the principles of honor, integrity, and the sacred codes of Cosa Nostra. Yet Leoni was running it with little regard for honor, integrity, and those sacred codes. Worst of all, he had helped send Omnio, the last Falcone, to prison for the rest of his life.

But all was not lost, for no one was craftier than Don "The Butcher" Falcone. He had one last trick up his sleeve. Like he had always instilled in King, life was really just one big chess game. To win, you always had to think three moves ahead. It was how he had fought his way up from the streets to eventually seize control of the entire Syndicate. And the one strategic move that had made him so successful was maintaining strong relationships with powerful and influential men. They had been integral to his success and longevity. Over the years, he had developed a knack for knowing which ones were corruptible, and spent his life building relationships with them by delving out exorbitant bribes and endless favors. Keeping such powerful friends on his payroll had helped him ascend to the position of Boss of Bosses, and kept him there for over three decades. But Leoni had learned from him. One of the reasons the Commission had backed him was because he had compiled his own stable of corrupted politicians, police chiefs and government officials. Yet what nobody knew, not Leoni or even the Commission, was that Don Falcone had an old friend who was more powerful than all of their connections combined, a friend who owed him a favor that dated back nearly fifty years. And it was time to finally call it in.


One month before his trial, Don Falcone boarded an airliner bound for Key Largo, Florida, where he paid an unannounced visit to his old friend, Stanley Dunn. During this visit, he presented Stanley with his dying wish.

The following week, Stanley Dunn, retired Floridian Senator and father of the current United States President, was sitting on his terrace reading the back pages of USA Today, when he noticed a small article highlighting news from Detroit, Michigan. The headline read:


**REPUTED MOB BOSS, PETER "THE BUTCHER" FALCONE, DIES IN HOUSE FIRE. NO FOUL PLAY SUSPECTED.**


Stanley stared at the headline with disbelief. Of all things, his old friend had died in an accidental house fire. *How ironic,* he thought. *The man survives two years on the battlefields of South Korea, close to a decade in prison, over thirty years as the leader of the Detroit Mafia, even prostate cancer, just to just to end up dying in a house fire.*

But as he set the paper down, his mind began drifting through their years of friendship. They had been through so much together. Words could never express how much he owned the man. None of his family would even exist if it weren't for Peter Falcone. Not his son, not his grandchildren, not even he would be alive if it wasn't for "The Butcher." He owned the man more than his life. He owed him everything. And because of it, he planned to make sure his old friend received his dying wish. The last Falcone would not die in prison.

*To be continued…*

**To purchase Volume 2 of TO BE A KING, visit:**

www.amazon.com/author/gunnerlindbloom

**Enjoy a sneak preview of Chapter 1 from TO BE A KING, Volume 2:**

# <u>CHAPTER 1</u>

DETROIT, BASEMENT OF DUCHESS
GENTLEMEN'S CLUB, THE DAY AFTER KING'S
RELEASE FROM PRISON

With tears in his eyes, King stepped back from their embrace and looked Vonni over. He was surprised by how little his faithful *protettore* had changed over the last eight years. Even at age 32 he still had the boyish good looks of his youth. And though he was only the manager of a seedy strip club in the ghetto, he looked like a Wall Street executive in his tailored black suit. It made King's heart swell with love just to look at him. Giovanni. "Johnny New York." The one man he knew he could always trust. For weeks now he'd known this day was coming, yet he had not expected to feel such an overwhelming sense of emotion. He had truly been reunited with his long-lost brother.

But he wasn't the only one feeling overwhelmed with emotion. Vonni was feeling the same as he looked King. Although, his beloved *capo* had very much changed in appearance. He now had the hardened good looks of a mature man. Years of heavy weight lifting had transformed his physique into a chiseled mass of muscle, with huge shoulders and arms bulging from under his suit. There were a few random grays at his temples, but they only seemed to accentuate his good looks. And though his dark irises were just as menacing as ever, his eyes were aglow with a level of intensity that Vonni had never seen before.

"Let me guess," Vonni said, gesturing towards his suit, "Jimmy Smith?"

"Of course," King said, adjusting his cuffs. "This one's off-the-rack, but good ol' Jimmy is having five more tailored for me as we speak."

Vonni had a thousand questions he wanted to ask, but they would have to wait for a more private setting. "So who's this lovely little lady?" he asked, offering Madonna a smile.

"My new accountant," King said matter-of-factly, glancing down at her. "Madonna, meet Giovanni Battaglia. He's the closest thing I've ever had to a brother."

509

"An accountant, eh?" Vonni said, looking incredulous. "I had no idea they came so beautiful... I would've gotten myself one a long time ago."

She appreciated the compliment but was a little unnerved by how he was looking at her, as if she were an enemy spy who had just infiltrated his lair. He was different from the other men they had visited today. For starters, he had an accent. New York, she guessed. And unlike everyone else King had introduced her to, he did not seem at all intimidated by him. There was no fear or nervousness in his eyes. Only genuine love and excitement. It made her wonder who he was and why he would be so suspicious of her.

"Thank you, Mr. Battaglia," she said politely. "That's very sweet of you. But I'll have you know, not all accountants are frumpy old women or balding men with glasses. We come in all shapes and sizes."

"So I see," Vonni said, offering her another smile, his reservations about her slowly evaporating. "But please, call me Vonni. The only people who ever call me mister are judges and lawyers."

"So..." she said, glancing at King. "I'm guessing the two of you have been friends for a long time?"

King offered him a grin. "He's been my *protettore* since we were, what, seventeen?"

"You were eighteen," Vonni corrected. "I was seventeen."

She looked at King, confused. "What's a pro... a pro-tett-ore? How do you say it?"

"*Protettore*," King said, forcing back a laugh. "It's Sicilian for, well, something like a bodyguard."

She looked at Vonni, still confused. He was a bit stocky but didn't look anything like a bodyguard. And King definitely did not look like he needed one. In fact, he looked like he could be a professional bodyguard himself. But she knew from working at the Players Gentlemen's Club that most bigshot Mafiosi were often escorted by at least one bodyguard, which she always

510

figured was more for show than anything. But now she was beginning to think that they actually had them for a reason.

"So, Madonna," Vonni said, glancing at King, "how is it that you know my paisan here?"

"I… well…" she began, but glanced up at King, unsure if she should tell the truth.

"I met her at Sal's place last night," King answered for her. "There I was, in the middle of eating my dinner, when suddenly out of a glowing shroud of mist she appeared like an angel from heaven."

"Wow, really?" she giggled, rolling her eyes. "I don't remember it being so dramatic."

King shrugged and looked at Vonni. "Okay, maybe there wasn't a shroud of mist. But I thought she was a cutie so I invited her over to have a drink with me. When she told me she was studying to be a CPA, I offered her a job."

"Aren't you forgetting something?" she said, giving him a look. "Like the part where you told my boss I quit before you even offered me the job."

"Well," he said, smiling at Vonni. "I figured she could make more money working for us without taking her clothes off."

"Us?" Vonni asked.

"Yes, of course, us. Who else is going to be my partner?"

Vonni suddenly felt a rush of excitement. The look in King's eyes, the inflection in his voice, told him what he was hoping to hear—his boss was planning to put the crew back together. It was the best news he had heard in nearly a decade.

"Well, partner…" Vonni said, gesturing towards one of the leather sofas in his office. "Sit down and make yourself at home. You know I'm not much of a drinker, but if there was ever an occasion to celebrate with a drink, this is it. And you'll stay for dinner. I got a decent chef up there. Old dago named Tony Cuirillo. Learned to cook behind the walls of Jackson. Did a dime for manslaughter back in the eighties. When I hired him, I taught him how to cook Sicilian style. He's good. I'll have him whip you up anything you want." He gave him a knowing look. "But let me guess: Steak Siciliano, medium, with a side of pasta? And don't worry, I make sure he always adds sugar to the *sugo*."

"Perfect," King laughed. "You know me so well, *amico mio.*"

"Patrón, *el padrone*?" Vonni offered, holding up the expensive bottle of tequila.

King plopped down on the sofa. "I'll take mine on the rocks," he said, gesturing towards Madonna. "But water hers down. She's driving."

"No thanks," she said, sitting down next to him. "Not a fan of tequila. But I'll take a glass of champagne if you have some."

Vonni opened a small refrigerator and removed a chilled bottle of Louis Roederer Cristal champagne. "Will this do?"

"Yummy!" she answered excitedly, recognizing the $250 bottle of champagne. "Cristal is my favorite!"

While Vonni poured their drinks, King sat back and took in his surroundings. It seemed the room was more of a lounge than an office. Though it was dimly lit, there was enough light to see its opulent decor. The polished wood floors were covered with ornate rugs. A marble-topped bar was stocked with high-end liquors. A huge mahogany desk looked like it belonged to a Fortune 500 CEO. Behind the desk was large a bank of security monitors streaming live footage of nearly every inch of the property. A series of framed photos of beautiful nude women adorned the walls. In the center of the room was a baize-topped poker table that was cluttered with playing cards, half-empty drinks, and ashtrays, some of which still had cigars smoldering in them. But the room's most impressive feature was a life-sized marble statue of an ancient Spartan warrior. Nearly naked and clutching a sword, it stood behind the poker table, poised for attack. King found the irony of what it represented to be comical in such a pretentious setting.

Vonni handed them their drinks and offered King a cigar. "Havana? I've been holding onto them for a special occasion."

King looked at the cigar suspiciously. "Havanas, eh? Let me guess, rolled on the laps of Cuban virgins?"

"Yes," Vonni answered, flashing him a smile. "How did you know?"

King raised an eyebrow. "Call it a hunch," he said, and then turned to Madonna. "Honey, would you be a sweetheart and wait for us upstairs? I need to have a private word with my paisan."

"I'll have a table readied for you," Vonni offered, snatching the phone off his desk. "Order whatever you like. On the house, of course."

When she hesitated, King patted her knee reassuringly. "Don't worry, doll. We'll only be a few minutes. When we're finished, we'll come up and join you for dinner."

"Alright," she said, standing to leave. "But don't take too long. Some of those girls up there looked pretty scary."

"I'm sure they don't bite," King chuckled, glancing at Vonni. "Just give us a few minutes. Order us some appetizers. Maybe some shrimp cocktail stuffed mushrooms. Yes, I could go for some shrimp and stuffed mushrooms. It's been a good two weeks since I had some fresh shrimp."

She gave him a confused look. "But you just got out of prison two days ago. You mean to tell me that they fed you guys shrimp in prison?"

He shot Vonni a look. "Oh, not everyone ate shrimp. Only some of us."

She knew she was missing something but decided to let them have their private time. "Well, I'll order you some shrimp cocktails and stuffed mushrooms. But please don't leave me up there alone too long."

"Ten minutes," he assured her. "That's all we need."

When she stepped from the office, Vonni locked the door so they couldn't be interrupted. "Spunky little thing. Looks a lot like—"

"I know who she looks like," King said, holding up a hand. "Purely coincidental. She just happened to catch my eye last night. Turns out she's actually got a head on her shoulders."

Vonni realized he had struck a nerve and quickly changed the subject. "So..." he said, dropping onto the sofa directly opposite him. "Goddamn, brother, you're really home. I feel like I'm dreaming or something. I can't believe that old fuckin' Senator really pulled it off. A presidential pardon!"

"Believe it," King said, taking a sip of his drink. "But I owe it to my grandfather. He saved that old Senator's life back in Korea. It was the least the guy could do."

Vonni tipped his drink to him. "To Don Falcone. He was a great man."

King tipped his glass to him and drank to the memory of his grandfather. "Indeed he was," he said, reminded of an old Henry Wadsworth Longfellow poem he'd once read:

*Lives of great men all remind us,*
*We can make our lives sublime,*
*And, departing, leave behind us*
*Footprints on the sands of time;*
*Footprints, that perhaps another,*
*Sailing o'er life's solemn main,*
*A forlorn and shipwrecked brother,*
*Seeing, shall take heart again.*

"Shit, man!" Vonni said, no longer able to contain himself. "You have no idea how much I've missed you."

"Oh, I think I do," King said, smiling at him affectionately. "Not a single day has gone by that I haven't thought about you."

"Eight fuckin' years," Vonni said, staring at him with genuine love. "It sure seems longer. I mean, so much has changed since you left. The Syndicate's all fucked up. Leoni's losing it. *Pazzo* for real! I'm not in the loop, of course, but I've heard rumors."

"Yeah?" King asked, savoring another sip of the expensive tequila. "What kind of rumors?"

514

"Well, for starters, some of the Families want Leoni out. He's made a lot of enemies over the years. I even heard Rubino and Toccio are ready to go to war with him. I guess he's killed a couple of their guys. Top guys, too. One was Johnny Jarjosa Junior. Remember him? He owned half the strip clubs in town and was a big earner for Dominic Fats Carazzo. Old man Fats knows Leoni had Jarjosa killed so he could take over all those strip clubs. That's how Leoni does it. He just whacks guys and claims their shit as his own. But I hear Fats wants his head on a platter over this Jarjosa business. I even heard Carzzo's kid, Big Paulie, killed Rafael Quassarani to even the score. And you know old Quasimodo was one of Leoni's top earners. Now all the Families are picking sides. A few guys have turned up missing. I'm guessing they got the business too. It's been crazy the last year or so. Even I've been watching my back. I'm telling ya, man, there's gonna be a war if Leoni doesn't tighten up ship."

King sat back and let this all sink in. Dominic "Fats" Carazzo was a stumpy little bespectacled mobster high on self-worth and low on morals. His primary means of income were escort services, strip clubs, and high-end prostitution. They were rackets King had sometimes been involved in, but usually tried to steer clear of. Even though he knew almost all the Families were involved in these rackets to some degree, he had never approved of exploiting women for profit. And he had not been afraid to voice this to Fats Carazzo before he'd gone to prison, which was why Carazzo had never been a fan of his and had always regarded him with such disdain. But as he now considered how they were posturing for war with Leoni, he was reminded of an old maxim his grandfather had taught him: *An enemy of your enemy is your friend*. Which was why he now made a mental note to pay Fats Carazzo a visit.

"Junior Jarjosa, eh?" King said, imagining the potential repercussions Leoni would face if the Commission knew he was whacking Made guys just to take over their operations.

"Yeah, and he ain't the only one. Remember Vinny Arpicci? Well, him and his half-brother, Paul Riggio, were moving pounds out of their dad's garage over there on Mack. Big weight. I'm talking hundreds of pounds. I guess they were getting it from some Lebanese cat who owned the pizza joint next door. And they were making big money until Anthony found out they weren't cutting him in. Cops found them double-tapped in some abandoned house. Down in the ghetto. Arpicci's other brother, Dennis, was so scared he took off to Arizona and has been hiding out there ever since. Not even his parents can find him. I'm telling you, Anthony is worse than Leoni. *Putana* rides around town on his high horse expecting everyone to bow to him like he's fuckin' King Kong. He gets drunk at the casinos and acts like he owns the fuckin' places. He bets on everyone's books but never pays. And who's gonna say somethin' to him? Nobody. They're all a bunch of spineless *cazzo*! A couple years back, he came here to play in one of my games and ended up shooting some *melanzani*."

"Why?" King asked, surprised his cousin had such a murderous streak.

"Because he thought the guy was marking cards," Vonni answered, making a gun with his fingers and aiming at the spot where it happened. "Bam! Shot him right the head. Right there at my fuckin' table. It took me months to get guys to come back in and sit down for a game. Cost me thousands."

King snatched up the guillotine cigar cutter that was lying next to a humidor on the coffee table. "Yeah, I heard Anthony has been getting out of control," he said, casually clipping the end of his cigar. "But it plays to our advantage."

Vonni produced a lighter from his pocket. "How so?" he asked, lighting the cigar.

King slowly puffed until the tip of the cigar was glowing red. "Well, first let me tell you about Jesup," he said, exhaling a cloud of smoke. "It's where I spent the last year. All the old bosses find a way to get transferred there because the weather is warm and

516

the whole place is on the take. I'm not exaggerating when I tell you there wasn't a single cop who wasn't dirty. We had everything in there. I'm talking the best food, booze, drugs, whatever a guy could want. Even women. I just happened to luck up and get transferred there about a year ago. I got tight with a bunch of old-time wiseguys from all over. Some had been locked up for decades—real shot-callers. Even a few guys who still run their Families from the inside. Guys who were on the Commission before they got locked up. Most of them knew my grandpa. A few even did time with him. One was a New York *caporegime* named Vittorio Salestro. A Colombo guy out of Brooklyn, your old stomping grounds. He's still got a couple years left on a twenty-year bit for murder, but before he got locked up he held a seat on the Commission. Right now, until he gets out, his son Gino is interim boss of the Columbo Family. But Gino keeps him in the loop. That's is how I heard about what's been happening up here."

"No shit?" Vonni said, leaning back on the sofa. "What a small world. I actually remember that name, Gino Salestro. I never met him, but I definitely heard of him. I never knew his old man was the fuckin' Boss, though. That's crazy. So, what else did the old man tell you about what's been happening up here?"

"A lot," King said, looking him in the eye. "He said the Bosses here are not happy with Leoni. Aside from his irrational behavior, I guess he's been double-dipping from the casino skims, not paying all the investors their due shares. Including some of the Commission *capi*. Even the casino owners are fed up and threatening to lock down the count rooms unless something is done about him. And from what I hear, because he's grown used to relying on the skims for most of his income, he's let his other operations slide. Don Salestro says his donations to the Corporate Fund have dropped in half over the last five years. He's also losing his grip on his political ties. I guess he stopped paying them because the casinos are making him enough money. He says he doesn't need their municipal

517

contracts anymore. But he's not the only one losing the municipal contracts. Without the city officials in his pocket, the rest of the Families are also losing their contracts. The mayor is just handing them out to his *melanzani* paisans… it's costing the rest of the Syndicate millions, some of which usually makes its way up to the Commission and The Corporate Fund. But this is the least of their concerns. What they're more worried about is the possibility of the Families banning together to take out Leoni. They know if this happens a war will erupt over who will replace him. That would bring way too much heat on the *borgata*. If the Feds start cracking down on the Families, the skims could be compromised altogether. So, Don Salestro told me they want something done about Leoni as soon as possible."

Vonni leaned forward with an incredulous look. "Wait, are you saying what I think you're saying?"

"Don Salestro liked me," King said, a conspiratorial glint in his eyes as he took a casual puff of his cigar. "We became very close over the last year. And before I was released he spoke to the some of the Round Table on my behalf. He personally vouched for me and my character. He even suggested to them I might be the one who can get things under control here in Detroit. So, thanks to his personal endorsement, I've been granted their protection. Leoni can no longer just bully me."

"Holy shit!" Vonni boomed, jumping to his feet. "Are you serious? The goddamn Commission wants you to take out Leoni?"

King held up a hand. "Whoa, slow down, killer. I didn't say that. They just think the other Families might respect me as a voice of reason because of who my grandfather was. But first I'll have to prove myself to them."

"Yeah?" Vonni asked, raising an eyebrow. "And how do you expect to do that?"

King shrugged. "You know how it works. Bring food to their tables. Money talks. If I want to win over the Syndicate *capi*, I'll have to put money in their pockets. But that's the easy part.

Once I earn their alliance, I'll make myself invaluable to them by manipulating the Commission however they see fit. That's how I'll prove I'm capable of being a Made *caporegime*. But we both know it's always about the money. And right now, Leoni is costing them a lot of it. The Commission, too. But if a war breaks out, they stand to lose a lot more. That's the only reason the Big Ten has left Leoni in place this long."

"So what first?" Vonni asked, returning to his seat, barely able to contain his excitement.

King took a pull from the cigar and exhaled several lazy smoke rings. "Oh, don't worry, paisan, I have a plan."

"Of course you do," Vonni chuckled, staring at him with genuine love. "Damn, man, I can't believe this shit. For a while there I really thought you'd given up."

King drained his drink and rattled the ice cubes around in his glass. "Now Giovanni, have you ever known me to give up on anything?"

"No, but when you told me to stop writing... Well, what was I supposed to think?"

"I had a reason for that. I was pretty sure the inspector at the prison was intercepting our letters. I think he figured out our system, because some of our go-betweens were saying your letters looked like they had been steamed open. I decided it would be safer for the both of us if nobody knew the president was giving me a pardon."

Vonni nodded his understanding. "I see your point. That's not the type of shit you want the Feds catching wind of. If they don't know about it, they can't appeal it."

"Exactly," King said, stepping over to the bar to refill his drink. "That's why presidents always wait until their last day in office before they hand out pardons. But forget that. I'm home now. Let's drink to the future."

Vonni tipped his drink to him. "To the future!" he toasted excitedly, looking around the room. "Because there definitely ain't no future in running this fuckin' shithole!"

519

King returned to the sofa and propped his feet up on the coffee table. "Vonni," he said, his voice suddenly somber and all business, "You have no idea how good it is to see you. We have so much to catch up on, but right now I need to know something..."

"What?"

"Money. How much do we have?"

Vonni quickly crunched some numbers in his head. "Well, like I told you in my letters, that investment broker you referred me to helped me establish a shell company based in Grand Cayman. Using a resident agent over there, we invested everything we had into a few solid stocks and mutual funds. The company made us some decent profits and managed to stay off the IRS radar."

King set his drink on the coffee table and looked him in the eye. "Vonni, you explained all of this in your letters. Don't be afraid to give me the number. I know you did your best."

Vonni took a sip of his drink and shrugged. "Just over two million," he said matter-of-factly.

King nodded, impressed. Eight years ago when he was sent to prison, he had left Vonni with just under a million dollars in cash. Since then, it seemed Vonni had more than doubled it. Unfortunately, they were going to need more. A lot more.

"Not bad, kid," he said, doing some quick math in his head. "It's a drop in the bucket compared to what we'll need but don't worry, we'll get more.

"And how do you plan to get it?"

"Don't you mean how do 'we' plan to get it?"

Vonni's face broke into a smile. "Oh yeah, of course. I just didn't know we were speaking French. *Oui oui, monsieur.*"

"Smart ass," King chuckled.

"I get it from you," Vonni said, tipping his glass to him. "Now tell me about how 'we' are going to get this money."

"Oh, I have a few ideas, but we'll have plenty of time to discuss them later." He pointed at the ceiling. "For now, why don't we go upstairs and join Madonna. I don't want to leave her up there by herself for too long. Like she said, some of those girls of yours did look pretty scary. No offense."

"None taken," Vonni laughed. "I'm fully aware of what kind of dump I run here. Shit, I'm scared of some of those girls myself."

King took in the room. "Yeah, well, it may be a dump up there but you sure did a nice job down here. Very *feng shui*." He gestured towards the marble Spartan warrior. "I'm diggin' Sparty over there."

"You like him?" Vonni said, regarding the sculpture with a touch of pride. "I scored him a few years back when one of Carlo's guys hit a big house in Grosse Pointe. I probably could've gotten ten grand for him, but thought he'd fit nicely down here."

"Well look at you," King chuckled, taking a sip of his drink. "Developing a taste for interior decorating in your old age."

"Thanks," Vonni said, matching his sarcasm. "It's become a bit of a hobby. I figured since I spend half my life down in this dungeon, I might as well spruce it up a bit. Helps me trick myself into forgetting what a shit hole I got upstairs."

"Yes, well, a lot of things are about to change," King said, getting his feet. "I predict your tenure here will soon be coming to an end."

"Meaning?"

"Later," King said, motioning towards the door. "Right now, you can catch me up to speed on everything over a few drinks and shrimp cocktails. We'll have plenty of time to talk shop later."

Vonni had a million questions running through his head, but knew King was right. They had plenty of time to discuss business. Tonight was a night to celebrate, to eat drink and catch up on lost years. But before they headed upstairs, he had to at least give him a little welcome home gift.

521

"Hold on," he said, peeling back one of the rugs on the floor, exposing a well-hidden safe. "I know you'll be needing some spending money." He then opened the safe and removed several packets of crisp $100 bills. "Here, take this. It's not much, but it's all I keep here in-house."

King took the cash and did a quick mental calculation. Five packets of $100 bills, $50,000 total. "Thanks, you know I love money," he said with a grin, citing Christopher Walken's famous line from the 1990 film, *King of New York.*

"Let me know if you need more. Tomorrow I'll call Billy and have him get you a new car. Anything in particular?"

King thought for a moment. "You know, I was thinking about changing things up. Maybe something German. So yeah... tell Billy to find me a nice 600 Class Mercedes. Black. Tinted. And tell him I want it fully bullet-proofed."

Vonni raised an eyebrow. "Bullet-proofed?"

"Yes, you can never be too careful. Because let's face it, paisan, we both know there's going to be people who aren't happy to see me home."

"Anthony?"

"He's at the top of the list."

"So, is there anything else you need me to do?"

"As a matter of fact, there is. Call the whole crew. Have them meet us here tomorrow night."

"What time?"

"Six. We'll make them dinner. I'm thinking *spiedini.*

"Is there any particular reason you want them here?"

"Yes, but I'll tell you when we're all together. For now, let's go upstairs and *mangia.* I'm starting to worry about Madonna up there. I feel like we might have tossed her to the wolves."


For the next two hours, they ate and drank and celebrated King's homecoming, entertaining Madonna with dozens of humorous anecdotes from their past. Of course, they didn't go into detail in front of her, but they also recounted many of their successful, as well as few of their not so successful, business exploits. They shared with her the story of how they first met, the day King had pulled Frankie Bommarito off Vonni in little Jackie's backyard. They talked of the many parties they had hosted at Club Vanzetti's, and their many travels. But what they talked about most was Don Falcone.

Madonna was captivated. With a room full of sleazy strippers performing lap dances in the shadows all around them, she listened with rapt attention as the two old friends spoke of men she had never heard off. Though they lost her from time to time when they spoke in Italian, she knew it was their way of keeping her from knowing what they were talking about. Nevertheless, she was intrigued by their interaction. She could tell they had a genuine love for each other. In fact, she had never seen two unrelated men share such a powerful sense of camaraderie. It was almost as if they could read each other's thoughts. Sometimes they even finished each other's sentences. And though they did not discuss their plans for the future, there was a certain glint in their eyes, a hint of excitement in their words, that told her that they had something big planned. It was almost as if they had a great secret they soon planned to make known to the world. She couldn't help but wonder what it was.

By the end of the night, both King and Vonni were fully drunk on alcohol and nostalgia. When Vonni walked him to the front door to see him off, he stood back and regarded him with tears in his eyes.

"Welcome home, *goombadi*," he said, his words slurred from the alcohol. "Today has been one of the best days of my life."

King embraced him in a powerful hug, then whispered in Italian, "*Saremo presto li conquor tutti.*" We will soon conquer them all.

"I am your *protettore*," Vonni responded in Italian. "You are my *capo*. I told you a long time ago that I would follow you into the depths of hell and smack the devil himself if he dared threaten you. And I meant it."

King patted his face affectionately. "I know you would, paisan," he said, his eyes welling with tears. "You're the only one I have ever trusted. You never gave up on me. And for that, I owe you my life."

"You owe me nothing!" Vonni said emphatically. "I took an oath and I intend to honor it till the day I die. I know you will become everything Don Falcone ever dreamed of. And it is my job to keep you safe while you do."

King hugged him one last time. "You are more than my *protettore*, paisan. You are my best friend, my true goombadi, my *fratello*. Thank you for having faith in me. I promise you, all the dreams we once had will soon be ours. Now is our time. Tomorrow begins a new era for the Falcone name. You just make sure everyone is here tomorrow night. For now, I go. Give Pamela and baby Omnio my love. I can't wait to see them."

"I will do that, paisan," Vonni said, finally switching back to English. "I can't wait till you meet him. He's such a smart little *bambino*."

"Must take after his mother," King joked.

"Yeah," Vonni laughed. "I say the same thing all the time. She's the beauty *and* the brains."

King looked down at Madonna, who was hovering next to him. "Speaking of beauty, you gonna be okay to drive?"

She smiled up at him. "I'm fine. I only had two glasses of champagne."

Vonni extended a hand to her. "It's been a pleasure meeting you, Miss Madonna. Please get him home safe. Tonight, *bella*, you are his *protettore*."

"I promise I'll get him home safe," she said, blushing, looking up at King lustily. "Trust me, I plan to take good care of him when we get home."

524

"Yes, I'm sure you do," Vonni chuckled. "Just don't wear him out too much. We have a lot of work ahead of us over the next few days."

"Good night, paisan," King said, giving him a firm handshake. "I'll see you tomorrow night."

"I'll make sure everyone is here," Vonni promised. "But get here early so you can help me make the *spiedini*."

King assured him he would, and then led Madonna out to her car. When he climbed into the passenger seat next to her, he removed one of the $10,000 packets of cash from his inside pocket.

"Take this," he said, thrusting it at her, his head spinning from the alcohol. "Tomorrow, I want you to use it to lease us some office space. If there's anything left, keep it. Consider it a signing bonus."

Then, without adding another word, he simply leaned back in his seat and dozed off, no longer able to fight the effects of the alcohol. For a moment, Madonna stared at the money in her hand. She had never met anyone who treated money with such indifference, as if it were just play money. Over the last twenty-four hours, he had given her almost $15,000 like it was nothing more than pocket change. And he was a man who had only been out of prison barely 48 hours. Staring at the money, she now remembered the beautiful mansion he had pointed out to her the previous night. At the time, when he'd expressed his intentions to buy it, she thought he was just trying to impress her with a pipe dream. But she now realized that King Falcone didn't have pipe dreams. He fully intended to buy that mansion.

**To purchase Volume 2 of TO BE A KING, visit:**

www.amazon.com/author/gunnerlindbloom

Printed in Great Britain
by Amazon

72525438R00317